WALKING ON BORROWED LAND

NUMBER NINE IN THE TEXAS TRADITION SERIES
James W. Lee, General Editor

Walking on Borrowed Land

William A. Owens

Introduction by William A. Owens
Afterword by James W. Lee

Texas Christian University Press
Fort Worth

Copyright © 1950, 1954, 1955, 1988 by William A. Owens

Library of Congress Cataloging-in-Publication Data
Owens, William A., 1905-
Walking on borrowed land.

(Texas tradition series ; no. 9)
I. Title. II. Series.
PS3565.W58W35   1988   813'.52   87-40266
ISBN 0-87565-028-7

Illustrated by Walle Conoly

To the Memory of

GRANT WOOD

who loved the spirituals in this book, who taught me many lessons about people, who gave me my best instruction in the methods of artistic form and expression.

INTRODUCTION

Writing a Novel—Problem and Solution*

Though I realized it only lately, *Walking on Borrowed Land* was growing from the time I, at the age of six, became aware of the conflict between white and black. We lived on a farm near Blossom, Texas, and had to pass the Negro school to get to our school in the middle of town. There was a strip of woods between white town and colored town. One afternoon I walked with my older brothers and some other boys through town. As we approached these woods, we saw colored boys coming from school.

"Let's chase the niggers—" one of the boys said.

And they did, off the road and through the woods, with shouts and tripping and throwing sticks. Too small to take part, I tried to keep up, afraid of what might happen if the Negro boys should find me alone. I was close enough to see their frightened eyes and tense faces as they took to their heels. We went on home laughing, but somehow I knew something wrong had been done.

As I grew older I became aware of many fascinating things about the life of the Negroes: their way of talking, their songs, their modes of worship. Every day I was kept aware by my family of the differences between white and black. On many a night I shivered before the fire as I listened to stories of riots and near riots in the past. As I grew older I discovered ways to learn Negro life at close range. I could go to Negro churches and stand outside or

---

Editor's note: William A. Owens's comments on the genesis of *Walking on Borrowed Land* were written shortly after the novel was published in 1954. The "Introduction" was published in *The Southwest Review* (1955) under the title, "Writing a Novel—Problem and Solution."

sit on my pony and watch the shouting and dancing. To my own people this was legitimate entertainment. Even more entertaining was a Negro baptizing. Sometimes the whole white community would turn out to watch the preacher and deacons dip white-robed men and women into muddy creek water. We knew the people well by name, for they worked, many of them, in the houses and on the farms of whites. For weeks after a baptizing there would be humorous recalling of how Aunt Nervy or someone else threw a fit when hauled out of the water.

When I was about twelve the chain gang camped near our farm. For several years I had seen wagonloads of convicts going along the roads, their feet bound with ball and chain, their faces sullen. Naturally I had a curiosity about these men. When their tent was nearby, I slipped in at night to listen to their songs and watch them dance. It was as much fun as a baptizing, and more exciting, for it was forbidden—I never saw another person from our community there except another boy who sometimes went with me.

For years I had sung "Sweet Chariot" as I rambled about fields and woods. Now I added some "sinful songs." From Negro convicts I learned "The Midnight Special":

> *If you ever go to Dallas*
> *You better walk right,*
> *You better not gamble,*
> *And you better not fight.*

I also learned one they called "The Crow." This they sang as a group. "Now tell me, where is the crow?" the leader would sing.

> *"He's in the hickory tree."*
> *"Now tell me, how do you know?"*
> *" 'Cause he told me so."*

Then all together they would sing:

> *Oh, where'd you get that mystery?*
> *from the old black crow in the hickory tree.*

At the age of fifteen I took what duds I had and went to Dallas to make my way. At work, at school, I was suddenly cut off from any contact with Negro life. Sometimes as I rode the streetcar through "Deep Ellum" on a Saturday night or a Sunday afternoon I saw crowds of Negroes along the tracks or in front of their picture show. I wondered about their way of life, but never attempted to find out.

At Southern Methodist University as I became more engrossed in the study of literature I became more aware of my interest in folk literature. I learned that other persons, Dorothy Scarborough particularly, had actually made studies of Negro songs. Her *On the Trail of the Negro Folk Song* set me to recalling all the songs I had learned back home and made me determined to learn more.

One night I rode the streetcar to the corner of Thomas and Hall, the center of Negro life in Dallas. The only white on the street, I walked slowly back and forth. It was a warm night and houses were open and the streets full of people. I listened to the voices and tried to memorize the phrases I heard. No one paid particular attention to me—I was ignored even more thoroughly than I had been at country baptizings.

As I walked along I heard women's voices singing:

> *So high you cain't git over it,*
> *So low you cain't git under it,*
> *So wide you cain't go around it,*
> *You gotta go in at the do'.*

I was near a church and the front door was open. Almost without thinking I stepped inside.

An usher met me. "We reserves a place for our brothers in white in the balcony," he said.

Though alone in the balcony, I felt completely at home. The people sang and shouted and danced. There were songs I had known long ago. There were also many new ones. I took down words and tried to memorize tunes. The preacher preached. Toward midnight the clamor of the meeting rose to a crescendo with the aisles full of shouting, dancing, sweating men and women. Then they began to drift away and I took the streetcar home, with a new purpose of recording every Negro song I could find.

For the next several years I recorded songs in Negro homes, churches, dance halls, and saloons up and down central and east Texas, the most rewarding area being the Brazos bottoms. The story of my recording machine frequently went ahead of me, and the people welcomed me with the greatest hospitality. My collection of recordings grew, as did my knowledge of Negro life. So did my sympathy for the Negroes. I think for the first time I really understood the handicaps under which they lived. I know I realized only then what a waste of talent was there.

I began casting about for a way to tell whites what I had found out about Negroes. I tried articles on Negro spirituals. I tried character studies of Negroes I had met. These writings seemed cold, without the passion I had begun to feel about the injustice of segregation.

Then came Pearl Harbor and I enlisted in the army as a buck private, an inferior position if there ever was one. After basic training I was assigned to work in San Antonio and, of all things, to interview some Negroes about an outbreak that had almost gotten out of hand. From there I went to Tulsa, where a more dangerous situation threatened. It was part of a general unrest.

During three months in Tulsa I talked to most of the Negro leaders in town. I also visited churches and schools. I talked to county officers and police officers. I spent many hours in city court listening to trials of minor cases. The Negroes always seemed to get the worst of things.

One hot afternoon I was driving from Muskogee to Tulsa when the idea of a novel about Negroes first came to me. It came with such clarity that I parked beside the highway and wrote out the basic plan that the novel eventually followed.

My study, my interviews now had greater purpose. I began assembling a mass of unrelated details.

But there was a war on and I was a soldier. I was suddenly shifted from Tulsa to Brisbane, Australia. For two years I fought the battle of the Pacific from Australia to New Guinea to Leyte and Luzon. There was no time for working on a novel, but there were times when I could find a sympathetic person to whom I could tell my story, and it grew with each telling.

The war over, I went to Columbia University as a place in which I could get training in the techniques of writing fiction. I got some help directly. I got a great deal more indirectly, from being in a climate in which one could say "I am working on a novel" without feeling shy or ashamed.

I think that from the beginning I had been converted to the point of view of the book, the waste and shame of segregation. But I had to put my themes down more specifically than that.

My basic theme was segregation in education. Negroes in the South are handicapped most because they are denied education. If Negroes could be educated, they could advance themselves more and avail themselves of whatever opportunities the whites yielded to them. I had already rejected "separate but equal" education as a fallacy. My most important task in the book was to show the falseness, the economic waste, the shame of this idea.

The Negro is in transition. In my own lifetime I have witnessed progress. I have seen Negroes move ahead. I have seen prejudice decrease in some areas, and new opportunities opened. Some Southern Negroes want to go ahead. Others—afraid of the wrath of whites or afraid of losing some of their influence in an all-Negro situation—want to hold back. Often Negroes have said to me, "Give us a hundred years or two. We are not ready to compete." Those who study the situation can understand, if not condone, these conflicting attitudes.

Religion in some of its forms is a retarder of progress, among whites as well as Negroes. Some Negroes exhaust themselves night after night dancing and shouting. Some preachers preach that Negroes should be content with their lot here because heaven awaits them by and by. On the other hand, other preachers, fully as sincere in their belief of rewards to come, preach that Negroes should try to achieve as full a life as possible on earth. Religious conflict thus became another theme to be developed.

My study had given me an insight into the Negro's superstitions, beliefs, music. I based the folk theme on the belief that the farmer has to plant three cotton seeds to get one to grow. This gave me an opportunity to approach the Negro through his folklore. It also gave me my title, *Walking on Borrowed Land*.

My next problem was selecting characters, for I had long felt that, to have validity, the novel would have to be expressed in terms of individuals who in their own actions and emotions would demonstrate what I wanted to say.

Almost from the moment I conceived the idea of the novel the main character was a Negro teacher. Having been a teacher myself in communities in which the white school board diverted Negro school funds to make white schools better, I was quite aware of some of the problems in education—segregated educations, that is. I also am strongly of the opinion that the best possibility for progress is in education of both Negroes and whites. So I chose Mose Ingram, giving him the name because Moses was a leader of his people and Mose was a common name for slaves, and Ingram because it could easily have been inherited from an Anglo-Saxon master. I perhaps was influenced also by the slave Mose who at the end of the Civil War forsook his people and freedom to stay with his owner, my great-grandmother. As a child I had heard many stories of his loyalty and goodness.

But Mose Ingram is a composite of many people. For some years in a small Texas town I had as friend a Negro school principal who had studied at Columbia and then had returned to do what he could for his people. He was a man of considerable ability, and so highly respected that when in the late afternoon he went for a walk through the business section along Main Street, white men frequently greeted him and stopped to pass the time of day. I deliberately gave him his years on a Mississippi plantation because I wanted to play somewhat on contrasts. I had chosen Oklahoma as my locale for the reason that the whole racial conflict seemed most sharply delineated there in a border state. By the same token, I had Mose go to Chicago to study in order that he might have an understanding of life in a less segregated area. I placed his age at forty-six because I needed a character with broad experience and mature judgment to carry the burden of the conflicts.

Josie, Mose's wife, is likewise a composite. Her name and physical characteristics come from the cook in a home I used to visit in a small Texas town. From the beginning I wanted her to represent those Negroes who have accepted emotional religion as the greatest good on earth, the sure key to heaven. Her thinking was borrowed from many sources. Once I visited in the Trinity River bottoms a cotton plantation on which the Negro workers were in an almost perpetual state of revivalism. The white owner hired the preacher and paid him well to tell the people to endure their hard life without complaint because everything will be better in the great by and by. To make sure the preacher kept his bargain, the owner had his white overseer sit outside the church on horseback to check on the sermons. Not all the workers were taken in, but there was almost no complaint. "He do be good to us about the church" became the answer to all criticism. In a dozen other places I heard the story of Ham, inspired no doubt originally by whites, and all Josie's other remarks about Negroes keeping "in place."

The idea of giving Mose and Josie three sons—Thomas, Robert, John—preceded the theme "one to grow," but the ideas quickly fused in my thinking. I also had in mind the Parable of the Sower, which I had often heard Negro preachers use as a text. I wanted the sons to represent the waste of good seed cast upon the barren social ground of Oklahoma. I also wanted to show that the climate is improving there. Out of the dozens of kinds of waste I could have chosen, I settled on two: waste of life as Thomas' life is wasted by an almost careless bullet, and the waste of talent, as Robert's musical talent is wasted. I made John a scientist, a doctor, because it seemed to me a Negro might have the greatest opportunity in science.

Thus in Mose's family I tried to individualize most of the thematic thinking of the novel. But I had to have other characters to help with the action and to support, even reiterate the themes.

Sister Brackett, the support for Josie in her loyalty to old ways and emotional religion, was drawn directly from real life. Before the war I met a Negro woman preacher who was pastor of a church in San Antonio and who sold hominy to customers in white town. She was a familiar sight in her fringed-top buggy. For several years I recorded her sermons and songs—songs she had for the most part composed herself. I suppose half the people in San Antonio knew Sister Crockett (her real name) in those days. She is now feeble with age and has given up both hominy making and preaching. Once after a recording session she said to me, "You gonna put me in a book?" "I don't know," I replied. "I'd like to." She bowed her head as if in prayer and then said, "I'd be thankful if you'd put me in a book." That I have tried to do, with all the faithfulness to details of dress, theology, speech, and manner that I could manage. I also found the character of Sister Brackett useful for carrying information back and forth across the tracks. In communities where rigid segregation is practiced, someone has to keep both sides informed of what goes on. A hominy peddler was a natural.

Mose also needed support for his religious stand, and for that purpose I imagined Brother Simpson, putting him together with traits drawn from half a dozen Negro ministers I had visited while collecting Negro spirituals. Fortunately for the people, the South has thousands of Brother Simpsons. It was sheer pain to write his death, but I had to write it to make it possible for Mose to have his one emotionally drunken night with Josie and Sister Brackett.

For support of Mose in his difficult school situation I developed the boardinghouse-keeper, Lora Dixon, who for me represents natural ability and a realistic attitude toward both whites and blacks under Jim Crow. I meant her to be the one Negro character who could recognize Mose's course and help him—fiercely at times—to stay on it.

Though the white side had to be presented, I tried to keep it to a minimum of characters. The John Carson of the first half of the book can be found on white school boards all over the South. There are fewer of the later John Carsons—those who recognize inequity and realize change must come—but there are some. I meant the white medico, Dr. Lewis, to be the actual spokesman for the position that John Carson assumes at the end.

In addition to their parts as actors, I meant the minor characters to support themes. Thus the music teacher, Cenoria Davis, herself a complexity in the Negro community, demonstrates waste of talent. Newspapermen Harrison Williams and Daddy Splane represent Negroes' waste of the opportunity to help themselves and each other. Frenchy, in addition to being like Sister Brackett a "messenger across the tracks," is the Negro who has half seriously, half mockingly adjusted to the situation. As thousands like him do in the South, he "gets along." Alan Carson, son of John Carson, represents, on the one hand, waste of talent as it extends to the whites and, on the other, an echo of the white conscience.

I must not suggest that these characters came so fully developed and purposeful into my mind. I have described them as they finally shaped themselves into the novel.

For the next step—the actual writing—I was entirely on my own. My natural feeling for the land and the people made me select the simplest possible style: the words had to belong to the people, the ideas they expressed had to be so lucid that the people could understand them without unnecessary exertion. Dialogue had to be in the language of the people, but because of my own aversion to language butchered for the sake of phonetic spelling I felt that I had to work with a few words that would suggest the flavor and then depend most on my own feeling for rhythm of expression. I found myself constantly searching my mind for words and phrases. I also eavesdropped on every conversation I could and recorded faithfully in my book possibly useful bits of dialogue.

For individual scenes I drew on my memory where I could and created new scenes when my memory yielded nothing.

The novel opens with Mose Ingram arriving in Columbus, Oklahoma. I knew the "arrival" scene had been used to the point of cliché. Nevertheless, I could see no other way to get Mose (and the reader) into the scene and to start the action. Recalling an arrival by train at Denison, Texas, I re-created it for Mose's arrival in Columbus—a town, by the way, composed of elements from Oklahoma City, Tulsa, and Muskogee and placed in my mind somewhere between Muskogee and Fort Smith, Arkansas. For this mythical town I drew a map and named the streets and located the buildings on them—tedious work but a distinct aid to visual memory, which I find necessary in writing. What I am saying, I suppose, is that I have to *see* my characters as well as details of scenes as I write.

I could tell how I arrived at every scene in the book. A few will serve the purpose.

I needed a scene that would demonstrate the quiet, dignified worship in Brother Simpson's church. For Mose's first attendance

I drew on a Communion service I had witnessed in the church of the Rev. I. B. Loud (now of Dallas) at Calvert, Texas. On that occasion four of us—three white Protestants and a Jew—knelt at the altar with the congregation while the minister, and two women dressed in maid's uniforms, served the bread and wine.

For Mose's active participation in the Methodist Church, I hit upon the idea of a building program. I must confess to several trials at various scenes before I imagined having the church people bring bricks. Once my imagination was working, I had only to call to mind dozens of collections I had observed in Negro churches, in some of which white visitors had taken part.

In order to create a sense of guilt on Mose's part, in order to have a basis for Josie to criticize him, I introduced what she would honestly have called blasphemy. The scene opens with the three sons trapping birds in the snow, progresses to an accident in which one boy cuts his wrist, and ends when Mose throws the Bible against the wall in anger. In my childhood whenever snow came— a rarity in northeast Texas—my brothers and I built deadfalls and trapped birds. The idea of using Scripture to stop the flow of blood came from a different time. I was passing a Negro cabin on a country road when a woman ran out and asked me to get help: her daughter was bleeding to death. I ran to the nearest house and found a white woman. When she and I went into the Negro cabin, the daughter was sitting in a chair with a washpan in her lap. The washpan was half full of blood. Blood was pouring from her mouth and nostrils. The white woman sat down beside her and began reading the passage from Ezekiel which is used as a folk cure.

In order to show to what extent Negroes sometimes become involved in emotional religion, I used a scene in which Josie beats her son Robert in the frenzy of a Holy Roller meeting. This scene was based on an account by an old Negro I met in the woods north of Beaumont in the spring of 1939. He told me that the devil doll came to a meeting in Beaumont, and the people became so excited they beat each other until the white policemen came and took the whole congregation to jail. The scene took little shaping to fit my story.

The burial of Thomas came out of my memory. When I was about seven I attended funeral services for a member of the Woodmen of the World, a white man, in Blossom. I recall all too clearly the faces of the people when the minister took a dove into the grave, and the screams of the women when the dove skimmed the earth. Later I heard that Negroes had borrowed this service and used it with even greater manifestations of grief.

As I look back over the scenes I realize that few of them were created out of whole cloth. I used the sound of "moaning low" I heard at funerals and in the cotton fields on the Womack farm in the Red River bottoms. I used glances, tones of voices, manners gleaned from a lifetime of living among the people.

That seems to me the work of the novelist: to make others see and know and understand a way of life.

Though I knew all along that parts of the novel would have to be revised, I was not prepared for what happened when I completed the first draft and read it over. I did not know enough to write such a book. What I did know was not presented well enough.

With my manuscript and notebook I went back over the area. My brother drove me over the countryside I had known as a child. I tried hard to recapture impressions, and noted them in my book. I went to Oklahoma City again and walked the streets of the Negro section. I went on to Tulsa. The two old men at the police department who had given me most aid before were both dead. The men who had replaced them were indignant that I wanted to question them about an old riot.

Day and night I walked the streets of Greenwood, the Negro section, hearing speech, observing atttiudes. Then I revised furiously.

At last I took a chapter to a Negro preacher and asked him to read it. He read it while we sat in his front parlor. He finished it and looked at me. "How come you know so much about colored folks?" he asked.

The answer which had been forming in my mind for a long time was suddenly clear: there is not much difference between blacks and whites in the South. Writers have too long emphasized the differences, which are minor and largely a matter of degree when we consider that Negroes and whites have the same religion, language, economic problems. They even share to a great extent the same folklore. The only actual difference is that created by an unnatural division called Jim Crow. It was a great relief to me to know at last that I could write in the area of human emotion, experience without having to divide my own mind into "white" and "black."

Elated, I went back to writing.

But I still had a lesson to learn. To demonstrate the theme of waste, in the first version I had a race riot in which thirty men were killed and a Negro town burned—a riot I had copied too faithfully from the Tulsa riot of 1921. As I had described it, the riot threw the whole book out of balance and made melodramatic the violence that is a part of the racial conflict. It took my literary agent and several editors to show me the error.

Once I recognized it I was able to write the death of Thomas in a remarkably short time, and I feel the book is much strengthened by centering attention on the death of one man. Is there a better way to demonstrate waste?

As I look back over this I realize how impossible it is to tell exactly how a novel was written. I can point out some of the devices. I cannot explain how I had to "feel" a character, a scene, a word even. I can tell how many hours I labored over a scene, but I cannot tell actually what happened when the scene came right. I don't believe my editors can either.

There is, for example, a night club scene in Chicago. They handed this scene back twice. Each time they said it was "too dramatic," "too staged." Their suggestions gave me nothing to go on. At last, in a kind of desperation as the deadline was approaching, I took the scene apart entirely and put it together again with a change in focus on characters. They greeted the rewrite with enthusiasm, and then explained that the scene was no longer "static"!

I am compelled to believe that writing "comes right" when the writer is willing to submerge himself completely in his people and their way of life.

I had to learn how to go back and walk with my characters the streets of Happy Hollow.

I'm walking on borrowed land,
This world ain't none o' my home.

Negro spiritual

1

THE train crawled across hot wind-parched prairies. Coach passengers leaned out the windows to catch a breath of fresh air, or covered their faces with damp handkerchiefs and fanned themselves with paper fans. A brown-skinned Negro in cowboy boots and wide-brimmed hat picked his guitar and sang:

"Call the number of the train I ride:
Number One, Number Two, Three, Number Fo',
and Five...."

Mose Ingram, tired of the hot cushions, tired of the weary-voiced singer, went to stand in the vestibule. Hot winds blew smoke and dust through the open doors, but he remained standing there, watching with smarting eyes the patches of brown grass and fields of cotton turning white in the September sun. He waved to cotton pickers dragging their sacks up and down mile-long rows. They shaded their eyes against the afternoon sun and waved back to him. Ahead, Mose saw a short low ridge that lay like a loaf of bread on the flat table of the prairie. Then he saw the smokestacks and rooftops of a town.

"Co-lum-bus . . . Co-lum-bus, Ok-la-homa," a porter called through the coaches.

A Pullman porter stopped beside Mose in the vestibule. "Coming into Columbus," he said.

"Columbus," Mose repeated thoughtfully, confidentially. "That's my new home."

Mose went back to his seat and brought two heavy suitcases to the platform. The blues man was singing again the words that had stirred the passengers to laughter and jeering when they pulled out of St. Louis the night before:

> "White man rides in a Pullman coach,
> Nigger man rides Jim Crow. . . ."

Now the words brought only hard silent smiles to the few passengers who still had a way to go.

All day long Mose had watched passengers, singly or in groups, separate themselves from the others and then stand on the station platform waving as the train pulled out. Now it was his turn. He smiled briefly at the remaining passengers and then turned his back on them to catch what glimpses he could of the town he had chosen to live in, to work in. To the north he saw a cluster of unpainted shacks beginning at the railroad tracks and stretching away to the hill. To the south were stock pens, a cottonseed-oil mill and, near the station, two-story houses with their backs turned to view.

"Don't look like much, do it?" the train porter remarked.

"A place to work——" Mose's words were lost in the clang of train doors and suitcases falling on metal.

The train pulled through the station and came to a stop with the locomotive and baggage car past the passenger platform and the Negro coach at the last stairway. Mose swung his suitcases to the station platform, waved to the coach he had left, and started up the ramp. Far ahead he could see the Pullman passengers, followed by a dozen redcaps, their arms pulled straight with heavy bags. Mose nodded good-by to the porter and started toward the waiting room. Smoke from the engine rolled around him and left another coat of soot on the red brick walls and tile roof of the station.

Mose passed the entrance marked WHITE WAITING ROOM and entered the COLORED WAITING ROOM. The room was hot, dirty and small enough for the dozen or so passengers to make it seem crowded. Smoke rolled through the windows and hung in a cloud against the ceiling. The smell of strong disinfectant rose from floors and brass spittoons.

Mose stood aside while other passengers dropped into compartmented seats. Then he dropped his suitcases and looked for a ticket agent for information.

Far away, as if from a domed cellar, he could hear a train caller in the white waiting room calling the trains. He could not make out the times of arrival and departure, or whether the trains were on time, but the names of towns filled his mind: "Mus-ko-gee, Tul-sa, Sa-pul-pa, Guth-rie, McAl-ester, Okla-homa Cit-ee. . . . "

A taxi driver came in and circled the waiting room. Without pausing he came up to Mose.

"Taxi, suh? Taxi to Happy Hollow?"

"What's that?" Mose asked.

"Colored section of town. Say, you must be from a long way off." Mose nodded yes.

"Thought I ain't seen you here before. Real name is Pleasant Valley, but white folks and most niggers calls it Happy Hollow. Names don't make much difference noway. Taxi's two bits."

Mose took up his suitcases again. "All right. You'd better take me there. Can I get a place to stay all night?"

The taxi driver circled the benches while he called out in the singsong of a train caller, "Pleasant Valley Rooming House, Genteel Rooms for Genteel People, Daily and Weekly Rates, Lora Dixon, Prop."

He winked at the others, who were laughing at his clowning. Then he stopped soberly before Mose, who had dropped his suitcases and stood between them.

"That's whut it say on the sign out front. It's a good place. Stays there myself. How long you gonna stay?"

"I don't know. I've come here to live——"

"If you knowed whut I know, you'd git right back out o' town—back where you come from. You come from St. Louis?"

"Chicago."

"Man, you better go back. You got it easy there. It's rough here—on us folks."

"My home's Mississippi."

"I ain't saying go back to no Mississippi. But Chicago. Man,

man." He shuffled a step and then turned to Mose again. "Whut kind o' work you do?"

"I'm the principal of the school."

"You is?" The taxi driver looked him over, sizing up the thick shoulders and muscular arms. "You'll be able to handle the big boys in school, but I don't know about the gals. Last principal we had run off with a slut——"

"I'm married."

"Him too. Staying with a gal at least. Whut's yo' name?"

"Mose Ingram. What's yours?"

"Professor Ingram," he said, emphasizing the *Professor,* "my real name is George Washington Comeaux, but all the niggers and most white folks jest calls me Frenchy. I'm from N'Awleens and they say I'm a Frenchy-looking nigger. Guess my grandmammy or somebody got mixed up with a Cajun. You say you from Mississippi?"

"Yes."

"You don't talk like no Mississippi nigger. Reckon that's from teaching."

Frenchy turned from Mose and circled the room again. He was a small man with kinky black hair and muddy skin. His thin lips and pointed nose must have come from his French ancestor, Mose thought.

"Last call for Happy Hollow."

His voice was startlingly full and resonant; for a moment he drowned out the train caller in the domed white waiting room. But there were no more passengers.

"Depression sho' nuff bad when folks'd ruther walk two miles than pay two bits taxi fare," he said to Mose. He took Mose's suitcases. "Us go this way."

They came out on the Main Street side of the station, at a distance from the circular drive before the white waiting room on which automobiles and taxicabs paused briefly and then swung up the low rise south to the modern buildings of the Columbus business district, to the churches and schools and homes of white Columbus.

Following Frenchy, Mose looked north over the shacks and sand trails of Pleasant Valley. He shuddered to see how positively the tracks served as dividing line.

"You ain't been here before?"

"No."

Frenchy paused at the curb. "Let me tell you. I been from N' Awleens to Atlanta, from Dallas to Kansas City, from Chicago to New York, and I say they ain't a purtier town nowheres than Columbus, Oklahoma. The streets is wide and clean. They got a hundred niggers doing nothing but cleaning them streets. They got big houses and yards—some yards big enough to plant a acre of cotton in. You'd never think they could build such a town on this ugly prairie. . . . "

As he talked, Frenchy put Mose's suitcases in a running-board rack and they took the front seat together. Frenchy looked at the vacant back seat and then glanced toward the station. Three women were setting out on foot, carrying heavy bundles. They looked at the taxi, their faces tired and downcast, and then walked on.

"Reckon I ought to take them," Frenchy said, "but my taxi's my business and I need the money."

He backed into the street.

"We going across the tracks," he said. "Over there, ain't hardly no streets a-tall—jest sand roads with row houses slapped together."

Mose was glad when the cab started moving. It stirred the hot air into seeming coolness and made breathing easier. They crossed the tracks and took a sandy road leading between junk piles and railroad yards. Clouds of dust rose from the wheels and drifted across the junk yards. The sun, slanted above the low hill, still broiled the earth, giving it a parched-crisp smell.

"How long you been here?" Mose asked.

"Ten year."

"Why do you stay, if you don't like it?"

"I got me a business. I done made me a place here. Ain't no use moving on and having to start all over again. It's tough here, but it ain't gonna be no easier for me nowheres else."

Past the junk yards, in an open lot between them and the first row of houses, Mose saw a low wooden building that looked like a dance pavilion. The doors and windows were open. Red and green crepe paper hung in strips from the ceiling. Over the entrance a sign swung in the wind: PEPE'S TAVERN. The green snake of the Mexican flag curled itself about the letters. The tavern looked foreign, out of place.

"He's Mex," Frenchy said. "Spick. Used to be a bootlegger. Now he's got this place—gonna make a beer joint out'n it soon as he can git a license. Man, ain't I glad prohibition done gone!"

A phonograph blared from the tavern—two male voices harmonizing on the words "Ay, Panchita" above the thump of guitars. Three colored boys stood with their elbows on the window sills looking in and listening.

"It's mostly a place for colored folks," Frenchy said. "Whites going there ain't out for no good. A few Mesicans hangs around to gamble, or to peddle the weed. They come and go with the railroad work gangs."

"How does he stay open?"

"Ain't nobody gonna close him. It's a place where all kinds o' folks can meet. Law ain't gonna touch that. But he ain't got it so easy, being a Mesican."

They reached the edge of Pleasant Valley—mostly sand-stained shacks, with here and there a painted bungalow. They passed a few people walking the sand road, but, on a Friday afternoon, it was still too early for many to be off work. Those they saw carried bundles on hip or shoulder. They stopped to chat at yards and porches; they stopped to wave at Frenchy.

Their faces changed, became sullen at the sight of a touring car coming from the direction of Reservoir Hill. Mose saw two white men on the front seat, their bodies erect, their faces tanned and serious under broad-brimmed hats. They slowed to pass Frenchy and raised their hands to him.

"The Laws," Frenchy told Mose.

"The Laws?"

"Ain't nobody else but. The man driving is Mister Hub Kelly.

He's the High Sheriff. The other'n is Mister Gus Blackledge, deputy in this *pre*cinct."

"What do you think of them?"

"I gits along with them. They need somebody over here like me, so they respect me. I ain't telling you all I know—jest enough to help you git by. Hub Kelly's a good man. He ain't giving no trouble to black or white. But you watch out for Blackledge. He ain't no good. I knowed him a long time and ain't knowed nothing good about him. When they's a knifing on this side or somebody whups somebody, Hub Kelly follows the law. He gits complaints filed and witnesses in court. He mighty nigh gits justice. Blackledge don't go to no bother. He pistol whups fast. He'd jest as soon shoot a man as look at him. When he starts shooting, folks takes to tall cotton. But I ain't a-scared o' him. He knows my place.

"I'm a friend to white and nigger the same," he continued. "It helps my business. But I ain't taking nothing from none o' them. That way I git along. I tell you, it ain't easy. Whites and blacks both still recollects the Tulsa riot in 1921. They scared spitless whut happened then might happen agin."

They turned onto a wider street leading to the center of dark town—the "Main Drag" of Saturday nights—where there were a few stores, a moving-picture show and "stands" for the sale of hot catfish sandwiches and barbecue.

"You remember whut it looked like from the station up the Main Street of Columbus?" Frenchy asked. "Well, you looking up the Main Street of Pleasant Valley. It winds around a right smart over here, but it's the same street. Different over here, ain't it? You say you come to stay. If you do, you gonna git all-fired tired o' this street."

He stopped in front of an old two-story frame house with sagging porches and board roof patched with squares of tin.

"This the Pleasant Valley Rooming House," he announced. Mose read the words on a rough sign nailed to an oak in the front yard. "Right here you in the middle o' Happy Hollow. This front porch's in spitting distance of the moving pictures, pool hall and funeral parlor. Most folks goes to all o' them some time or other. You ain't got to wait long to git acquainted."

As Mose lifted his suitcases down he saw an old buggy pulled by a little red pony coming along the road from Columbus. The buggy top was flat and rectangular, upheld by four metal pipes and gaily fringed in red. Across the top, white signs hand-painted in red letters announced: JESUS SAVES, JOHN 3:16, HOMINAY FOR SALE.

"Who is that?" Mose asked, his eyes wide and staring at the driver.

She was a dark woman above average in height. She had on a flowing black dress like a priest's cassock, a clergyman's collar which held her chin high, and a widow's black veil caught around her kinky white hair and falling over her shoulders. Her lips clucked excitedly as she urged the pony to get along to Happy Hollow.

"Sister Brackett," Frenchy said offhandedly as he carried Mose's suitcases to the porch. "She's the pastor of the holy-roller church—and bound to save everybody. She peddles hominy over in white town for a living."

"E'ening, Frenchy," she called, halting the panting pony in the yard, and then: "E'ening, Brother. Who you?"

"I'm Mose Ingram, the new principal of the school."

"Well, amen, praise the Lawd," she said fervently, rolling her eyes upward on the prayer. "You look educated—you sound educated." She examined him carefully with frank eyes. "Is you?"

"I hope so."

"Is you saved?"

"Yes," Mose answered respectfully. It was like being in Mississippi again, where a man's heart, a man's soul were public property to be examined, discussed.

"Sanctified?"

"I don't know," he said doubtfully.

"Then you ain't. Anybody that's sanctified knows it. It's jest like being clubbed over the head. The Spirit hits mighty hard—and you knows when you been struck."

Her voice was toned for a sermon, Mose recognized. He waited for her to begin her text. Instead, she leaned over to see that her skirts were tucked around her feet so her ankles wouldn't show. Then she spoke again, in a conversational tone.

"I knowed you wus coming," she said. "Miz Carson tole me Mister Carson done hired us a new principal. Mister Carson's the School Board——"

"Yes, I've had letters from him. Do you know him?"

"Sho' does. Been selling hominy to him and Miz Carson for twenty years. They good Christian people——"

Frenchy interrupted her. "He owns the biggest men's wear store in Columbus—got the biggest prices too. Why, man, it costes you a dollar to turn around in his store. And niggers? He ain't got no use for them a-tall. If a nigger go in that store to buy, he gotta go in at the back door and come out the same way—like going in white folks' houses."

"Hmph!" Sister Brackett coughed. "Any nigger worth his salt would go in the back door anyway. That's nigger manners."

"Any handkerchiefhead nigger," Frenchy shot at her.

Footsteps on bare floors stopped their argument. A big hand pushed the screen door open. A big woman in a blue uniform followed the hand. Her face was broad and dark; her hair, tied up in a red-striped towel, reeked of peach-tree pomade.

"E'ening, folks," she said. "What's the ruckus?"

"Brought you a new boarder," Frenchy said, his shoulders raised in a mischievous swagger. "I'll take my rake-off at supper. He's the new principal." Mose bowed toward her. Frenchy continued. "Miz Dixon runs the boardinghouse and teaches the primary grades in school."

Before a breath could be caught, Sister Brackett's tongue lashed out like a whip. "Sister Lora Dixon! You been had yo' hair straightened agin." Her white false teeth chopped the words off one by one. Her whitened eyes set in anger. "I've a mind to git right out'n this buggy and preach you a sermon. You a fine example for the po' little child'en in school. You with yo' skirts halfway to yo' knees and yo' hair straight and stiff as a board. Whut you needs is more praying and less fixing."

Lora Dixon leaned her heavy weight against her door facing and waited for the tirade to be over. Mose could see that she had heard all this before and expected to hear it again—coolly, stolidly, minding her own business.

Sister Brackett stopped lacing her and turned to Mose. "Brother, you got a wife?"

"Yes, ma'am."

"Child'en?"

"Three boys."

Sister Brackett allowed a hush to come. Her hands shook, her face grew troubled. She studied Mose's face searchingly. Then she turned to Lora Dixon. Their eyes met. Sister Brackett lowered her head ominously.

"One to grow." She let the words fall like a prophecy.

"Yes, Lawd." Lora Dixon sighed.

Frenchy laughed, a mocking giggle, breaking the mood in an instant. Sister Brackett hissed at him and then spoke to Mose, forcing him from the dark thoughts she had raised.

"Brother, I hope you a Godly man—more Godly than the las' one. He come here with one woman and lef' with another—a gal at the beauty parlor, the one where Sister Dixon gits her hair straight. Whut church you belong to?"

"Methodist."

"Well, you can hold to gitting saved, and backsliding, and gitting saved agin the rest o' yo' life if you want—but not me. I'll take the good old holiness way straight to heaven on a narrow path and never turn back. I'm the pastor of the Pentecostal Fire-Baptized Holiness Mission, amen. We'd like for you to come to our church. It's a little edifice over there. Ain't much to look at and no piano, but we got the true religion. And when the Reverend—that's my husband—lif's 'Old Hundred,' it's awful close to heaven——"

"Too much holiness around here to suit me," Frenchy interrupted. He looked at Mose. "They's a night train back. I'll help you catch it if you want to."

Mose shook his head slowly. "I'll stay."

Frenchy climbed into his taxi again and headed toward Columbus.

A pall of red dust gathered on the road behind him and drifted across the rows of houses. Lora Dixon shielded her face with a towel.

"Frenchy's a sinful nigger," Sister Brackett said sadly. "He wus brought up by the Catholics in N'Awleens. He's got his place here, but he's got a hard, ain't-a-caring way about him."

But his words had brought her back from the mount of holiness and left her facing a calm man, a stolid woman, in the middle of Happy Hollow. The spell broken for her, she clucked her pony to a start and creaked on down the road.

One to grow! Mose turned her prophecy in his mind after her fringed-top buggy had disappeared among the shacks and chinaberry trees. *One to grow.* Mose thought of cotton-planting time in Mississippi—a row of one-mule cotton planters lined up, Negro field workers setting planter plates. "You got to plant three seed to make one grow," they said. Mose saw himself following a planter down the row. He saw his three boys playing in the new-turned earth. Curious, he thought, her bringing up this old belief.

Not so curious, he thought again, looking across the quarters, seeing the houses built on barren ground, sensing the tensions of the people living in them.

The prospect was more desolate than he had anticipated. But he could not turn back. He had to face his own weaknesses, his own strength in taking up life in the irony of Happy Hollow.

2

Mose picked up his suitcases and followed Lora Dixon into a long room that extended across the front of her house. On one side it was boardinghouse-dining room with a long table, cane-bottomed chairs in rows along the walls, an open cupboard stacked with dishes. The other side was boardinghouse-living room, from which boarders could watch food come from kitchen to table. Lora Dixon walked toward rough stairs rising awkwardly at the back of the room. From the bottom of the stairs Mose could see the kitchen, where a tall dark woman pushed cooking vessels around on a wood stove. She was frying salt pork. Hot grease spattered on the stove lids and burst into flame. The smell of burning grease followed them upstairs and hung in the narrow hallways.

Lora led Mose to a small room with a window looking out on the hydrant square—a room so small that it seemed crowded by the rusty iron bed, cane-bottomed chair, and washstand with its white porcelain basin and pitcher.

"Frenchy's got the next room," she told him. "Ain't no bathroom. You got to go outside, out back. How long you want the room?"

"About a week. I'll move as soon as I can find a house and bring my family."

"Where they now?"

"They're still at Penrose Plantation in Mississippi."

"You ain't no Mississippi nigger." Her voice was cool, appraising. The way she said "nigger" grated on Mose. "You sound like a Yankee nigger to me," she continued. He felt her curiosity, her distrust. It was more than the distrust of a landlady for a new board-

14

er. It came, Mose knew, from division by section, by locale, as well as by color. He had felt it in Chicago, in the way colored acquaintances had called him a "down-home nigger."

"I'm full 'down home,' " Mose said. "I was born and raised on a plantation in the Mississippi Delta. My wife and three sons are there now. They have never been any place else."

"You didn't jest come from Mississippi?"

"No, ma'am. I came from Chicago. I been in school there."

"You mighty old to go to school."

"Forty-six next month, but when I ought to a been in school I was geeing and hawing old Beck down a cotton row...."

Lora smoothed the sheets on the bed. A fine mist of dust rose from them, hung in the close air, formed a red film on her hands. She brushed the dust away and wiped sweat from her face with her apron. Then, after saying that Mose could eat with her as soon as he had washed up, that her other boarders would not be in from work until after sundown, she left him alone, with no apology for the dust, the heat, the dark discomfort of the room.

"Precious Lawd, take my hand ..." Lora sang as she went heavily down the stairs. A woman's voice in the kitchen took up the melody with her. With the song Mose knew he was "down home" again. He hummed with them as he stripped to the waist, poured water into the basin, splashed his gritty face.

Mose had the body of a farm hand, the face of a man given to much thought. He was tall and straight. His muscles, toughened by years of hard work on a cotton plantation, were those of a lifter of cotton bales. Only around his waist was there a flabbiness. His face—soot-black, broad, heavily lined on forehead and cheek—had a thoughtful look until he smiled. Then his mouth opened wide to show strong white teeth, and his eyes brightened. His hair, close cropped and kinky, with a light sprinkling of gray, fitted his fine head like a fleecy cap.

Mose was still humming "Precious Lawd" when he went down to supper. Lora was waiting for him at the table, her chair angled across from the plate she pointed to for him. It was like being in the servants' kitchen at Penrose Plantation again. The table was of planed oak, worn smooth and white with many years of scrubbing. The dishes were white hotelware, the knives and forks bone-handled. Even the food was the same: corn bread, black-eyed peas, salt pork, boiled cabbage, and pepper sauce in a quart fruit jar.

"How long have you taught here?" Mose asked Lora after he had helped his plate.

"This makes twenty years. Folks say I nearly own the school." She laughed warmly, noisily, no distrust in her voice now. "I ought to in that time. I've seen a lot of teachers come and go, and spanked most of the kids in town."

"Where did you go to school?"

"Right here."

"I mean, where did you get your training to be a teacher?"

"Ain't had none. The year I was sixteen one of the teachers took sick and quit. Being the biggest girl in school, they hired me to take her place, and I jest stayed on. I layed off to go to Langston summers, but jest didn't. But I ain't missed going off to school none. You don't need it to teach kids to read and write, and that's about all we try to do here. Sometimes we don't try that very hard."

"But in an eight-teacher school——"

"Don't kid yourself, Professor," she said, her laugh harsh again. "It ain't really eight teachers."

"Mister Carson said——"

"It don't make no matter what Mister Carson said. It ain't really eight teachers. We jest got four teachers besides the principal. Each teacher gets ten dollars a month extra to hire a girl pupil to help her. It looks good in the papers to say eight teachers. Makes it look like equal education. It works out all right that-a-way, I reckon. White folks seem satisfied. They don't want their darkies educated too good nohow."

Mose saw again the letter from John Carson offering him the job, the words "eight-teacher school" standing importantly alone. They had had a part in his decision to come to Columbus. "Eight-teacher school"—with only four teachers. Again he felt the frustration, the futility that had driven him from a one-room school in Mississippi to the university in Chicago, that had dogged him down the city streets, that had sent him back south of the Line. Frustration mixed with anger when he spoke.

"Why don't the colored people protest?"

Lora laughed scornfully. "Protest! You done forgot you ain't in the North now. Niggers protest? You lived all your life in Mississippi. You know a nigger ain't got no right to kick about nothing. You forgot you down home again. They call this part of Oklahoma 'Little Dixie.' Some ways it's tougher 'n Old Dixie. We live trouble enough as it is, without'n stirring up more."

On her words Mose stopped eating, pushed his plate back. She was right. For a moment he had let his memory lag.

"What have the principals before me done?" he asked more humbly.

"Hmph! Nothing. They been a bunch o' handkerchiefheads—too busy shining up to the whites to draw their little pay. Las' one run off with another man's wife."

"So I hear tell. Who are the other teachers?"

Lora pushed back her plate and leaned her elbows on the table. She took her left index finger in her right hand and started counting.

"I'm the primary teacher ... and you can depend on me. I got my faults, but you can depend on me."

"I believe that, all right."

"The intermediate teacher is Cenoria Davis."

"Can I depend on her?"

Lora looked toward the kitchen and then leaned closer to Mose. "If I don't tell you about her," she said in a low voice, "somebody else will, and you might as well get it straight the first time. But don't tell nobody I told you. She boards here with me and I ain't aiming to get in trouble with her. You don't act like the talking kind."

"I'm not."

"She was the wife of Jackson Davis, the principal last year. They come from the South somewhere—Louisiana, I reckon. Ain't nobody ever knowed them here before. Law', what a couple they made! He was tall and dark, she was tall and light. Ain't nobody around here can touch her for looks. Things went fine at first. They went to the Methodist Church and took a active part. He was president of the choir and she played the piano. Then the word got out that he was fooling around with a little dark gal down at the beauty parlor. Cenoria come to school one day and said we ain't got no principal. He done run off to New Orleans with that Cluris. That night Cenoria moved over here to the boardinghouse, and far as I can find out she ain't heard o' him since. Ain't no letters from him, I know."

She sucked black coffee down her throat and met Mose's gaze frankly, her eyes sure of her audience.

"Law', it nearly broke her heart when he done her that-a-way. She went around dazed like somebody with the weed—not talking much to nobody and grieving her eyes out. Nothing seemed to help her but her music. She'd go over to the schoolhouse at night and play in the dark. Ain't nobody ever played the piano like that. Law', she made it talk, and every word it said was about the misery in her soul. From where I set right here I could hear her thumping that jazz like she'd break her thumbs and fingers. Sounded sometimes like drums a-beating, sometimes like a wild thing wailing. Then she'd come to her room and pace the floor——"

"Is she all right now?"

"I reckon so. She don't go to the schoolhouse no more at night, and the only playing I hear her do is at church on Sunday. She looks peart and purty agin. Lots o' folks thought she'd get in trouble, but she ain't yet. I ain't blaming her for having man trouble. Law' knows, I had plenty of that myself."

She stopped suddenly, the subject cut short.

"And the other teachers?"

"Fannie Mae Williams teaches maid work."

"Maid work? What's that?"

"Well, a couple o' years ago the white ladies of Columbus complained on account of the maids they were getting didn't know nothing about maiding. So the School Board started maid training for all the girls—you know, washing clothes, cooking, scrubbing floors, tending young'uns. Now they want to start a course like it for the boys so's they can learn how to fix cars and porter. They don't mind if their colored he'p cain't read or write long as they can do white folks' work. Fannie Mae's uncle is Harrison Williams what owns *The Neighborhood Eye*. When she ain't teaching, she keeps house for him and helps with the paper. The other teacher is Sister Daisy Simpson. Her husband pastors the Methodist Church. She teaches what's left over."

"I trust she's reliable," Mose said with a laugh.

"Law', ain't nobody better 'n Sister Daisy. Onliest trouble with her, she don't know nothing."

"Are all the teachers here now?"

"Will be Monday morning when you ring the bell. All here now but Cenoria. She's visiting over at the City."

Mose stood up and stretched his hands over his head. Lora looked at the white shirt clinging wet to his shoulders.

"You big enough to handle sassy boys," she said, "and you look like you'll do it all right—but, man, you got to show this town a lot o' things before they'll believe you the right man for principal. You got to show you ain't after every slut what comes along. You got to show you ain't no booze hound. What's mostest, you got to show you ain't no handkerchiefhead, that you got guts enough to stand up to the white folks and get the equal education they always talking about."

"I'll fight for equal rights," Mose said quietly. "That's why I'm here. But I have to fight in my own way."

She studied his face deliberately, seemed to like what she found there. "No matter what you do here, life ain't gonna be no bed o' roses for you, Mose Ingram," she said, "but I reckon you can get along if you try hard enough and walk the straight and narrow. Would you like to see the schoolhouse?"

"Yes, ma'am."

She took a key from over the kitchen door and gave it to him. "You better keep this one," she said. "You the *man* now."

3

LEAVING Lora at her table, Mose, in a crow-black suit and white shirt with standing collar, dressed to the dignity he must maintain, paused for a moment on the porch to get his bearings and then stepped into sand shoe-mouth deep. It was cooler, now that the sun was behind Reservoir Hill and Pleasant Valley in shadows. It would be cooler still when the blessing of darkness spread over a too-bright land.

Workers, their dust rags, mops, shoebrushes laid aside for the night, converged on Happy Hollow from white town and country. From Columbus came the men who worked in the cotton-oil mill and railroad yards, the shine boys and porters from hotels and office buildings, women in uniform who served in the white houses in town. On they came, walking, quietly or noisily, laughing, singing, scowling, each carrying his little bundle of provender for the night, the women clutching their "totin's" from white folks' tables. Along the trails from the country the cotton pickers straggled, their canvas sacks over their shoulders, the women with bright rags tied around their heads.

With their return, shacks came to life. Thin streams of wood smoke rose from chimneys and stovepipes. Odors of cooking food—salt pork frying and cabbage boiling—mixed with the smell of houses closed up all day. These were soft, warm, human smells, much like those Mose had known in the "quarters" at Penrose Plantation. They aroused children to laughter, women to song. From a shack behind the boardinghouse Mose could hear a woman singing:

"Sometimes I'm both toss-ted and driven,
Sometimes I know not where to ro-o-a-oam,
I've heard of a city called Heaven . . ."

Her words were smothered in a baby's wail, but Mose found himself concentrating on what should have been the last in the refrain—"Home."

Mose crossed the street, stopped before the closed picture show long enough to read the posters announcing a Western feature for Saturday night, and took one of the paths through the hydrant square. Men, women, children with the gravity of men and women, with pails and jugs in their hands, waiting their turns at the sluggish stream, stared curiously at him. Frenchy and Sister Brackett had spread their news well. Respectfully the people said "E'ening, Professor" as he passed. He smiled at a little boy who looked him over and said in a low sharp voice, "Man, he's big—heaps bigger 'n the las' one." The hum of their laughter followed him to the schoolhouse.

It was a new rectangular building of cheap red brick set in an acre square. The grounds, uncared for all summer, were covered with scraggly grass and rubble. Toward the back fence purple thistles thrust their thorny heads above the grass. Mose stopped to read the name—PHILLIS WHEATLEY SCHOOL—cut in block letters in a concrete slab above the entrance.

Not a bad building at all, Mose thought as he inserted the key in the lock. He compared it with the one-room frame building on Penrose Plantation. Pleasant Valley was a promotion from that. He wondered what the white schools in Columbus were like. Probably as good as any he had seen in Chicago, he thought. The door yielded with a fine grating of sand.

Mose drew the smell of books and chalk dust deep into his lungs. He saw that a pencil sharpener inside the front door needed emptying. He took it to the drum stove and poured out a handful of shavings. The faint smell of dry cedar clung to his fingers. He went through all the four rooms on the ground floor, touching a desk here, straightening a shade there, wondering about a rocking chair behind one teacher's desk. Two rooms were separated by a sliding partition. He slid the doors back and studied the auditorium they made. Not big enough to hold all the children that ought to be in school, he thought, not big enough for the community center he hoped to make of the school. He went to the second floor. Here there were four more rooms and an office with PRINCIPAL above the door. Mose felt more at home than he had since he first left Penrose Plantation. He pulled a chair up to the desk and sat down.

"Feels just right," he said to himself, half amused. He leaned back and looked out the window over the part of Pleasant Valley that stretched from the schoolhouse to Reservoir Hill. Dozens and dozens of shotgun houses formed irregular lines to the edge of the slope, some rising bare and ugly from the Oklahoma prairie, some half hidden in clumps of oaks and peach trees. From these houses, with smoke from cooking fires rising in straight columns above them, flowed the life with which he was to intermingle, whose channel he had determined to turn. Facing him at last was the task for which he had been called, for which he had left an old way of life, for which he now felt fear and trembling and firm resolve. Alone, in this schoolhouse opened for him, he repeated again his ideas for redeeming the Southern black: Educate him . . . teach him to read and write . . . help him to be his own teacher, lawyer, doctor, technician . . . help him to better jobs and higher standards of living . . . help him to lift himself above the slavery of the South. Those ideas sounded fine in Chicago, he thought, but there was a hollowness in them in Columbus, where girls were trained to be maids, boys educated to be porters. Not so good, he thought. It was a hard task he had set for himself, but he had put his hand to the plow.

His thoughts were broken by footsteps on the stairs, a voice at the door.

"Evening, Brother. Can I come in?"

Mose looked up to see an aged man in Prince Albert clothes standing in the doorway.

"I'm Brother Simpson, pastor of the First Methodist Church, Colored," he said as he advanced toward Mose's desk. "They told me the new principal was at the schoolhouse, so I come over to talk with you awhile and pass the time of day."

Mose offered his hand, then brought in a chair for his visitor. Brother Simpson sat with his face to the window. The light was still strong enough to mark the deep lines of his thin face and to turn his hair to yellowed cotton. His eyes were sunken and sharp— the eyes of a holy man. Mose was reminded of the Prophets. This might be Isaiah, or Jeremiah, or Hosea come to talk with him. Hosea most likely, Mose thought, for his face was marked by suffering, his eyes lighted by kindness.

"Been pastor here long?" Mose asked.

"More than fifteen year, winter and summer."

"You must know the place well."

"Like the pages of my Bible Book. I've seen a lot of things go on here. It ain't a peaceful town. Lord knows it ain't."

"What makes the trouble?"

"Lots o' things. Columbus is a new town. Oklahoma's a new state. A lot o' things ain't organized yet. Being new, it's a kind of battleground. Negroes fight for what they want and whites fight to keep them down. They call it 'Little Dixie,' but it's too far north for the Negroes to be like what you've seen in Mississippi or Alabama. It ain't far enough north for Negroes to have any of the freedom they'd get in Chicago or New York. They're always see-sawing."

"Any open friction?"

"Not to amount to anything. White folks leave us alone as long as we behave ourselves and don't disturb them. Most of the colored folks're from down home and glad enough to stay in their place. Living close like this, we got to get along. But we got some trouble-makers over on this side, and we got some *emancipated* folks that've been up North and want to act big-britches when they come back. They stir up bad blood yelling about race."

"Any troublemakers among the whites?"

"A few we know about. It used to be all the whites 'd come after us. Now it's only a few. Most of them are young bucks that like to come over to Happy Hollow on Saturday night and scare niggers to have a little fun. They ride up and down the streets squirting soda water on folks, but they's mostly harmless. They's a few ugly ones—like Blackledge. He's a deputy in the High Sheriff's office and, man, how he hates niggers! Sometimes he eggs white boys on to stir up trouble with colored boys. Says it helps keep us in our place. You'll know it's him by the way folks shut their doors when he comes on this side. Little kids run inside and hide when they see Blackledge coming."

"I saw him pass this afternoon."

"Then you know about him. He won't bother you long as you say 'Yes, sir, Mister Blackledge' and 'No, sir, Mister Blackledge' and do what he says."

Brother Simpson ended with a shrug, and then lifted his eyes to the glow behind Reservoir Hill. "It seems mighty peaceful in Pleasant Valley tonight," he said, "but you and me've lived in the South too long. We know that any day the hate can grow like fire in a dry pasture—like it did in Tulsa not so long ago."

As darkness grew positive, Brother Simpson talked of his wanderings from Tennessee to Indiana to Oklahoma, of his hopes and failures as a pastor. When he first came to Pleasant Valley he had dreams of a red brick church trimmed in white and with a white steeple reaching so high it would have to be seen by the white folks in Columbus. In the prosperous years following the war, he had raised enough money to build the basement of his church—money donated by Negro soldiers returned from France, by members of his congregation who did without food to add a few bricks to their church, by white churches in Columbus as a part of their missionary offering. When the basement was completed they all had hopes of continuing until the last shingle was on the steeple and the last blue and amber panes in the windows. But the seven lean years that came would soon be twice seven. They no longer spoke of when the church would be completed.

As Brother Simpson talked of the time of building, with the men of the congregation working together laying bricks, spreading mortar, to the rhythm of spirituals rising from within them, Mose found himself wanting to add his own strength to raising that white steeple. These were not Hebrew children making bricks without straw in the land of Egypt; they were not primitive blacks building a straw temple to some unknown god in the jungle; they were followers of Jesus raising an altar to Him. Mose knew their need to raise it high and white—like a finger pointing at Jim Crow Christians. He knew, or thought he knew, the depth of guilt segregation made for the whites.

"Will you worship with us in our church, Brother?" Brother Simpson asked, laying his hand on Mose's knee.

"If God wills. But I can't promise for my wife and sons. I hope they will come. I'd like my sons brought up in your church. I want them to know there's something besides cotton-patch religion. I want them to feel the reverence, the dignity—a dignity I didn't know about till after I left Mississippi."

"Ours is a quiet service, with singing of hymns, reading the Scriptures, praying together. We discourage folks from going into trances and talking in unknown tongues. If a sister wants to shout, we let her shout, but we don't set up a brass band for her to holler and dance by."

Mose remembered their church on Penrose Plantation, in a house that had once been a part of the quarters. He remembered the meetings he had attended since childhood—meetings made up chiefly of singing and shouting and dancing. He remembered the hot summer nights when crops were laid by and the dog days were on them—nights when men and women danced themselves into exhaustion in the sawdust, and penitent sinners threw themselves on the ground to bellow out their sins. He remembered, with hot embarrassment, the night Josie received the gift of tongues and lived for a brief moment a new Pentecost. It had taken all night to bring her out of the trance that followed. Shamefully he remembered the ruckus he raised the night he got religion.

He remembered his first summer in Chicago—days and nights of searching for peace in store-front churches—his relief in finding at last that worship could be quiet, contemplative.

"I like quiet, reverent worship," Mose said, "but I don't know about Josie. She was brought up in the holiness religion—she's never known any other kind. It may be hard for her to change."

"She could go to the holy-roller church. They whoop and holler over there every night. You'll hear them starting up after while. They's a Baptist church here too, but they ain't got a regular parson and don't many people go to it. They done been weaned over to Sister Brackett and the Holinesses. Spiritualist preachers come and go, selling their holy incense and handkerchiefs sprinkled with holy water...."

Mose leaned out the window and looked at the yellow squares of lights from the houses. Reservoir Hill was a darker shadow against the dark sky. He sniffed the faint odor of dew on dusty grass and trees.

Brother Simpson talked on, his voice quiet, his questions probing. "It ain't ordinary," he said, "for a Mississippi Negro to get as much schooling as you got. It ain't ordinary for a man to have as much understanding as you have. I'd like to know how you managed."

Mose faced the *why* again, as he had often in the past few months —faced it and talked to Brother Simpson as he had learned to talk to himself, simply and honestly.

"I was born and raised on Penrose Plantation in the Mississippi Delta. My mammy and pappy died of swamp fever when I was a baby and I was brought up in the plantation kitchen, with everybody nussing me. When I was old enough I went to the plantation school. Reading and writing came easy to me. Before I was twelve I was writing letters for folks that couldn't write—and verses for memory books. After I was twelve they sent me out to be a field hand, but I kept on studying. One day Miss May—she's the owner of the plantation now that all the others died off—sent for me to come to her sitting room and read for her. It was a big room on the second floor with windows looking above the magnolias to the cotton fields, in a part of the house I'd never been in till that day. Miss May was sitting on a sofa wrapped up in a white shawl. I sat on a footstool and read to her from Jefferson Davis' *Rise and Fall of the Confederate Government.* Then I wrote 'Miss May Penrose' on a slate with all the flourishes I knew.

" 'That's fine,' Miss May said and held the slate up for Josie to see. Josie was learning to be her maid then, and has been her maid ever since. I don't see how Miss May will get along without her now. Miss May and Josie mirated over the writing and made me write 'Josie' on the other side of the slate.

"Miss May told me that day she wanted me to go to school and be a teacher so I could teach the plantation school. She helped me a lot with money and clothes. I went to a small Negro college in Mississippi. After I graduated I married Josie and taught the plantation school for ten years. During those years I was satisfied to stay with my wife and sons, teaching colored children to read and write and grow up to be good workers on Penrose Plantation. I had a mule and cotton patch of my own and raised a crop every summer. Then I began wanting to study more, but there was no place for me to study in Mississippi. I began wanting to go up North. Josie discouraged me. She thought I had enough education as it was. She had been taught only enough to read the Bible to Miss May. She argued against my going, against the idea of change. She was afraid of what would happen to me if I went up among the Yankees. I might be killed. I might forget to come home. 'What will Miss May think?' she asked. Miss May hated Yankees worse than anything in the world.

"One day I went to Miss May and told her what I wanted to do. She hemmed and hawed and then said I could go summers, if I would come home winters to teach the plantation school. She even lent me money each year to go on. She'd always say 'I know this takes you farther from home' before she handed me the money.

"I went to Chicago because it was about the nearest place to Mississippi I could get what I wanted. There was a white professor there who knew all about Negro writers—old Doctor Thompson. I wish you could talk to him. I studied under him—Dunbar, Frederick Douglass, Sojourner Truth, all the others. I would read what they said about slavery and then talk about it to Doctor Thompson. He was one white man who could understand what they had to say. At last I got so full I had to think of some way of doing what I could for my people."

"Why did you come to Columbus?"

"There are a lot of reasons. I couldn't be satisfied any more at Penrose Plantation. I just had to get away from there. Every fall when I came home to Mississippi I hated it more. I saw more clearly what the whites are doing there. This was my last summer and I had to make up my mind. I could stay up North, or I could go back home. The offer at Columbus was the last one I had. I took it because of the location. If I went back to the Deep South, I couldn't do much. Too many things stand in the way. Violence is too easy. If I went north, I would be running away. So I came here. You said this place is a battleground. Well, I expected that, and I'm here to help in the fight. When you look at all the angles, there was no choice."

"I understand you, Brother, and I'm glad you're here."

The two men stood together. Brother Simpson went before Mose down the stairs, feeling for the steps in the darkness. It was quiet and cool outside. Only a few lights glowed in shacks and stands, a few gleamed bare on the posters at the picture show. From a distance Mose heard men and women singing a spiritual, stamping out the rhythm on the floor with their feet.

"Sister Brackett's church," Brother Simpson said. "They'll be at it most of the night." He took Mose's hand. "Your job will be just like wrastling a elephant—no place to take hold. . . . Where you going to start?"

"With the white folks first. Cain't much be done down South till the white folks want it done. I'm going to see Mister John Carson tomorrow morning. Then I'll know where I've got to work—and what I've got to work with."

Brother Simpson said good night and turned away, leaving Mose to lock up the schoolhouse for the night.

4

MORNING came through the boardinghouse window with a searing glare of sun and sky. "Gonna be another scorcher," Lora Dixon said to Mose at breakfast. "Gonna be another hot damn day," men called to one another on the streets when Mose was on his way to Columbus to talk to John Carson. Mose felt the heat pulling the moisture from his skin, leaving a feel of drying leather.

It was Saturday and Pleasant Valley was getting ready for "Sa-a-dy night." While the sun still cast long shadows, women worked furiously sweeping yards, hanging out clothes, cleaning and dusting. Men lined the porch at the barbershop, waiting to get their scalps peeled. Women, in loose dresses and bright head rags, clustered about the door of the beauty parlor. Those without money for the beauty parlor combed and straightened one another's hair on their front porches. Skillful hands heated heavy steel combs over alcohol flames and pulled them through mats of woolly hair. At times a breath of scorched hair and peach-tree pomade showed that not all the hands were skillful enough. But slight matter. The ritual of "Sa-a-dy night" must be observed.

Sister Brackett passed Mose in her buggy, on her way to white town to sell her hominy—white crocks beside her, white crocks crowding her knees. Frenchy drove by with his taxi filled with a pay load. A watermelon peddler rocked along the street in a rickety wagon, calling out

> "Chicken am good,
> Possum am fat and very fine,
> But give me I wisht you would
> The watermelyun smiling on the vine...."

A minstrel without the trappings of the minstrel show, he added his own street cry to the minstrel song:

> "Buy yo' watermelyuns from Zack...
> M-m-m...
> Rattlesnakes ez ripe and sho' nuff fine...."

He stopped singing long enough to raise his hat to Mose.

All along the way people tipped their hats or bowed and said, "Good morning, Professor"... "Kinda warm here, Professor, but you'll git used to it." That's nice, Mose thought. Nice and friendly. They knew who he was and wanted to make him feel at home. Josie would like these people. It was a fine place to bring his family.

From the station up Main Street Mose walked close to the curb, ready to move out of the way of whites he met, ready to step into the gutter if his space should be needed by a white man—not feeling inferior, merely observing a lifetime of training in Mississippi. What Miss May considered "good nigger manners" in Mississippi would no doubt be acceptable in this Columbus, which seemed to be made up of all the Columbuses in the Deep South. The sidewalks were not marked FOR WHITES ONLY, but Mose read the signs there in the eyes of the whites he met. He knew it was better for him here in Columbus to remember his place. Negroes who got out of their place got in trouble. He had seen that often in Mississippi. He had seen it in Chicago as well, he remembered wryly.

Along his way Mose saw many Negroes "in their place." At the Columbus Hotel Negro doormen in blue-and-red uniforms opened doors for white patrons, whistled taxis to the curb. At the Columbus National Bank a Negro in gray cotton uniform polished brass plates on the doors. Negroes carried bundles, shined shoes, washed cars, rolled wheelbarrows of concrete. Mose saw them until his perception was dulled. He had seen them all his life "in their place" as servants to white men.

Mose found the back door of CARSON BROTHERS, CLOTHIERS and entered, hat in hand. Salesmen and customers mumbled around racks of fall suits and hats. Mose stood near a counter of work clothes waiting to ask for Mr. Carson. The smell of denim overalls carried him back to his boyhood on Penrose Plantation—to new overalls at cotton-picking time. A slender boy wearing the freshman cap of the University of Oklahoma walked back and forth in a shiny leather jacket. A large gray-haired woman watched him with a bored look on her face. A clerk rubbed his hands over the boy's shoulders, smoothing the jacket into a mold over his slender form. A middle-aged Indian turned himself slowly before a three-way mirror, studying the effect of a broad-brimmed Western hat set squarely on his head. He tried his braids in front, behind, and then looped them at the back of his neck. His eyes were dull, his lips barely articulate, but the clerks waited on him deferentially.

No one noticed Mose until a Negro porter came by with his arms loaded with freshly pressed suits. "What you want to buy?" he asked Mose. "Duckings?"

"Nothing. I want to see Mister Carson about——"

"Oh, you the new principal. Frenchy pointed you out to me." He laid the suits on a counter and asked Mose to follow him upstairs to Mr. Carson's office. "I wisht I had a nickel for every dollar that Indian's got," he said.

The office was on a balcony overlooking the store. Mr. Carson sat at a desk where he could keep an eye on his clerks and customers. Mose stood at the end of the desk until Mr. Carson looked up.

"What you want?" Mr. Carson demanded gruffly.

"I'm Mose Ingram. You hired me as principal."

"So you're the new principal. It's about time you showed up. I was afraid you wouldn't get here in time for school to start Monday. Well, I'm mighty busy on Saturday morning, but I reckon I'd better take time to talk to you a little. I've got the school ledger right here."

Mose remained standing at the end of the desk. He knew that he would not be asked to sit down for the interview. Mr. Carson did not look like the kind of man who would ask a Negro to sit down in his office, even if the Negro was a teacher. Mr. Carson was a Southern business gentleman. He would keep Negroes in their place. He might be kind in his own way, Mose felt, looking at him, but his own way was strictly Jim Crow.

"We'll talk about you first," Mr. Carson said as he opened the ledger. "I didn't like the idea of hiring a nigger sight unseen, but there wasn't anything else to do this time . . . and you seemed the best of the lot. But there's some things I want cleared up before we go any further."

"Yes, sir."

He took up a letter and flattened it on his desk. Mose could see the signature: Enoch Thompson.

"A lot of good things in this letter, but they don't apply down here. We're not looking for a research student or an expert on Negro poetry. He obviously don't know how we do things down here."

He suddenly glared at Mose fiercely. "You are a Mississippi nigger, ain't you?"

"Yes, sir."

"You got the manners of a Mississippi nigger all right, but you don't talk like one."

"I was born and raised there. Maybe going to school in the North makes me talk different."

"Maybe so. Anyway, I hired you because of the letter I got about you from Miss May Penrose. She sounds like a real Southern gentlewoman. She said that you were a good nigger on the plantation for her, that you run a good school and that you know your place. Can you live up to her recommendation?"

"I'll try to, sir."

"All right. Now, another thing. You got to stay away from the women. The one we had last year was a regular boar shoat. We cain't have anything like that again. Understand?"

"Yes, sir."

"Now tell me about your family."

"I have a wife and three sons. Josie, my wife, was personal maid for Miss May on the plantation."

"So Miss Penrose said. How old is your oldest son?"

"Thomas is fifteen."

"Is he a likely nigger? If so, I could give him a job here in the store shining shoes and sweeping up. He could get to be a porter when he's a little older."

Mose hesitated, and then decided to speak at least a part of his mind. The hesitation saved him from spilling the bitterness touched by Mr. Carson's offer, calmed him for speaking reasonably of his plans for his sons.

"Thank you for the offer, sir, but Thomas is going to be a lawyer. He'll need all his time to study. He'll——"

"A lawyer?" Mr. Carson asked incredulously. "What in hell good is a nigger lawyer? Answer me that if you can. Better let him be a porter. Then he can make a living and stay out of trouble. But a lawyer. I'll be goddamned. I suppose the other two want to be bankers."

"Boys change their minds sometimes. Right now Robert wants to be a minister and John a doctor," Mose said quietly.

"Being a nigger preacher's all right. But nigger doctors and lawyers—I ain't got much use for them."

"Yes, sir," Mose said, knowing nothing else to say.

"Now take my son Alan. He finished down at Norman last spring and is going to start to law school this fall. There will be a job for him when he gets through—working in a law office here in town, or running for some office. He could be a judge someday. Ain't nobody ever heard of a nigger judge—or a nigger lawyer. Have you?"

"Yes, sir."

"Where?"

"In Chicago."

"I guess it's all right to have nigger lawyers in Chicago, but it's different in Columbus. You better change his mind and make him be a porter. It'd be a heap better in the long run. Mark my words."

"Yes, sir."

"Where you going to live?"

"I don't know yet, sir. I'm looking for a house."

"I've got just what you need—a three-room house only a little ways from your school. Kinda small, but big enough for your family. Ten dollars a month, take it or leave it."

"I'll take it," Mose said uncomfortably. He wanted to end the interview as quickly as possible without offending Mr. Carson, to get away and think things over again. A part of his plan was to stand firm when he could, yield when he must, but at all times to avoid open friction with the whites.

"Now, to the school business. As principal you will get one hundred dollars a month. That's a lot of money for a nigger in this town. Four of the teachers get eighty a month apiece, but they'll have to hire their assistants out of that. The assistants get ten dollars a month. Understand?"

"Yes, sir."

Mose understood much more than he could say at the moment. He knew that school funds were apportioned by the state on a per-capita basis. He knew that the amount spent on Negro education in Columbus that year would be far below what they were entitled to. But the account books were kept by white folks, and colored folks could never know how much they were entitled to. He knew this, and remembered his conversation with Lora Dixon the night before. Now was the time he should protest, demand more money for the school, demand real teachers instead of substitutes. He dared not, for he feared his own anger. He accepted the situation as it stood, feeling that there was nothing else for him to do, wondering what any other colored man could do in the circumstances. Later—yes, later, when he had established himself—then he would speak his mind.

"Your Yankee professor said you were an expert in Negro poetry. Well, you won't need that here. We try to teach the nigger kids how to read, write and do the kind of numbers they'll need in a filling station or shine parlor. We ain't got time or money for any fancy education for them. You don't believe any of that fancy stuff about uplifting niggers, do you?"

Mose was not prepared for this question. He felt himself at a great disadvantage. He thought of the reasons he had given himself when he left Chicago and came south to teach—reasons he had repeated to Brother Simpson the night before. He thought of the things he wanted to do. But if he spoke them now, Mr. Carson would drive him out of his store—perhaps out of town.

"Not fancy, sir—just a solid education," he equivocated, and wondered how far he could dissimulate without becoming himself an Uncle Tom, a handkerchiefhead.

"Then we agree. Last year we put in a course in maid work at Phillis Wheatley—ain't that the damnedest name for a school? Gotta get it changed sometime—so the white ladies can get maids of some account to them. It seemed to work out all right, so we'll keep it up this year. Next year we ought to start teaching the boys how to be porters and waiters...."

Mose remained silent, his mind busy with an unhappy decision: it was better to let things pass on the surface, not to tell the whites what he wanted to do, better to teach on the sly the things he was bound to teach. Then he might at least wriggle in the Jim Crow strait jacket.

"Got anything else on your mind?" Mr. Carson asked. "If not, I'll get back to work. Saturdays are busy days."

"Yes, sir. I need to borrow some money to bring my family from Mississippi."

"Never saw a nigger that didn't need money for something or other. How much do you need?"

"About a hundred dollars."

"You'd better go over to the bank—the Columbus National Bank. We keep the school funds there. See Mister Brown and tell him who you are. I'll telephone him you're coming. Is that all?"

"That is all, sir."

"Then you start school Monday morning. I'll come by before the week is over to see how you're getting along."

"Thank you, sir."

"See here, Mose. I'd advise you to talk more like a nigger. It'd sound a lot better in Columbus."

"Yes, sir."

"We've had a lot of trouble with nigger principals. You stick by us, we'll stick by you."

"Yes, sir."

Mose bowed respectfully and left the office. As he walked along the street toward the bank he felt remorse because he had not spoken out to Carson, had not told him all he felt about coming to Columbus and the work he wanted to do for his people. But the remorse faded into the reality that he was not likely to find one sympathetic white man in Columbus. He tried to recapture the confidence and hope he had experienced in the schoolhouse the night before, but that was impossible under a glaring hot sun on the streets of white Columbus. The elephant was indeed too big to grapple with.

"A man's got to be strong," he told himself as he walked along. But something had happened to his strength. On the streets of Chicago he had learned how to be a free man with a purpose in life. Here in Columbus he was already beginning to slink along the streets and shy from dangerous encounters.

"Can't keep on feeling this way," he muttered.

He came to the bank and hesitated outside the plate-glass window. He looked inside at the tellers in their neat cages and at the officials in their leather upholstered chairs in the front office. He watched a Negro porter pushing a broom across the smoothly polished terrazzo floor. His fear of banks made him tremble slightly. Banks catch a man and hold him tight. But there was no other way. He straightened his shoulders and walked through the door. He crossed the smooth, slick floor and came to a mahogany rail. Behind the rail was a mahogany desk with MR. BROWN on a neatly lettered sign. He paused in front of that desk.

"What do you want?" Mr. Brown asked, looking up.

"I want to borrow some money. I'm Mose Ingram, principal of the school. Mister Carson said he'd telephone you——"

"Yes, he called. How much do you need?"

"A hundred dollars, sir."

"That's a month's salary."

"Yes, sir, but I need it."

"Got anything for collateral?"

"No, sir."

"You expect me to lend you money on your name?"

"That's all I've got, sir."

"When can you pay it back?"

"You can make it for three months, sir."

"Very well. But see that you take care of it properly. Your salary checks will be drawn against this bank. We will hold them until you have made proper settlement of your account. Agreeable?"

"Yes, sir."

Mr. Brown took a note form and filled in the details in purple ink. As he wrote he talked to Mose.

"Carson said your wife was coming here to live."

"Yes, sir."

"Said she was a maid back in Mississippi."

"Yes, sir."

"Well, I've been thinking. My wife needs somebody to work for her steady. Maybe your wife would like the job. It'd pay three dollars a week and totin's."

He pushed the note over for Mose to sign. Mose held the long desk pen in his fingers for a moment as he thought about the offer of a job for Josie. He stooped over the desk and wrote his name on the dotted line.

"Well, sir," he said slowly, "I don't believe Josie will have time for a job. We have three children for her to take care of——"

"But she worked in Mississippi."

"Yes, sir, but that was different. Miss May just about raised her. It wasn't like working for somebody. And the children could stay about the house. Here we wouldn't have anybody to look after the children."

"As you like. But if she ever wants a job, let me know."

Mr. Brown opened a drawer and took out a stack of new ten-dollar bills. Carefully he counted out nine, pausing each time to wet the tip of his finger with his tongue.

"You pay the interest in advance," he said. "That's customary here."

Mose opened his mouth to protest, but closed it again, knowing the futility. He took the bills, thanked Mr. Brown, and left the bank.

"In debt again," he said to himself bitterly. "Always in debt. On the plantation it was debt for seed and faring, and pay back high at picking time. Here it's still debt, with interest too high for any man to pay. I'll always be in debt here. I'm tied to Columbus now like a pig tied to a post."

He remembered the offer of a job for Josie. For a moment he thought she could help pay off the debt. Then he thought of the salary. *Three dollars a week and totin's.* The picture of her walking along the road from Columbus with a bag of "totin's" under her arm made him glad he had refused.

Mose found himself at an open square called in every Southern town the "Cotton Yard." White farmers, a handful only, with their wagons drawn up in rows, watched resignedly while cotton buyers thrust long knives deep into the bales and brought out handfuls of test lint. They pulled at small bits to check the length of fiber, and then threw the leavings to the wind. It was waste for the farmers— enough for a plug of chewing tobacco or a snack of candy for the chaps at home—but they dared not object. Then an old Negro—old enough to have been a slave, humble enough to have been a slave— came with his cotton sack and gathered the waste, which the Cotton Yard keeper sold back to the cotton gins for baling.

Mose watched the scene, an old one for him, for a moment, marveled that in Oklahoma poor whites seemed little better off than Negroes, and then took himself—all the diverse things he had been that morning—back to Happy Hollow.

5

SATURDAY lunch at the Pleasant Valley Rooming House was a hurried, noisy meal, with the places at the table filled, while more customers waited in the living room or on the porch, crowding in for the Saturday two-bit special. A white man, a dime-a-week insurance salesman, worked on the porch, collecting dimes, signing new policies—a part of the scene, but aloof from the Negroes who composed it, obviously as unfeeling about them as they were about him.

Mose ate hurriedly, then caught Lora Dixon on her way from the kitchen.

"I rented Mister Carson's house."

"Which one? He's got about twenty on this side."

"He said it was close to the school."

"Oh, that one. It ain't much."

She led him to her front porch and pointed out the ridgepole. "That's it. That shotgun house with patches of green roofing and the flue with a bucket on top." Mose followed her finger and located the house, on another street and two blocks away. "It's the onliest empty house up that way now," Lora continued. "They call that Mulberry Street. It ain't got no sign, but that's the name."

"I'll go have a look," Mose told her.

He walked past the Methodist church and turned west on a street so narrow it was hardly a street at all. The houses, no more than shacks, squatted in irregular lines, with ugly patches of grass and weeds between, with here and there an umbrella chinaberry tree to hide the ugliness. There was no one to speak to Mose as he passed by, the people having withdrawn into the shadows of their houses

39

to rest through the heat of the day. Their gardens wilted in the sun; their chickens, a few gamecocks and hens, dusted themselves under chinaberry trees.

The house was the last one on the street. Past it, the street became a thistle-grown path leading to the fields flanking Reservoir Hill. From the outside it was a low house with boxed walls of unpainted pine and a roof too sharply pitched. A shed porch, added as an afterthought, looked like a shabby hat pulled low over the front door and window. Mose tried to peer through the window, but the dirty pane only mirrored his sweating face. He pushed the front door open and stepped in.

He stepped out again as quickly, gasping from the hot air and unbearable stench. He fanned the door a few times and then propped open the windows in the front room. The last occupants had left without cleaning up. A litter of rags, newspapers, broken bottles covered the floor. Children, using it as a playhouse, had brought in branches from trees and clay from the road to build a fort. The fragrance of drying willow leaves, a fragrance he had loved in brush arbors at revival-meeting time, lost itself here in the heavy odor of filth. Mose was sure he smelled chinches. Cracks in the walls must be full of them, he thought. He would have to wash the house with lye water.

Take it or leave it, John Carson had said. Mose's first impulse was to leave. But where else to go? Except through the rooms of this house.

The front room was about fifteen feet square, with a door in front, another leading to the second room, and a window on each side. In one corner a brick flue rose naked from the floor through the ceiling. The pine walls were bare and dirty. Mose went to the second room, like the first except that it had no flue. The third room, half the size of the other two, was kitchen, dining room, pantry and, on Saturday night at least, would have to serve as bath. The ceiling was partially torn away and he could see blue sky through a hole cut in the roof for the stovepipe. The floor was spotted with rancid pork fat dropped by many a careless cook. From the back door a trail led to an outhouse at the back of a weed-grown garden.

Mose was on a plumb bob that swung from wrath to despondency to resignation. He hated the circumstances that prevented him from going to John Carson, from throwing in his face the promise he had made. He dreaded bringing his family here. He remembered their cabin on Penrose Plantation—no larger than this house, but clean and neat, and comfortable with the many things Miss May had given Josie. He thought of the tenement kitchenette he had shared on the South Side of Chicago. This was worse than any other home he had ever had, a dismal place to set the future in.

But he had no choice, other than to make the place as livable as possible before Josie and the boys arrived. He would have to start to work at once if he wanted the house ready in a week. It would have to be scalded and scrubbed inside and out. He would have to paper walls and ceilings. There was no money to buy wallpaper. Newspapers would have to do, if he could find newspapers. He went back to the boardinghouse to borrow pots and pans and scrubbing brushes.

"That place is a frightful mess," he told Lora. "Ten dollars a month for a pigpen."

"Ain't no wonder. Last one lived there was a crippled beggar—a filthy old man smelling like a goat."

"I've got a lot of work to do before Josie gets here. She is used to Miss May's clean rooms and kitchen, and her own neat cabin. She won't live where there's dirt and filth. I thought you might loan me some things to work with, and I'll clean it up this afternoon."

Mose carried over the kettle and pails, broom and mop, soap and corn-shuck scrubbing brush Lora lent him. Then he carried water from the hydrant in the center of Happy Hollow until kettle and pails were full.

"Nothing like carrying water to make you appreciate running water," Mose said to Lora. He thought of ways to get John Carson to pipe water to the house. A hydrant in the yard would help.

By the time he had a fire under the kettle, most of the people in Pleasant Valley knew that the principal had rented the house and was readying it to bring his family.

Brother Simpson came across from the parsonage, his Bible in his hand. "Evening, Brother," he said to Mose. "I see you getting ready to work, so I come over to watch the fire for you and keep the kittle going. I can read Scripture and think on my sermon while the fire burns."

"Thank you," Mose said to him, and to Lora Dixon, who came wearing a work apron and with her hair tied up in a towel. "It's neighborly of you to help."

Mose poured lye into a pail of water. With this flesh-searing mixture he washed down walls and floors.

"That'll kill the chinches," Lora assured him.

She brought fine white sand from her garden and sprinkled it on the wet floors. Mose scrubbed with the corn-shuck brush—making the rough pine floors white except for patches around the stove, where fire had popped out and burned dark holes and grooves.

As he scrubbed, Mose worked off some of the morning's distemper. His eyes readjusted to the perspective of Jim Crow and brought John Carson and all Columbus into focus. He approached more reasonably the handicaps he had set for himself. He was glad to have Brother Simpson tending his fire, Lora Dixon lending a hand. With them he felt more secure, more confident. They lived and worked under Jim Crow. So could he.

Late in the afternoon Sister Brackett stopped her buggy outside and came back to the kitchen, where Mose and Lora were scrubbing at grease spots on the floor.

"E'ening, Brother. E'ening, Sister," she said. "Heard you wus going to move here and come by to see. That's nice. We'll be neighbors." She took Mose by the arm and led him to the back door. "You can see the top of our church right over that chainyberry tree. Me and the Reverend stays in the first house the other side of the church. We want you to make our church and house jes' like yo' own, amen."

Mose stopped work long enough to show her what he planned to do with the house. She held the edges of her black skirt from the damp floor as she walked.

"We'll have to eat in the kitchen. The stove'll be here and we can put a small table there. Won't be a table big enough for us all to eat at once, but a heap better than eating off a drain board in a kitchenette, like I've been doing. We can use the middle room for a bedroom. It's big enough for two beds. We'll have to make down a bed for Thomas in the front room. It'll be crowded, but we can manage for a while. What I need now is enough newspapers to paper the walls."

"I got a stack you can have," Sister Brackett told him. "I'll go fetch them right over." She went to the porch and then turned back. "Cenoria come home from the City this evening."

Sister Brackett returned with her buggy loaded with newspapers. Brother Brackett sat beside her on the seat.

"The Reverend," she said to Mose when they entered the house. Brother Brackett extended a feeble hand for Mose to shake. "I'm po'ly, Brother, po'ly," he mumbled. "I'm jest gitting over a spell o' the shakes."

He was tall and thin with a high arched nose and high cheekbones. His hair, almost gray, hung in straight locks over his collar. A Gullah, Mose thought; or maybe he had some Indian blood. It was easy to see that malaria had left him a wreck of a man.

Sister Brackett had a small bundle tied up in a white cloth. "Sweet-smelling yarbs," she told Mose as she tied the bundle to a nail on the wall. "May it bring good luck to yo' house." Then she hung a motto over the door. Stepping back and raising her hand, she read the words in her preaching voice: "Be Vigilant." For Mose her motto had more shades of meaning than she could have dreamed.

By nightfall Mose was ready to start papering. He boiled flour paste in a pot. With a brush he spread paste on the wall and laid newspapers over it. Darkness came. He borrowed a lamp from Lora Dixon and worked on. Brother Simpson left to prepare for his Sunday services. Sister Brackett and Brother Brackett went to their church, where people were already gathering for Saturday-night meeting. After they had gone, Lora told Mose that she was going to the picture show.

Mose glanced briefly at the newspapers as he unfolded them. Most were copies of the Columbus *Times,* a white daily. Sister Brackett had begged them from her white customers to wrap hominy in. There were also copies of *The Neighborhood Eye,* a colored weekly dedicated on the masthead to printing the news from the blackjack hills and vales of Little Dixie. These he put aside to read when he rested, to find in them, if he could, the temper of the people. Carefully he pasted the papers on the walls, keeping them straight and right side up, remembering a youthful frustration in a cabin papered crazy-quilt. Around the room the headlines ran, with a few words and phrases establishing a pattern: FDR, the New Deal, NRA. Slapping flour paste on the walls of a shotgun house, laying on newspapers instead of wallpaper, Mose thought of what "New Deal" could mean to the Negroes of Happy Hollow—and to the white farmers in the Cotton Yard, for that matter.

Mose papered two rooms before midnight, and then sat down to rest. The kitchen would have to wait. He put the copies of *The Neighborhood Eye* by the lamp, arranged them chronologically, and thoughtfully read them, from the social notes of communities he had never heard of before to the advertisements for skin whiteners and hair attachments. In a church notice he read, "Bring your new handkerchiefs, new aprons, and a new water glass to be blessed. You will receive a blessing if you just walk in the door of this church. You can also be developed out in the spiritual unfoldment psychic study. License granted upon completion of the course." It was from a spiritualist church in Tulsa. Among the classified ads he found one for blessed holy articles from India recommended for miraculous healing, for peace of mind, for overcoming enemies. "Voodooism in another form," he said to himself sadly.

In the column for the lovelorn he read, "My boy friend is in Chicago and I have a baby girl for him. How can I get him to marry me?" A man complained, "I'm unhappy about my lot in life. I married, but not for love. Now this wife gained weight so fast she weighs two hundred and fifty pounds. That's too much meat for me...."

More shocking still were the local news items of Pleasant Valley, which boldly wove stories of scandal and gossip about names Mose had heard in his short stay. Here, for all to see, was the sorry story of Jackson Davis and Cenoria, told boldly and with shadings that chilled Mose and aroused his anger. Through several issues he traced the observations and imaginings of unnamed correspondents: Jackson Davis had been seen going into the beauty parlor at two in the morning. Question: What beauty was he going after? The question was answered several issues later with a report that Davis had gone off to New Orleans with a beauty named Cluris. Another question: How come Cenoria did not go after him? Mose had some questions to ask himself about this puzzling woman. How could she stay on in Happy Hollow? How could she face *The Neighborhood Eye?* He turned through the remaining issues, searching for her name, finding nothing more than brief notes that she was visiting in Boley or in the City.

"Man," Mose said to himself, "a paper like this is a fine way to start a community free-for-all." He studied the name Harrison Williams, Editor, and remembered that Fannie Mae Williams was one of his teachers. He decided to see Harrison Williams as soon as possible. One item of gossip could destroy his further usefulness in Pleasant Valley.

Mose blew out the lamp and closed the door. He stood in the darkness of the porch and looked and listened. Lights still showed in most of the houses in Pleasant Valley, Saturday night not being over till dawn. From Sister Brackett's church came the sound of singing and praying and dancing. The rattle of a tambourine jangled at him as he walked along. Ahead was the Methodist church, dark and still. To the left, Sister Brackett's, with the people singing the songs of the plantation and his childhood. He felt himself waver to the left. For a moment he thought of stopping by just to sing some songs with them. Instead, he went toward the boardinghouse, toward the "Main Drag," where lights still glowed in house and stand, where the stillness was broken by the sound of sinful songs, of laughter, of billiard balls clicking against one another.

6

Mose sat on the boardinghouse porch the next morning and watched Sunday-dressed people gather at the Methodist church. It was fortunate, he reflected, to be able to look at the community objectively—before faces and names combined into persons to be loved, feared, trusted, admired, respected, pitied as they revealed themselves to him.

When the singing began he put on his black coat and went over. From the outside the basement structure looked like a flat box half dug into the red earth. He tried to imagine what the builder had in mind when he drew his plans. Mose glanced through square open windows at the singing, fanning people. He passed through the square door and became one of them. He felt cramped by low ceilings and crowded benches. But the others did not seem to feel the narrow room. Brother Simpson stood in the pulpit leading them in singing "Brighten the Corner Where You Are." A clear electric bulb, hung from the ceiling behind him, cast shadows on his sweating, gleaming face, made hotter a room already stifling. A light-skinned girl at the piano kept ahead of the singers, pulling them along with heavy bass runs and furiously pounded melody. She must be Cenoria Davis, Mose decided. Her face was turned from him and hidden by a mass of black hair worn low on her shoulders, but he could feel what Lora Dixon had said about her music.

"Morning, Professor," Brother Simpson shouted above the singing. "They's a *re*served seat for you right here in the amen corner." He pointed to a vacant seat in the front row.

A young man wearing a "Vice-President Usher" arm band took Mose by the arm and led him to the seat. He found himself seated next to a row of little boys with polished faces and woolly topknots.

On the other side was a fat little man with gray hair and wide gray mustaches.

"Morning, Brother," the little man said, leaning over to shake hands with Mose. His skin was smooth and dark across his cheeks and chin and crinkled like fine black crepe around his eyes. His teeth were like yellow grains of corn set in red gums. "Glad to see you at church. I'm Vice-President Elder. My name is Joe Johnson. I'm a railroading man."

Mose opened the hymnbook handed him by an usher and began to sing. His bass voice, full and deep, found the tempo of the piano, became the undercurrent of a rising flood of song.

"Step it up faster," Brother Simpson shouted.

Mose felt the people catch the rhythm, saw Cenoria Davis watching his hand. It was like the days when he had led revival-meeting singing down home. They came to the end of the song, but Cenoria kept playing. As if commanded, the people rose to their feet and sang the song through again. Mose enjoyed it as he had never enjoyed singing in Chicago churches.

When the song ended, Brother Simpson looked at Mose and then at the congregation. "Mighty good singing!" he exclaimed. "But ain't no use trying to wear one song out. We got plenty more in the book." He waited for his laugh from the crowd. "If our new brother can teach as good as he can sing, we done got us a good principal. Brother Mose, I here and now appoint you a member of our choir. You can bass it."

"Move up, Brother," Elder Johnson urged him.

"Thank you, Brother Pastor," Mose said, and took a seat in the front row of the choir to the left of the pulpit. He looked into the faces of a good part of Happy Hollow, and liked them. The feeling of being at home came to him, stronger than he had ever felt it in Chicago. Josie ought to like these people, he thought.

"Brethren and Sistren," Brother Simpson began, "this is Communion Sunday and, as has been our custom for many years, we will have a short sermon and a long testimonial service. Let us stand and sing the Doxology."

"Praise God from whom all blessings flow . . ."
With reverence and thanksgiving forever praise Him.
"Praise Him all creatures here below . . ."
Praise Him all creatures, black and white, black as well as white.

Mose followed the words with his lips, half consciously with his mind, being occupied with thoughts of the time and place enmeshing him.

The pastor led them through their regular order of service, reading the morning prayer, the Apostles' Creed, and then the Parable of the Sower: "Behold, a sower went forth to sow . . ."

Mose held his attention on the reading of the pastor. But at another level of his mind he heard Sister Brackett in her buggy, saying ominously, with confidence in her gift of prophecy, *One to grow.*

"And when he sowed, some seeds fell by the way side, and the fowls came and devoured them up: some fell upon stony places, where they had not much earth: and forthwith they sprung up, because they had no deepness of earth: and when the sun was up, they were scorched; and because they had no root, they withered away. And some fell among thorns; and the thorns sprung up and choked them: but others fell into good ground, and brought forth fruit, some an hundredfold, some sixtyfold, some thirtyfold."

Like words from far away and long ago the reading fell on Mose's ears. Uppermost in his mind, crowding out the words, the cotton-planting scene sharpened into focus. The pastor's words were faint in the roar of the men: *You got to plant three seed to git one to grow.* Three boys, rich brown like cotton seeds when the hulls have been cut away, rose from the ground and chanted with the men.

"Who hath ears to hear, let him hear." Brother Simpson finished the passage and began reading the interpretation given by Jesus.

Mose found himself translating the words to his own place, his own time. How thorny, how stony, how barren the Oklahoma earth for him and his sons! How many vultures waited for those who fell by the wayside! Was there ever a place for him to send his roots deep, for him to possess the land and bring forth fruit? And through all his meditations ran the theme of waste—waste of life, waste of talent.

Mose forced himself from his own dark thoughts to the words of Brother Simpson. He has real religion, Mose thought, real humility, real understanding. He was like Hosea himself in the pulpit, not preaching a sermon but telling children of the mercy and goodness and love of God—and the infinite peace of those who accept His Word.

"Brothers, Sisters," Brother Simpson said, "as we go into our testimonial service I would ask that our prayer be in the words of the Psa'mist when he said, 'Let the words of my mouth and the meditation of my heart be acceptable in Thy sight, O Lord, my Strength and my Redeemer.' We have in our midst today a stranger —a new friend. He has come among us to be the principal of our school. It is right and fitting that he should be the first to bear testimony for our Saviour. Brother Mose Ingram, stand up right where you are and tell the congregation what is in your heart about God."

Mose stood and addressed the congregation. "Brothers and Sisters," he began, "I am a stranger in this place but not a stranger in the house of God."

"Amen, Brother," the elders rasped.

"From my childhood on Penrose Plantation in Mississippi I was glad when they said unto me, 'Let us go into the house of the Lord.' When I was a student up North I did not forsake the ways of the Lord, but went to church every Sunday, even if I had to go to white churches where I was the only colored person in the congregation."

"Did you, Brother? Hear him, Brother! Amen, Brother," the people chanted.

"And everywhere I went I found God. People's got different ways of worshiping, but it's still the same God. In Mississippi colored folks sometimes shout and dance in the presence of God, sometimes go in trances and talk in unknown tongues. White folks up North just sit in their pews and keep silent when they feel the Lord is near. But black or white, we are the children of God, walking together toward the fields of glory."

Emotion built up, burst into a spiritual led by Elder Johnson, who, with face beaming, toes tapping, sang

> "Walk together, child'en, won't you get ready?
> Walk together, child'en, won't you get ready?
> Walk together, child'en, won't you get ready?
> They's a great camp meeting in the Promised Land."

Mose found himself drowned out as a hundred voices took up the song and made it cumulative with "Sing together, child'en" . . . "Clap yo' hands, child'en" . . . "Pray together, child'en." When they sang the refrain "Walk, walk, never tire, Walk, walk, never tire," Mose heard a high soprano singing treble in clear, sweet tones. It was Cenoria Davis, seated at the piano still but with her hands idle in her lap. Her black hair was now a frame for her face. Her skin was smooth and pale, her eyes the color of her hair. She seemed out of place, a wild canary among starlings. Her eyes were half closed, but Mose knew that she was studying him while she let her voice wander above the others like a lost spirit.

When the song ended, Mose sat down and Elder Johnson testified how the Lord had been good to a railroading man. While his voice still clung to a word, a woman—Sister Lacey the Pastor called her—stood up and started singing "I am a po' pilgrim, traveling through this unfriendly world." Others joined her and forced the elder to end his testimony. Sung down, he took his seat again. Then the woman told how for many years she had the miseries and took liniment every day. After she started walking in the Light, the blessed Gospel Light, she had not taken another drop of liniment, and she had strength for hoeing and picking cotton every day.

The gray-haired, the venerable stood, one by one, began a spiritual, told of religious experience in church, at home, in the cotton patch. With the simplicity of children they revealed their deepest emotional experiences. There was none of the mass hysteria Mose had seen on the plantation or in the store-front churches in Chicago. Brother Simpson had been right: they did not set up a brass band for the people to dance and shout by.

Zack ended the testimonial service, his watermelon peddler's song discarded for the moment for the words and paddle-wheeler rhythm of "The Old Ship o' Zion."

> " 'Tis the old Ship o' Zion,
> 'Tis the old Ship o' Zion,
> 'Tis the old Ship o' Zion,
> Git on boa'd, chile, git on boa'd. . . .
> It will land you to the place of jester. . . .
> Git on boa'd, chile, git on boa'd. . . . "

Brother Simpson brought them quickly to the Communion service. Two ushers lifted aside the lectern at which he stood, exposing to full view the Communion table with its snowy-white linen. Two old women came from a back room wearing black dresses, white aprons, and white caps with black ribbons on their frizzly gray hair. They had been chosen to wait at the table of the Lord and had borrowed their uniforms for the day from white homes in Columbus. Reverently they lifted the white covering from the table and folded it between them. Then they stood at either end of the table, ready to pass bread and wine as the pastor needed them for the service. It was a humble scene, a reverence-compelling scene, before which Mose bowed his head.

Brother Simpson followed the Communion service in a Methodist Episcopal hymnal, taking licenses here and there as the emotion of his people rose or faltered. His voice was deep, stirring, his call to the altar persuading. Mose went to the rail and found himself kneeling between Elder Johnson and Cenoria Davis. Her pale hand gripped the rail beside him, but she kept her eyes to the floor.

Brother Simpson took the Bible and read, with the congregation fitting words into the rhythm antiphonally.

"Jesus took bread . . ."
"Bless the Lawd."
"And blessed it . . ."
"Praise His Holy Name."
"And gave it to the disciples . . ."

"*A-a-amen.*"

"And said, take, eat; this is my body . . . "

"*M-m-m-m.*"

They kept humming, their voices rising and falling in patterns of thirds and sixths, while Brother Simpson passed along the rail and dropped broken wafers into outstretched palms. He passed the plate back to the old women. Then he took a napkin on his arm and a silver goblet in his hand.

"For this is my blood of the new testament . . . "

"*Hallelujah, King Jesus.*"

"Which is shed for many for the remission of sins."

"*M-m-m-m, Lawd.*"

"God bless you, my brother. God bless you, my sister," he said, going from one to another, leaving a taste of red wine on eager lips.

Communion ended, the two women came forward and covered the table again. Brother Simpson stood before it with bowed head.

"Brethren," he said, lifting his eyes to his people again, "it is now time for our offering for the poor. As you give, remember the words of the Master how He said it is more blessed to give than to receive. We will sing our parting song, and you will drop your offering on the table as you march by, amen."

Cenoria struck a chord; the people shuffled forward, singing

> "Good-by, I'm sorry to leave you,
> Good-by, I'm sorry to leave you,
> Good-by, I'm sorry to leave you,
> Gonna leave you in His care."

Mose joined the line marching slowly past the table. He fingered the coins in his pocket. Then he took a dollar bill and dropped it, tightly folded, on the table.

Outside the church, he stopped for a few minutes to shake hands with the elders.

"Come to dinner at my house," Elder Johnson urged.

Mose watched Cenoria Davis come out, pass him and, with eyes averted, walk rapidly toward the boardinghouse.

"Another day, Brother," he replied to the invitation.

Mose walked around the church, busying himself with estimating how much time and money would be required to finish it and to build a high white spire. Then, his mind still on the puzzle of Cenoria Davis, he walked slowly to the boardinghouse, humming to himself the remainder of the parting song:

> "Gonna leave you with the Prayer Book and the Bible,
> Gonna leave you with the Prayer Book and the Bible,
> Gonna leave you with the Prayer Book and the Bible,
> Gonna leave you in His care."

7

THE puzzle of Cenoria Davis was still with Mose when he came down to breakfast Monday morning—deepened by the fact that she had not come to any meals on Sunday, had at no time joined the other boarders in the porch rockers. Mose supposed she had spent her time in her room. Grieving over what? Mose asked himself, if grief it was.

Lora Dixon was preparing lunches for her boarders. The early risers, the ones who had to be at work in Columbus at six, had already gone, with the taste of soda biscuits in their mouths and bags of soda biscuits in their hands. For those to come, Lora put a row of lunch bags on the dining-room table. Mose, with a cup of black coffee in his hand, watched her split biscuits and slip slabs of side meat between the halves. A burning lamp on the table glowed uselessly in the gray-blue light from the windows.

"Hear you going to have a school opening this morning," Lora said curiously.

"Yes, ma'am."

"Hear you invited Brother Simpson and Sister Brackett."

"Yes, I invited them yesterday."

"What they going to do?"

"Well, I thought one could give the invocation and the other the benediction. Isn't that customary?"

"I don't know what's customary where you come from, but I know what Sister Brackett'll do if she gets a chance. She'll turn it into a holiness meeting. She'll jest take the bits between her teeth and head straight for the Promised Land. Law', last year Principal Davis asked her to give a little talk first day of school. First thing you know, she was prancing up and down the aisle hollering and shouting like kingdom come. Before it was over, she had most of the children bellering and crying with her. It might nigh broke up the first day of school."

"Thanks for warning me," Mose told her. "I guess I'd better ask her to give the benediction."

"Well, I'm jest telling you, she's mighty easy to get started, and once she gets going, ain't nobody can stop her till she's done wore herself out. You know how holinesses is about school. They think it's sinful for folks to read and write. They think the devil waits for folks between the covers of a book. She'd like a chance to put the fear of books in the children. Cain't you take back your invitations?"

"Not this late. But I can keep her from putting on a show. I'm a God-fearing man myself, but I have outgrown that kind of religion. We've got to keep it out of the school. It's holding our people back."

"I hope you can. Folks'll think a heap better of you if you do—the right kind of folks will."

"I'll keep a grip," Mose promised.

When Mose came out of the boardinghouse the sun was already up. Pleasant Valley was as fully astir on Monday as it had been on Saturday, but the holiday spirit was lost. Smoke from a hundred breakfast fires collected in a hazy bank along the ridge of Reservoir Hill. Children stood sleepily around the hydrant, waiting their turns to draw buckets of water. Cotton pickers, with sacks slung across their shoulders, walked along the roads toward the country, the women holding their skirts tight about them to keep them from touching dew-wet grass. Men in the uniforms of bellhops, filling-station attendants, bank porters slapped their feet dismally toward Columbus. Those who came near Mose spoke.

"Morning, Professor," they called, or "Morning, Elder," if they had been to the Methodist church the morning before. "Didn't know schoolteachers got up so early. . . . Don't whup too many today." Their jokes, their laughter had the listlessness of Monday morning.

On the school ground, a half-dozen boys batted a ball back and forth in two-eyed cat. Their twine ball was sodden with dew and dropped dead after a few feet no matter how hard the bat stroke. Their bare feet and legs were wet with dew; blades of green and yellow grass stuck to their dark skins. "Morning, Professor," they said to Mose, shyly, and went on with their play.

Mose opened windows, swept floors, carried out rubbish left from the year before. Each teacher was her own janitor, but Mose could not wait for them. He wanted the school to be ready for the opening exercises, which he had set for ten o'clock. His muscles were stiff from his work on Saturday, but his spirit was free. It was good to be at last working at his task.

Lora Dixon arrived first. She had changed from her blue uniform to a red crepe dress. As much at home in her schoolroom as in her own kitchen, she set to work cleaning windows and blackboards. Sister Daisy came next, white-haired and motherly, but obviously vague as to her responsibilities as a teacher. Fannie Mae Williams, a tall husky woman in a white cotton uniform, arrived with several girls from her maid-training class. The girls washed and rewashed windows, dusted and redusted, to show Mose how well they had been trained. Mose, standing in the doorway to escape the confusion they created, saw Cenoria Davis come walking leisurely across the hydrant square. She looked pale yellow in a canary cotton dress.

"Good morning, Mrs. Davis," Mose said cordially and put out his hand. "I enjoyed your playing at church yesterday."

She touched his hand briefly and said a soft good morning. Mose followed her into the auditorium, where the other teachers waited.

"You all know Mrs. Davis," he said lamely.

"Yes, sir, we all know her," Fannie Mae Williams said.

Cenoria seemed to wince at her inflection on *know*. Mose sensed their intolerance for her position, her behavior, most of all, for the lightness of her skin. More trouble here than I expected, Mose thought. He wished he had never seen *The Neighborhood Eye*— fervently wished Cenoria Davis would go, to New Orleans, anywhere. Pleasant Valley had enough problems without her disturbing presence, her more disturbing appearance, he made himself add.

As he talked to the teachers briefly and outlined his plans for the school year, he tried to see each in relation to her work, not in relation to neighborhood frictions that had shown themselves. Sister Daisy, he decided, was too old for the job. But she would keep on teaching as long as she liked. The wife of the Methodist pastor would be considered a good teacher and a good influence in the school. Fannie Mae Williams was dull of eye, but she seemed capable and willing. He looked at Cenoria Davis again, sitting a little apart, seeming very much alone and lonely. He would have to use great care in dealing with her. He turned to Lora Dixon—knew she was the ablest of the four. He was sorry she had not taken teacher training, but he knew she was a good teacher without it.

"I got my faults, but you can depend on me," she had said. Mose knew he could, no matter what happened.

At ten Mose rang the bell Miss May had given him long ago for the plantation school. He counted heads quickly, found near a hundred, most of them under thirteen. The others were picking cotton or working at odd jobs. They would enter school in November or December and stay for a month or two. Mose knew that a Negro boy in the South had to get what education he could before he was fifteen. After that, he got caught by the cotton fields, shine parlors, filling stations. The girls were little better off. They drifted away with men or became servants for white folks. Only a few finished high school; fewer still went to college. He knew also that Negro college training in Oklahoma was in no sense equal. Facing the children in his charge, he compared them with the colored boys and girls he had seen in Chicago going to high schools and colleges.

Mose took his place at the front of the auditorium. The teachers stood along the walls, ready to quell any mischief-maker. Brother Simpson came in and sat on the front row. Sister Brackett, with her long black dress freshly washed and ironed, followed him and took a chair at one side. Mose shook hands with them; then he went through the auditorium shaking hands with the parents who had come for the opening. A prosperous-looking man came in and took a chair at the back. Mose introduced himself.

"I'm Harrison Williams," the man said, "editor of *The Neighborhood Eye.*"

"Glad to know you," Mose told him. "I want to pay you a visit real soon."

Mose looked at Cenoria Davis standing at one side, perfectly cold, unresponsive, except for the tightness of her lips. Mose thought he saw hatred in her eyes, thought he understood it. He wondered how many others in the room had lips as tightly drawn because of *The Neighborhood Eye.*

There was a whispering as the people eased themselves into the small seats. Mose extended his right hand with palm down, the signal for prayer, and said, "Brother Simpson." Brother Simpson knelt on the floor at the front of the room. Sister Brackett knelt beside her chair. Softly he began the invocation.

Sister Brackett began praying with him, following the custom of her church, in which all pray together. Her voice rose higher than Brother Simpson's. He raised his voice. She prayed louder. Mose saw her suddenly as the symbol of the fettering emotionalism Negroes had to leave behind. He saw now what Lora had meant. He stole a quick glance at Lora. She stood against the wall with her head bowed but with her eyes raised toward Mose. Brother Simpson came to the Lord's Prayer and the pupils and teachers recited with him. But Sister Brackett did not join them. She was lost in her own supplication.

"Lead us not into temptation," they prayed together.

She shouted, "Glory, glory, praise His Precious Name!"

"Deliver us from evil ..."

The word *evil* seemed to strike her ear like a hammer. She lifted her hands above her head and slapped them together. Her words became an unintelligible gibberish as they tumbled from her lips. Brother Simpson brought his prayer to an end. Her voice boomed louder in the silence. When she realized the others had stopped praying, she stood up and mopped her face with her handkerchief. "Hallelujah!" she shouted. Then she started toward the speaker's stand.

Better stop her quick, Mose thought. "Let's sing 'My Country 'Tis of Thee.' " Cenoria Davis picked up the melody on the out-of-tune piano. Sister Brackett's words were lost in the shuffle of feet as the people rose. But she did not sing. She sat down and stuck out her lips.

By the time the song had dragged to a ragged close, Mose knew that Sister Brackett had been headed off for the time being. He looked at the rows of children facing him, the boys with their scalps close-clipped or shaved, the girls with their hair wrapped and tied with ribbons.

"What is the name of this school?" he asked.

"Phillis Wheatley," they yelled.

"Why is it called Phillis Wheatley?"

They looked at him blankly. No one knew the answer. They looked at one another, at their parents, Harrison Williams, Brother Simpson.

"Ask Brother Simpson," they said.

"No—" Mose laughed—"I won't ask Brother Simpson, but I will tell you the story of Phillis Wheatley, so it will be in your mind every time you come to this school."

The children leaned forward to listen. Mose saw Harrison Williams fish in his pockets for note paper and pencil.

"A long time ago while our people were still in slavery a man by the name of John Wheatley lived in Boston. In those days Boston was one of the cities where white slave traders could sell the Negroes they took captive in Africa. They had a big market place and Negroes were put on the block just like people sell hogs and cows now. One morning John Wheatley went down to the slave market to buy his wife a Negro girl."

"Do tell!" a woman exclaimed.

"A new boatload of slaves had just arrived from Africa. Mister Wheatley watched them as they were led in chains to the auction block and auctioned off to the highest bidder. They brought out a little girl eight years old. She was tired, hungry and nearly scared to death. She had been kidnaped from her father and mother in

Africa and brought all the way to America. She wasn't much to look at as she stood there wearing nothing but a rag around her waist and crying her eyes out. But Mister Wheatley liked her looks and thought she would be a good slave for his wife, so he bought her and took her home with him."

"How much did he pay for her?" a boy asked.

"The books don't say how much he paid for her. The point is that he bought her, that in those days a Negro could be bought and sold like a calf or a bale of cotton. Now Mister and Mrs. Wheatley were good Christian people. They named her Phillis and brought her up almost like a daughter. They taught her to read and write English and Latin. Then she started making up poems. She wrote one of her poems to George Washington. They say she was the one who said Washington was first in war, first in peace and first in the hearts of his countrymen. He liked her poem so much he invited Phillis Wheatley to come see him at his headquarters. The Revolutionary War was going on, but they say she went anyway. Her poems became so famous she was invited to England, where she was entertained by royalty. It was a wonderful thing for a Negro slave girl to be entertained by lords and ladies. After that, she came back to the United States.

"Phillis Wheatley died when she was thirty-one. During her twenty-three years in America she was transformed from a primitive African girl to a cultured Christian woman. Her master gave her her freedom because of the progress she made. She stands as one of the great spirits of the Negro people. This school was named Phillis Wheatley to remind colored children of her greatness. I have told you her story to show you what one Negro child did, to suggest what you may do."

He looked down at the sober faces, the quiet hands.

"What church did she belong to?" Sister Brackett demanded.

Her question, distracting as it was from the mood Mose had meant to create, caught him without a reply that would silence her. "I don't know," he said lamely, "but while she was in England she spent most of her time with Methodists."

"Hmph!" Sister Brackett snorted. "I don't see why you sanctify her when she wusn't sanctified herself. It ain't your lot on earth what matters. It's what you store up for yo'se'f in heaven——"

Brother Simpson interrupted. "Her story is an inspiring one, no matter what church she belonged to. It reminds me of a song we ought to sing. It's a song that ought to be on the lips of every Negro child in the South. Could you h'ist the tune for 'Oh, Freedom,' Sister Davis?"

She played the opening bars; Brother Simpson began singing.

> "Oh, freedom, oh, freedom,
> Oh, freedom over me,
> And before I'd be a slave
> I'd be buried in my grave,
> And go home to my Lord and be free."

They sang the song through once, twice, three times, with increasing volume, increasing fervor. Mose knew the opening exercises had come to more than he had anticipated, that he should close on this peak of enthusiasm, though he would have to leave much unsaid. He turned to Sister Brackett. "Will you pronounce the benediction?" he asked.

She prayed a short prayer and then swept out of the room. "I got my hominy outside," she said to Mose as she left.

Mose looked up to see Lora Dixon with her hand outstretched to him.

Opening exercises over, visitors departed, Mose set to work reestablishing the order disrupted by the sudden departure of the former principal. Records had not been completed; final report cards were never issued. He had to depend on a child's word, a teacher's word, his own judgment in assigning classes.

Children in the primary grades, when he called for them to stand, ranged from five to fourteen.

"Miss Lora, do all these belong in your room?"

"Most do. Some I don't know."

Mose pointed to the oldest girl in the group. Her body had the contours of a fully developed woman. Her face was sullen, her eyes dull.

"She's been in my room off and on several years."

"Have you ever promoted her?"

"I didn't have a chance. She never come enough."

"Can you promote her now?"

"Not her. She cain't spell 'cat.' "

The children laughed. The girl rolled her eyes and pulled at the back of her dress. Mose thought of the theories of education he had learned at the university. How few applied here! Resignedly he told Lora Dixon to march her children off to her room.

"Equal education!" he said quietly, bitterly.

Then he called for the children in the intermediate grades to stand. "Can you read?" he asked.

"Yas, suh."

"Write?"

"Yas, suh."

"Do you belong in Miss Cenoria's room?"

"Yas, suh."

He turned to Cenoria Davis. "They are assigned to you for the time being. We'll have to give tests and make shifts on the basis of results."

When the primary and elementary teachers had marched their groups away, no more than thirty were left. None claimed to be above the ninth grade. Mose could see that work for the upper three grades in high school would have to be planned on an individual basis when the children came—if they ever came.

He announced that girls studying maid work with Fannie Mae Williams would be excused from other classes one period each day. They would study reading, writing, arithmetic with the other teachers.

A girl bounced to her feet. She was overgrown, belligerent. "I ain't gonna do it," she said angrily. "I ain't never gonna be nothing but a maid, and you don't need arithmetic maiding."

Mose argued, and then yielded to her obstinacy. He finally agreed that girls could spend all day with Fannie Mae Williams studying washing, ironing, cooking, cleaning. "That's what white folks wants," the girls offered as their logic.

To Sister Daisy Simpson he assigned all the classes in spelling and geography. Then he took the eighth and ninth-grade work himself.

By noon of the first day the children were assigned to classes and teachers had assumed their responsibilities. While he ate the lunch Lora Dixon sent over, Mose worked at problems of textbooks, lesson plans, record systems.

Wednesday afternoon soon after lunch Mose heard laughter and the sound of feet scraping on the floor. Leaving his own students, he ran down the stairs. The noise was coming from Sister Daisy's room.

"Jabbo, you shet up and let Roscoe bound Oklahoma."

The voice, high and shrill, was not Sister Daisy's. There was a silence and then a boy's voice. "Oklahoma is bounded——"

A book skidded across a desk and crashed to the floor.

Mose slipped quietly into the room. Sister Daisy was asleep in her rocking chair with a handkerchief over her face. Emmy, the girl who helped her, stood before the class, shouting angrily, "Roscoe, you——" She slapped him across the face. "Leave Jabbo alone and bound Oklahoma."

Startled, he dropped his hand and began. "Oklahoma is bounded on the north by Kansas and Colorado, on the south by Texas."

Emmy saw Mose and, terrified, began shaking Sister Daisy. "Wake up, wake up!" she cried. "Here the principal."

Sister Daisy roused herself and pulled the handkerchief away. "What you want?" she demanded of Mose.

"I heard a noise and came to see if you needed help."

"I ain't needing no help," she said defensively. "Emmy and me makes out all right. I has to have my nap right after dinner, so Emmy does the bounding. She makes out all right."

"If it wasn't for Jabbo and Roscoe——" Emmy began.

"We'll talk it over after school," Mose said, "in my office. You take over now, Sister Daisy."

That afternoon, with his four teachers and their helpers, he outlined a plan of teacher training. Every afternoon after school they would meet for an hour of study of reading, writing, arithmetic, geography, history, and methods of teaching them.

"You can count me out Wednesdays," Sister Daisy said. "That's missionary-society day."

"If you do the study I set," Mose said firmly.

Then he talked of the task facing them.

"We talk a lot about equal education," he ended. "We expect a lot from the whites. We deserve a lot from them. We must never forget how much responsibility rests on our own shoulders."

8

A WEEK had passed; it was Saturday again, better for Mose than any "Sa-a-dy night," for his family would arrive on the afternoon train from the South. The house he had moved into would then be a home.

It had been a hard week, a week of "working like a nigger"—the phrase came back from his Mississippi childhood, made him smile. Days he had worked as teacher, janitor, handyman. Nights, after supper at the boardinghouse, he had gone to his rented house to finish cleaning up and papering the kitchen. He bought a cookstove and heater at a secondhand store near Columbus station. He bought beds, tables, chairs from his neighbors in Happy Hollow—castoff pieces rickety but still usable. With new pine boards he built a table for the kitchen. At the Happy Hollow Grocery he bought a coal-oil lamp and set it on the table in the front room. At night he worked by its light, painting the tables and chairs coffee-brown. His neighbors came nightly, partly to help, partly to take him into Happy Hollow living.

Sister Brackett came once, brought a picture of the Sacred Heart and hung it over the front door, never realizing in her Protestant heart that it was a Catholic picture, that it was in a way one of the idols she preached against. With heavy fingers she rubbed the tarnished gilt frame, trying to make it bright again.

That morning, Saturday morning, Mose stayed at home to make final preparations for Josie's coming. The teachers came to help. Lora Dixon brought a loaf of bread fresh from her oven; Sister Daisy, an embroidered scarf for the chest of drawers in the middle room; Fannie Mae Williams, a bracket lamp for the kitchen. It had been in the office of *The Neighborhood Eye.* "We don't need it no more, now we got the office electrified," she explained. When there was no more work to be done, when they had polished every particle of dust away, they stood around talking to Mose about Josie and his sons. They made jokes about Mose and Josie, hearty, good-natured jokes filled with understanding of husband-wife relationships.

"Man, you must sho' nuff love that woman," Lora Dixon teased, "to want to do all this for her."

"I like her a right smart," Mose said, lapsing into plantation talk.

Lora Dixon, husbandless herself (Mose knew already the gossip that her husband had left her long ago to take up with a tricky woman), stared at Mose's upper body. He had pulled off his shirt, and his undershirt made a mold for the muscles of his back and chest.

"I'll bet you some sweethearting man," she said. "Yo' wife sho' ought to appreciate you." She laughed and the others laughed with her. But Brother Simpson came in and the joking was over. No telling what he might think. Mose was glad he had come. It was too easy for jests like Lora's to be given a sinister meaning in *The Neighborhood Eye.*

Toward noon, Cenoria Davis arrived, with what Mose considered dramatic timing and effect, wearing her canary dress and carrying a vase covered with yellow crepe paper filled with long-stemmed yellow cosmos. Shyly she said, "I brought these for Mrs. Ingram. I thought they'd cheer her up, coming so far." Then she went away again, hurriedly enough to reveal her extreme self-consciousness with the others. A week had passed and Mose was as puzzled as ever by her. But now he felt sympathy as well. He read too easily the glances of the other women, the way they looked at her, as if they distrusted a pale skin and good looks. Her husband had left her, gone off with another woman, but not because of her looks. Why would a man take up with her, then leave her? the women asked. When would another man take up with her, leaving wife and children for the touch of her light skin, the feel of her slim body? Mose had not yet talked with her, because of her aloofness, but he knew she was a lonely woman, out of place in Happy Hollow. Among hearty women she seemed fragile, like the flowers she had brought and placed on the table in the front room.

Mose gave himself too little time, heard the train whistle when he was near Pepe's Tavern, saw black smoke rolling across the prairies before he could get to the station. The train pulled in while Mose was still outside the station. He waved to Frenchy waiting in his taxi, ran through the colored waiting room, found his way impeded by passengers going and coming on the stairs.

Before he could get to the front of the train, to the colored coach, he saw Josie coming down the steps, looking large and flustered in Miss May's blue-flowered dress and white lace hat. Miss May's clothes again. Mose had never seen her dressed up when she was not wearing one of Miss May's castoff dresses. This one was better than most. It was tight for her and pulled at the seams and folded into wrinkles above her hips. But it was good material and held her ample flesh in. She had added a piece of white cloth that came high on her neck. Between this and the white hat her face shone like a piece of wet coal. Her arms were stretched outward around two bundles wrapped in brown paper. She turned back without seeing Mose and shouted directions to Thomas and Robert, who followed close behind her carrying a tin trunk.

Thomas, looking taller and heavier after another three months of farm work, came down the steps backward, holding the trunk almost level with his shoulders. Robert, balancing the other end, looked out, saw Mose hurrying along the ramp. "Papa," he yelled and pushed the trunk down faster.

"Look out for that trunk," Josie bawled. "It's got my dishes in it."

The trunk was another piece of Penrose Plantation. Mose had often seen it in Miss May's rooms, had often rested himself on its curiously wrought tin top.

Mose pushed toward them. Thomas and Robert set the trunk down and, with Josie, stood guard over it. John, looking small, shy, bewildered, came down the steps, his feet guided by a porter.

Mose reached Josie first, put an arm around her waist, tried to kiss her on the mouth, reached only her moist cheek. He could see that she was tired and cross after the long journey.

"How are you? How did you stand the trip?" he asked anxiously.

"I'm all right." Her tone was indifferent, her manner as awkward as if she was speaking to a stranger. He thought of the days when they were boy and girl on the plantation, keeping company. She had been as neutral then, on the maidenly advice of Miss May.

He turned to his sons, who held back behind their mother. On the plantation they would have rushed on him, perhaps have clung for a moment, but in the strangeness of the station they seemed unwilling to move. None of them touched him; a sack of candy lay in his pocket undisturbed.

"Frenchy's waiting outside with a taxi," Mose said awkwardly. "We'd better go."

"Be careful of Miss May's trunk," Josie warned again. "She give it to me for a parting gift," she said to Mose. "It's got all our belongings in it. Which way we going?"

Mose took Josie's bundles and led them through the station to the taxi. Josie gave Frenchy an unfriendly "Good e'ening." Frenchy helped Thomas and Robert wedge the trunk between the seats. They sat on it and Josie climbed in after them. Mose and John sat with Frenchy.

"Last call for Happy Hollow," Frenchy yelled from habit. He started the motor and bumped them across the tracks.

"Smells funny here," John said, sniffing the hot air.

"Oil mill," Frenchy explained.

Mose told them how the cooking oil was pressed from cottonseed and boiled in big vats. Sometimes there was no smell but that of hot cottonseed oil in Columbus.

"But it's a fine place," he reassured them.

"Ain't half as good as Penrose Plantation, I'll bound you," Josie argued. They were soon on the "Main Drag" of Happy Hollow, stirring up dust that rolled over shacks and chinaberry trees.

"You'll like it well enough, once you git acquainted," Frenchy told them.

Lora Dixon was on her front porch to wave to them as they went by. A Saturday crowd around the hydrant shaded their eyes to stare at them. Frenchy turned onto Mulberry Street and chugged his taxi through the sand to the house.

"This where we gonna live?" Josie demanded.

"Yes," Mose answered doubtfully, feeling defenseless, seeing again the shabbiness of the house.

"Hmph! Nigger shack," Josie snorted. "I've got a good mind to turn right around and go back."

"It's the best I could do now," Mose told her, his voice full of disappointment at this sorry home-coming. "It's better inside. Let's go look around. We can fix it up some more."

He took John by the hand and Josie by the arm. Thomas and Robert followed, the trunk swinging between them. There was a rattle of dishes and then Josie's sharp voice reproving them. "Miss May says three moves is worse 'n a fire," she added. She watched them until they had set the trunk safely on the porch. Then she followed Mose inside. She looked at the newspapers, smooth and clean on the walls. She kicked at a splinter on the hard-scrubbed floor.

"Ain't much in it," she remarked as she went from the first room to the second. She stopped beside a bed and tested it with a ponderous hand. The springs gave way under her weight with a rusty creak. "Which bed we gonna have?" she asked.

"That one," Mose answered. "I thought we could put Robert and John in the other one and make down a bed for Thomas in the front room."

"That may suit me, and again it may not," she said. "Maybe I'll make me a bed down in the front room and let Thomas sleep with you. You been gone so long it don't make no difference."

Mose looked at her for explanation, but she went on to the kitchen without looking at him. She was more than cross and tired from the trip, he decided. Three months away from her, and she was going to sleep alone in the front room. She was standing in the kitchen. He looked at the lines of her body under the blue-flowered dress. Three months is a long time.

Josie opened the oven doors, looked in the cupboard.

"There's enough food cooked for tonight," Mose told her. "Our neighbors brought in a lot. I bought some more. They brought fried chicken, bread, baked sweet potatoes. You won't have to cook at all tonight."

Josie looked at the dishes of food. She went back to the front room, where the boys had left her trunk. She opened it and began taking out keepsakes from Penrose Plantation. She took out the hen on a nest made of white milk glass. Miss May had given it to her for a pin tray when she was a little girl. She shook the pins in it and set it on a table. She unwrapped plates, cups, saucers.

"Git me some water," she said to Thomas. "I gotta warsh these up tonight so's we can eat."

Mose took two buckets and went with the boys to the hydrant. It was late afternoon and many people waited their turns. They spoke to Mose, stared at his sons. Thomas and Robert stood close to Mose, watching the buckets fill up.

"Better 'n the well back home," Robert said. "You don't have to pull no rope."

Josie washed the dishes and set them on the white cloth she had spread on the table.

"Looks mighty good," Mose told her, still trying to console her for the uprooting.

"It looks all right," she admitted. Her eyes were downcast and she let the corners of her mouth droop. "But I sho' nuff wisht I was right back at Penrose Plantation this minute."

"You'll like it better when you know some people," he tried to persuade her. "Nobody'd like it at first. It's new country. But you've got good neighbors—Lora Dixon, Sister Daisy Simpson, Fannie Mae Williams. They're all teachers and good women." He realized that he had purposely failed to mention Cenoria Davis. "You'll like them. First thing you know you'll be having porch parties and inviting a lot of women. There's a fine church to go to. I went last Sunday. It's the Methodist church, and they've got a mighty fine pastor—Brother Simpson. He preached as good a sermon as I ever heard. It seemed to me like a worshipful congregation. You wait till tomorrow and see whether you like it or not."

"Ain't they nothing but Methodist churches here?"

"Yes. There's a Baptist church, but they don't have a pastor now, and there's the Pentecostal Fire-Baptized Holiness Mission. Sister Brackett's the pastor over there. She brought us that picture and motto. But I thought we ought to try the Methodist. The pastor is a fine old man, and he conducts a quiet, reverent worship service—the kind I'd like our boys to get used to. You'll go tomorrow, won't you?"

"Ain't seen a Sunday yet when I didn't," she flared at him.

Thomas came in and stood by the table where Josie was placing their supper. "We wants to look around."

"We *want*," Mose corrected him. "You're not on the plantation now. You must speak correctly."

"We want to look around," Thomas said again, somewhat chastened.

"Not tonight," Mose told him. "Wait till tomorrow and I'll take you for a walk before church. Tonight we'd better stay home and get things straight in the house."

Thomas stood in Josie's way with his head hanging down and his mouth open.

"Shet yo' mouth," Josie snapped at him. "You want to be a loose-lipped nigger when you grow up?"

Thomas left the room without speaking to his mother.

When the food was ready, Josie called them to supper. She and Mose sat with John at the table. Thomas and Robert sat in the kitchen door with their plates on their knees. She put the lamp on the corner of the table to give them more light.

"Miss May sho' hated to see us leave," Josie said. "She said she'd druther see me laid in my coffin and took down to the burying ground than to see me step on that train to come to Oklahoma. I felt jest like her. She's been like folks to me all my life. She'll worry a lot about us. She said it was bad luck for us to break up and start all over again this late in life. She come jest as fur with me as she could, and when the train pulled out she was standing by the tracks waving her hand...."

Her talk of Miss May carried them through eating and putting away the dishes. They went to the front porch and sat in the gathering darkness. She still talked about Penrose Plantation, recalling pleasant moments of their life there, putting the blame on Mose for denying her the privilege of going back. But her sons were hardly listening. They were finding interest in new things. From their porch they could see the lights of the picture show. They could hear people laughing and joking as they paid their money and went inside. They begged Mose to take them, but he would not—not on their first night in their new home.

Josie had less patience with them. "Wash yo' feet and git to bed," she ordered them. They took a basin of water to the back door and, without play, without laughter, scrubbed their feet and legs.

Josie went in and made the beds ready. Mose could hear her spreading quilts for a bed on the front-room floor. After the boys had gone to bed—Thomas in the middle room—all was quiet and Mose and Josie could hear praying and singing at Sister Brackett's church.

"Sounds like real religion," Josie said. "If I wusn't so dog-tired I'd go over and set a spell with them."

She went to the end of the porch to listen to the singing. Mose went and stood beside her. After a while they could hear the singing no longer. Mose moved nearer Josie and let his hand slide down the small of her back and caress the roll of flesh above her tight waistline.

"Is you trying to sweetheart with me?" she snapped.

Mose dropped his hand.

" 'Cause if you is, you might as well forgit it. While you wus off North, I come to a new time of life—a new way of thinking. I prayed to God and he give me a new blessing. It put me above carnal sin. It don't allow nothing of the flesh. A long time now you been going one way, I been going another. It used to worry me, but it don't worry me no more. I know my feet been taken out of the miry clay and set on solid rock."

She walked away from him and went inside. "I'm going to bed," she announced, "and I mean right now."

Mose sat on the edge of the porch and listened while she undressed and lay down on the pallet on the floor. Long after he could hear her deep breathing in sleep, he waited in the darkness, plagued by new questions, new doubts. He had taken her from the plantation, but he feared that the plantation was too deeply ingrained in her, that she would never rise above the way of Negro life it represented—in superstition, in religion, in Miss May's white folks' moralizing. The road he had chosen was not easy—that he knew. It would be ten times harder with Josie pulling against him.

9

Josie awoke grumbling. In the early-morning light she shuffled barefoot through the house putting away bedclothes, cooking breakfast. When the sun rose a hot ball in a hard blue sky she railed at the things she hated: the sun, the heat, the dryness, the dust, the bareness. She wished aloud for the oaks and magnolias that shaded Penrose Plantation. She wished for the soft light filtered through layers of green leaves. She wished . . .

Mose, unable to bear more, walked out of the house. His three sons, like him dressed in white shirts, dark pants and black shoes, trailed him down the street. "Little Mose" they had all been called on Penrose Plantation. "Little Mose" they were sure to become in Happy Hollow. Mose strode ahead, relieved to get away from Josie's complaining voice, but dreading the task before him.

Thomas caught up with him and walked beside him. He was tall, his head reaching above Mose's shoulder. He was heavy of build like Mose, but his face was more like Josie's. It had the unyielding quality Mose had come to dread in her. Thomas did not want to talk. He walked with his eyes straight ahead, his mouth tightly closed. Nothing of the "loose-lipped nigger" in him this morning, Mose thought.

Mose chewed a stem of grass to wash away the taste of soda biscuits and white gravy he had swallowed for breakfast. Looking back, he saw that John had white from soda biscuits on his cheeks. Mose stopped to brush it away. "Old Flour Face!" He laughed with good humor he did not feel.

John laughed too and rubbed his sleeve across his cheeks and eyes. His eyes were dark brown, the shade of his own, Mose thought. Mose turned to Robert. His eyes were the reddish-brown of buckeyes, like Josie's.

Mose took the road to Reservoir Hill—the road he had seen cotton pickers striding along in the mornings to the fields, dragging themselves along home in the evenings. He had chosen this road with the task before him in mind.

From all his worry that night before had come one decision: he must tell his sons at once what being Negroes might mean in Columbus, Oklahoma. He had to explain a new sort of segregation to them, if he could. He had to point out the barriers of a Jim Crow world—the places where Negroes were forbidden to walk, stand, sit—the little signs so great in import: FOR WHITES ONLY. Most important, he had to make them understand, as much as he could, the effect of these little signs on the white man's conscience, the black man's pride.

He had planned to give them a few weeks in Pleasant Valley and then try to tell them one by one, but with Josie pulling against him he felt it better to begin at once. But how? How does the colored parent tell his child he is different? How does any parent tell his child that a clubfoot or a harelip sets him apart? How does any parent tell his child that life, fair in the beginning, may turn harsh, cruel, destroying? He knew that many Negro parents never attempted, preferring to let their children learn the hard way.

As he tried to fit his thoughts into words, he felt his own shortcomings, his own lack of understanding. He knew what it was to be a Negro in a Jim Crow world. He had felt the slur, the slight, the stinging word, though not the whip nor the lyncher's wrath. But experience had not given him a code of behavior that Negroes could live by until Jim Crow can finally be overcome. He had no better rule of conduct than his father had, or the slaves before him: "Yas, suh, Boss. No, suh, Boss." He had no more to give his sons now confronted with these artificial barriers.

For a moment he wished that he had never taken them away from Penrose Plantation. There the pattern was established; there they could have lived their lives out without being awakened to the full hardships of Jim Crow. He regretted his thoughts immediately. Better to be here with eyes open to pain than living there like the generations of slaves before them.

They left the road and climbed a narrow path up Reservoir Hill. As they climbed, their shoulders burned in the heat, their eyes in the brightness. Mose led them to a ledge swept bare by the wind. From it they could look across Pleasant Valley and pick out buildings in Columbus. They stood in a tight group looking over the town.

"I'm hot as a nigger at election," Robert said and scrubbed his face with his handkerchief.

"Me too," John agreed.

Mose took the opportunity—took it bluntly, boldly, in a way he had never planned, in a way thrust upon him by the necessity of the moment. "Where did you learn that saying?" he asked.

"All the niggers on the plantation says it," they told him.

"All the *niggers?*"

Mose tried to put into the word the sting he felt when he heard it spoken by white folks, the bitterness he had stored up in a lifetime of being a *nigger* in a white world. The boys heard the change in his voice and stared at him, their eyes alive with questions. They did not know at first how to answer him.

Thomas was the first to venture. "All the *nigras,*" he said.

"Nearer right." Mose compelled himself to smile again. "But it's still got some sting. If you can learn to say *Negro,* you'll be right. When you say it, just look at your knee and say, 'Knee, grow.' Then you'll get it right."

"What's wrong with nigger?" Robert asked. "That's what Mama calls us."

"It's all right when she calls you nigger. It's no more than calling you boy. It's not all right when white folks call you nigger. She doesn't mean anything by it, but they say it with a knife in the throat. They whittle it down till it means something low and vile and mean. You've never heard the word said like white folks here are going to say it. I'm mighty afraid you'll hear it that way soon."

"Miss May always called us niggers back home," Thomas argued.

"She's white folk, but I don't think she meant anything by it."

"That was different. When you were at Penrose Plantation you were with Negroes all the time except when you were with Miss May. You saw her only when you went up to the big house. There you were living just like black folks did in time of slavery. The only difference is, Miss May couldn't buy or sell you. But it's not the same here. There you were colored people belonging to the plantation, living among colored people, in a way made comfortable by generations of good slaves. You were a part of the life. It was not a good life, but you belonged. Here you are Negroes, in a minority. Some white folks'll call you niggers, or jigs. It'll be different when they call you nigger. You'll know the difference when you hear it—you'll feel it. Just step over the bounds and you'll hear it."

Mose raised his arm and pointed over Columbus. He pointed out the station where they had arrived the day before, the First Methodist Church with its globular domes of red tiles, the Columbus Hotel, the cotton-oil mill. His finger traced the railroad track through town till the ends were lost in the prairie.

"The railroad track separates whites and colored here like a high stone wall," he said. "In the morning the gates are opened so colored servants can go through. At night, when white folks' work is done, the gates are closed again. That wall is called the color line. This side is called Jim Crow. White folks sometimes crawl over it at night. Negroes never do."

"Why, sir?"

"Segregation was made by white men, because they consider themselves superior. I've told you many times how whites went to Africa and captured our people to sell them into slavery. Since the beginning of America, the white man was the owner, the colored man the slave. The Civil War was fought to right the wrong, but the wrong is not yet righted. We celebrate Eight o' May, June Teenth, and all the other emancipation days, but we're still not free. We live in a land owned by white men, where white men make the laws. They let us borrow the land as long as we obey the laws. They make laws saying we can't live in Columbus, so we can't live in

Columbus. Negroes can go to Columbus to work for white folks or to buy their goods, but they can't go there to live. That's Jim Crow law—and Negroes still have to obey. I'm telling you this not because of my own bitterness, or because I want you to feel bad, but to prepare you for the day when some white man calls you nigger and you feel your blood boil up and hate grow in your heart. I know it will come to you as it has to me. You've got to hold in."

He clamped his teeth shut. Already he had shown more feeling than he had intended. There must be a better way for a man to tell his son he is black, he thought. His sons looked at him as they had never looked at him before, their eyes disturbed with questions. He knew by their looks that his talk was not beyond them, that they already knew the color of their skins and felt the effect of being different. Their questions, he knew, could be answered only through their experience on a Mississippi plantation. They had to be lived with, worked out. Now he had to reassure them if he could. He pointed to the tracks again.

"You have to remember only one thing. The railroad track marks the line between blacks and whites. Long as you don't cross over, you won't get into trouble. I don't want you to cross the tracks without me. You won't need to, if you keep in school and study hard. You'll see boys your age going over with shine boxes under their arms. They'll tell you how easy it is to make money around the station and hotel. I don't want my sons shining shoes. Not that shining shoes is bad. You've got better things to do. Understand?"

"Yes, sir."

Mose paused a moment. "When you meet white folks on this side, you'd better say 'Yes, sir,' and 'No, sir,' and step out of the way."

"Yes, sir."

Mose looked at his watch. "We've got an hour before church. That will give us time to walk to the tracks and back. I want to show you the dividing line."

They came back to the road at the foot of Reservoir Hill. From there they cut across fields to the tracks. As they walked on the ties toward the station Mose talked to them of the effect of segregation on whites, of the guilt they felt because segregation violated the teachings of Christ, the precepts of democracy they professed to believe. He spoke of whites, North and South, who because of what they believed or because of conscience tried to treat Negroes better.

"The white conscience is a growing thing," he told them. "It'll gnaw and gnaw at people, feeding on their hearts, till they'll make things better for us. But we have to do our part. We have to deserve. That's why we left Mississippi—for a chance to do our part. Things will change in Mississippi. They've got to. They'll change faster here."

They came to the road from Columbus to Pleasant Valley. From it Mose pointed out their narrow boundaries. Then they started home—past the junk yards, past Pepe's Tavern, closed and quiet on Sunday morning. Other people walked the road now, on their way to church.

"We'll get your mother and join them," Mose told his sons.

When Mose and his family arrived at church Brother Simpson was already in the pulpit. The choir was half filled, and ushers worked at recruiting more singers. One of them met Mose and Josie in the doorway.

"Yo' seat's a-waiting, Brother," he said to Mose. And then to Josie: "Sister Ingram, you must have a fine voice."

"I sings a right smart," Josie replied. She allowed him to escort her to a chair in the choir.

"Alto or soprano?" he asked.

"I sings tribble."

He seated her on the front row with the sopranos. Mose, in the bass section, could watch his sons sitting together near a window. He could see Josie in one of Miss May's dresses and a hat Miss May had always worn to funerals.

Brother Simpson opened a hymnbook and laid it on the lectern, opened another and handed it to Josie.

"We will open our worship this Lord's Day by singing 'Amazing Grace, How Sweet the Sound,' " he announced.

Cenoria Davis turned the pages of the hymnbook until she found the number. Then she played the closing measures and a chord. Josie held her hymnbook, waiting for the tune. Mose knew she could not read the music, could barely read the words. But it was a familiar song on Penrose Plantation. Brother Simpson held up his hand to choir and congregation. Before he could give the signal, Josie opened up in a powerful voice. Startled, he held his hand, but the others took up the song, two full beats behind her. Cenoria Davis accented the rhythm heavily on the piano, but Josie paid no attention. She was singing as she always had on Penrose Plantation, unhampered by books, notes or piano. Mose tried to attract her attention, to frown her into silence, but she had closed her eyes and lifted her face toward heaven. By the time the congregation reached the last measure of the first stanza, she had started the second. She kept her pace through all four stanzas. Then she sat down, leaving the choir struggling through a ragged amen.

Mose felt the sweat gather on his face and run down on his collar. He remembered his words with Brother Simpson about dignity and reverence in worship. From the look on her face, he knew that Josie had been near shouting during the song. He recalled the last time he had seen her shout down home—remembered and winced. "Straight from the cotton patch," people would say if she let herself go here.

When the service progressed to the Apostles' Creed, Mose realized that he should have explained the order of worship to his family, that he should have explained the words to Josie. She had never heard parts of the service before. That was not the way of religion at Penrose Plantation, where the pattern of worship followed the emotions of the members.

"I believe in God the Father Almighty, Maker of heaven and earth," Brother Simpson recited, with the congregation mumbling after him. When they came to "I believe in the Holy Ghost; the holy catholic church" Josie expelled the air from her lungs in a hiss.

"Popery!"

Mose heard her and shook his head at her. She did not see him. She was glaring at Brother Simpson. Brother Simpson had heard her, but he kept on going to the end of the passage. When the choir went into their sevenfold amen, Brother Simpson turned to regard Josie.

"Miss May hates Popery," she said in a loud voice.

"Sister——"

"Say what you will, Brother," Josie said, stepping forward for emphasis, "Miss May hates Popery, and I hates it too. All them men they call Father. Whut I'm here to tell you is that my Father is in heaven. He ain't no earthly father wearing long black skirts to hide his cloven hoofs and tail."

Josie sat down and stared above the heads of the congregation straight out the front door. She said no more, but the order of worship had been broken. Brother Simpson did not preach a sermon. Instead he explained the Apostles' Creed. Again and again he came to the word *catholic* and tried to show her that it meant *universal*. But Josie would have none of it. The fear and hatred of Catholicism had been too deeply ingrained in her. She sat with puckered mouth while he talked.

For their closing song the choir sang "By and By, When the Morning Comes." Josie dropped her hymnbook. She did not stoop to pick it up. She knew the words already. She did not know what the notes—like little blackbirds strung along wires—meant anyway, and cared less. People were singing long before anyone decided to write the notes down. On the second chorus she felt like singing "tribble." Her voice rose high and quavering as she sang a third above the sopranos, at times independently of them as she followed her own sense of harmony. On a high note her voice faltered and broke. Josie stopped singing and sat down.

After the last benediction, Robert went over to the piano. Cenoria Davis was playing a hymn for the postlude. He listened and watched her slender fingers glide up and down the keys. With gentle fingers he caressed the notes she was not using.

"You play the piano?" Cenoria asked.

"Ain't touched one before."

Mose saw them and wanted to hear what they were saying. Watching Robert finger the keys, he was sure it was about music, though he had not known before that Robert had an unusual interest in music. He was surprised that Cenoria Davis, who treated others so coldly, should be so warm and friendly with Robert. But he could not join them now. He had to go after Josie, who had left the church without speaking to anyone. He caught up with her in the middle of Mulberry Street. He walked beside her, not knowing what to say.

"They pitches their tunes too shallow," she complained. She said no more about the service. Mose decided to hold his explanations for a better time. No point in talking to her when she was too stirred up to listen.

In the afternoon Josie sat on the porch in one of the white uniforms she had worn when she worked for Miss May. Mose had gone to the church for a meeting of the elders—gone without mentioning the morning service. She had waited for him to speak to her, to scold her, but he had said nothing, leaving her to wonder when he would speak. To Miss May she had always said, "We never fuss—jest speak each other out, then we through." She missed speaking out the trouble growing between them. Feeling that the argument would come soon, she was trying to recall all the things Miss May had said about Popery.

Her sons sat on the porch with her, occupied at first with the books Mose had brought them from school. They soon tired of the books and put them aside. Then they sat staring across what they could see of Pleasant Valley.

Josie was puzzled by their quietness. "Whut's fretting you young-'uns?" she asked.

Thomas leaned against a post and cleared his throat self-consciously.

"Mama," he asked, "what makes *Negroes* different from white folks?"

"Is that whut's fretting you? I done told you before, lots of times. The Lawd made it that way when he made white folks white and black folks black. He done it 'way back in the time of Noah, when he made Ham black and Shem and Japheth white. Boy, you a son of Ham. You black, and you better not forget it."

"I don't recollect the story too good," John said.

"Then I better tell it to you agin. It's something every nigger's got to know."

Sure of her convictions, sure because Miss May had made her so, Josie began her talk on the question of black and white without the doubts that had hounded Mose.

"You all know the story of Noah and the ark?"

"Yes, ma'am."

"You know how Noah took two of every living thing on the ark?"

"Yes, ma'am."

"And you know how the Lawd caused it to rain for forty days and forty nights, amen, and after the world was destroyed He brought the ark safe to rest on dry land?"

"Yes, ma'am."

"Then the Lawd told Noah and his sons that He wouldn't destroy the earth by flood no more, but next time He'd burn it up with a unsquenchable fire. He told them that the seeds of Noah would inherit the earth. Well, you'd a thought Noah and his sons would a been content to behave theirselves after that. But they didn't. No, sir-e-e-e. By now Noah was an old man, but he went out and planted some grapes and made wine. Then he drunk wine and got four-eyed drunk. He was so intosticated he went in his tent and pulled off all his clothes and laid there naked as a jaybird. Ham went in and seen his father drunk and naked. He laughed like a fool at Noah and went and told Shem and Japheth about it, and they were ashamed. Shem and Japheth took a robe between them and walked in backwards and covered Noah up. But the harm wus done. Noah woke up and found out Ham had seen him and laughed at him. He cursed Ham and told him that him and his children gotta be servants for Shem and Japheth and their children."

"Is that the truth, Mama?"

"Miss May say it's the truth, and I believe her. She say that's why black folks got to be servants for white folks. That's why niggers got to look up to white folks. They got to look up to white folks and be humble. Miss May say they ain't nothing worse 'n a uppity nigger."

The old story, worn thin as it was, echoing as it did both the authority and the conscience balm for white slavers, stilled the disturbing questions Mose had raised.

"That ain't the way Papa said it," Thomas said. His tone asked that she take away the questions entirely, restore life to the simplicity of Penrose Plantation.

"Don't pay no mind to what he say. He done been up North and got a different consideration. When Miss May and the Bible say something true, it's sho' nuff fact."

Sister Brackett drove her buggy into the yard and stopped. Holding a fold of her skirt in her hand, she climbed slowly down over the buggy wheel. With stately stride she crossed the yard to the porch.

"E'ening, Sister," she said to Josie. "I'm Sister Brackett. You heard of me?"

"Yes, Sister, I hear tell of you. Good e'ening."

"I done come to applaud you for standing up for the truth in church today."

"You hear about it?"

"Hear about it? Honey, every colored person in Columbus done heard about it by now."

Sister Brackett sat in a rocker and rocked back and forth. She rubbed her face vigorously with a black handkerchief. Sweat had run down and dampened the edges of her clerical collar. She talked to Josie, but she used her sermon voice and raised it loud enough to be heard by the boys, who had taken their own conversation to the other end of the porch.

"Honey," she said, "the trouble with the world today is they's too much of this highfalutin religion. Whut we needs is to get back to God. We ain't needing no fancy books and creeds and prayers to go sweeping through the pearly gates. All we got to do is know and love God. That's what I preaches to my white folks I sell hominy to every day. I tell Brother Simpson every time I see him he ain't gonna lead people to God with a lot of hocus-pocus and idol worship. That's too much like Rome for me. Lawd a mercy, how I hate the thought of Rome!"

"You right, Sister," Josie agreed. "Amen, you right. I'm glad I up and told them flat what I thought about Popery. Miss May say priests is got horns and hoofs."

"They say that's true, Sister."

"And that them nuns has to lie down in their coffins and swear their vows."

"I hear that too, Sister. The Lawd only knows whut goes on when nuns and priests get together."

Sister Brackett looked at the boys and then rocked her chair closer to Josie's. With heads close together and their voices pitched to the level of a gossip's, they repeated to each other the stories about sin among Catholic clergy.

When the last dread story had been repeated, they talked of what faith meant to them—their faith that taught resignation on earth so that greater treasures might be stored up in heaven.

"I ain't bothering my spirit none about things on this earth," Sister Brackett said. "I ain't a-caring if white folks does have everything. All I needs is vittles to hold my body together and clothes to cover my nakedness. I can do without here long as I git to enter the pearly gates, amen."

"Amen."

"Folks here always hollering about change. All the hollering in the world ain't going to make no difference with white folks."

"What is to be will be," Josie said resignedly. "I'm reconciled to my lot in this world below."

They bowed and clucked together.

"Honey," Sister Brackett said, a new tone in her voice, "why don't you come to our church tonight? It's a real church, without'n spot or wrinkle. When we gits to preaching and singing, the glory rolls till it bounces on the ceiling. You ought to hear it."

"I'm coming," Josie promised. "I'm coming tonight."

Mose came up Mulberry Street while they were still talking. He walked slowly, giving Sister Brackett time to go before he reached the porch. But she waited, a look of satisfaction on her face—the look of the successful proselyter.

"I'm going to hear Sister Brackett tonight," Josie told him at once.

"She won't hear no Popery in *my* church," Sister Brackett said belligerently. "Nor none of this talk about change. We cain't waste time in this life. We got to prepare for the glory of the next."

She wiped her face with her handkerchief and rose to go. Carefully she straightened the folds of her long black skirt. Then she looked at Josie's uniform.

"Honey," she said, "yo' skirts's mighty short for a God-fearing woman."

10

SCHOOL over for the day, Mose sat in his office checking reports from his teachers, making plans for the following day. Mose liked the schoolhouse when it was a beehive of teachers and pupils busy at learning. He liked it almost as well in the late afternoon when the building was quiet, as it was now—when he could sit in his office and ponder problems, make plans.

Robert waited for a moment at the office door and then came to stand beside Mose's desk. "I waited to walk home with you," he said.

Mose rubbed his hand over Robert's burry head, and for some reason remembered the superstition of white folks that rubbing a Negro's head brought good luck.

"That's nice of you. We can go when Mrs. Dixon brings up her report."

He rubbed the fleece again to brush the superstition from his mind. He studied the boy's eyes, trying to understand the mind, the spirit behind them.

"What part of school did you like best?" Mose asked.

"Chapel, sir."

"Chapel? Why?"

"I liked the piano. I'd druther listen to it than eat."

Lora Dixon came up the stairs with her day's reports, interrupting them at a moment when Mose would have liked to draw Robert out more on his love of music.

"You wait outside on the transgressors' seat," Mose told him. "Then we can walk home together."

Outside his office door Mose had placed a hard, straight-backed bench. Above it he had hung a sign: THE WAY OF THE TRANSGRES-

SOR IS HARD. But Robert's face, under the sign, was not that of a transgressor. It was that of a sensitive young boy. He could hear Mose and Lora Dixon talking about reports, but his mind was not on them. It was on the chapel service with Cenoria Davis playing school songs on the piano. He had felt an ache at church the day before, an ache that became stronger during the chapel music. It returned to him now, rising deep within him and spreading outward until it centered in his finger tips. He knew it could be eased by touching the piano keys. He stretched his hands wide and studied each finger. Perhaps his father was right. Perhaps he should be a minister. Then he could always play the church piano.

Lora Dixon stood in the doorway talking to Mose, but no longer about reports. "Your boys took to school like fleas to a hound-dog cur," she was telling him.

"Young people do have a way of adjusting."

Mose said it quietly, modestly. But he felt more than that inside. He had brought them to school that morning shy, diffident, "country." By noon they were at scrub ball with the others. Soon the "country" looks would be gone, the last marks of Penrose Plantation erased.

His thoughts were interrupted by heavy footsteps on the stairs, by Harrison Williams' head above the landing.

"Evening, Mister Williams," Mose said.

"Evening, Professor. Evening, Lora."

He shook hands with Mose and then Lora. Lora gathered a folder of papers and started downstairs. "It's time to get supper on the table for my boarders," she apologized.

"Lucky boarders," Williams said. "I always tell people the best food in the world is at Lora Dixon's. Mighty good grub." He raised his voice to make it carry to her at the foot of the stairs. Then he turned to Mose. "How's school?"

"Fine."

"How do your folks like Happy Hollow?"

"Finest kind. One of my boys is outside now. Robert, I want you to shake hands with Mister Harrison Williams, the editor of *The*

Neighborhood Eye." Robert shook hands with him shyly and returned to the bench.

"Mighty fine boy," Williams said. "He'll be a credit to you someday."

Mose felt insincerity in the man's voice, felt it and disliked him for it. What kind of game is he playing? he thought. How could the editor of *The Neighborhood Eye* find anything good in Happy Hollow?

"Have you seen my paper?" Williams asked, accepting the chair opposite Mose.

"Couldn't help seeing it." Mose laughed. "Our kitchen is papered with it."

"It must about set the walls on fire."

That's better, Mose thought. At least he knows the kind of news he prints—and can laugh about it.

"I want to thank you for the story on the school opening," Mose said. "I thought it was a good story."

"I'm glad you liked it. I kind of liked it myself. I don't often get anything as good as Phillis Wheatley to write about. Most times folks just send in a lot of trash."

"Why do you print it?"

"That's what people want. They's a lot of knifing and killing and rape in Oklahoma, and folks want to know about it, so I give it to them. A colored newspaperman has a hard enough time making ends meet anyway."

"Negroes have a lot of things to be proud of. You could write about them. You could write protest. We've had some fine leaders—Douglass, Dunbar, Du Bois. I've got a trunkful of notes——"

"I done wrote about old Booker T. till folks is tired of him. They're tired of hearing about good niggers. They want something new."

"Give them something new. Give them a picture of their own lives. I've looked at Columbus. I've seen the shame of their living. You could hammer away at it."

"Not in Little Dixie. You cain't say nothing that'll rile white folks. We got the finest white folks in the world right here in Columbus, but they don't want no stirring up race. It'd be like lighting the fuse on a powder keg. Colored folks here don't want to hear about race either. They ain't interested. They got their own little world."

That's worse, Mose thought. He's got all he needs to be a regular back-seat-driving Uncle Tom.

"How long you been here?" Williams demanded.

"Ten days about."

"I been here nigh sixty years, and you tell me what to write. I was born here when it was Indian territory. My father and mother were slaves of Creek Indians, freed after the war. I ain't got Indian blood, but a lot of colored people here have. I've lived hand to mouth in a Jim Crow world a long time. It took me a long time to learn to rock with the blows. It ain't been easy. I got this paper. It gives me a good living, and I'm going to hang on to it. I got to write what they'll read."

Mose saw how futile it was to continue his argument, how awkward it might be to antagonize Harrison Williams.

"One thing about Oklahoma puzzles me," Mose said to change the subject.

"What's that?"

"The Indians. As far as I can see, they're treated exactly like white folks."

"They are white folks—by law. When Oklahoma was applying for statehood, a lot of Indians didn't want it. They wanted a state all for Indians—wanted to call it Sequoyah. The whites outtalked them. They passed Jim Crow laws against the colored people. Then they passed another law making Indians honorary white men."

"Why don't you write that story? Won't Negroes read it?"

"They might, but it won't affect them none...."

The sound of a chromatic scale run by fleet fingers jerked Robert awake and sent him running downstairs to the auditorium. He forgot Mose and Harrison Williams, forgot the talk between them. He found Cenoria Davis playing from a big book. He had never heard music like it before. The heavy chords seemed to strike like blows in the pit of the stomach. He crept closer, close enough to make out the words, but they were strange words, in a language he had never seen before. He crept closer still, let his fingers silently caress the upper keys.

"Hello," Cenoria Davis said as she turned a page. "Which one are you again?"

"Robert. I was at church yesterday."

"I remember you. You liked the piano."

"Yes'm. What is that you're playing?"

"It's a Bach chorale."

Her words were as unfamiliar as those on the page.

"Can I hear it again?"

Her fingers again followed their well-remembered paths up and down the keyboard. Her face was bent close to the piano—too close for her to read the page. She seemed to be listening intently, to be freeing her own spirit in the feel of the notes. Robert watched her in awe. He had seen light people before, but never anyone her color. She was beautiful. He wanted to touch her hands when they came to rest.

"Where did you learn to play?"

"In a convent in New Orleans."

"You Catholic?"

"Not now. Don't guess I ever was. I was an orphan and the Sisters took me to the convent when I was ten. They put me in their school. I wasn't much good in the lessons they set for me, except in music. When they found I liked to play the piano, they gave me extra lessons and let me practice all I wanted to. They said they wanted me to play for church."

"Did you ever?"

"No. Before then I left the convent and never went back again. But I kept on playing the piano. I remembered the hard lessons Sister Theresa set for me. I always tried to play like she said."

"Don't you never play no blues songs? Like 'When You Go to Dallas'?"

"Sometimes . . . when I get real low. Then they come to me and

I have to play them to get them out. Mostly I play songs for church and the pieces Sister taught me."

Robert struck the keys lightly. He let his fingers run down the keyboard. When she did not object, he hammered the notes, handfuls at a time, and laughed at the sound.

"Do you like the piano so much?" she asked.

"Yes'm."

"Would you like to learn to play?"

"Better 'n anything."

"Then I'll teach you."

"What'll it cost? I ain't got no money."

"It won't cost you anything. If you really like music, I know how you feel. I felt the same way when I first went to the convent. The Sisters would play the piano and I would hide in corners to listen. They found me listening so often they let me play."

"Could you show me something now?" he asked shyly.

With the sure touch of a musician who is also a teacher, she placed his fingers on the keys. "This is middle C," she began.

They were still at the keyboard when Mose and Harrison Williams came downstairs. It was dusk in the room. Harrison Williams glanced at them and hurried away. Mose came to the piano and looked down at the notes and staves she had drawn for him. Cenoria saw him and shrank from Robert as if she feared a rebuke from Mose.

"Miss Cenoria's going to give me piano lessons," Robert said to Mose.

"Do you mind?" she asked.

"Not if you teach him church music—the kind you've been playing. He won't have time for blues or jazz. He won't need them when he grows up. But how'll he pay? I can't afford——"

"I won't charge him anything. He likes music too well not to have a chance to learn. It'd be a shame to see his talent go to waste."

"That is very generous of you. If he's got talent, I'd hate to see it wasted."

An awkwardness stopped Mose's speech, seized all of them.

"All right, Robert," Cenoria said. "Tomorrow after school we'll have the first lesson. It's time to go home now."

She left the schoolhouse quickly and took the short cut past the hydrant to the boardinghouse. Mose closed and locked the building for the night. Then they went along Mulberry Street, Mose sedately, Robert skipping to a rhythm Mose could not hear.

11

Hot winds from the south blew on through September, keeping midday temperatures near a hundred in the shade, keeping the air dry and dusty, giving Josie many hours of sharp complaining, of longing for the moist greenness of Mississippi. Then there was a lull in early October before the wind came from the north, when the days and nights were alike—hot, dry, enervating. Mose explained to her that Oklahoma, the part called Little Dixie, lay in the zone where the winds blew for months from the south, and then for months from the north. All they could do was wait for change. Mose had not yet learned himself how violent Oklahoma weather could be, or what a force it could be in the lives of her people. He had not yet lived through the nagging heat of August dog days, or the bitter sweep of a blue norther across Oklahoma prairies.

Mose was working late at school when the first change came. The air had been unbearably muggy during the day. When he left the schoolhouse he saw a low-lying bank moving from the north. By the time he reached home the north wind blew, bringing great drops of rain to spatter the dust of Mulberry Street, bringing a fresh breath of air to cleanse the lungs, raise the spirit. For a moment Josie forgot to complain about Oklahoma. The boys raced one another through house and street in wind and cloud and gathering darkness.

Good weather held through November, with nights clear and cool, with days breaking into soft moist fog that hung in clouds along Reservoir Hill. By noon the fog would fade away into clear blue sky and reveal the burnished reds of oak and sumac. For a time it was a pleasant earth under a friendly sky. People in Happy Hollow, living close to weather, noticed the ever-strengthening north wind and said that the good days would not last. Josie stuffed rags into cracks in walls and floors, but she could not reach the roof to close holes through which blue sky showed by day, bright stars by night.

Mose set up the heater in the front room. Every afternoon, after Robert's piano practice, the boys had to go up the trail toward Reservoir Hill to pick up wood for the heater. They saw other colored people with their buckets and sacks, walking the railroad track, picking up scattered pieces of coal dropped from passing tenders. They begged to go with them. It was easier than picking up sticks among the brush and thorns of Reservoir Hill. But Mose would not let them. Times were hard, and they had no money for wood or coal, but Mose would not let them join the coal pickers. "It looks like scavenging," he told them.

A December morning broke with gray sky and fog heavy enough almost to be a mist. During the morning it cleared enough for the sun to shine dimly, far to the south, but the threat of storm remained in the air.

"Gonna be a norther," people said to one another as they passed shivering on the street.

They gathered what fuel they could, stuffed cracks, nailed boards over broken windows.

"Gonna be a norther," the teachers and children told Mose at school.

"Blue norther coming," people warned him when he was on Mulberry Street again. "Better git in a lot of wood. This ain't no Mississippi cold snap. This a sho' nuff norther. It'll freeze the marrow in your bones." Happy Hollow drew itself into a tighter ball, waiting for the north wind to strike. "Nothing between us and the North Pole but a bob-wire fence," people joked to Mose.

Thomas and John went straight from school to Reservoir Hill. Mose, seeing how low their woodpile was, called Robert from the piano and joined them. Though it was only four o'clock, it was almost dark when they went up the slopes of Reservoir Hill looking for sticks. Threat of cold brought them closer together, united them in a brotherhood against storm. Mose, with his heavier strength, broke branches. The boys dragged them out of the brush to the trail. They worked feverishly, excitedly, gloating over each stick, making a game of piling up wood.

"This's more fun than picking up dirty old coal," Thomas said.

"We ain't got to be scavengers," they told Mose. "We got plenty of good wood."

They piled their arms high and staggered down the slope. Mose went first, loaded with enough heavy sticks to keep the fire going till bedtime. Thomas and Robert followed close behind him. John trailed behind, struggling with an armload of light branches.

"You tote the kindling, Little Mose," they had told him.

They warmed their fingers briefly and then went for a second load. They filled the box beside the stove and piled more on the porch. They were on Reservoir Hill a third time when a light flurry of snow came, borne on the rising north wind.

"Time to go," Mose called to the boys. "No sense in freezing."

Their arms half full, they hurried down the hill, glad to escape the wind that cut through their clothes like knives. Josie, with a lamp in her hand, opened the door to them anxiously.

"I thought you'd froze up there," she said.

Josie helped them brush off the snow. She helped them take off their outer garments. Then, while they rubbed warmth into one another's hands, she gave them cups of scalding "pot likker" from a kitchen kettle. Mose felt a difference in her, as if the cold had frozen her back to a need for human warmth, a need to draw closer to her husband and children. Like the ice that burns, it had melted her frozen feelings, frozen by the heat of a too sanctimonious summer religion.

Mose watched her while she cooked supper, marveled at her change to the Josie of pleasanter days in their cabin at Penrose Plantation. Her lips lost their pout, her voice its tone of complaint. Even her hands had a happy sound as she slapped together her special supper: batter cakes, ham gravy, ribbon-cane sirup.

"Pass the 'lasses," Josie said to Mose at the table.

Mose and the boys looked at her, burst into laughter at the well-worn joke. "You must say *mo*lasses," he corrected her.

"How can I say *mo*lasses when I ain't had no 'lasses yet?"

They roared at the joke and made it last them through supper.

After the dishes had been put away, they gathered around the heater and built up the fire till the sides glowed. The storm howled with a fury gathered across a thousand miles of plains. The walls swayed and creaked in the wind. Sleet hit the board roof like shot and rattled off the eaves. Hominy snow sifted between boards in the roof and lay like coarse sand on the cold kitchen floor. But they were snug and warm around the stove.

While Josie popped corn in an iron skillet, the boys played "William Tremble Toe"—as they had often played it winter nights on Penrose Plantation. They spread their fingers on Mose's knees, and Thomas slowly tapped each finger while he recited with exaggerated stress:

> "William Tremble Toe
> Was a good fisherman;
> He catches hens,
> Puts them in pens—
> Some lay eggs,
> Some lay none.
> Wire, brier, limber lock,
> Three geese in a flock—
> One flew east,
> One flew west,
> One flew over the coocoo's nest.
> O-u-t spells 'Out goes he,
> You dirty old dishrag, go!' "

Robert was "it" first and waited for Thomas to set a forfeit. Mose had watched them pay by standing on their heads, kissing their toes, jumping through a broomstick back in Mississippi. He wondered what they would do here.

"Mock somebody," Thomas at last decided.

"Yeah, mock somebody," John yelled.

Robert stood before the stove a moment making up his mind. "You'll have to guess who," he said.

While the others tried to guess, he walked across the room, seated himself with knees crossed, cleared his throat, walked again.

"Papa?"

"No."

"Brother Simpson?"

"No."

He walked past John and brushed his hand across his head. "Mighty fine boy," he said with a quick look at Mose. "He'll be a credit to you someday."

The others failed to guess, but Mose roared at his remarkably good caricature of Harrison Williams.

Then, between reaching their hands into a dishpan of popcorn, they played clubfist with Josie. Thomas put a fist on Mose's knee, with thumb up. Robert grabbed his thumb and they built—fist, thumb, fist, thumb, with Josie's fist at the top of the stack.

"Take it off or knock it off?" Thomas asked.

"Knock it off," she challenged him.

While Robert and John held their fists firm, Thomas and Josie tussled with each other over the game. With a sharp crack on her knuckles, he broke her grip. The game ended in tear-squeezing laughter.

A chill gripped the outer edges of the room, made them huddle closer to the stove. They talked of Christmas and what Santa Claus might bring. They recalled the fine Christmases they had spent back home at Penrose Plantation. For once Josie did not talk of going back to Mississippi. Instead, she opened a whole new field of imagination for them.

"What do you 'spect Miss May gonna send for Christmas?" she asked.

Midnight came, with the wind still howling, the sleet rattling. Josie shivered through making the two beds in the middle room. Then she made her own pallet close to the stove. All the time she was making it, the boys grabbed at flying sheets and quilts, happy to find her playful again.

Josie took the Bible from the table and handed it to Mose. "You read it," she said.

Mose looked at her in surprise. It was the first time she had suggested family Scripture reading since they had come to Pleasant Valley. He took the large leather-bound book in his hands and slowly turned the pages.

"What do you want?" he asked.

"Psa'ms."

He turned to the First Psalm and read slowly:

> "Blessed is the man that walketh not in the counsel
>   of the ungodly,
> Nor standeth in the way of sinners,
> Nor sitteth in the seat of the scornful.
> But his delight is in the law of the Lord;
> And in his law doth he meditate day and night.
> And he shall be like a tree planted by the rivers
>   of water ... "

While he read, the boys sat quietly on Josie's pallet, listening to the sonorous words of the Hebrew poet. After the Psalm, Mose prayed a short thanksgiving. It was as if he had come home from a troublous journey and found peace and quiet in his home.

"Time for bed," Mose announced, rising from his chair.

Robert and John pulled off their clothes by the warmth of the stove and raced off to bed in their underwear.

Josie poked at the pallet. "That floor gitting mighty hard," she said without looking at Mose.

The room was so quiet Mose could hear coals breaking and shifting in the stove.

"Gonna be mighty cold tonight," she said.

Mose said nothing. He held his face against a windowpane and tried to measure the remaining strength of the storm.

"Want me to sleep on the pallet?" Thomas asked.

Josie said nothing, but sat staring at the dying glow of the stove. Mose wanted to touch her, to tell her to come back to her own bed, but he remembered too well the sharpness of her words since she had come from Penrose Plantation. He went to the cold room and undressed. He crawled between cold sheets. He could hear Josie and Thomas mumbling in the front room, but could not make out their words. With a sudden stirring, Josie blew out the lamp and came to the middle room. He could hear her pulling off her dress. She came over to the bed and touched his shoulder.

"Move over," she told him.

"Why?"

"So's I can have yo' warm place. If I got to stay in Oklahoma, I might as well stay comfortable."

Mose moved over and she climbed heavily into bed.

12

IT WAS January and new snow was falling on old snow, proving Josie's weather saying right. "If'n the snow stays on the ground three days, it'll snow agin before it melts," she had said. "Mark my words." While Mulberry Street was still mud and ice, gray clouds came again and laid another layer of soft white snow over the ugliness of Happy Hollow. It drove the coal pickers, bundled now into moving balls of rags, farther and farther from town, up and down the railroad tracks after the trains had run. The hard summer had turned into a harder winter. People without jobs or food talked of Roosevelt and relief. They waited in lines in the basement of the courthouse to get a little help—more often to hear that relief would come soon, when the machinery could be set up. They would have to wait a little longer, not in the warm courthouse but in row houses made colder by the burden of snow.

The rick of wood Mose bought for Christmas was already burned up, and the ashes, carefully saved by Josie, had been taken to Sister Brackett for her to use making hominy. Thomas led Robert and John farther and farther up Reservoir Hill picking up sticks. With numb fingers they scratched in the snow for pieces of wood big enough for the heater. They wasted energy and sticks throwing at birds in the bushes.

In the late afternoon, tired from beating snow and ice from the sticks, tired from dragging their loads down Reservoir Hill, they thought they had enough wood for the night. They warmed themselves by the heater and watched snow pile higher on the windowpanes. As they watched, birds came nearer and nearer the house.

"I'm gonna catch me a snowbird," Thomas bragged.

"You cain't neither."

"I bet I can."

"How you gonna do it?"

"Gonna build me a deadfall."

"You know how?"

"Watch 'n see."

"What'll Papa and Mama say?"

"They don't care. Papa's still at school working on the stove. He say he won't be home before dark. Mama ain't gonna git back from Sister Brackett's much sooner. She wouldn't care if she was here."

Thomas borrowed the heavy oak board Josie used for ironing. While Robert and John watched from the porch, he raked away a patch of snow the size of the board, leaving a rectangle of wet brown earth in the midst of the whiteness. He placed the board over the rectangle and propped it up on a stick trigger he had whittled into a figure 4. He tied a cord to the trigger and adjusted it for easy tripping. He sprinkled bread crumbs on the ground under the trap and ran for the warmth of the house.

Robert and John moved to a window; Thomas lay on the floor in front of the partly opened door, the trigger cord tight in his hand. At first the birds stayed as far away as the garden. Then some sparrows fluttered around the trap. They hesitated, and then warily pecked at the bread crumbs.

"Nothing but sparrows," Thomas complained.

"There's a jay bird," John shouted.

A blue jay lighted on a picket fence. A cardinal perched himself, a red shivering ball, in a bare chinaberry tree. Robert saw them and began drumming a rhythm on the windowpane. "Cain't get a redbird, a bluebird'll do," he sang jeeringly. Enjoying Thomas' annoyance, he sang through the refrain, "Skip to my Lou, my darling."

"Shut up," Thomas commanded. "You'll scare 'em away."

They waited tensely while the sparrows took more and more of the crumbs. Then the blue jay dropped down among the sparrows. With them he edged forward, stretching his neck to reach the crumbs. When he thought they were far enough under the trap, Thomas jerked the string. The jay flew away, a streak of blue against the snow.

Thomas ran to the deadfall and lifted it. "Got one!" he shouted. He took out the crushed sparrow and set the trap again.

"You cain't eat no sparrow," they told him.

Thomas laid the sparrow on the floor beside him and took slack out of the trigger cord.

A redbird perched on a paling and eyed the brown spot of earth.

"Wish we could catch him," John whispered. "He'd be good eating."

A flock of snowbirds landed near the porch and picked along toward the deadfall. The cardinal swooped past their grayness and picked at the crumbs. Step by step he edged under the deadfall. The boys held their breath, waiting. With a quick jerk Thomas pulled the cord.

"Got him!" they yelled.

Thomas brought the bundle of crumpled red feathers to the house. Robert took the bird and stroked the feathers smooth. "What'll we do with him?" he asked.

"Skin him and broil him."

"Let me skin him," John begged. "I'm gonna be a doctor, so I got to learn how to operate. You catch more birds while I gut him."

He laid the bird on a board and punched a hole in the skin with a pocketknife. But the blade was too dull. He tried a butcher knife from the kitchen. The blade was too large.

"I'll get the razor," John whispered to himself. "That'll cut all right."

Thomas and Robert were intent on a flock of snowbirds around the trap. Quietly he opened the drawer where Mose kept his shaving things. He took the razor out and opened the blade, feeling his flesh on edge at the touch of the cold steel. He glanced at Thomas and Robert. They had not seen him get the razor. With the end of the blade he slit the skin through red breast feathers. Red blood flowed over the feathers, stained John's hands. Carefully he opened the skin and peeled it from the body. He held the bit of raw flesh up for them to see.

"Better gut him," Thomas told him, still without seeing the razor.

John laid the bird on the board and started to slit it open. But the razor slipped, and John stared with surprise to see it sink into his left wrist. Before he could cry out, blood spurted over the bird and board. It drenched his clothes, splotched the floor. His small-boy whimper turned Thomas and Robert to him. They saw the blood and forced him onto a chair.

"He'll bleed to death," they whispered to each other in terror. "What'll we do?"

They mopped at the blood with handkerchiefs. They tried to stop the flow by squeezing his wrist with their hands, but the blood still came in spurts.

"Better go get Papa," Thomas told Robert.

When Robert jerked the door open he found Josie stamping the snow off her shoes on the front porch.

"What's happened?" she demanded. "You look like you seen a ha'nt." She pushed Robert before her into the room.

"John's cut hisself. He's bleeding to death!" they cried.

John, calmer than they, held out his wrist for her to see.

"The Lawd a mercy," she prayed. "My boy's dying! My boy's dying!" She folded him in a close embrace, smearing her own clothes with blood. "Robert," she cried, "go on and git yo' pappy. Thomas, you go git Sister Brackett."

Alone with John, knowing something had to be done soon, Josie, without waiting to take off her cloak, ran to the kitchen for a wash-basin to catch the blood. As she ran she thought of remedies for stopping bleeding. She recalled having seen old women on the plantation put soot on wounds to stop the flow of blood. With her fingers she dug at the caps of the cook stove, scraping off soot with her nails. She piled it on the cut, but the blood washed it away faster than she could daub it on. Soot mixed with blood and made black streaks in the basin.

"God save us," she prayed. "God save my boy!"

Her prayer was stopped short by a memory. Miss May had told her a long time ago that reading a verse from the Bible would stop the flow of blood. She grabbed the Bible and took it to the window. Quickly she turned the pages of the Old Testament.

"Ezekiel . . . Ezekiel . . . Where's Ezekiel?" she muttered. "That's the book . . . got the book . . . now whut's the chapter and verse?"

Her eyes found the word *blood* and then the beginning of the verse. Tracing each word with her blunt forefinger, she began reading in her slow voice:

"And when I passed by thee, and saw thee polluted in thine own blood, I said unto thee when thou wast in thy blood, Live; yea, I said unto thee when thou wast in thy blood, Live."

She looked at John holding his wrist over the basin. "That'll stop yo' blood, son," she reassured him. "You only got to believe it will."

She took up the words again, repeated them, made them a sing-song chant. Her voice got louder, her feet began a dancelike tapping.

Sister Brackett burst through the door, her black veil flapping, her dress caught tight under Brother Brackett's heavy overcoat.

"What's yo' trouble, honey?" she demanded. She did not wait for Josie to answer. The blood and Scripture told her all she needed to know. "Read, Sister, read," she implored. Then she turned to John. "Pray, son, pray. The Lawd'll take care of His own."

Sister Brackett fell on her knees beside John and began praying at the top of her voice. Josie read louder, shouting the word *Live* in a frenzied, frightened cry. "Yea, live!" Sister Brackett took up the cry. John, terrified at last, leaned his head over his bleeding wrist and bawled. Thomas, who had come in with Sister Brackett, leaned against John and sobbed. Reading, praying, crying, they watched the blood flow unchecked.

Mose ran in, with Robert close behind him. He looked at John and saw how the blood was spurting—saw how soon the blood would be drained from his body. He stared at the two women in their frenzied supplications. In sudden anger he passed by Sister Brackett and came to Josie. He jerked the Bible from her hand and flung it against the wall. He caught her by the arm and pulled her to her feet.

"Good God, woman, do something!" he shouted. "Can't you see how he is bleeding? Get me a clean sheet quick. Thomas, you go get Doctor Lewis as fast as you can. Frenchy's at the pool hall. Make him take you."

Thomas grabbed a heavy coat and started for the door. Sister Brackett interrupted her prayer long enough to be practical. "Doctor Lewis ain't coming without'n you send him the money," she said. "He's the onliest doctor that'll come to Happy Hollow, and he ain't coming without'n he gits his money."

"Wait," Mose said to Thomas. He took five dollars from the sugar bowl. "Give him this—all of it if he wants it."

Thomas took the money and ran.

Josie, too startled by Mose's violence to speak, picked up the Bible and straightened out the crumpled pages. Gently she put it on the table. Then she got a sheet out of Miss May's trunk and gave it to Mose. Sister Brackett prayed again, but she watched Mose from the corner of her eye, ready to dodge if he should turn his wrath on her.

Mose tore the sheet into strips and made a tourniquet. He put John on a bed and bound his arm above the elbow.

"Heat water, Josie," he ordered. "The doctor'll want some."

Josie went to the kitchen and built a fire in the stove. Sister Brackett lowered her voice through the Lord's Prayer. When she had ended her "Amens!" and "Praise the Lawd!" she gave Mose a hostile glance and went to join Josie in the kitchen. Mose heard them muttering together. "One to grow," Sister Brackett repeated. "He may be the first." Then he heard Sister Brackett leaving by the back door.

"God bless you, Sister," Sister Brackett said, "and let not the hand of the blasphemer fall upon you."

Mose went to change the tourniquet, saw that John was resting quietly, that the spurt of blood had changed to a gummy drip. He took the razor, wiped the blade clean, honed it for a moment and then returned it to the drawer. He took the skinned bird and threw it out the door. In the gathering darkness he watched a flock of sparrows picking the ground around the trap clean.

With relief Mose saw Dr. Lewis hurrying along Mulberry Street, Thomas a respectful two paces behind him. Mose had seen him often before going down the side streets and back alleys of Happy

Hollow, had as often heard his story. Most of his life he had been a country doctor riding a mustang pony over Oklahoma prairies. He looked like a sawed-off cowboy; he walked unsteadily on legs bowed by long years in the saddle. He had given up his country practice and moved to town, but to the white people of Columbus he was "that country doctor" who still carried his pill cases in saddlebags. After he began taking Negro patients, he became "that nigger doctor" and lost most of his white patients.

He dropped his saddlebags on the porch. "Hello, Mose," he said. "Frenchy couldn't get up this street in that open-air taxi of his, so I had to walk from the corner. Times like this, I wish I had my old nag again. She never stopped for snow. How's the boy?"

"Mighty weak, sir, but the blood is beginning to clot."

Dr. Lewis stopped on the porch long enough to kick the snow from his cowboy boots. Then he went to the middle room, where John lay under a pile of quilts.

"Get me a lamp," he ordered brusquely.

Josie brought a lamp from the kitchen and stood with it at the foot of the bed like a statue carved in coal.

"Let's see now, let's see now," Dr. Lewis said. He took John's hand, turned it to the light, picked at the caking around the cut. "Sut," he said disgustedly. "A bad cut and you try to stop it with sut." He stared at Mose and Josie, watched them wince at his words.

His probing brought a fresh spurt of blood. John jerked his hand away, tried to stop the blood by burying his hand in the sheets.

"There, there, son," Dr. Lewis soothed him. "It's not as bad as that. We'll have you fixed up in no time. First, something to kill the pain."

He took a hypodermic needle and slid it under the skin in John's arm.

"Here, you hold this lamp," Josie said to Mose. "I cain't stand to see that done to my own flesh and blood." She covered her eyes with her apron and stumbled to the kitchen.

Dr. Lewis took curved needles and silk threads from his kit. "It'll take a few stitches, and then a few days in bed to recover from the loss of blood. Nothing to worry about at all. How'd you do this anyway?"

John looked at Mose, smiled guiltily, said nothing.

"John's going to be a doctor, sir," Mose told him. "He was practicing dissection on a redbird with my razor."

The doctor laughed. "Probably ruined the edge."

Mose and the boys laughed less heartily, mostly from assurance that John would be all right. Josie put a grim troubled face in from the kitchen, but she did not laugh.

"So you want to be a doctor."

"Yes, sir."

Dr. Lewis caught the edges of the wound with a curved needle, pulled the thread through, tied a quick knot.

"A nigger doctor?"

"Yes, sir."

"Well, I've never seen one, but, God knows, we need them. I've been the only doctor coming to Happy Hollow for years now. I've sewed up more niggers than any other doctor in the country and been on more nigger granny cases. It's too much for an old man like me. I need help. I'd like a colored doctor to help me."

He finished the stitches, wrapped the hand in gauze, brushed John's fleece lightly with his hand. "No more playing with razors," he warned him.

When he had his saddlebags packed again, Dr. Lewis came back to John's bed. "What you say interests me a good deal. It's time we had a colored doctor in Columbus. In about a week you come to my office to get the stitches out. I might have an old scalpel to give you."

After the doctor had gone, with two dollars in change jingling in his pocket, Josie stood beside the bed rubbing John's face with her hand. She looked at Mose reproachfully. "The Book," she said. "You oughtn't to a flang the Book. Bad luck comes to them whut blasphemes the Bible. . . ."

Mose knew that in a moment of anger he had inflicted a wound for which there was little healing.

13

BEFORE the third day passed, the north wind died down to a chilly breeze, the sun came out, the snow became watery white and then faded away altogether, leaving Pleasant Valley its natural reddish brown, with mud and slush underfoot. "It's like I say," Josie reminded them. "Snow melted before the third day, so it ain't gonna snow agin soon. I'll bound we don't have no more snow this winter. I seen geese going north yistiddy. I'll bound we have a early spring...."

John's hand healed quickly. After a week Mose took him on foot to Dr. Lewis' office to have the stitches removed. They walked up Main Street in Columbus, passed the Columbus Hotel and turned down a back alley. There, at the back of a frame building that was drugstore and doctor's office, Mose had seen a line of Negroes waiting to go up to the doctor's office for "blood-purifying shots." There, among garbage cans and empty packing cases, Negroes waited their turn to climb the outside stairs. White patients, the few who came, entered through the drugstore, and for them there was little waiting.

Mose and John waited their turn in the alley and then climbed the stairs slowly, for the steps were rickety, the rail unsteady. They entered the colored waiting room, a dimly lighted room with a row of cane-bottomed chairs around the wall. Dr. Lewis had his office in a narrow space between the white and colored waiting rooms. They could hear his gruff voice, and then a man's whining complaints.

"Doctors' offices don't have to be this gloomy," Mose said to reassure John.

He tapped a bell on a table and they sat down to wait.

Patients came and went from the white waiting room, share croppers, oil-mill workers, the poor of white Columbus. Then Dr. Lewis opened the door and thrust his head out. His face was flushed red from the heat of a gas stove; his bony skull shone red through a mist of white hair. He saw John and let his eyes brighten for a moment.

"Well, come on in," he ordered, more sternly than necessary, Mose thought.

Mose, going first, took in quickly the details of the sparsely furnished office, warmed by the yellow-red flames of an open gas stove, the white waiting room on a balcony, the drugstore below. A ragged old man was struggling with a heavy coat. White trash, Josie would have called him. Not much fee from him, Mose judged. No wonder the doctor's office was bare and shabby. Niggers and white trash don't have much money for doctors.

Dr. Lewis placed John on a chair and cut away the bandages. With curved scissors he snipped the stitches and then jerked them out. John winced with each jerk, but did not cry. Mose liked the firmness, the gentleness of the doctor's hands.

Dr. Lewis caught John looking at the worn instruments lying on a table before him. "Still want to be a doctor?" he asked.

"Yes, sir."

"Been fooling with your daddy's razor any more?"

"No, sir."

"I wouldn't be surprised if you did. Razors and niggers seem to go together." He laughed a humorless laugh, not inviting Mose and John to join him.

When the stitches were all out, Dr. Lewis studied the scar, seemed pleased with his work. Then he went over to his table of instruments. He took a scalpel and tested it with the edge of his thumb. He drew the blade along his hairy forearm, shaving it clean.

"Still sharp enough to shave," he said. "Here, boy, take it with you. It ain't new, but it'll be good enough for you to practice operating with. But be careful what you cut with it. Don't go around whittling on desks—or other niggers." He looked at John and winked.

"No, sir," John said.

"You're too young to be any help to me now, but in a couple of years, come around to see me. I'll give you a job cleaning up here and helping with patients. You'll get some experience and help me too. Most of my patients are niggers. I might as well have a nigger to help me."

Mose found no offense in his way of saying *nigger*.

"Where you going off to school?"

"I've thought of Wiley College, down at Marshall," Mose replied for him.

"I meant medical school."

"I don't know, sir," Mose said. "He can't go to any of the medical schools in Oklahoma."

"I know," the doctor said. "Jim Crow. You've got to go out of the state. It's tough enough going to medical school under the best of circumstances. Jim Crow makes it tougher. When the time comes, I'll do what I can to help——"

He was interrupted by the tapping of the bell in the colored waiting room. He replaced the bandages on John's hand, touching the dark skin as if he found no offense in it. Mose understood his gruffness—perhaps understood his kindness. A lifetime of riding horseback over Oklahoma prairies in weather mostly harsh, and now a dingy office in a back street. Gruffness, even bitterness, can come from disappointment, kindness from watching human suffering.

"No need to bring him back unless there is trouble," Dr. Lewis told Mose. "You can take the bandages off in a few days."

For Mose and John the scalpel was more than a worn-out medical instrument; it was a symbol for the future. With his father's hone, John smoothed the tiniest nicks from the edge. He polished the handle till it shone like old silver. He held it in an outstretched hand to test the steadiness of his nerve.

Josie came home from Sister Brackett's while he was still fondling it.

"Look," he said excitedly. "Look what Doctor Lewis gave me!"

"Whut's that knife?" she demanded.

"A scalpel—to operate with. He said he would give me one."

"I wouldn't dast take it!" Her face was troubled, her voice ominous.

"Why?"

"It's bad luck to give a knife. It'll cut yo' love in two. I ain't never seen it fail. Give a knife and bad luck comes. Ain't no telling whut trouble that thing'll bring. Here, give it to me."

Reluctantly he handed her the scalpel. She took it and put it in the drawer with Mose's razor.

"Don't you never let me see you meddling there agin," she warned him. "Troubles comes in threes. We had one already. Law' only knows whut's coming next. . . ."

When John's wound had entirely healed, leaving only a darker line on his dark skin, Josie still kept her heart wounds open, wounds made when Mose flung the Bible against the wall.

"God will smite you," she told him day after day. "God will smite you for yo' blasphemy."

Her tones became more bitter, more reproachful. When they had gnawed deeply into his own consciousness, Mose humbly apologized to her.

"Don't say you sorry to me," she told him. "Go prostrate yo'se'f before God. . . ."

Her constant upbraiding finally gave him a sense of guilt. He began to blame himself for having thrown the Book. His reason told him that there was no guilt—told him that for Josie and many another like her the Bible was magic, a thing to conjure by, like a bag of hide and hair and bits of nails. But emotion was more deeply seated than reason.

Nightly Josie told him of a way out of his troubles—through sanctification at Sister Brackett's church. She herself had received the "second blessing," was now beyond the touch of sin. She had put on the white dress, the symbol of the "saints" in Sister Brackett's church. If Mose could only see the way, she prayed.

She moved back to the pallet in the front room, leaving Mose to lie beside Thomas and wonder whether reason could prevail in a world bound by superstition.

One night, unable to stand his fruitless searching longer, unable to listen to the shouting and singing at Sister Brackett's, Mose walked down Mulberry Street to take his problems to Brother Simpson. He found Brother Simpson and Sister Daisy sitting on their porch in the dark. Mose sat on the edge of the porch and leaned against a post. Sister Daisy went inside to light a lamp and remained, leaving the men to talk.

"Josie says I blasphemed against God," Mose began. His voice was low, troubled.

"How, Brother?" Brother Simpson asked.

Again Mose went over the details of the day John cut his wrist, the details that led to his throwing the Bible against the wall.

"It's superstition—nothing but plain superstition," he argued.

"I agree with you, Brother," Brother Simpson said. "No amount of Scripture reading will stop blood. But you desecrated the Book. No man's got the right to desecrate the Book."

Mose's words became a wounded cry. "Then you think it's blasphemy?"

"I don't know. I wish I did. I wish I could relieve your suffering. It calls to my mind old Moses. In anger he broke the tables of the law God had given him. The Bible say he waxed hot and cast the stones out'n his hands and broke them. You know the suffering he went through before God forgave him and made new tables. You know God helt him back from the Promised Land. Brother, in anger you flang the Book agin the wall. You got to pay somehow. It may be your conscience. It may be worse. God grant your suffering won't be more 'n what you can bear. . . ."

Overwhelmed at last, Mose left Brother Simpson and walked through the dark streets of Happy Hollow, searching for peace, searching for a sign. But they were denied him.

When he came back past the pool hall, Frenchy saw him and ran after him. "I seen Cluris," he said.

"Who's that?"

"The gal Jackson Davis run off with. She's come back."

Mose was too submerged in his own problems to respond immediately to Frenchy's concern.

"Davis might come back too," Frenchy said. "He's got a wife here. Cenoria. He could raise a mighty big ruckus in Happy Hollow."

"Where did you see Cluris?"

"She's staying down at Mama Jo's."

For a moment Mose had a picture of an old barn of a house down by the tracks. He saw rows of painted women—rouge glowing darkly on dark skin—in poses on a porch. Cluris had stepped down a long step from her job in the beauty parlor.

Frenchy seemed to follow his thoughts. "It's a sho' nuff comedown," he said. "And she's got over three thousand hours in cosmetology too."

Mose walked home along Mulberry Street, Cenoria's troubles a light ripple over deeper currents. The singing at Sister Brackett's rose in a crescendo. Could that be a sign? He uttered an emphatic "No!" and walked on.

14

IT WAS Sunday morning—an end-of-May morning when Oklahoma is in calm spring, lush spring, before hot winds from the southwest burn and scar. Mose sat on his front porch making plans for the week ahead. One more week of school, one more Friday, one final exhibition of songs and speeches and drills and his first session as principal of Phillis Wheatley School would be ended.

Josie had picked a mess of turnip greens from the garden and was washing them in the back yard—washing them extravagantly in seven waters as Miss May had taught her, though it meant backbreaking work for Thomas and John to bring enough water from the hydrant. They begged Mose to make Robert help them, but he was at the schoolhouse playing the piano, practicing his part for the closing exhibition.

Mose finished his work, glanced at his watch. It was still an hour before he would gather his sons for services at the Methodist church, an hour before Josie would put on her clean white dress and go to Sister Brackett's.

Mose watched a new automobile come along the road from Columbus, watched it work like a beetle up and down side streets, pausing every so often at houses. He did not recognize the car, but the route was the one John Carson took one Sunday morning a month when he came to collect rent on his houses. The car skidded in thin mud and turned onto Mulberry Street. It was a large car, almost as long as the shotgun houses in Happy Hollow.

The driver leaned out and called, "Good morning, Mose."

It was John Carson with his son Alan.

"Good morning, sir. You got a new car?"

"Yep. We're going up North among the Yankees this summer. I thought I'd better get a car that'd get me out if they gang up on me."

Thomas and John came from behind the house in time to hear his hearty laugh. They grinned at him, and then stopped near the car, their images reflected in its shiny sides so that Mose saw four boys, eight buckets.

"Did you know the schoolhouse door's open?" Mr. Carson asked Mose.

"Yes, sir. I let my son Robert practice on the piano on Sunday mornings."

"You have not reported that to the School Board."

"No, sir. I didn't think it was necessary. I'm sure he'll take care of it. But if you think——"

"Ain't no telling what the Board members'll say—and they'll blame me. They say I'm too easy on niggers anyway. Let's go over to the schoolhouse. I want to inspect it. I got to make my spring report at the next Board meeting."

Mose motioned Thomas and John to go back to Josie. Then he stepped reluctantly off his porch. They were going to take Robert's greatest pleasure from him. "I'll meet you at the schoolhouse," he said.

Mr. Carson turned his car around and overtook him. "Get on in the car," he said.

Mose got in the back seat. He sat uncomfortably on the edge of the cushion, bringing as little of his soiled trousers as possible against the upholstery. He rolled his sleeves down and wished for his coat.

John Carson parked in front of the schoolhouse and led them across the strip of wet sand toward the entrance. For a moment Mose was able to see father and son in sharp contrast. John Carson, with his robust body, his healthy tanned face, his roach of white hair, was a good frontier type. Men had moved west, Boomers and Sooners, taken the prairies, left them in fee simple for sons like him. But in this case the vigor did not extend to the third generation. Alan, at twenty, was slender, pale, effete. His movements were unsure, his blue eyes too intense. Mose had heard him described as a student. He had, in fact, been in law school down at Norman. Sister Brackett had spread the news in Happy Hollow that he had endangered his health by studying too hard. Mrs. Carson had told her over a sale of hominy. He did look unhealthy, Mose decided, but it was the unhealthiness of frailty rather than overwork.

Their attention was caught by a series of opening chords and then a melody carefully phrased. It was "March of the Men of Harlech," which Cenoria Davis had chosen as the accompaniment for the girls' flag drill and freedom tableau. Every afternoon for weeks Robert had played the march while Cenoria Davis guided ten little girls through a flag drill and taught them their poses for the last triumphant moment, when they would stand in white dresses and with flags held high, a picture set in the frame of the stage and illuminated by red tableau powders. At that moment Thomas—selected best pupil of the year by the teachers—would step forward and lead the audience in the pledge of allegiance to the flag. Mose found himself thinking that at last Robert had mastered a tempo suitable for the drill.

Robert turned at the sound of footsteps on the bare floor, and stopped playing when he saw John Carson entering the auditorium. He stood up quickly.

"Wait a minute, boy," Mr. Carson said. "Who told you you could play the school piano?"

"My father."

Robert looked at Mose for assurance, saw a stolid mask set with stern eyes.

"I'm afraid the School Board won't like it," Mr. Carson said. "You'll have to stop."

Robert let the piano lid fall shut, closing off the hours he liked best. He shuffled his bare feet miserably against the floor. He turned wide eyes to Mose for help. Finding none, he took some sheets of music and slid away from the bench.

"When can I practice for the exhibition?" he asked Mose.

"The what?" Mr. Carson demanded.

"The exhibition."

Mose explained the closing exercises he had planned. In a voice that should have been sharp with pride but had been made dull as a froe, he told Mr. Carson of Robert's part in the exhibition.

"If you'll let him practice this week," Mose said, "I'll take full responsibility for the piano and school property."

"Oh, all right, then. This week and no more. But take good care of the piano. It's public property."

"Yes, sir."

Robert had moved to Mose's side, and they stood facing each other, father and son, father and son, segregated subconsciously by generations of Jim Crow tradition.

"Can you play blues?" Alan asked.

"No, sir. I'm not allowed to play that kind of music."

"Can you play spirituals?" It was Mr. Carson who asked.

"Yes, sir. Some."

"When I was a boy down by the Arkansas I used to hear the niggers singing spirituals." Mr. Carson's voice was suddenly friendly. "It was mighty pleasant in the late afternoon to hear them singing in time with their hoes. They'd keep singing a song till it got in your blood and you couldn't keep from singing with them. One I remember was 'Swinging on the Golden Gates.' Can you play it?"

"A little."

Robert slid back onto the bench and raised the piano lid. His long fingers paused for a moment on the yellow keys, his bare toes sought and found the pedals. He glanced at Alan Carson, who leaned against the end of the piano watching him. Robert touched the keys lightly and his distrust, his fear of white men went away for a moment as he followed the tune. He played the song through once and came to the refrain again. Mr. Carson suddenly began singing.

> "Oh, wake me, shake me,
> Don't let me sleep too late;
> Gonna fly away in the morning
> To swing on the Golden Gates...."

He finished the refrain and laughed self-consciously. "That takes me back," he said. And then to Alan: "That's something you missed by not growing up on a cotton farm. Town niggers don't sing like country niggers. I can still hear old Aunt Mary showering down on 'Sister Lou, Brother Joe, Aunt Maria done caught that train and gone.' She was my mammy and I loved her like my own mother. What's your name, boy?"

"Robert, sir."

"You play pretty good. How long you been playing?"

"I started last fall when we first come here."

"You've learnt mighty fast. Can you read music that good?"

"No, sir. I don't have to read it for songs like that. They just come natural."

"Can you play 'I'm up on the Mountain and I Cain't Come Down'?"

It was Sister Brackett's favorite song. Robert had often seen her bring her whole congregation to shouting and dancing with its words of faith, its syncopated jump-up rhythm. As his fingers searched out the melody, he began to feel the song as Sister Brackett felt it. His feeling poured into his fingers racing up and down the keyboard, into his toes stamping a passionate rhythm. Alan moved closer, sat on the end of the bench.

Mr. Carson went over to Mose. "Say, Mose," he said when the music stopped, "you got a real musician here. You know, it's a funny thing. My boy Alan has studied trumpet ever since he was knee-high, but he cain't play nothing without the notes right in front of him. I've spent a pile of money on music lessons, and he cain't play nothing but a few jazz tunes."

"I am proud of Robert," Mose told him. "I want to keep him studying music if I can. Not much he can do with it in Oklahoma, but I'd like him to have it."

Robert let his fingers experiment with chords. Mr. Carson turned to Mose again. "I've just been thinking," he said. "There's an old piano in our basement Robert can have if you don't care. Then he can practice at home all he wants to. It ain't much, but it's better than nothing at all. I got it when I fixed up a playroom for Alan and his friends. But nobody ever used it. Alan never brought friends there."

"I don't have the money to buy it, sir."

"That's all right. I'll give it to him. He can pay me off by playing spirituals at the club sometime. We haven't had a nigger program in a long time."

Mose was remembering a bit of folk wisdom: *Touch a white man in the right spot, he'll give you anything he's got.* John Carson had been touched by Negro spirituals as countless white Southerners had been touched before him. It was, in fact, traditional for him to be touched by spirituals, traditional for him to be paternal in giving away things he no longer needed. Mose could not refuse the piano. Robert's look told him that.

"That's certainly generous of you, sir," Mose said in a tone that even Miss May would have approved.

Robert let his fingers hold a chord, let his face show his pleasure. The possibility of having a piano at home had never occurred to him before.

"Well, Mose," Mr. Carson said, "let's have a look at the upstairs."

They went out of the auditorium and up the stairs. Robert let his fingers wander up and down in broken chords. Alan stood listening to the unusual pattern of harmony. Difference in color, difference in age disappeared. For the moment the piano was all that mattered.

"I'll help you move it," Alan promised him. "We can get a

truck from the store. You come to our house tomorrow morning. You can play some more for me then. I want to hear you play our grand piano."

Mr. Carson came back with his watch in his hand. "Time for church, Alan. Let's go."

Mose watched Alan walking with his father. He noted the spoiled droop of his lips, the pinch of loneliness around his eyes. "Something eating that boy," he said to himself.

Monday morning at nine Robert hurried up the back drive to the Carsons' back door. Over and over he repeated the manners Josie had told him: "Go to the back do'... take off yo' cap... scrape yo' foots... act like a nigger oughta act...."

Alan answered the bell. "Come on in," he said eagerly. "The truck won't get here till ten. Come on and play the piano."

Shyly Robert allowed himself to be led through the kitchen and hallway to a large parlor. It was the largest room he had ever seen—larger even than the one at Penrose Plantation. Alan opened the grand piano and sat beside Robert on the bench. Robert touched the white keys and let his fingers tingle at their touch. Then he began "March of the Men of Harlech."

"Don't play that," Alan commanded him. "Play spirituals—and play them hot. Nobody here but us."

As he played the spirituals, trying variations in syncopation and harmony he had never dared try before, he forgot that he was a little Negro boy in a white man's house. He forgot everything except the tunes he played and the eager face of the white boy on the bench beside him. What makes him like this? he thought. How come he's different from the others?

An hour passed, and then another, before the spell was broken by two Negro truckmen from the store. Alan took them to the basement and helped them roll out an old player piano. The player mechanism was broken, but Robert found the tone, the action better than in the one at school. Eagerly he helped them lift the piano to the back of the truck. Then he stood beside it, letting his fingers form chords.

"I can't go with you," Alan told him. "My father expects me at the store. But I want to hear you play again. Can I come to your house?"

Robert hesitated, surprised at the question. He remembered his father's talks about Jim Crow. He saw white faces in cars racing the streets of Happy Hollow late at night. He thought of Josie. What would she say if a white boy came to their house? "Po' white trash."

Alan saw the hesitation. "Maybe you can come here sometime—when my folks aren't at home," he said.

"Maybe," Robert said doubtfully.

"That is what I hate about Oklahoma," Alan said angrily. "A person can't go where he likes. You've never been up North, have you?"

Robert played while the truck rolled through Columbus and Happy Hollow.

Josie watched them unload the piano, her voice heavy with grumbling. "Ain't like no white man to give niggers a pyanner," she muttered. "Mark my words, ain't no good gonna come from it."

Robert was too excited to heed her. He cleaned the keys with a cloth and then filled the room, the house, the neighborhood with 'I'm Up on the Mountain and I Cain't Come Down."

As he played he thought of Alan Carson's love for blues and spirituals. If only Alan could hear Cenoria Davis play . . .

15

ON Penrose Plantation, Mose had his own way of spending the long summers: with his own mule, plow and cotton patch. But in Happy Hollow, when he closed the schoolhouse door after the final exhibition, he had nothing to do, no way to bring in money for faring. He could have joined the cotton choppers going out before sunup to neighboring farms. He mentioned working on a farm to Brother Simpson.

"That won't look so good—not here in Happy Hollow," Brother Simpson advised him. "Folks expects you to have more standing."

For a week he worked at the schoolhouse, cleaning it, putting it in shape for the fall opening. Then he worked on his own house, patching the roof and straightening sagging blocks. John Carson had agreed to let him owe the summer rent till fall if he would make the repairs without charge.

One morning in the middle of June Mose woke with the realization that he had three months of idleness stretching ahead of him. He sat on his porch while the sun came up, while Josie baked biscuits and made flour gravy, and made up his mind to try for a job in Columbus. He dressed in his black suit and white shirt and walked to Columbus.

From the station to the bank to the courthouse he went looking for a job, but the only work he could find was shining shoes or washing dishes in the hotel restaurant. "Depression's worse 'n ever," people told him. "Times is sho' nuff hard. No work, not much *relief*." White folks were having tough going, Negroes tougher.

Mose came to a corner where colored women sat in rows on the curb, leaned in groups against the wall, waiting for white women to come hire them for a day's work. They wore work dresses and every type of head rag and, to Mose, seemed a pathetic caricature of all the pictures of Southern Negro women. It was almost noon, and still they waited, hot, tired, dejected. If a job did come now, they could not get in a full day, and their pay might be two bits and totin's.

Mose passed the relief headquarters in a warehouse, saw two lines of people—Jim Crow here too—waiting their turns for rations of sowbelly and black-eyed peas.

As discouraged as any person he had seen that morning, Mose turned his feet toward Happy Hollow. For him there was no work, no money. He would have to borrow at the bank. That meant more bondage, more trouble. Mose remembered again Josie's prophecy, felt again his own burden of guilt. Was this the bad luck for his blasphemy? Was this a part of the suffering Brother Simpson talked about?

Mose, after wanderings that had taken him to Reservoir Hill and back, found himself standing in front of the First Methodist Church, Colored. As he studied the unfinished basement, his eyes adjusted to a new sight, a clear sight: a handsome brick church on this foundation, a white spire rising into the blue sky above Reservoir Hill. This might be a sign, he thought. He looked toward Columbus and then back again. The vision was still there, but clearer. "Yes, it is a sign," he said aloud for no one to hear, and felt the guilt grow less. "The church could be built this summer," he reasoned with himself. All they needed was a leader, and he had been given a sign.

Mose went to ask for Brother Simpson and found him returning from a country graveyard where he had held a funeral. The old man was tired and dusty from walking. They sat in the shade of the porch.

"We ought to get the church finished," Mose said.

"Course we ought to get it finished," Brother Simpson agreed.

"Ain't nothing in the world I want more, but how we gonna do it when times is so hard?"

"I've been over to Columbus today looking for a job. I saw a lot of Negroes over there looking for work—most of them not finding anything. Among our own members we've got plenty of free labor if we can persuade them to work on the church in their time off. If we could only get the bricks and boards and cement . . . Do you know how we could get the stuff to work with?"

Brother Simpson studied the question, his eyes on the brick foundation. "We *could* call on our brothers and sisters in white to help us," he said slowly, diffidently. "They ain't failed yet to give something when I asked them. They most always help a Negro church—think religion helps keep us in our place. It's not like asking for money for Negro schools or charity. But times is hard for them this day and time. But, well and all, it's been a long time since I asked them for anything—nigh on to fifteen years. They were mighty holpful then. . . ."

It was nearing sunset, and their neighbors—those who had worked and those who had been unable to find jobs—trudged back along the road from Columbus, tired, dispirited, bitter. From his front porch Brother Simpson pointed to them.

"Look at my po' people," he mourned, "tired, ragged, hungry. Nothing to solace them but religion, and only a basement to find it in. I'm getting old now and not much account. Won't be long now till I'll have to leave the pastoring to somebody younger and stronger than me. It would warm my heart good to see that church built while I'm still pastoring. . . ."

For Mose the sign became a positive, driving force. "Let's get the elders together tonight," he said. Within an hour he had his sons going through Pleasant Valley to call the elders together.

Tired, skeptical, the elders came to the church. So many times before Brother Simpson had called them to make plans for finishing the building. Now he stood before them again, an old man, and repeated his dream of red church and white spire. Seeing their apathy, Mose tried to stir them. He argued the good sense of building while labor was plentiful and materials cheap. He called on Harrison Williams to support him.

"In hard times," Harrison Williams said, "people forget their troubles working together."

"Where'll we get bricks and cement?" The elders came back to the same old question.

"From the white folks is the onliest place I know," Brother Simpson answered.

"Let's ast them," the elders agreed at last. "Ain't no harm done in asting. White folks with no more feeling than a gaspergoo will give money to build a colored church."

The decision to build once made, they settled down to plans with new spirit. They appointed Mose chairman of the building committee. Then they appointed committees of men and women to wait on the white people of Columbus for offerings.

"I'll use my front page next time for the church," Harrison Williams promised. "I think I can persuade the Columbus *Times* to run an editorial for us."

Their enthusiasm for building grew as they talked.

"It'll be like a big revival," they assured Brother Simpson.

Mose went with Brother Simpson to call on Dr. Martin, pastor of the First Methodist Church in Columbus. They found him in his office, sitting in a leather chair with an electric fan blowing on his feet. "He looks like a preacher," Brother Simpson had said of him. Mose saw his heavy-set body, his florid complexion, his carefully cut clothes. He looks like a banker as well, Mose thought.

"Good morning," Dr. Martin called heartily and rose to shake their hands. Then he made sure they were comfortably seated. "What can I do for you, Brother?" he asked Brother Simpson.

Mose thought fleetingly that his tone was that of a major prophet speaking to a minor prophet.

"You remember we built the basement of our church and didn't have the money to finish?"

"Yes."

"Well, we want to go on. We want to go on till the last brick is laid—till the steeple stands pointing to heaven like a beam of light."

"That's a worthy cause," Dr. Martin said, "one my church would like to take part in. We feel a grave Christian responsibility toward the Negroes in our town. How do you plan to work?"

Brother Simpson presented their plans in detail, with clarity, with earnestness—raised in stature, Mose thought, by the high seriousness of his purpose.

"We've done some alterations ourselves in the last year," Dr. Martin said when Brother Simpson and Mose had no more to say. "Would you like to see our church?"

He led them through a narrow hall connecting his office with the main auditorium. He helped them to admire the tall stained-glass windows, the darkly varnished pews, the altar with its single gold cross and snowy linen. It was a beautiful church—a jewel on the red clay and sand of Oklahoma. They expected nothing so fine for their own church. They'd be fortunate if they got a few red and blue and amber panes to shed color on the morning worship.

"The main dome rises above the altar," Dr. Martin was saying. "We have recently installed twelve great bells in the belfry."

Brother Simpson looked at him quickly. "Seems like you had one big bell before," he said. "Seems like I used to hear one big bell tolling on Sunday mornings."

"Yes, we did. One of our members gave us the new ones."

"What'd you do with it when you got this whole steepleful of bells?"

"It's in the churchyard, out back."

"Ain't being used?"

Mose noticed a sudden change in Brother Simpson. He was no longer one minister talking to another. He was a black servant about to ask a favor of his white master.

"You don't reckon we could see it?" he asked hopefully.

"I don't know why not."

Dr. Martin led them to a back lawn. There lay a great iron bell, rusty and half grown over with grass. Brother Simpson raised the heavy iron clapper and let it fall against the side. The bell gave a deep sound, but the resonance was lost in the earth. With shrewd eyes he looked at Dr. Martin.

"It don't sound so good on the ground, do it?" he asked.

"No, it doesn't."

"It wants to be up in a steeple to sound good, don't it?"

"Yes," Dr. Martin agreed.

"I always wanted a bell in my church," Brother Simpson said humbly. "I like to hear it on Sunday mornings telling my people to drop their work and come to church. I like to hear it in the evening telling them another day's work is over. Most of all, I want one when I die—to toll out the number of years I worked and toiled on this old earth. You white folks got twelve bells and don't need this one. You reckon we could have it to go in our steeple when we get it built?"

"I don't know. That'd be up to the elders and congregation. They might give it to you, if they saw you were really getting your church built. I'll tell you, let's wait till we see how far you get along. Then when you're making progress, I'll bring the matter before our board. As far as I am concerned, you could haul the bell away today."

Later in the afternoon Mose and Brother Simpson walked home through Happy Hollow.

"We gonna get us a bell," Brother Simpson said to all he met. "Tell the people we gonna get us a bell."

Their campaign in Columbus was quiet, orderly, thorough. Men dressed in their Sunday suits went to the bank and stores to ask for money and building materials. Women with tin cups in their hands went from back door to back door, asking white housewives to give their nickels and dimes.

The gifts were varied and more plentiful than Mose had anticipated. A man from the white Methodist church gave them the bricks from an abandoned well, if they would take them out and fill the hole. Mose sent Zack with his wagon and men to help him.

They brought the bricks, muddy and moss-grown, and stacked them on the vacant lot beside the church. The manager of the oil mill gave them the bricks from a crumbling wall. A lumber company gave them enough secondhand siding for the spire and agreed to sell them cement at cost.

No one in Columbus was overlooked. Businessmen met one another with the question "You been hooked for that nigger church yet?"

On through June they worked like pack rats, but when Mose and Brother Simpson estimated the pile of bricks they knew that they were still short. The campaign had not been turned on Pleasant Valley yet. They knew there were enough loose bricks on their side of the tracks to finish the church. But how to get them? How to make people give up doorstops and warming bricks? The appeal had to be unusual.

Brother Simpson searched through the Old Testament, found the story of Jacob's altar. He brought it to Mose. "Brother, I want you to make me a sign," he said.

Together they worked out a sign and set it before the church, where all the people of Happy Hollow stopped to read:

> AND JACOB TOOK A STONE, AND SET IT UP FOR A PILLAR. AND JACOB SAID UNTO HIS BRETHREN, GATHER STONES; AND THEY TOOK STONES, AND MADE AN HEAP.
>
> ALTAR RAISING SERVICE
> EACH PERSON BRING ONE BRICK
> FIRST MONDAY NIGHT IN JULY
> LET NO ONE COME WITH EMPTY HANDS

"That ought to bring us bricks," Brother Simpson said. "Now I'm gonna invite our white friends in Columbus. I set it on Monday night on purpose for that. We want us a bell."

A red-hot sun set on an outdoor makeshift altar, raised at the last minute because the crowd seemed sure to overflow the basement. Mose and a crew of men strung lights on poles, moved benches outside for choir and honored guests, set the piano on a separate little platform. Crowds gathered to watch or help. Sister Brackett stopped her pony long enough to form her own opinion of the service.

"We gonna have us a church with a bell," Elder Johnson told her.

"Hmph!" she said, and went on home.

Before it was dark enough for lights, Cenoria Davis went to the piano and played spirituals. Choir members arrived early, took up the songs, drew others with their singing.

"We got people from all the churches," the elders told Brother Simpson, who was waiting in the basement to make a proper entrance.

"The Devil's church too?" he asked with a smile.

"The Devil's church too. We got folks tonight I ain't never seen at church."

White people from Columbus, invited and uninvited, began arriving in their cars. They parked along the streets with their windows rolled down, eager to hear the singing, to see the ceremony, but not eager to risk a touch of dark flesh.

"Make 'em pay," Sister Daisy, in charge of the women ushers, urged. "Hold yo' plates under their noses till they pay."

Dr. Martin had arranged for the honor guests to come in a body. They came, when it was full dark, when the crowd had filled the lot and pushed into the dusty streets on all sides. Mose watched them file in: Dr. Martin, Mr. Brown, Mr. Carson, Dr. Lewis, ministers, lawyers, merchants, the strong men of Columbus. They looked the part of benefactors—with the exception of Dr. Lewis, who was, as usual, shabby and weather-worn.

The women with collection plates waited eagerly for the white guests to be seated. From them would come the best money offering of the service. Sister Daisy watched with wily eyes, whispered briefly with Lora Dixon.

"Wait," Sister Daisy cautioned her ushers. "Don't ask them for nothing yet. They'll just nickel and dime you to death. We got to ask them for change till they ain't got no quarters and fifty centses left. Then they got to put dollars on the plate. You watch me."

With a determined face she approached the white men. "Evening, Doctor Martin," she said. "It's a great honor to have you with us this evening. Could you give me change for fo' bits?"

Frenchy came in and pushed his way into the row back of the white visitors. Mose could not remember having seen him at church before; nor could he remember having seen him in the dark coat and white pants of a Happy Hollow dandy. Mose saw the ease with which Frenchy talked to the white visitors and was glad that he was near them—to give his comment on life across the tracks.

The elders opened the church door, and Brother Simpson stood for a moment with a bright light shining down on his white hair. Then he marched up a cleared aisle to the altar, the singing of the choir setting a measured pace.

> "We are climbing Jacob's ladder,
> We are climbing Jacob's ladder,
> We are climbing Jacob's ladder,
> Oh, love, love, love.
>
> We are climbing higher, higher,
> We are climbing higher, higher . . ."

They paused for Dr. Martin to give an invocation. Then, since it was not a part of the regular service he had planned, Brother Simpson asked for the money offering. The choir took up the song again; the collection takers made one more round through the crowd. Sister Daisy herself went down the row of white visitors. Solemnly they laid their bills on her tin plate. At Brother Simpson's signal, Sister Daisy, with an air of having worked her mine fully, led the ushers past the altar, where they stacked their plates on a table.

Brother Simpson took his Bible and opened it at a red silk marker. Then he raised his hand for silence.

"I wish I had his dramatic sense," Dr. Martin whispered to Frenchy.

"Brothers and sisters, both in white and black," Brother Simpson said, "we have worked hard to gather the wherewithal to complete this house of worship. We have all made sacrifices, but none greater than God would have us make. Our brothers and sisters in white have been a great help and comfort to their darker brethren. In so doing, they are showing the true Christian spirit. Tonight we are coming to the symbolic part of the building of our altar. We are glad they are here to partake of it with us. In this ceremony to transpire, we follow the path trod by the Israelites of old."

He cleared his throat and looked at his elders. "Amen," they said in subdued voices.

"We been working with a sign to goad us on—a sign from the Bible. Tonight I'm gonna read that sign from the Book to begin our ceremony."

In a voice that rolled over the crowd and echoed from the walls of Happy Hollow, he read, "And Jacob took a stone, and set it up for a pillar. And Jacob said unto his brethren, Gather stones; and they took stones, and made an heap."

He paused for the words to take effect. "Amen," the elders chanted.

"Brothers and sisters," he said, "we ain't got stones to build with, but we got bricks. When they said they was no more bricks for us in Columbus, I asked you to search yo' own hearthstones and bring us a brick. I asked you to make one more sacrifice for the Lawd. Tonight we gonna lay our bricks on the altar for God. Let no one falter."

Cenoria Davis swept the keys with her fingers. The elders moved the table from in front of Brother Simpson, leaving a wide, clear space.

"Jacob took a stone, and set it up for a pillar," he read again. Then he took a smooth red brick and laid it on the improvised altar. "Like Jacob of old I am setting up a brick for a pillar. Now let the choir sing, and you march by and lay yo' bricks on the altar. . . . "

Cenoria Davis led them in improvised words.

"Lay yo' bricks upon the altar,
Lay yo' bricks upon the altar,
Lay yo' bricks upon the altar,
Oh, love, love, love. . . . "

The elders rose, marched past the altar, left their bricks in a haphazard column. The line became snakelike and reached out into the street as men, women, children crowded into it, each bearing a brick. Fascinated, the white visitors watched the pile grow.

"Didn't know there were that many bricks in Happy Hollow," Dr. Lewis said. "Where'd they get them?" he asked Frenchy.

At that moment Sadie Maple, Mrs. Brown's cook, was laying a white-enameled brick on the altar.

"That one looks like it come from Mrs. Brown's flower bed," Frenchy said with a quick smile. "Wouldn't be surprised——"

"I'll be dogged if I don't believe it did," Mr. Brown whispered in amazement.

Their attention focused on the bricks rather than on the people; they made a game of guessing the real contributors.

"There's one from the courthouse drive."

"That yellow one looks like it came from the walk at the Gulf filling station."

"That green one must be from Sinclair."

The marchers kept coming; the stack grew higher and higher. Mose was certain they had enough bricks now to raise the walls, perhaps enough to discard the irregular in size and color.

Mr. Brown saw another one from his wife's flower bed. "That's stealing," he whispered to Dr. Martin.

"Not stealing," the minister replied good-humoredly. "Let's say appropriating—for a legitimate cause."

"Shouldn't we speak to them? Let them know we know?"

"I think not. Tomorrow Mrs. Brown will miss a brick or two from her flower bed; the filling-station man will find a brick gone; some other people will miss a few. But what they miss they can mend."

"But we are encouraging stealing, dishonesty."

"The slave always has the right to take what he needs, when his master has not provided it. I'm not going to say a word, and I'd rather no one else did. Let them have their church without bother from us. They deserve it." He paused, looked at the rapt faces of the marchers. "Furthermore, I've made up my mind on something else. I'm going to give them our old church bell tonight."

When the last marcher had laid his brick on the altar, reaching above his head to do so, Brother Simpson looked at the stack and then at Mose. "That enough bricks, Brother?"

"Plenty."

"Then say, Amen!"

Dr. Martin stood up with hand outstretched.

"Speak, Brother, speak," Brother Simpson called to him. "Speak yo' heart right out."

Dr. Martin went forward and faced the crowd. He stood beside the bricks and rested his hands on them. "What I have to say won't take long," he began.

"Say it, Brother, say it if it takes all night," the people urged him.

"First, I want to say that this has been an inspiring service."

"Say it, man, say it," they chanted.

"The next thing I want to say is that my church has a bell——"

At the word *bell* Brother Simpson started toward him.

"After seeing your service tonight," Dr. Martin continued, "I want my church to give you that bell—on condition you'll be good niggers and go to church."

"Amen, we will, we will," they promised.

Brother Simpson reached Dr. Martin and grasped his hand. Tears stood on his cheeks and glistened in the light.

"Thank you, Brother, thank you," he cried. "Another one of my prayers is answered. All my parson years I wanted a church with a bell. Oh, Lawdy, that bell's gonna sound sweet when it's rung on Sunday morning—and sad at night when it counts out the years for somebody dead. Lawd, I've tried hard to serve you. Now I'll die easy, knowing a bell will toll out my years for all the folks to know how faithful I been to the Lawd. A new church. A big bell." He raised his eyes. "Thank you, Lawd, thank you. . . ."

His words were drowned in a spiritual that burst spontaneously from the people:

"Oh, it just keeps a-leaking in this old building,
It just keeps a-leaking in this old building,
It just keeps a-leaking in this old building,
I believe I'll have to move,
I've found a better home...."

Brother Simpson stood, his head bowed to the overwhelming feeling of his people. When they had sung themselves out he said, "Amen, brethren, how true that is! We gonna move to a better home—with painted pews and a steeple with a bell...."

Mose remained until after midnight, helping to count the offering, larger than they had expected, helping Brother Simpson compose a letter to the Columbus *Times* thanking the white people for their generosity. When he walked along Mulberry Street he heard a few cars on the road to Columbus, racing with their mufflers open. Young white boys out for some fun, he thought, and then dismissed them, his mind being occupied with plans for building.

Mose climbed wearily into bed beside Josie and then sat up again quickly when he realized that Thomas was not at home. He recalled having seen Thomas last when he laid his brick on the altar. Why was he not at home? Where in Happy Hollow could he be at this time of night? Mose was at the point of getting dressed to go look for him when Thomas came creeping through the kitchen door.

"Where have you been?" Mose demanded.

"They called me nigger," Thomas said bitterly.

"Who called you nigger?"

"Some white boys in a car. They called me nigger and squirted soda water on me."

"What'd you do?"

"I yelled for them to come back. They'll come back some time, and I'll be laying for them."

Mose laid his arm across Thomas' shoulders, tried to teach him the resignation he should feel when *nigger* was flung at him as a bitter taunt.

"Don't fight back, son," he begged. "Don't ever fight back, alone. You can't win. You'll only get a deeper hurt."

Mose soothed Thomas to sleep. Then he lay awake with the problem till dawn.

"That is always the way," he told himself. "Some white people do what they can to help us—a few tear us down. . . ."

They built the church during July and August. Cotton was chopped and corn laid by. Times were still hard in Columbus and work at a standstill. So there were many hands to clean bricks, mix mortar and lay bricks one on top of another until the walls were raised. Under the direction of Mose and Brother Simpson they worked with a fervor that bordered on frenzy. In a short time cotton would be ready to pick; gins would run again; cottonseed oil would boil at the mill. The church had to be finished before then— before workers had to go on to paying jobs. They worked all day; they strung lights on their scaffolds and worked at night, taking time off only for sleeping, or eating the food the women brought them.

They sang as they worked, to the rhythm of hammer and trowel and wheelbarrow. At times the songs were not songs but the "moaning low" they did in cotton fields in the hour before sundown. In a lull a singer would improvise a tune and follow it like a thread up and down the scale. The others would join him, humming strange harmonies in thirds and sixths, each person following his own little variations, with the tunes crossing and recrossing to create a wild throbbing beauty in the night. The working and singing brought them closer and closer together.

"What church you belong to?" they asked one another jovially.

"The *Methodist* church—the one with the bell."

At last the roof was finished and the spire painted a glistening white. Quietly Mose and Brother Simpson left work and walked past the railroad station, the bank, the white First Methodist Church. From all those places they could see the spire pointing upward like a thin white finger. Satisfied, they went back to their task.

September came, and the afternoon set aside for hoisting the bell to the steeple. Most of Happy Hollow came to help or to watch.

Sister Brackett drove her buggy into the churchyard and watched the men raise the bell slowly with block and tackle. Josie, who had stayed away from the church until this afternoon, came and stood beside her. Mose and Brother Simpson stood idle at last.

"That steeple's mighty purty," Sister Brackett said to Mose, "but take care, Brother, that it ain't a finger pointing at pride in yo' heart. You cutting mighty high on the hog these days. Take care the Lawd don't trim you down."

"Ain't I been telling him that?" Josie demanded. "Many a time I been telling him it ain't right to worship a building like he do this one."

Mose heard their remarks, smiled at them. Before him was a positive sight—a bell being drawn slowly up the side of the building. Thomas, with a new white rope, was holding the bell away from the walls.

"I always hear," Sister Brackett continued, her voice pitched to dark prophecy, "when a house is built, somebody's gonna die."

"Me, too," Josie agreed solemnly.

Mose stood with his face away from them, hoping to avoid being brought into their talk.

"Say, Brother Mose—" Sister Brackett drew his attention when the bell was at last in the steeple—"when you gonna ring that bell?"

"Tomorrow morning to call people to worship."

"Well, all I got to say is, I hope you ain't gonna have to ring it for somebody dead before you get to ring it for church. You know what I hear——"

"When will you leave off your superstition?" Mose demanded sharply.

"Call it what you will, Brother," Sister Brackett shot back, "but mark my words. That bell's gonna toll the death of some member of this church before snow falls."

The bell in place, the bell rope threaded through the iron loop, the people drifted away toward their homes. Josie and Sister Brackett left together, Sister Brackett leading her horse and buggy behind her. Their voices came back to Mose a doleful chorus, and he became aware that not all his feeling of guilt had left him.

16

AFTER breakfast the next morning Mose moved his chair out to the front porch and, with Bible in hand, sat contemplating the new church. Between his house and the church stood other shotgun houses, low on the ground but tall enough to hide the lower part of the church and the yard still marred from building. They were shabby little shacks, but Mose hardly saw them as his eyes studied the red brick walls, took in the shingled roof and shot upward with the white spire into the blue sky. With pride in a job well done, he focused his eyes on the latticed half of the steeple and made out the shape of the bell.

Thomas, dressed in white shirt and dark trousers, came to borrow Mose's watch to ring the bell by. He was the janitor of the new church—an arrangement Mose had made to help him forget the incident with the white boys. Often Mose had said, "Don't harbor the hurt. That happened a long time back now. It won't help to harbor the hurt."

As often Thomas said, "No, sir, I'm not studying them," but the hurt was in his tone as deep as ever.

Mose worried over the brooding, the obstinacy in his face. He sought to penetrate more deeply into his son's mind—to find his own part in helping the boy adjust to Jim Crow. He hoped the church, the bell, would give him new pride in Happy Hollow.

"Ring it at exactly nine-thirty," he said. He took his gold watch from his pocket and handed it to Thomas.

"Yes, sir."

Thomas took the watch and slipped it into his watch pocket. He studied the effect of the shiny black fob against the dull black of his trousers. Then, with a seriousness gratifying to Mose, he walked down Mulberry Street toward the church.

At exactly nine-thirty the bell rolled its iron tones into the shimmering hot air, and echoed back from the slopes of Reservoir Hill. Each tone, each echo seemed to belong to Happy Hollow.

Josie came from the kitchen and stood on the porch to listen. She wanted to hear the bell; she wanted to remind Mose of Sister Brackett's prophecy, of what he had said to her about old beliefs.

Mose overlooked the frown on her face. "Sounds good, doesn't it?" he said.

"It sounds all right," she answered in a dead voice.

"Makes a fellow want to go to church," he pursued.

"It don't make me want to go to church a whet more 'n I did anyway. It ain't bells nor churches whut preaches or saves folks' souls."

"No," he agreed, "it isn't, but a nice house of worship and a bell to remind the people it's church time ought to make more come to church."

"It ought to, but I bet it don't. I say Sister Brackett's right. She say you trying to educate folks away from the true religion of the spirit. She say you bounden to a idol worship—you worship altars and bells instead of God. You and Brother Simpson . . . and all you Methodists." She twisted her hands in her apron. "Mose, when we wus on the plantation you wus a good cotton-patch Christian. I ain't seen nobody that could outreach you in praying and singing and shouting. Now you got education, but you lost the spirit. Heaps of times I've wisht we wus back down home."

"Education doesn't make you lose the spirit," Mose argued, "though it may make you change your perspective. The spirit will be with us in church today. If you don't believe it, come and see."

"Don't reckon as I can. I done promised Sister Brackett I'd be vice-president usher. . . . "

One afternoon in late October Sister Brackett came loping her pony up Mulberry Street. Mose, home from school, busy stacking a rick of wood on his porch, saw the flying lash, the straining pony. Something really wrong now, he thought. She stopped the buggy, climbed down over the wheel and trotted across the yard, calling to Mose and Josie.

"Brother Harrison Williams is bad off," she proclaimed. There was a positive note of triumph in her voice.

"What's the matter with him?" Mose asked.

"Don't know. He was taken sudden—struck down sick as death at work in his office." She rolled the words on her tongue as if they tasted sweet. "Fannie Mae called Doctor Lewis, and he's jest gone over. They say his fever's high and he's out'n his head most of the time."

She's glad he's sick, Mose thought. She'll be gladder if he dies—in time to fulfill her prophecy.

"I'll go offer to help," Mose said soberly, and took his hat from a nail behind the door.

"He's a Methodist member, ain't he?" Sister Brackett asked, holding him a minute longer.

"Yes."

"Ain't no snow fell yet, is they?"

"No," Mose jerked out shortly, and then stifled his breath on hot words.

Mose left Sister Brackett and Josie talking in low tones in the kitchen. He knew the things they were saying to each other. Sister Brackett had been saying them widely in Happy Hollow since the new church had been built. She had said them till people believed them. In awe they told one another how often her predictions had come true. Maids took her words to the white kitchens of Columbus, brought them back strengthened because white women had clucked over them.

"She ought to be stopped," Mose said aloud on Mulberry Street. He knew, however, that to stop her kind, a great section of the Negro people would have to be stopped.

Harrison Williams was a sick man. Mose knew that as soon as he entered the bedroom and saw the drawn face almost hidden in a pile of quilts and pillows. He did not need to see the distress on Fannie Mae's face, or to hear Dr. Lewis' short, whispered instructions.

"Glad you're here, Mose," Dr. Lewis told him. "We've got a tough pull. If his heart holds out, we'll make it all right."

Dr. Lewis left, and Fannie Mae prepared the room and herself for a long battle. Her face was full of worry, but she was calm, efficient in her work. Mose could see how fiercely determined she was to hold onto Harrison Williams—saw, and for the first time began to understand her. In school she had remained quiet and shy, teaching maid work, doing a maid's work in the building—working on a temporary certificate that had expired, unable to get another if anyone questioned her qualifications. Mose felt sorry that he had mentioned her lack of a certificate. If maid work had to be taught, she was as good a teacher as he would ever find.

Bit by bit, as they sat watching over the sick man, Fannie Mae told her story. Her parents had died when she was a young girl, and she had been forced into maiding. She had worked in white homes all through Little Dixie. When his wife died Harrison Williams brought her to Pleasant Valley to keep house for him and got her a job in the school.

"He took me out'n maid work and made me a teacher," she said. "Now he's gonna die . . . and I'll have to go back to maiding again."

Mose tried to convince her that her job was safe, that he and all the parents were well satisfied.

She shook her head sadly. "Someday some white man'll say my certificate ain't good and you got to fire me, and you got to. Uncle Harrison could stand up for me, with the paper and all, but they ain't nobody else. . . ."

His illness developed rapidly into pneumonia. For days he lingered between life and death, fighting—most of the time without knowing he fought. Then pneumonia gradually relaxed its grip and he returned to listless life. Sister Brackett and Josie would not believe in his recovery. In the stars and in signs they sought the answer to when he would die. They pressed Fannie Mae for details of his illness, sighed with deep satisfaction when she confessed that she had found the beginning of a crown in his feather pillow.

"Doctor Lewis say he'll be up again soon," Fannie Mae insisted hopefully.

But they shook their heads. Death was coming to him soon. The crown in his pillow proved it. Mose argued with them, but time was on their side. Harrison Williams was an old man already. He had almost lived out the time allotted to man.

Toward the end of November Harrison Williams sent for Mose. Mose found him sitting in a chair in front of the fire, a shriveled old man now, trembling and shaking, the confidence and smoothness all gone. Fannie Mae, home from school, hovered about him, anxious that he should not tire or get chilled in the cold air.

"Evening, Professor," he said. "I called you to give me some advice. The time has come at last when I have to give up my paper. It ain't been out in a month. I don't think I'll ever be able to get it out again. I've got to sell."

He showed Mose an advertisement he had run in Negro newspapers in the South and North. Then he handed Mose half a dozen letters.

"Times is sorely," he said. "I got several answers but only two bids."

"Which one offers the best paper?"

"A man in Chicago named Amos Evenly."

Mose read the letter. Evenly had received backing from a national Negro organization. They were lending him the money to buy and print a newspaper that would educate Negroes and inform them of their civil rights. He planned to fight discrimination through legal measures—through the courts. "Oklahoma seems to me a good place to publish such a paper," the letter ended. "Farther south, I'd be licked before I started. Farther north, papers are already established. My backers agree with me. They have authorized me to make what I think is a high bid. . . . "

Mose was pleased. How near the words were to his own when he decided to come to Columbus! He knew the organization backing the paper well and trusted its aims, its leaders. He was also disturbed. A Negro editor with liberal views would have a hard time in Columbus. He could not go far before the whites would fight back. Perhaps Amos Evenly had not heard of the trouble in Tulsa. Perhaps he had never heard of the difficulties a Negro editor in the City had met.

"He'll have trouble," Mose told Harrison Williams, "but the right kind of man could do a heap of good here."

He read the other bid. It was from a doctor of spiritual science who wanted to make Columbus a center for his church and sales service. Mose studied the letterhead: "Daddy Splane, Holy Articles from India and Jerusalem." He read again the claim that Daddy Splane, blindfolded, could tell a person anything he desired to know.

"If you've got Southern Negroes at heart," Mose said, "Evenly seems the best man to take it over. I hope that he is a man of good judgment, that he will know what is best for our people."

"He says he wants to help the race. That ought to be enough. That's what you said, and you done all right."

"I know. But I'm used to Jim Crow and 'Hey, nigger, git off'n the sidewalk.' He may not be. He may not be willing to get along with the whites. You and I know that anything we gain has to come through the help of Southern whites, or at least with their consent—not through pressure from the North."

"Your words make me think on trouble. It's a great responsibility to sell my paper. I'd better talk to Brother Simpson too." He held the two letters on his knees. "You seen Daddy Splane offered more money. . . ."

A few days later Fannie Mae came to Mose's office. "I got a favor to ask, Professor."

"What is it?"

"Uncle wants you to help publish one more edition of the paper before he lets it go. He say he wants to give his farewell to Pleasant Valley and tell his subscribers the paper's gonna belong to Daddy Splane."

"Daddy Splane?"

"Yes, sir. The other man couldn't meet Daddy Splane's offer."

Harrison Williams revealed again, Mose thought, but he kept his thoughts to himself.

"It's a big favor to ask, but I thought you might help. I don't know much about it, and Uncle's too po'ly."

For a week Mose worked after school every day helping Fannie Mae get her material ready. For his own part, he wrote about his favorite Negro character—Sojourner Truth. In the simplest language possible he wrote the story of this woman who had talked the evils of slavery through America, who had risked her life taking runaway slaves up the Underground Railroad. When he had finished, he read it to Harrison Williams.

"Put that on the front page—with my farewell," the old man said.

Mose searched the office for enough material to fill the sheets. He dug through stacks of letters and penciled notes for personal items. The more he read, the angrier he became. The crudely scrawled unsigned notes were filthy, scandalous, evil.

In a locked drawer he found a sheaf of items worse than the others. These he took to his office to ponder over, with his door locked. Each was a new revelation of the character of Happy Hollow, of Harrison Williams himself.

His anger became personal when he read:

How come Cenoria Davis stay in school late every day? Mighty funny she always got one big boy to stay in. Is some more pounding besides the piano going on? Ask her how come she don't go after men and leave the boys alone.

Mose's first impulse was to stop Robert from taking piano lessons, to forbid him to have anything to do with Cenoria Davis. But, he reasoned, the trouble lay not with Robert or Cenoria. It was with the scandalmongers, who could make evil of anything. He turned another sheet.

Better warn the menfolks to keep away from Sister Brackett. She got the power to do anything bad to men. She can lay her hands on a man and take his manhood away.

Another form of Sister Brackett's power in Happy Hollow. With a little voodoo added to her religion, she could prey on the fears of her followers. If the Lord wouldn't still her enemies for her, her voodoo would. No wonder "Look out, nigger, don't you hoodoo me" became as fervent as a prayer.

Mose pondered bitterly a barely legible note:

Ask the Professor what kind of licking a nigger's got to do for a white man to give him a piano—boots or higher up.

He had often wondered what Happy Hollow thought of John Carson's gift to Robert. Did accepting it make him the handkerchiefhead they seemed to think him?

He searched the pile, found only one other note that mentioned him personally:

How come the Professor and his wife are the same as brother and sister?

In a cold fury Mose took the sheaf of papers to the stove in the auditorium and thrust them among the coals. At least Daddy Splane would not have them to begin his career in Pleasant Valley.

One gray day in late December Mose worked at the school until dark. Then he went home to a supper of bread and milk. Josie had already gone to Sister Brackett's for prayer meeting. Robert had gone with her. Thomas and John hugged the stove, reading.

Mose ate his supper by the stove and took up a book. They were interrupted by footsteps on the porch, a hard knock at the door.

"Open the door."

It was Brother Simpson. He came shivering into the room, his overcoat drawn tightly around him, a white shawl wrapped around his head.

"I just come from Brother Williams'," he said.

"How is he?" Mose asked.

"He died a little while ago."

"Died? No!"

"Yes, Brother. Fannie Mae come running for me about dark to say he is worse. I went right over. He was already unconscious, and died before Doctor Lewis got there. He said it was a heart attack, brought on by the pneumonia."

"You going back over?"

"Soon as I can get something to eat. I told Fannie Mae I'd sit up all night."

"I'll go over now," Mose said. "There'll be a lot to do." His mind was on the pile of letters in the newspaper office; they had to be burned. "But wait—the bell?"

"We'd better ring the bell," Brother Simpson said slowly. "Brother Williams was a member in good standing—an elder. Go ahead, Thomas. Ring the bell. Count the years right, and remember you're ringing for a good man. Fannie Mae done talked to the insurance. This gonna be some funeral when he gets funeralized."

Thomas buttoned up his coat and slammed the door behind him. Brother Simpson pulled his shawl tighter around his ears and stepped into the night, eager to get started on plans for the funeral. Mose, not agreeing fully that Harrison Williams was a good man, but aware of the circumstances that made him what he was, put on heavier clothes and found his flashlight. He was on the porch ready to go when the first note of the bell rang out on the cold air. He stood reverently while the bell tolled out slowly to sixty-four. Mose tried to push aside the scandalmongering, tried to see that in his way, his Negro way in a Jim Crow world, Harrison Williams was a good man.

Mose thought of Sister Brackett and Josie at prayer meeting. He could imagine their exchange of glances when they heard the bell. He could almost hear them whisper to each other, "Ain't I told you, Sister?"

As he walked rapidly toward Harrison Williams' house Mose felt fine flakes of snow on his face—the first snow. He brushed them away and thought that again time was on the side of superstition.

17

Mose sat in his office. He was thinking of his work in the time he had been at Phillis Wheatley, taking his own inventory, making his own resolutions. Progress had been slow, but it had been made. It was now an eight-teacher school, though not all the teachers were the best-trained. He considered the roll before him. Lora Dixon and Cenoria Davis had both been away for study during summer session. Sister Daisy was no longer on the roll. Mose had finally persuaded John Carson to dismiss her and her rocking chair. Her place had been taken by Emmy Johnson, who had been away to Langston for a year. Fannie Mae Williams had expanded maid work to include sewing. Effie Hightower, one of the girls he had trained, taught high-school English. Elgie Mays had come in the fall to teach algebra; Cloys Carr relieved him of high-school history. It was a good staff, one he could depend on.

The building was in better condition, the grounds better kept.

His mind turned to plans for new courses: typing and shorthand for the girls, though there was not a secretarial job for Negroes in Columbus; shop work for the boys——

He heard steps on the stairway and then a knock at his door. "Come in," he said without turning from his view of Happy Hollow and Reservoir Hill.

"Professor Ingram?"

"Yes." Mose turned quickly.

"I'm Daddy Splane. I've come to take over the paper."

"I beg your pardon," Mose said, rising and extending his hand. "I thought you were one of the children."

Mose stood looking at his visitor. He was an old man, a little old man, dressed in tuxedo, tucked shirt and black tie. His small head and face seemed smaller under a turban of pale-blue silk. *Daddy Splane, Doctor of Spiritual Science.* Mose knew at a glance the reason for the bizarre costume. He tried to discern the mixture of blood that made him. His skin was light brown, his eyes dark. His nose and lips were thin. A lot of white blood in him, Mose thought—Irish, English, German. Enough for him to pass if he tried.

"When did you get in?" Mose asked.

"Today. I came as early as I could. I don't want to miss a single issue."

Mose tried to see the man against the background of Happy Hollow. His clothes, his manners were different. But Negroes were used to those who dressed a part to make living easier. He could dress as he pleased. The test would be in how he behaved as a Negro.

"Nice town, Columbus," Daddy Splane was saying. "A nice town, judging by what I've seen."

"Have you seen all of Happy Hollow?"

"Not yet."

"It may not look so good when you've seen all of it. You ever lived Jim Crow?"

"Plenty. But I have ways of getting around it. I just put on my turban and pass as a Hindu. No trouble at all."

"Don't people suspect?"

"Some do. They're afraid to make trouble. They know I'd go to court."

"That wouldn't do you much good in Oklahoma."

"No, but they don't want the bother. So they let me ride in the Pullman, eat in the diner. I live good, tip heavy. They don't give me no bother. Money gets me most places I want to go."

"It won't get you far in Columbus, if you live in Happy Hollow."

Mose felt his distrust grow. Any Negro who would desert his race for a few considerations, a few comforts would be a hindrance in Happy Hollow. Yet Mose felt impelled to tell what he knew of their situation.

"Did you ride out with Frenchy?"

"Yes."

"You might ask him about Columbus. You ever lived in the South?"

"No." His hesitation was slight, only enough to make Mose wonder, to make him watch for traits of speech, manner. "But money talks in the South, just like it talks in the North."

"Well, it's not like the North. Let me warn you of that. Trouble brews easy here—trouble between blacks and whites. You heard of Tulsa?"

"No."

"They had a riot. 1921. It was bad: people killed, houses burned. It's uneasy here—like Tulsa. All the time it's like sitting on a powder keg, with white folks holding a match. We're working to make it better, but it takes time. What did you come to Oklahoma for? You say you're not a down-home?"

"To teach my faith, set up a spiritualist church, sell my holy objects from the East, publish a paper——"

"Have you seen *The Neighborhood Eye?*"

"Several issues."

"Do you expect to print that kind of gossip and slander?"

"I expect to combine spiritualist doctrine with what the people want to read. Any harm in that?"

"White folks in Columbus didn't mind what Harrison Williams printed. They sometimes sent nickels by their maids to get *The Neighborhood Eye* so they could have a good laugh."

"Some of my best customers have been white folks. I've sold them hundreds of holy handkerchiefs. I'm going to set up a mail-order business——"

Mose stopped him impatiently. "Negroes like you make me wonder. You hold back the race."

"What're you doing to help?"

Mose shifted in his chair and looked across to the bleak slopes of Reservoir Hill. It was sunset, with a flush of red in a gray world. Smoke rose from chimneys and flues in blue-gray spirals. Gray houses seemed to settle into a gray earth. He thought of that first evening when he sat in his office and talked to Brother Simpson of why he had come to Columbus. He thought of his successes, failures. The church had been built; other buildings must come. Better homes, better streets. He spoke slowly.

"I'm a Southern Negro, born and raised on a plantation in the Mississippi Delta, where my father and mother were slaves and where my people still live in slavery almost as real as before the Civil War. God knows I have seen and felt the misery and violence of slavery. I have known the fear inspired by black bodies hanging from white-oak limbs, and the fearful sound of bloodhounds at night tracking down some tortured soul. I have lived in the North also. I have tasted the freedom of the North. I have also known the poisonous hatred between races in the North."

He paused and gave Daddy Splane a searching look. "You ask me what I am doing for our race. My answer is: all that one Negro in Oklahoma can do. I teach the children to respect their race, to have pride in their people. I teach them to prepare themselves, to make themselves worthy of their opportunities. I hoped *The Neighborhood Eye* could be used——"

"That's not my way. I have a different kind of message to preach."

Mose would not be stopped. "Every day I work for better schools, homes, churches. That's not much, but it's a big job for one man. I expect others to join me. Among the ones I teach there may be ten, a hundred, a thousand to carry on the fight where I leave off. At some time the wall will break—here in Oklahoma. You could join me."

Daddy Splane got up. "Not me. I don't have time for race. I've come here with a message of peace from the East."

Mose shut his teeth on his words. There was no sense in a fight between them, no matter the circumstances that had placed them in Happy Hollow, no matter the differences between them.

"If we stay here," he said quietly, "we've got to learn to work together."

Thomas finished sweeping and stood quietly in the doorway

listening to Mose describe incidents of friction between colored and white in Columbus. Mose watched his face grow grim, bitter. He had learned hard lessons early.

"This is my son Thomas," Mose said to Daddy Splane. "He is going to be a lawyer. He's seen the trouble here. Tell him what the white boys did to you."

Thomas began quietly, diffidently describing the gangs of white boys who crossed the tracks at night to cause trouble. He told how they raced their cars through the streets, laughing, shouting when Negroes had to hide behind trees and houses. As his feeling grew his voice became louder, more intense.

"One night they stopped me," he said. "They called me nigger. Without any reason they called me nigger—like I never been called nigger before."

For the moment Daddy Splane seemed affected. "What a story!" he said.

"Many more like it in Happy Hollow," Mose assured him, "and worse."

"How far along in school are you?"

"I have another year after this. Then I want to go to college down in Marshall."

"Then what?"

"Law school up North. Ain't no place in Oklahoma for me to study law. They've got a good school at Norman—no Negroes allowed."

Daddy Splane's interest in Thomas passed quickly. He talked of his plans to turn the front room of Harrison Williams' house into a church. He talked of plans for the paper.

"When do you expect to run your first issue?" Mose asked.

"On time. Frenchy told me you helped prepare the last copy."

"Yes, I did."

"Would you help me get my first one ready? It's strange, but the old man didn't leave hardly anything in his files. Looks like somebody had gone through and stripped them clean. I need help on personals and local news stories. . . ."

Mose and Thomas walked with Daddy Splane back to the Pleasant Valley Rooming House. Brother Simpson stood at the porch talking to Lora Dixon in the winter twilight. They stared at the blue turban and bade Daddy Splane a cool good evening.

"You going along home?" Brother Simpson asked Mose.

"Yes."

"I'll walk a ways with you."

Brother Simpson walked along between Mose and Thomas. "What do you make of Daddy Splane?" he asked.

"One more obstruction," Mose said sadly. "He's not interested in race. He's interested in Daddy Splane. He claims he can help people fight evil and pain with holy water, blessed handkerchiefs. He claims he's got a message from the philosophy of the East."

"How could a man come to such a belief?"

"I don't know. He claims he never heard of a turning plow or a cotton sack, but I have a feeling that he's from down home, that he has seen the day when he could pick four or five hundred pounds and lead the field hoeing. Something's gnawed deep at him some time or other. When you find that out, you'll know what keeps him from admitting he's a down-home, what makes him lie to pass, what makes him exploit the simple-minded with his spiritualism and bundles of holy handkerchiefs. He won't help us step forward. He may make us step back."

18

ONE spring afternoon Mose left the schoolhouse just before sundown and walked home along Mulberry Street. The sun was warm and bright. People along the way stabbed the earth with forks, slashed it with hoes, planting their early gardens. They paused from their work long enough to say "E'ening, Professor," and then went on filling the air with the smell of freshly dug earth. Mose could see Josie in her garden bending and stooping as she dropped seeds into small brown furrows. He was reminded of spring gardening in Mississippi and, forgetting for the moment the differences between them, he went down the rows toward her, carefully stepping in her tracks to avoid the newly seeded beds. When he was near enough he could hear her mumbling garden wisdom handed down from generation to generation.

"Dark of the moon for root crops . . . light of the moon for top crops . . . Good Friday for string beans . . . "

Still planting in the moon, he thought. Still bound by sayings from childhood.

She heard his feet in the soft earth and stopped. "Whut you want?" she demanded, a blaze of anger in her voice.

"Lordy," he said, surprised, "don't get cranky. I just wanted to see what you're planting."

"Hot pepper," she snapped.

She touched the two matchsticks in her wropped hair, where she had placed them at noon to keep headaches away. She knew that Mose would want her to throw them away and take aspirin. He'd been like that since he first went up North. Finding the matchsticks crossed, she dropped her hands to her hips.

"Is you got something mean, low-down and nasty to say to me," she said, "now's the time to say it."

"How come?"

"You got to be mad when you plants hot pepper if'n you wants it to be hot. I got to git mad as a burnt-toed cat enduring the time I'm planting these seed. You got to do something to rile me."

She stood with hands on hips waiting for him to do or say something that would rouse her anger. She touched the matchsticks again. But he refused to humor her. He had come to ask for peace, not anger. He laughed at her gently and turned toward the house.

"Plant pepper some day when you're mad already," he told her.

From the house Mose could hear music. Robert was playing the piano, as he did every afternoon. Mose went through the kitchen and to the front room. The shades were drawn, the room in half-light. Robert was playing from memory, with his head bent low, his eyes closed. Mose listened to the deep, religious tones and recognized it as something from Bach he had often heard Cenoria Davis play in church. He wondered what white folks in Columbus would think if they heard such music coming from a shotgun house in Happy Hollow. Fascinated, he eased into a chair and sat watching the long dark fingers on the keys, himself conscious for the moment of blackness.

Robert had pulled off his shoes and was pressing the pedals with bare feet. His head bobbed slightly to the rhythm. He was fifteen—nearing sixteen—but he looked older. Mose wondered about his talent for music, from whence it had come. From his father? His mother? Or was it a gift from his race? Whatever the source, Mose was thankful for it. With it Robert would be asked to play in the white churches and clubs of Columbus. Mose leaned back in his chair to listen to the music and to dream of Robert playing in the white First Methodist Church. Darkness deepened in the room until he could see Robert as only a light blur against the mahogany. He could not follow his fingers on the yellow keys. But he could respond to the sound that rose and fell—emotion-guided from whisper to crescendo to whisper again.

Josie came in from the garden and slammed the kitchen door. She struck a match on the door facing and lighted a lamp, making a faint yellow glow on one side of the darkness. Robert kept on playing without looking up.

"Robert," Josie called, "you go wash yo'se'f for prayer meeting. Make haste now and git yo'se'f clean."

"Yes, ma'am," Robert answered, but he kept on playing till the music rose in a final crescendo.

"That's mighty fine music, son," Mose told him. "Mighty fine music. You've learned a lot. If you keep it up, you'll go a long ways."

Josie, her shoes cast off, her feet making light scuffing sounds on the floor, brought the lamp and set it on the piano. "Robert," she scolded, "you scrub yo'se'f clean now. You ain't taking no nigger stink to Sis Brackett's prayer meeting."

Mose was suddenly angry. How often they had come to conflict over holy-roller meetings! How often Josie had prevailed! "Robert," he asked, "do you want to go to prayer meeting? If you don't, you can stay at home and play the piano."

Robert looked at Mose and then at Josie. Josie glared at Mose, on the defensive. Robert could tell how she had persuaded him to go. Thomas and John could tell how they had begged off with the excuse that they had to work at the schoolhouse late. Her anger matched his. She had the right to take her own son to prayer meeting if she liked.

"You like Sister Brackett's prayer meeting, don't you?" she demanded of Robert.

"Yes, ma'am. I like the music."

"Ain't I telling you?" she said to Mose belligerently.

Mose did not answer her. The problem could hardly be solved in open argument, he had conceded to himself. Robert left the piano and went to the kitchen.

Josie crossed the room and stood in front of Mose. Her voice rose angrily. "You make me so mad. You and yo' holy Methodism. Well, I'm here to tell you Sister Brackett's church is as good as yo' high and mighty Methodist any day. And I'm telling you I'm gonna take Robert any time he wants to go. You got Thomas and John tied hand and foot to the Methodist church. But you ain't got Robert. He's too much like me. He know the true religion when he see it." She caught her breath, bobbed her head furiously. "Man," she exploded, "I ought to plant hot pepper right now!"

She stalked to the kitchen and back again. "I don't know why he fools around with music like that," she said, pointing to the sheets on the piano. "It don't make no sense to me—and it sho' God ain't purty. I'd druther he'd play jump-ups. You can git feeling in them."

"The music he's playing..." Mose began, and then stopped, the will to argue lost. He could tell her again of the music he had heard in white churches up North, but it was no use. The only music she knew she had learned on a Mississippi plantation. Mose was afraid that was all she would ever know.

"Give me a song I can sing," she said as she returned to the kitchen, taking the lamp with her. "That's music to me. Hurry, Robert."

Mose sat in the dark room listening to Robert changing his clothes and putting on his shoes. Josie was in the kitchen setting food on the table for him and Thomas and John. As she worked she sang a song they had often sung on Penrose Plantation.

> "If religion was a thing that money could buy,
> Hand me down the silver trumpet, Gabriel,
> The rich would live and the po' would die,
> Hand me down the silver trumpet, Lawd."

Robert hummed with her till they came to the refrain. Then he joined in the words.

> "Oh, hand me down, hand me down,
> Hand me down, hand me down,
> Hand me down the silver trumpet, Gabriel,
> Hand it down, throw it down,
> Any old way to git it down,
> Hand me down the silver trumpet, Lawd."

"Hallelujah, that's music in my ears," Josie said as she came to the room where Mose was sitting. She brought the lamp and set it on the piano, lighting again his sober face. She took her Bible from the table. "Come on, Robert," she said. "Us late already."

Robert followed Josie along the dark street, her large body in the white dress a blurred shape before him. He stretched his legs to keep up with her. When they turned onto the street that led to Sister Brackett's house they heard singing.

"Meeting's done started," Josie lamented, and increased her pace.

They were singing "Daniel Saw the Stone." Josie started singing with them as she hurried along the street. The rhythm stirred Robert's blood and quickened his pulse. He began singing too. They were still a block from Sister Brackett's house.

"You sing lead and I'll sing tribble," Josie said over her shoulder.

Robert took up the melody and she sang the third above. He overtook her and walked with his head close to hers, listening intently to the harmony, feeling her warmth and the warmth of her religion. He puzzled over the argument between her and Mose. What difference did the church make as long as it had music? Had these words anything to do with religious belief?

> "Daniel saw the stone that was hewed out'n the mountain,
> Daniel saw the stone that was carried out'n Babylon,
> Daniel saw the stone come tearing out'n the wilderness,
> Tearing down the kingdom of the world. . . . "

They opened the front door of Sister Brackett's house and found her front room full of kneeling, praying, singing people. Sister Brackett, in her priest's black robe, was at the far side of the room and facing the front door. A clear bright light hung just above her head drew their eyes toward her. Her black veil was thrown back from her face and her eyes sought heaven as her words rolled forth in prayer. The song became an accompaniment for her words—became wordless itself, became sounds, sounds built upon sounds, to a rhythm that grew faster and faster.

"Oh, Lawd, sanctify us tonight," Sister Brackett prayed above the singing. "Let us not go away from this altar till every saint has received the second blessing. Oh, Lawd, let us not go . . . "

Josie crossed the room and knelt near Sister Brackett. She was still singing tribble and Robert could hear her powerful voice high and clear above the others. Robert found a corner and knelt in it, among the old men. He tried to bow his young body to a level with theirs. He covered his face with his hands and hummed his own harmony. He could not understand what Sister Brackett was praying for, but he liked the music. Nothing he played on the piano stirred him as this rhythm did.

The song came to an end.

"Amen, Lawd, thank you, Lawd, shout glory," Sister Brackett chanted through the large white rag she wiped across her face. Brother Brackett raised his eyes and said, "Amen, Lawd—hah!" His voice rang like a woodcutter's ax on a frosty morning. "Praise the Lawd . . . and amen," the others prayed, keeping their faces to the floor.

"On yo' knees, child'en," Sister Brackett commanded.

They cowered lower before her, breathed the dust of the floor.

"Raise yo' hands, child'en. . . . Hands heavenwards, child'en."

They raised their hands high above their heads—hands that trembled as they raised them.

"Lower yo' hands, Brothers. . . . Lower yo' hands, Sisters. . . . Bow yo' heads to the floor, child'en. . . . Close yo' eyes, Brethren. . . . Humblify yo'se'fs before His holy name. The Lawd's coming down on a big white cloud. Bright like a light the Lawd's coming down here to this room. The Holy Ghos' gonna descend right down. The Holy Ghos' gonna enter the hearts of everyone here. Bow yo' heads down, child'en. . . . Open yo' mouths, child'en. . . . Say to the Lawd, sanctify me. . . . "

Tongues loosened in prayer, filling the room with the sound of voices in supplication. Robert could hear Brother Brackett and Sister Brackett above the others, leading, exhorting. He could hear Josie praying, "Sanctify me, Lawd . . . renew my heart with Thy great blessing." But Robert could not pray. He could not bring himself to their frenzy. He bowed his head lower, but his eyes could not leave off their seeing. Josie was almost prostrate on the floor, her white dress crumpled and wet with perspiration. Her head rag had slipped off and her hair stood wildly about her head, from which the matchsticks were at last gone. Near her Sister Brackett knelt with her face toward heaven. Tears ran down her face. Sweat dripped onto her priest's collar and wet the edges.

The prayer subsided into an incoherent murmur.

Brother Brackett began singing another song, softly at first in his deep bass voice, then louder as the others joined him.

> "Oh-oh-oh-oh, somebody touched me,
> Oh-oh-oh-oh, somebody touched me,
> Oh-oh-oh-oh, somebody touched me,
> And it must a been the hand of the Lawd."

While they sang, Brother Brackett sat back on his heels and talked to them. "Brothers, Sisters, you got to work hard for the Holy Ghos'. It don't come easy. You got to pray hard. You got to sing hard. You got to humblify yo'se'f before the Lawd. We singing a song, Brothers. We singing a song, Sisters. The Holy Ghos's waiting to come to yo' hearts while we sing this song. . . ."

"Increase the spirit, Lawd," Sister Brackett implored.

But the spirit was not increased. The praying, singing people knelt closer to the floor, some rolled in the dust, but the spirit did not come in. They prayed and waited, but no one sprang to his feet to dance with joy with the Holy Ghost. Something was wrong. They all felt it. Somebody was standing in the way.

"Who among us is guilty of sin?" Sister Brackett suddenly demanded.

"Not me, Sister. Not me, Lawd," they shouted.

"Who's been having truck with the Devil?" she persisted.

"Not me, Sister. Not me, Lawd."

"They's a sinner in this room," Sister Brackett said in an accusing tone. "Let him stand up. Let him confess his sins. Till he do, the Lawd won't come down. Speak up, sinner, and tell yo' sins."

Covertly they eyed one another as they bowed their heads to the floor and mumbled, "It ain't me, Sister. It ain't me, Lawd." Robert felt their eyes on him—accusing, naming—and bowed lower to the floor. A feeling of guilt swept through him for a thousand things done or left undone. He longed to escape their burning eyes.

Brother Brackett rose to his feet and looked down on them. When they saw the wrath on his face they groveled lower before him. It was like the wrath on the face of the Lawd.

"Let the guilty one speak up," he ordered.

They waited in silence. But no one spoke.

"Brethren, we got to make a test. We got to know where the Devil's hiding. See this crack in the floor?"

He pointed to the center of the room where two boards had pulled apart. Their hypnotized eyes followed his pointing finger.

"We all gonna git on this side of that crack and pray. When you know you not the guilty one, you will cross over on yo' knees to the tother side. Search well yo' heart. Make sho' you free from sin before you moves."

They crept across the room and clustered around Brother Brackett. Robert found himself at the front of the group with his knees almost on the crack.

Brother Brackett brought a chair from the kitchen, placed it astride the crack at one side of the room. "Keep yo' eyes closed while you pray, Brothers and Sisters," he urged. "Don't be a-spying on one another. Let every saint see only what's in his own heart. Now we gotta have somebody set in this chair to see they ain't no fudging ahead, no holding back, and to give the hallelujah when we all crossed over."

Sister Brackett studied their faces deliberately, and then spoke. "Let Robert, the son of Sister Josie, set in the chair. He the youngest. He ought to be the purest. He ain't had time to do much in the sin line."

"Amen, praise the Lawd," the others shouted.

Brother Brackett took Robert by the shoulders and seated him on the chair. Robert looked up at Brother Brackett with puzzled eyes—asking the meaning of this strange testing, begging that the burden be shifted from his shoulders. But Brother Brackett was too busy with arranging. Robert looked at Josie, found her wrestling with her own burden.

"Keep yo' eyes on that crack," Brother Brackett said to Robert, "and when they all crossed over, shout hallelujah."

Brother Brackett knelt near the crack. Sister Brackett began singing "Oh-oh-oh-oh, somebody touched me." They all began singing and praying with her. Robert watched Brother Brackett, Sister Brackett and Josie cross the crack on their knees. The song leapt on: "Feel the fire a-burning, Lawd, somebody touched me. . . . "

Robert found himself staring at a man against the wall—a man he could not recall having seen before in Happy Hollow. He was small and wiry and soot black. His white shirt, wet with sweat, clung to his arms and ribs. He crawled toward the crack on his knees and then retreated, crying, "No, no, Lawd! Don't torture me, Lawd!" He put his forehead against the floor and begged for mercy. He leaned back on his heels and let the tears roll from closed eyes down his cheeks. He opened his eyes again and fixed them on the crack. Then he forced them along the line until they came to Robert. He stared back at Robert with red bloodshot eyes, like a madman's.

"Look, Brother, look!" he screamed. He jumped to his feet and cringed against the wall.

"What is it?" Brother Brackett demanded. Their prayers interrupted, the others turned to look at him.

"The doll," he cried. "See it? See, it's running along the crack."

"What doll?"

"The little black doll—the devil doll."

"Lawd a mercy," they wailed.

"There it goes!" the man yelled. "There it goes under the chair. The Devil's after Robert. Robert's the sinner. Oh, Lawd, the Devil's in Robert! We got to beat the Devil outa Robert."

The man fell upon Robert with flailing hands. In a wild frenzy the others sprang to their feet, lifted their hands. They shoved and pushed him till he was on the floor in the middle of the room—lying on his face, cowering under the falling blows. He could not see. All he could hear was the hysterical shout of the people. Then he remembered Josie.

"Mama," he begged.

He twisted upward, saw her face. She was above him with her hands lifted to strike him. Her eyes were closed and her mouth was working. "Old Devil gotta go," she was saying. Robert shielded his face from her blows, but her big rough hands struck his arms and shoulders. Sister Brackett stood over him with hands raised. Brother Brackett slapped him with broad palms. Robert lay on the floor and hid his face in his hands.

"Papa," he whimpered. "Where is Papa?" But no one heard him.

Suddenly the little man was on his feet again. "The Devil's gone now," he shouted. "I got the spirit of King Jesus in my soul. The spirit done touched me—hallelujah!" He danced around the room, slapping the wall with his hands.

"Oh-oh-oh-oh, somebody touched me," the people sang as they danced around the room. They danced in trances, with eyes closed, with panting breath. Losing all sense of direction, they bumped into one another again and again as they whirled about the room.

Robert crawled out among them and found the front door. Josie danced past without seeing him. He felt her blows on his face again.

He got out of the house and into the street. In his blindness he bumped into a car. He heard people in the car laughing. White folks, he thought bitterly. White folks come to watch niggers git religion and cut up. He had to get away. He had to get home to Mose.

"Feel the fire a-burning, Lawd, somebody touched me," he heard them singing as he fled down the street.

19

ROBERT was still running when he turned up Mulberry Street. He saw a light burning in the front room at home. Mose had not gone to bed yet. Needing help from the accusations, the stinging blows, Robert drove himself on, toward the glow of the light, the quiet of the room. He crossed the porch in two steps and jerked the front door open, bringing to a standstill the life inside.

Mose sat forward in his chair near the stove, holding his hands out to the fire he had kindled to take away the chill of the spring night. Across from him stood Zack, his clothes black and grimy from the coal he hauled in his wagon to Happy Hollow. He had come to get Mose to sign for a load of kindling, and held the receipt drying in his hand. John bent over a table with a book and a glass of milk. Thomas, coming from the kitchen, stopped still in the doorway.

"Papa!" Robert panted. He ran across the room and sank to his knees by Mose's chair.

"What is it, son? What's the matter?" He stood up anxiously and lifted Robert to his chair.

"Papa, they beat me."

Mose thought of white boys looking for fun in Happy Hollow. "Who beat you?"

"They did. The people at prayer meeting. All of them. Brother Brackett, Sister Brackett, the old man and—and Mama!"

"Mama? What for?"

"They say I'm a sinner, that I got the Devil in me."

Mose, feeling the boy's trembling, knowing well the experience he could have gone through, knelt beside him and put his arm around his shoulder. He saw the fear in the boy's eyes, the bewilderment in his face. He felt his own anger rising—at Josie, at himself. He blamed himself for letting Josie take him to Sister Brackett's. He swore that he had given in the last time. He could not change her, but he could keep his sons from the frenzy of the holy rollers.

Gently Mose helped Robert take off his wet shirt; gently he draped a cotton blanket over his shoulders.

"What happened?" he prompted softly.

Robert leaned toward the stove and shaded the light from his eyes with his hand. At first it was a calm recital of the prayer meeting, but when he came to describe the test for sin his body trembled, his voice shook. He sprang from his chair and paced the floor while he told them of the Devil doll, of the beating. His voice grew calmer as he described the little old man who claimed he had seen the black Devil doll.

"Folks sometimes imagine things like that when they get worked up," Mose told him. "Like they stick pins in dolls to punish their enemies. What's the old man's name?"

"I ain't heard them say."

"That's Huz Ellis—from out at North New Hope Chapel," Zack told them. "I seen him, but ain't to say know him. He walk in here at night to go to meeting. Folks say he ain't right in the head. Folks say he kinda crazy-like. Always seeing visions and things. Jest like the holinesses to believe a crazy man."

Mose turned to Robert again. "Josie hit you too?" he asked.

Robert was not willing to talk about her part in the meeting. He admitted that she had struck him, but did not describe the look on her face, the frenzy that made her like all the others. His own face still a puzzle, Robert turned the questions on them.

"Why did they do it?" he asked.

Mose hesitated and shook his head sadly.

"I want to know. Cain't anybody tell me?"

"Wait till I think how to say it," Mose said.

He tried to put into words his own thoughts on the question. It was a part of the compounding that made the Southern Negro: elements of African primitivism, Christian fundamentalism, evangelical emotionalism, voodooism—elements impossible to analyze or measure, elements easily exploited by fanatics. If he could answer Robert's question complete, he knew, he would have more understanding of why progress was slow in the South. He knew that he would never be able to say it in words Robert would understand. But he could at least give a clue.

"People search for God in many ways," he said slowly. "Some find Him in sticks and stones and idol worship, some in the quietness of a Christian church. Sister Brackett's people have to have dancing and shouting and falling in trances. They have to beat the Devil out . . ."

He paused, at a loss for more to say. "You understand?"

Robert spoke a low "Yes." He seemed quieted, comforted.

Mose resolved to work out a better answer. Then he reluctantly decided to prohibit where he had failed to explain.

"My son," he said, "you must not go to Sister Brackett's again. No telling what they'll do when they get crazy with religion. I will take you to church with me, or you can stay home and play the piano. You don't want to go back, do you?"

"No, sir, I don't want to go back. They'd beat me again. I couldn't stand to be beat again."

Robert pulled the blanket closer around him, crouched closer to the stove. "Why does Mama go?" he asked Mose.

"She was brought up that way—in Mississippi. She knows no other way to God." His voice became kind, compassionate. "You must not blame her. She meant no harm."

Robert quiet with his own thoughts, Mose spoke to Zack. "I don't know why the holinesses have to make such a show of their religion."

"Well, to my mind, they's two kinds of folks in the holinesses: them that's done done everything in the sin line and then haul off and git holy, and them that ain't got good sense. 'Scusing me, sir, I don't mean to say nothing agin Miz Ingram—jest agin holinesses.

They keep on saying they without sin. The Bible say he that say he without sin is a liar and they ain't no truth in him. That's what I think about the holinesses. I ain't saying Miz Ingram's one or tother o' these. I ain't saying nothing agin Miz Ingram. I do say, the man that claimed he seen the Devil doll is crazy as a bedbug."

"Josie is not like the others," Mose said, still groping for the meaning of her behavior. "I know she hasn't sinned much. I know she's a good woman. I think it lies in a deeper need—a need for self-expression. She's used to cotton-patch religion, like all the others at Sister Brackett's. That's the kind we had on the plantation down home. They put on white uniforms and cut themselves off from all other kinds of thinking. I belonged to it myself when I was young, but I broke away—going to school, going up North, seeing what other folks thought made me break away. Seems like Josie'll never break away, no matter what other choices she has. I don't know . . ."

Mose let his voice trail away. He suddenly felt disloyal talking about Josie.

After a long silence Zack stood up and folded the receipt with clumsy fingers. "Reckon I'll be going now," he said. "I got to work tomorrow. Ain't much more coal hauling. Then it'll be summertime agin and watermelons to peddle."

Mose went with him to the door and closed it behind him, glad for a little time alone with his sons before Josie would come home. He stood waiting by the door until he heard the rattle of trace chains and the sound of wheels on gravelly sand. Then he turned their talk to the prayer meeting.

"There was white folks outside Sister Brackett's," Robert said. "In cars outside looking in, listening. I heard them laughing when I come out of the house. I run into their car in the dark. They saw me and laughed some more. I——"

Thomas hopped from his chair and stood facing Mose and Robert, his outward calm broken for the moment, his fists clenched at his side.

"Why don't they keep their dirty white hides on the other side of the tracks?" he cried. "Why don't they stay where they belong? They want Jim Crow. Why do they break it? They ain't got no business coming over here spying on colored people and laughing at them. No matter how colored folks act, whites ain't got no business making fun of them. I'd like to break their heads, the dirty sons of——"

"Thomas!" Mose shouted. "Don't you use language like that. Not in this house. You hear me? I don't like it. I won't——"

"I don't give a damn whether you like it or not. I'm damned well going to say it. That's what they are—and worse. Coming over here watching us, ganging up on us, squirting us with soda water, making us look like monkeys . . . " He glared at Robert. "Alan Carson's one of them."

"How do you know?"

"I saw him. I was in front of the picture show with Jabbo and Roscoe and saw him."

"He must've come to hear the music," Robert said.

"Music my——"

"Son, son!" Mose tried to quiet them. "That kind of talk won't get you anywhere. The Bible says, 'Take not the name of thy Lord God in vain.' That means for colored as well as whites."

"To hell with the——"

Mose grabbed his arm and shook him to silence before he could speak the word *Bible*. With viselike fingers he gripped the boy's shoulders and turned him till they were facing each other. They stared at each other like strangers, in a new relationship set up by this first revolt of son against father.

"Son," Mose began again, "you're not going to use language like that in my house. I don't care how angry you get. It's blasphemy." The word stabbed at Mose sharply, a probe in a badly healed wound. "I won't have you blaspheming in my house. Where did you learn such talk? At the pool hall?"

"It ain't hard to learn hate words. Stand on the streets and you'll hear enough from colored people to know how deep their hate has grown. Listen to white folks talking to niggers. You'll hear the hate words come. I learned the words easy. It's hard to keep from shouting them at every peckerwood you see on the street. It's hard to keep from writing them on every wall and curb in the whole town of Columbus."

Mose, seeing how deep the hurt, the hate had penetrated, released his grip on the boy and returned to his chair. "Sit down, son," he said soothingly. "We've got to talk this thing through."

Thomas sat down and stared at his bare feet.

"When we came to Pleasant Valley I tried to tell you what being a Negro in a Jim Crow world means. I have tried to keep you from being hurt."

"I'm not blaming you. You've done what you could. The trouble is, you're just about by yourself on one side. On the other side are all the whites, and the colored people the whites have mistreated. You're so set on making things better, you ain't been listening to what's going on around you. If you'd listen one night at the pool hall, you'd know how deep the trouble is. You'd know more of how I feel."

The anger had gone out of his voice. He seemed again a thoughtful son talking to his father.

"I didn't know your hate had grown so much," Mose said sadly. "You must stop it from growing now. If you don't, it'll be like a scrofula that grows and grows and never heals. Sometimes there's no cure at all. Sometimes the end's a white man's rope over a white-oak limb. You don't want that, son. You don't want that."

Touched by the sad seriousness in his father's voice, frightened at the mention of the lyncher's rope, Thomas took his father's hand. "What must I do, Papa?"

"Turn away from hate, from anger. Work hard, study hard. Make things better when you can. Don't talk the way you talked tonight."

"My voice wouldn't reach far."

"It'd reach Columbus. Whites find out who's against them. Promise you won't talk like that again."

Thomas got up and paced the room. He paused before Mose.

"I'll try to keep my mouth shut." He glanced past Mose. "How about Robert?" he asked.

"I ain't never said nothing like that," Robert said intensely.

"I don't reckon you will. You got your friends among them."

"Thomas! Robert!" Mose intervened. "You must not say such things to each other. You've got to stand together. More than most brothers, you need to help each other."

The quarrel averted, Mose turned the talk to future plans—to education first, and then to the work they would do to help in the fight against Jim Crow.

"You'll be leaving Happy Hollow soon," he said to Thomas. "You'll have two years in Marshall and three up North. You'll have time to forget some of the hurt you've felt. When you come back you'll have more understanding of what our job is—and more patience to work and wait."

To Robert he said, "Your time will come later. You've been hurt tonight. You've got to put that aside."

In the quiet of the room Mose studied the faces of his three sons. Each had new adjustments to make, strength to restore. What mattered to Mose was for them to stand together. Together they would carry on the fight.

"My sons," he said, "there are many problems for us to solve— problems we can't solve tonight. Go to bed now and sleep. Every day we'll find what answers we can."

Long after the boys had crawled into bed, Mose sat up waiting for Josie, to talk with her about their sons, to get her help if he could. They had to pull together, of that he was certain, if they wanted to turn their sons away from trouble. Since they had come to Pleasant Valley, they had been like a seesaw unevenly weighted, never balancing, always upsetting each other. His anger toward her died down with the dying ashes in the stove. He could hold anger, but not for long.

Toward midnight she pushed the front door open and came quietly into the room. Her dress was wet with perspiration and streaked with dirt. She had tied her head rag over her hair again but had not cleaned the dried tears and grime from her face. She walked across the room without speaking and laid her Bible on the table. She watched Mose furtively as she dragged quilts into the room for her pallet. She turned her back on Mose and silently spread the quilts on the floor.

Unable to bear the silence longer, Mose spoke. "Robert came home some time ago."

"Sho' nuff," she replied in a dulled tone.

He waited again, but she said no more.

"You must have had quite a meeting," he ventured.

"It were."

"Robert said he was beaten."

"He were."

"He said they claimed he was possessed of a devil."

"He have evidence thereof."

"Where do you think he could have got a devil?"

Josie stopped and glared at him with bloodshot eyes. Mose caught a gleam of cunning.

"He might of got it from his papa."

Her words were deliberate, insulting, meant to rouse his anger. Mose felt himself getting hot, but managed to keep his voice controlled.

"Josie," he asked, "why can't we get along together like we used to back at Miss May's? We need to—for our sons' sakes."

Briefly he told her of the scene with Thomas, of his swearing at white people, his near blasphemy with the Bible.

"You ain't treated the Book none too good yo'se'f," she reminded him.

He ignored her comment. "We had good times when we worked together," he continued. "Now we're always pulling against each other. Why is that?"

"I ain't a-standing in the way none."

"No, but your religion is. Josie, why don't you give up going to Sister Brackett's church? It saps your strength, drags you down.

They tried to drag Robert down tonight. Why don't we all go to Brother Simpson? A family together. Then we could get a grip on the boys again—help them get straight. Why can't we?"

"You listen, Mose, and I'll jest up and tell you flat. The Lawd spoke to me tonight and told me to tell you. A nigger ain't gonna git nothing in this world no matter how he do, so he better store up all he can for the next. That's whut I'm a-doing at Sister Brackett's. A-storing up treasures for the next world. Where thieves neither break through nor steal. Mose—" her voice became soft, pleading, as if she were pleading with a sinner at the mourner's bench—"if you wus doing right, you'd be right there along with me. You'd be helping bring our boys along with us. Mose, I remembers whut a fine Christian man you wus on the plantation. I remembers the prayers you prayed and the songs you sung. God remembers, too. He ain't forgitting one bit, hallelujah. Mose, at prayer meeting tonight I been promised something by the Lawd. I been promised you'll be brought back to see the true light. Lawd, I'm waiting for that glory day. Amen."

She raised her hands to the ceiling, danced a quick shuffle around the room and sank with her face in a chair. Mose, unable to endure her wailing words, went to the middle room and closed the door behind him. Whatever peace he had known in Happy Hollow seemed forever lost.

20

MOSE rose from a sleepless night and dressed in the chill half-light of the room. His sons were sleeping peacefully—as if they had already shed the hard experiences of the night before. Thomas and Robert slept on a bed together, their bodies stretched full length side by side. Mose remembered them sleeping the same way on a pallet at Penrose Plantation. In sleep their faces had the innocence of childhood, unmarked by fear or hate or pain. As he looked at them, Mose thought of ways to help them over the hard road ahead.

John roused himself enough to spread fully in the space Mose had left. Mose let his hand slide down the boy's cheek and rest on his shoulder.

"You can sleep a little longer," he whispered.

Mose went to the kitchen and built a fire. He put coffee on to boil and sliced side meat into a skillet. He mixed battercake dough and put a pitcher of molasses on the table.

The sun still not up, Mose sat on the back steps with a cup of black coffee and looked across Reservoir Hill. He thought through again what had happened the night before. Josie had been against him many times since they had come to Happy Hollow. Now the whole family seemed torn apart by the changes they were going through.

"If Josie could only see things different. If I had a wife that went with me . . ."

He found himself wondering what life would be like if Josie

was not his wife. If, instead, he had Lora Dixon. Or Cenoria Davis. In a half-dreaming mood, in an illusion created by morning fog and hot coffee, he rejected completely the image of Lora Dixon. But he held tenaciously the image of Cenoria Davis. He allowed himself the pleasure of lingering over the imagined feeling of her firm body. He thought of how often Josie had forsaken his bed to sleep on a hard pallet—a sanctified wife. With Cenoria . . .

The oil-mill whistle blew cold and shrill.

"Fool," he chastised himself. But the dream would not be completely dispelled. "Blubbering fool." The words made a roaring noise in the morning stillness.

He was in a new trouble, a trouble he had never anticipated before.

What to do now? Should he go back to Mississippi and ask Miss May to take them in? Could he and Josie make a better go of it there?

He felt rather than saw the oaks and magnolias lining the lane to Penrose Plantation. He saw Josie and himself, both tall, lithe, strong, walk down the lane at dusk and stand, hand in hand, while the preacher said the ceremony from his seat in a buggy. He heard firm voices exchanging promises. He watched a man and woman walk back along the line of trees to take up their life together.

He looked at the housetops between him and Reservoir Hill. Smoke was beginning to rise from chimneys and flues. Happy Hollow was waking up. It was workday again. In every house people faced hardships, many of them greater than his own. They had to go to Columbus to work—to be colored help in white men's houses, stores, shops. He thought of what they must feel. . . .

Resolutely he pushed the dreaming aside. "Love, honor, obey . . ." The only course left to him was to bring his family together again and go ahead.

The smell of burning fat recalled him to the breakfast he was preparing. He poured batter into the hissing skillet. Then he called Thomas, Robert, John.

"Up right now and get your clothes on. Battercakes a-cooking—soon'll be done."

He went to the front room. Josie was still sleeping on her pallet, a sheet pulled across her face to shut out the light.

"Josie, you better get rolling if you want battercakes."

"How come you wake me up?"

"I made battercakes and wanted you to have your share."

He went back to the kitchen and turned the cakes. As fast as they browned he put them on plates and spread them with molasses. Thomas and Robert took their plates and sat together in the back door. Mose felt no resentment from the night before. John sat at the table. Josie took a plate and sat beside him.

Mose stood at the skillet with his spoon raised. "How do you like your battercakes?" he asked her.

"God, I like 'em," Robert mimicked.

His voice, his expression made them see the old woman on Penrose Plantation who had said the same of eggs. They all laughed.

"It sounds good to hear folks laugh in the morning," Mose said.

"Sounds good to me any time," Josie added, her voice a little thawed.

When breakfast was over they remained at their places, as if waiting for something to be said. Mose waited a moment, and then spoke slowly. "It's good to be like this together. It's good to feel like a family. Sometimes we see things different ways. That's human. Sometimes we say things we oughtn't to a said. Seems to me we've been going every which a way. That's not right. It'll hurt us. Whatever happens to us, we've got to remember we're a family. We've got to stick together."

The boys looked at him and then at Josie. She took her time, as if her mind needed to be made up—or as if she wanted them to understand how much depended on her. Mose watched the change in her eyes.

"It's the sho' God truth," she said convincingly. Then she pushed up from the table. "You all clear out o' here," she said in a softer tone. "I got work to do. Dishes to wash, beds to make..."

As he walked to school with the boys playing around him, Mose felt that they did want to be together again, and was glad. The facts of life in Columbus had not changed, but they could be better faced.

Mose called his teachers to the final meeting of the year.

"Two weeks more of classes," he reminded them, "and then the exhibition. I've gone over the program with Mrs. Davis. I think it's the best we've ever had. You have co-operated well. I know you will help make it a success."

As usual, Cenoria Davis sat at one side of the auditorium, apart from the others. Mose noted the chill her name made. He noted his own feelings. The dream of the morning returned with the clarity of experience. For a moment he felt that he had held her body against his.

"Ain't we always?"

Lora Dixon's voice brought Mose to the present. A feeling of guilt made a hot band around his head. He pulled his thoughts together and continued speaking.

"We've made some progress, I believe. Last year we had a regular tenth grade for the first time. This year we have the eleventh. Next year we'll have a full high-school program."

"That's gonna sound might nigh like equal education," Lora Dixon said.

"That's what we're working for."

"Jest don't let white folks know about it," Lora added.

"Ain't it the truth," the others agreed.

"They'll find out, but till they do, we'll go ahead."

After the meeting Cenoria and Lora left the building together. Mose, in his office, overheard Fannie Mae Williams and Emmy Johnson talking at the foot of the stairs.

"I don't know how Lora stand her," Fannie Mae said. "The way she calls folks nigger——"

"She better not call me nigger," Emmy interrupted. "She too bright in color to call anybody nigger."

"She call me nigger, I'll snatch her baldheaded."

On the day before the closing exhibition John Carson and Dr. Lewis came to see Mose at school. Mose was waiting for them, with the budget for the following year spread on his desk.

"Doctor Lewis has been appointed to the School Board," John Carson announced.

"That's good news, sir."

"We thought it was about time. He knows more about Happy Hollow than anybody else in Columbus."

Dr. Lewis took Mose's hand and gripped it firmly. "I've watched your work, Mose, and decided you need more help."

"Thank you, sir."

John Carson walked ahead of them through the rooms. "The School Board has no complaint, no fault to find with what you're doing."

"Thank you, sir."

He paused at Mose's desk and studied the budget sheets. "At the meeting last night we approved your budget as it stands—with one exception."

Mose wondered where the cut would come. "What's that, sir?"

"We voted funds for you to hire a Spanish teacher."

"Spanish? Why Spanish? I asked for a man to teach shop, mechanics——"

"State law requires a foreign language in high school. Ain't nobody ever heard of niggers studying French, so we decided on Spanish. It's a part of the equal education you people are always asking for."

"We want equal education. We want our children to get good training. But Spanish! Why Spanish when we need other things so much more?"

John Carson bent over the budget sheets a moment and then

faced Mose. "The decision's made. So you look around for somebody to teach Spanish."

"Yes, sir."

Dr. Lewis studied the figures on the budget sheets. He took a pencil from Mose's desk and divided the total cost by the number of children. "Christ, this school costs!" he said.

"What the hell can we do about it?" John Carson asked belligerently. "You cain't have whites and niggers in the same school in Oklahoma."

"I'd like to know why not. I went to school with colored children in Kansas. No black ever rubbed off on me. If people knew what this costs them . . ."

For a moment the two men faced each other squarely. Mose, from the opposite side of his desk, knew how emotional the problem was for each.

"Say that a few times and you know what people'll call you," Carson said.

"I know, I know." Dr. Lewis was the first to relax. "You got anything else to show us, Mose?"

For the first time Mose had heard a white man south of the Mason-Dixon line speak out. The moment must not be lost.

"Yes, sir," he replied, and led them outside to the back of the building. "There is a place for an addition. Looks like we'll use this building a long time. This'd be a good place for shops."

The two men talked together, calculating costs and how the building might be done.

"We'll see," John Carson said, "but not this year."

Mose walked to the car with them.

"How about that doctor son of yours?" Dr. Lewis asked.

"He's coming along fine."

"Well, tell him I've still got an eye on him."

Mose watched them go and then went to the back of the building again to imagine how the shops would look.

21

School over, Mose set up a rigid schedule of work and study for himself and his sons. "No idle minds in this house," he told them. Mornings he tutored them in subjects not taught at Phillis Wheatley School. Afternoons he and Thomas worked at the school, cleaning, repairing, painting—receiving themselves the money provided by the School Board for the work. Robert and John worked in their own yard and garden. People stopped on the road to say, "You doing wonders with that old place."

"Not long till September," they said as they worked. "Not long till Thomas'll go down to Marshall."

They folded into Miss May's trunk the dark suit from John Carson's store, the shirts Josie had starched and ironed.

Only in the evenings were they free. Sometimes the boys went to the picture show. Sometimes Thomas played pool with Jabbo and Roscoe. Sometimes Robert sat on Lora Dixon's porch talking to Cenoria Davis. Mose, seeing them there, felt he belonged with them, but could not bring himself to join them. Night after night he waited at home for Josie, who sang and danced late at Sister Brackett's.

On those nights Mose sat alone thinking, planning. In the beginning of this summer, when work was more plentiful, when faring was easier, Happy Hollow seemed a quiet place, a peaceful place. Times were not so hard. His neighbors seemed happier, better fed. The worst of the depression seemed over.

He watched his sons come and go and felt proud of them. In other circumstances they might still be humped over a cotton row. For the moment the idea of Negro progress was revealed to him in his own family: father, a slave; son, a teacher; grandsons, men who would work with words, music, science. Tremendous strides in three generations.

Yet the Negro was still in transition—in Oklahoma as well as in Old Dixie. Some, seizing whatever opportunity the white man offered or permitted, stepped forward. Others held back, afraid of change, afraid of breaking taboos established by generations of white masters, afraid of being caught themselves in the sporadic outbursts of hate. . . .

One evening Mose heard excited talking in Mulberry Street. He went to the porch and saw three boys approaching at almost a gallop: Thomas, Roscoe, Jabbo. They stopped at the steps, out of breath.

"You hear what happened?" Thomas panted.

"No. What?"

"A killing. Murder in cold blood——"

"Out at Old Elam——"

"White man killed a Negro boy—Bubber Mason. We got the news and went to see——"

"You shouldn't have," Mose said gravely. "You never know what might happen. I don't remember Bubber Mason."

"I ain't to say I know him," Roscoe said. "I seen him pass through sometimes."

"Did anybody see it?"

"Two colored men——"

"They told us——"

"Wait," Mose said. "One at a time. Thomas, what did the men tell you?"

"He worked out there in the hay for a white man. Mister Burkes. Yesterday he got overhet in the hay and went to lie down in the shade. Mister Burkes caught him and cussed him and sent him back to work. Bubber ain't meant to be sassy, but he said he wasn't going to be cussed and pushed around. After work everything seemed all right and Bubber went up to the store for a bottle of orange. He stayed around the store awhile not saying much to anybody. About dark Mister Burkes came up on horseback. He hitched to a tree and went in. He took a pistol out of his pocket and held it in his hand. Several white folks was in the store, but they didn't say anything——"

"Now let me tell," Roscoe interrupted.

" 'Bubber,' Mister Burkes said, 'I'm gonna kill you.'

" 'What fuh, Mister Burkes? I ain't done nothing, Mister Burkes.'

" 'You throwed rocks at my house.'

" 'I ain't throwed no rocks at yo' house, suh. Honest to God, I ain't, suh.'

"Then Mister Burkes pushed him agin a showcase.

" 'Don't lie to me, Bubber,' he said. 'You throwed at my house right after sundown. My wife says she seen you and knowed you. I ain't going to have no nigger throwing rocks at my house scaring my wife and children.'

" 'I ain't done that, Mister Burkes. I swear to God I ain't. I been right here at the store since we left the field. Ast——'

" 'Don't you call me a liar, Bubber.'

"Then he raised his pistol and pointed it at Bubber's heart. Ain't nobody else said a word.

" 'Don't shoot me, Mister Burkes. Please don't shoot me,' Bubber said. 'Honest, Mister Burkes, I ain't throwed no rocks at yo' house. Swear to God. I sassed you in the field, but I ain't meant no harm by it. I ain't gonna do it agin. Don't shoot, Mister Burkes, don't shoot!' "

Thomas took up the story. "He started going down on his knees just as Mister Burkes pulled the trigger. The bullet slanted down through his groin. They sent for a doctor, but it wasn't any use. He died before daylight, still laying on the store porch."

"Did he throw the rocks?" Mose asked.

"Can't nobody say. Nobody saw him but the woman. They say she is awful nervous."

"A horrible story," Mose said. He looked at the boys facing him in the twilight. Their faces were drawn, their eyes angry.

"It ain't right," they said bitterly.

"It's all wrong," Mose tried to comfort them. "I hoped that was all past in Oklahoma."

He heard other voices on the street, and then others began arriving: Brother Simpson, Lora Dixon, Cenoria Davis, Robert, Zack and a stranger they called Bo. Soon the porch and yard were full of people. Roscoe and Jabbo talked with them awhile and then went home to supper. Over and over Thomas told the story. Mose, watching the crowd, saw their anger rise.

"I calls it awful," Zack said.

"Me, too, people."

"What we gonna do?" the man called Bo asked.

His question changed their mood. Fear, apprehension became stronger than anger.

"Tell everybody what happened," Mose said. "Get people on their guard. Ask protection from the law. Thomas, you go get Frenchy and Daddy Splane."

Thomas left at a run. More people came up Mulberry Street when Sister Brackett closed her church. They crowded together and told the story over and over.

"It do seem a waste," they said, "to kill a boy like that."

They talked of the need for justice, for revenge. They talked of getting help from up North. They hoped that whites in Oklahoma would be outraged. As they talked, the feeling of frustration and futility grew. "Ain't no use talking," some said angrily. "Talking ain't gonna change Little Dixie."

Daddy Splane arrived, his head bare, his turban looped over his shoulder. "What you want me to do?" he asked Mose.

"Run an extra. Let people know about this. Every Negro newspaper in the country will pick it up. So will a lot of white papers up North. All you have to do is tell the story. It's enough to arouse feeling. We'll get help from outside."

Long after Daddy Splane had gone back to his office, Frenchy came in his taxi. "Soon's I got the word," he explained, "I went to Columbus. I couldn't find Mister Kelly. He went out to Old Elam with Blackledge. At the courthouse, they say come tomorrow."

The people drifted away in groups, talking of locking doors, barring windows....

Early in the morning Brother Simpson and Mose went to the courthouse. A crowd of white men stared at them from the station. Another crowd had gathered on the courthouse steps. The Sheriff was not in. Neither was Blackledge. They waited for a time and, getting no definite information on when they might see the Sheriff or on what was being done on the case of Bubber Mason, they went back to Happy Hollow.

A crowd had gathered outside Daddy Splane's. "Waiting for the extra," they said. "Ought to have it any minute now."

Mose and Brother Simpson joined the crowd and waited. "No, we didn't see the Sheriff," they repeated again and again. "No, we ain't found out anything." Neither mentioned the men gathering at the station and courthouse.

Frenchy came with a copy of the Columbus *Times* and opened it for Mose and Brother Simpson. On the second page there was a brief statement that Roy Burkes, a farmer in the Old Elam community, had shot and killed Bubber Mason, a colored farm hand, in self-defense at a country store near his home. Burkes had been released on his own recognizance.

"Lying bastards!" Frenchy swore. "Filthy lying bastards! Killed him in self-defense, they say."

"Do tell," the people cried derisively.

Daddy Splane came out with a stack of newspapers on his arm. He passed copies around at a nickel each.

Mose bought a copy and searched the front page. In a box in a middle column was the headline: BUBBER MASON KILLED BY WHITE MAN. The story was brief—too brief to present the injustice—and told without passion. In a box immediately underneath it Mose read: *Get your holy water glasses from Daddy Splane. Be blessed by this great spiritualist leader.*

Angrily he turned away.

"That ain't gonna do no good," people said to one another.

They took the papers, read them, and threw them crumpled to the ground. Then they turned their back on Daddy Splane. At street corners, on porches, people gathered in groups to talk angrily. Mose, walking the streets in anxiety, heard their bitterness lashing out in sharp words:

"Bubber Mason killed in cold blood!"

"Ain't it a terrible shame!"

"They calls theirselves Christians and kills in cold blood!"

"I'll be so glad to git away from down here. Washington, California, New York—any place so it ain't here!"

"I calls myself as good as any white man."

"I'm gonna kill me a paleface one o' these days."

"I seen Blackledge——"

"I scringes every time I see Blackledge."

Mose heard their remarks, let their anger burn in his brain. With a leader they would form a mob. They might march on Old Elam. They might march on Columbus itself, where there were stores with guns and knives and ammunition. With a leader like Bo, no telling what they'd do.

Mose, knowing he had to quiet their words before they became a din in white men's ears, stood near the hydrant and talked to those who gathered.

"Brothers, friends," he implored, "be calm, be quiet, be peaceful. Let's wait and see. The way you're talking, you'll rouse anger——"

"That's what we aims for," a voice shouted.

"The whites'll strike back——"

"Let 'em strike."

"We got guns."

"We got bullets."

Frenchy stopped his taxi in the street and pushed his way to where Mose stood. His face was grim, his eyes frightened. He raised a shaking hand to ask for silence, attention.

"They want a fight," he said. "I seen white men gathering. You better go home, or they'll be a fight."

Mose stood beside him and talked. "Bubber Mason is dead. Killing some white men won't bring him back. It'll get more of us killed. We got to hire a lawyer, take the case to court——"

"Ain't no justice in courts."

"Bullets is the best justice I know."

For an hour he held them. Then the men withdrew to the pool hall, leaving only a handful of women and children around the hydrant.

A man from the oil mill ran through the streets crying, "Git yo' weepons. Meet at the pool hall. Us going!"

Heavyhearted, frightened, Mose went to Brother Simpson. He found the old man kneeling behind his door praying.

"You don't need to tell me how the feeling's going," Brother Simpson said. "I seen it all day darting like flames."

For them there seemed only one way—call the people to church, let them soothe themselves with singing and praying. Mose went to the church and told Thomas to ring the bell.

At sunset the bell rang stridently, calling people from angry talk. Slowly people broke away from the gathering groups and came to the church. Mose stood with Brother Simpson at the entrance, welcoming them as they came.

Mose waited till he heard singing at Sister Brackett's church. Then he went and begged her and Brother Brackett to hold their people in meeting till the danger had passed, till they knew the mob at the pool hall had broken up.

Mose did not stay at either service. From Frenchy he had heard that white cars would patrol the streets of Happy Hollow that night—cars sent by the Sheriff to keep down trouble. Through the dark streets he walked alone, passing quickly by silent houses, pausing to listen where people still gathered to talk. With satisfaction he saw Sheriff Kelly's car cruising through the streets. He stood in the shadows, avoiding a meeting in Happy Hollow. He also saw Blackledge's car. There were others, some with sawed-off shotguns plainly showing.

When it was near midnight, when the only people on the streets were white men in cruising automobiles, Mose went to the pool hall to talk to the few men who had not yet given up the idea of revenge.

He found them moody and morose, drinking black coffee and beer and grumbling at the interference. "It's you," they said to Mose. "It's you that helt us back."

They glared at him and then turned to the man they had decided to follow. "What you say, Bo?" they demanded.

Mose faced the long-bodied, thin-faced stranger. He still knew little about him except that he had drifted in a few weeks before and set himself up at the pool hall. Mose knew his voice from the low, intense "Eightuh from Decatuh" he had heard in crap games.

"How come you call prayer meeting?"

His voice was as low, as intense.

"To prevent trouble, bloodshed. To keep the people in check."

"It's a good handkerchiefhead trick. You kept us from paying back the white folks for Bubber Mason."

"Maybe. I don't know. Perhaps I kept some of you from getting killed. You saw the white cars on the streets?"

The men nodded yes.

"You saw the shotguns?"

"Ain't we, though!"

To the men willing to listen, Mose talked of why he had come to Columbus, of why he stayed, of how returning murder for murder was not the solution.

"Your kind of justice would destroy what I set out to do."

"How come you say that?" Bo asked.

"It's the way I feel. Our ways of fighting are different. You don't seem to object to violence, bloodshed. I do. We've seen too much of that already. We've got to work without it."

"What you want'll take a thousand years. You'll hammer your life out and not make a dent."

"You may be right." Mose spoke quietly, seriously. "Ten more like me may try and fail—a hundred, a thousand maybe—but ten thousand and more won't all fail. That is my way—slow, steady, sure. Yours is hot——"

"It's swift. That's what I like about it. I want to live to see the change."

One of the men spoke up. "I jest wants to live."

"Man, you is right," the others said, laughing.

The tension broken, Mose said good night and walked up Mulberry Street, knowing the threat of a rising was over.

The day following was calm in Happy Hollow. People met to talk of Bubber Mason, of the rising that had been averted. Frenchy came from Columbus with word that the case of Bubber Mason would be brought before the grand jury. There might be an indictment, there might be a conviction, but the people doubted it. They had to get what comfort they could from the fact that the case would be recognized by the courts.

That night Kelly and Blackledge, in separate cars, patrolled Happy Hollow. Mose kept his sons at home, but he stood on Lora Dixon's porch to watch the patrol cars pass. There were also cars driven by white boys. They passed slowly while the boys peered into the life of Happy Hollow.

The following night there were no patrol cars, but the white boys came again. They raced through again and again with exhausts open, motors backfiring. Finding no sport because the streets were deserted, the houses shut, they circled a few times and then headed back toward Columbus.

Within a week all was quiet and Columbus and Happy Hollow seemed settled again into an uneasy truce.

On a Saturday night Mose allowed Thomas to go with Roscoe and Jabbo to see a Western, with the promise that he would come home as soon as the show was over.

Mose read for a time and then went to the kitchen to shell a basket of peas he had picked from the garden. John was already in bed asleep. Robert was playing the piano. Sometimes when he paused Mose could hear the singing at Sister Brackett's. They were staying late tonight.

There was the sound of pounding feet on the sand road. Mose started toward the front door in time to hear footsteps on the porch. The door burst open and Thomas stood before them, with tears streaming down his face but with no sound of crying in his throat. Mose saw his face writhing in pain, saw the drops of red spotting his shirt.

"What is it, son? What is it?" he demanded.

"Pepper. They burnt me with pepper."

Mose sniffed the red spots, then touched them with his tongue. Louisiana hot sauce. Thomas was covered from head to foot with liquid fire.

Too stunned to talk, Mose grabbed a bucket of water and with his handkerchief began cooling his son's eyes and lips.

"What happened?" he asked when the burning had slackened.

"A car came by and some white boys yelled, 'Nigger, nigger, get home, nigger.' I yelled back. They drove back and squirted me with squirt guns full of pepper. It hurt so bad I couldn't see."

Mose clenched his teeth on the things he wanted to say. "I'm sorry, son," he said gently. Then bitterly: "It was a mean, low-down thing."

Robert went to the kitchen and returned with a bowl of soft butter. "This might help."

Mose took off the cold packs and greased his face and body with butter.

Josie came in and listened while Thomas repeated his story. "I been telling you," she said. "You ain't got no business having truck with white folks."

When the burning was all gone, when Thomas was at last soothed to sleep, Mose went through the streets of Happy Hollow. There was no need for him to look now. The houses were all dark; cruising cars no longer shed their lights on the sandy roads. But Mose walked on.

As he walked, he considered the problem of Thomas. The hate was burning in him, deeper than ever before, searing the tissues of his soul. Something had to be done to save him.

Mose determined to talk to Blackledge, to ask him to keep the white boys on their side of town. He decided also to send Thomas to Marshall at once if the college would accept him ahead of schedule.

His sons set to their morning task, the letter to Marshall posted, Mose asked Frenchy to take him to find Blackledge. On the way, Mose told Frenchy of what had happened to Thomas the night before.

"This town is heading for trouble," Frenchy said. "Let a bunch of young bucks like that run wild and you sho' gonna have trouble. I ain't blaming you for talking to Blackledge. He could put a stop to it if he would."

"I know he could."

"How do Thomas feel?"

"I'm worried about him. He gets a grudge, he's likely to hold it. I've never seen him like he was last night. If this keeps on, I'm afraid of what he might do."

"I wouldn't blame him, no matter what he done, but he's on the under side here."

"I've told him that. I've just got to keep a close watch on him till I can send him down to Marshall."

They found Blackledge parked in front of a restaurant, listening to his car radio.

"Good morning, Frenchy," he said when they were alongside him. "What you want?"

"We want to talk to you."

"Well, park that open-air taxi and come over here."

They stood on the sidewalk a respectful distance away. He took off his Western hat and leaned out the window. A fiddle band played "Heel and Toe Polka" on the radio.

"Now what?" Blackledge asked.

"I want to report some trouble on our side," Mose said.

"What kind of trouble?"

"White boys have been coming over at night frightening our people. I want to ask you to keep them away."

"They done any damage?"

"Not that I know of, sir."

"Hurt anybody?"

Mose told of what had happened to Thomas. Blackledge laughed as if he had heard a pleasant joke. "Oh, that's nothing to worry about. Just boys' pranks."

"You ever been burned with hot sauce?"

"No, but the burning can't last long. Boys have got to have a little fun—play a few pranks."

"Boys' pranks can become men's crimes," Mose said earnestly.

"What you mean?"

Frenchy spoke up. "You let the white boys get away with a prank like that, they'll try something worse next time. Colored boys resent the pranks and try to fight back. Before long you've got trouble."

Blackledge looked at Frenchy and then at Mose. "Our boys're not like that," he said. "I always say, they ain't a finer bunch of boys nowhere than we have right here in Columbus. Oh, they'll play pranks all right, but they don't mean nothing by it. They don't mean no harm. They just want to get a laugh. That's all. I done the same sort of thing myself. We used to go down the sidewalk Saturday nights making niggers get off, but we didn't mean no harm by it."

Mose felt his throat tight, his body rigid. "What about our boys?"

"Tell them not to let it bother them. Tell them they've got to take a little off the white boys. Tell them that's the way it is."

He gave Mose a look that made him feel *nigger* to the bone.

"I'd keep them off the streets at night. Be good for them to stay home anyway. I'd warn them not to talk back. If white boys cause any real trouble, it'll be because some nigger talked back."

"You won't do anything else?"

"I didn't say that. Right now there's nothing else to do."

Mose turned to go.

"I been watching your boys," Blackledge said. "You better show them the straight and narrow. They're getting uppity."

"Yes, sir."

Mose paused at the curb to wait for Frenchy.

"I ever tell you anything wrong?" Frenchy asked.

"No."

"Our folks're stirred up. Wouldn't take much to set them off."

"They ain't been that much trouble."

"It don't take much. It didn't take much to git things going in Tulsa. You know how they go once they git started."

Blackledge laughed. "Niggers won't start nothing. They know too well what they got at Tulsa."

Mose and Frenchy drove slowly back to Happy Hollow.

"Not much you can do with a man like that," Frenchy said.

"No, not much. Only thing for us to do over here is keep our boys off our streets as much as we can."

22

ONE evening just at dark Sister Brackett came clucking her pony along Mulberry Street. A full moon rose over Happy Hollow, hiding the ugliness, casting a silver glow on road and roof top. Mose and Josie, sitting in the quiet of their own front porch, heard her wheels in the gravel, saw her in the moonlight like black-robed fate.

"How come she so het up?" Josie asked.

Not having an answer, Mose waited for her to halt her pony in the yard. She climbed down and rustled her long skirts across the rough, uneven grass.

"Whut's wrong, Sister?" Josie asked. "You ack like bad news."

"You know where Robert is?" she demanded.

"He say he gonna play the piano for Mister Alan," Josie said. "Ain't he there?"

"No, he ain't. He's down at Pepe's Tavern, down at that den of iniquity."

"Do tell!" Josie's voice was tense with worry.

"What's he doing there?" Mose asked, his own voice anxious.

"Playing the piano like he ain't got but tonight to play it in—playing songs I ain't never hear tell of before."

"Who's he with?"

"I ain't been able to see all of them from my buggy, but Cenoria Davis is one of them. I seen her setting there through a wide-open door. My old eyes tells me they's a white man or two hanging around there—waiting for black wenches to come up from the tracks, I expect. One thing I can tell you flat. Ain't nobody down there for no good."

"I'd better go down and get Robert," Mose said quietly. He brushed the sand from the soles of his feet and reached for his shoes.

"I knowed that boy's in the path of sin," Sister Brackett said. "Any nigger that'll take up with white folks like he do is bound to be on the road to ruin." She looked scornfully at Mose. "You all the time say you gonna make a preacher out'n him. I want to say to you, Brother, he done backslid from Methodism. His foots is in the miry clay of sin. The Devil done kotch him for sho'."

"Lawd a mercy," Josie moaned. "I know he's weak. Pray for him, Sister, pray for him."

"That's what I'm gonna do right now," Sister Brackett promised her, "soon as this Methodist gits out'n my way."

Mose tied his shoes, saw that Thomas and John were reading at the kitchen table, and gave her room. She knelt on the porch with the moon on her face, her black skin shining softly in the mellow light.

"Oh, Lawd," she prayed, "didn't you deliver the Hebrew child'en from the fiery furnace? Lawd, didn't you go to old Daniel when he down at the bottom of the lion's den? Lawd, I'm talking to you. Here we got one of our child'en in a den of iniquity to whut a lion's den ain't no danger a-tall. Oh, Lawd, you jest step down there——"

Blaming himself for giving too much of his attention to Thomas, for letting Robert go his own way too freely, Mose raced down Mulberry Street. He went toward the pool hall, hoping to find Frenchy there. He passed the Methodist church, its spire a soft silver in the moonlight. He passed the dark picture show and hydrant. He found Frenchy's taxi in front of the pool hall, heard Frenchy's strident voice above the bumblebee hum of other voices on the dark porch.

"Come here, Frenchy," he called.

"Who that? Professor?"

"Yes, Frenchy."

"What you want?"

"I want to talk to you. Can you come here?"

Frenchy came out and leaned against a fender while Mose repeated what Sister Brackett had told him.

"I want you to take me down there."

"Sho'."

"They say it's tough."

"It's tough all right, but I ain't minding that. I been there plenty of time before. Ain't never got hurt yet."

On the way, Frenchy was talkative, full of stories about the things that happened to a Negro taxi driver in a Jim Crow town. Mose, brought suddenly to consider the narrow fringe in which whites and blacks crossed the color line, asked why white men crossed the tracks.

"Women," Frenchy answered. "Dark meat."

Mose wanted to know more about the women.

"You mean the women in the houses?" Frenchy asked. "Well, first they's Mama Jo's. She's got the fanciest place, with lots of girls and beer and dancing. It's a sho' nuff sporting place. Then they's more down the tracks. In them they's jest one girl to a house, with her name over the door and a show window for her to set in. They got them houses fixed up mighty nice for white customers. Each one's got her own parking place in back—so white men can drive their cars in without being seen."

"Do they ever use your taxi?"

"Sometimes. Not often. They too scaid of gitting left over here. Them that ain't got cars mostly hires a white taxi."

"Do they always have white customers?"

"Some do, some don't. Ain't no black men allowed to go to their houses. Sometimes they walk the streets looking for a coon they can take to the bushes. If they got colored friends, they go down to Pepe's for beer and cigarettes, and meet their friends———"

"You mean they mix with folks—where Robert is now?"

"Professor," Frenchy said with a laugh, "you spend too much time in church. Lots o' things goes on at Pepe's. You'll see."

Frenchy drove slowly past Pepe's Tavern, turned at a junk yard and came back again.

"Stop here," Mose told him when they were squarely in front of the open door.

Like a peep show, Pepe's Tavern was open to Mose. It was a

fairly small rectangular room with tables in the front and a bar counter across the back. Electric bulbs shone dimly through red and blue crepe-paper shades. Streamers of green and yellow crepe paper hung from the ceiling and swayed lightly in a breeze stirred by moving people.

At one side of the room, at an old piano, Robert sat hammering out tunes—blues tunes, tunes Mose had never heard him play at home. Mose saw him, and then saw a couple come out of the crowd around the bar and begin a dance in the open space in the middle of the room.

"Hmph! Cluris," Frenchy said.

Mose looked at the lithe dark girl in a red dress dancing a slow shuffle with a boy younger than she, a boy flashily dressed in white trousers and flowered shirt. Cluris. The name reminded Mose of Cenoria. He looked for her, saw her sitting at a table near the piano. She had on a pure-white dress. She had loosened her hair and it hung like black silk over her pale shoulders. Absent-mindedly she tapped the rhythm, but her eyes were on the dancers. Their bodies, molded into each other like a primitive carving, moved in a slow, suggestive rhythm.

"Dry job," Frenchy explained to Mose.

Beyond them, alone at another table, Alan Carson watched the dancers intently. Light filtered through red crepe paper lent an unnatural crimson flush to his blond hair and fair face. Robert cut the tune off with a minor chord. The dancers stopped, separated. Cluris gave a quick, impudent shake of her rump at Cenoria. Her gesture was lost, Cenoria having turned to Robert.

"There's Pepe now," Frenchy said.

Mose looked behind the bar, saw a Mexican with the swarthy skin and heavy jowls of a Yaqui Indian. His coarse black hair hung over his brow; his mustache was a black line against his dark face. His mouth straight and unsmiling, he watched over till and customers.

"He's a tough *hombre* all right," Frenchy said. "He has to be to keep things straight where whites and Mexicans and niggers mix together. With bootlegging and women, you got enough to make any *hombre* tough. It's a wonder the Ku Kluxers ain't got him a long time ago. Might be a good thing for this town if they would."

Mose jerked the taxi door open.

"You going in, Professor?"

"I've got to get Robert. You want to go?"

"I sho' do."

Mose strode through the door and felt the people turning toward him: Pepe at the bar, Cluris dancing again, Cenoria at her table, three schoolboys playing dominoes at one side. "The Professor!" people whispered to one another. "What's he doing here?" Cenoria half rose from her chair, whispered to Robert, who kept hammering at the keys as if nothing could stop him. She sat back in her chair and turned her eyes away from Mose.

Mose marched across the room to the piano, leaving Frenchy behind speaking to Cluris, to Pepe. Mose laid a hand on Robert's shoulder. "What are you doing here, son?" he demanded.

Robert stopped playing and looked up, his look as unresolved as the chord he had left. He looked quickly to Cenoria Davis, to Alan Carson. His expression became hard. "Playing the piano," he answered sullenly, and then: "Cain't you see?"

"Don't you sass me, son," Mose told him sternly. "You're mighty big now, but not big enough for that."

With one hand he turned Robert from the piano and pulled him to his feet. "We're going home," he said. "We're going home and talk. I've got a heap to say."

"Yes, sir." His voice was still sullen, unyielding.

"Frenchy, you ready to go?"

Mose led Robert to the door. Frenchy came from the bar and joined them. Suddenly Mose left them and walked back to the table where Cenoria Davis was sitting.

"Cenoria," he said firmly, "I will be at my office at ten tomorrow morning. You will come then to talk about tonight."

A look of scorn came to her eyes. She allowed a faint smile to come to her face. "You thinking of firing me, Professor?" she asked mockingly.

"I—I don't know exactly what I'm thinking," Mose said slowly. "All I'm asking now is for you to come to my office and talk to me."

"I'll be there. I'll miss my trip to Boley to be there, but I'm not taking no lip off'n you nor nobody else."

Mose turned from her and found himself looking directly into the fevered eyes of Alan Carson. He felt a new anger rising. Alan Carson was to blame also for what was happening to Robert. Mose clenched his teeth, turned away. Alan Carson was white. He could not reprove a white man—here or anywhere else.

Back in the taxi, Mose, hearing a voice at the window, turned to see a dusky woman peering in.

"Treat me to a beer, mistuh," she was saying. "I'll show you a good time if'n you'll treat me to a beer."

Mose touched Frenchy's arm. "For God's sake, let's get out of here!" he said.

On their way home, Robert huddled silent in a corner of the back seat. Frenchy, primed by their experiences together, talked of the kind of life he had seen at Mama Jo's, at Pepe's Tavern. He told of the obscenities he had seen young boys exposed to.

"Ain't nobody willing to mess with Pepe," Frenchy said. "He'd knife you and never bat an eyelash."

"What about the police? Why don't they arrest him? Put him out of business?"

"He pays off too well. Too damned well. I ain't never seen him pay, but I know he do. I seen Blackledge come and go many a time. He know damned well what goes on there. Something's keeping his mouth shut. Looks like money to me."

"Does the High Law know what's going on?"

"I 'spect he do. He ain't a-caring long as it's in nigger town. Ain't no whites gonna care what goes on over here—not till some white man gits sliced up. Then they'll be a stink."

Mose was silent for a moment, his mind on what he had to do about what he had seen. "I'm going to talk to Hub Kelly tomorrow," he said. "I'm going to see if the High Sheriff can't do something about Pepe."

"He may listen to you, but I doubt it. Blackledge didn't."

"I'll try anyway. Then I've got another job. I've got to tell John Carson that his son's been hanging around Pepe's."

At home they found Josie on the porch talking to Thomas and John. Mose was glad Sister Brackett had gone. A man needed to be alone with his family at a time like this. He got out of the taxi and pulled change from his pocket.

"I ain't a-wanting money for this trip," Frenchy told him. "Keep yo' change for a time you need it."

Frenchy drove back to the pool hall. Mose and Robert walked slowly to the edge of the porch, where the others waited in moonlight bright as day.

"Where'd you find him?" Josie asked.

"At Pepe's Tavern, like Sister Brackett said."

"Ain't you ashamed of yo'se'f, Robert?" Josie asked him. "Ain't you ashamed to be seen at a place not fit for a dog?"

Mose sat on the edge of the porch and leaned against a post. Robert sat on the steps below him, his face bent low over his knees. Earnestly Mose told them of what he had seen at Pepe's Tavern. "It's no place for a good boy."

"Don't talk to me about religion no more," Robert interrupted.

"How come?"

"I just ain't got no call."

"Ain't I knowed it," Josie said. "Ain't I knowed the way you taken leads to Sodom and Gomorrah. Ain't I knowed it from the day you turned him away from Sister Brackett's."

Knowing how easily Josie could go from discussion to tirade, Mose changed the subject. What had to be said to Robert he would say when they were alone.

"Alan Carson was at Pepe's," Mose said.

His words surprised Josie, angered Thomas.

"What's he hanging around there for?" Thomas demanded. "Seems to me like he'd have better things to do than hang around with niggers and Mexicans."

"He do ack like white trash," Josie agreed.

Thomas, pacing the porch with angry tread, talked louder than he needed to of Robert's meetings with Alan Carson. "Ain't nothing but harm in it, Robert," he insisted. "White folks ain't out to do you no good. There ain't no such thing as a nigger lover. They all want something. You know how they feel. You know what they do. Why cain't you stick to your own kind?"

Leaving his words to burn like acid, Thomas stomped off to bed. Josie and John followed him. Robert looked at Mose, waiting. "No more talk tonight, son," Mose said gently. Robert sneaked away like a whipped dog.

Mose sat in the moonlight and traced the pattern of the man in the moon, as he had when he was a child. But there was no answer from the moon to the questions he asked.

23

WITH troubled mind Mose walked the long road from Happy Hollow to Columbus. He walked alone, though before him and behind him his neighbors plodded through dew-dampened sand going to do their white folks' work. He walked alone, the better to think out the task he had set for himself—the task of asking Sheriff Kelly to clamp down on Pepe, the task of telling John Carson that his son was on the downhill path.

He passed Pepe's Tavern, ugly in the bright morning light, grimy with dust and coal smoke. Doors and windows were shut tight. Pepe, in his room at the back, would be sleeping late. What kind of conscience could a man like that have? Mose asked himself. None, he answered. He peered through the dusty windows, had his vision stopped by red crepe paper. But nothing could shut the scene of the night before from his mind.

Mose passed the cottonseed-oil mill and railroad station. He climbed Main Street, passed the hotel and bank. A few colored people stopped their work to speak to him. Whites passed him by as if he had not been on the sidewalk. Seeing their cold faces, their averted eyes, he recalled an old rule of conduct he had heard from black men: "Hate their guts but stay out'n their way."

Mose found himself walking past John Carson's store. He thought of talking to Carson first, of asking him to help close Pepe's Tavern. He started toward the back door, but changed his mind and turned at an angle across a side street. The problem was not really Carson's. It touched him through Alan, and no more. All he had to do was keep Alan away. It was not trash on his doorstep. It was in nigger town—across the tracks. No white person in Columbus need feel concern about Pepe's Tavern—unless his son got the great pock from a black wench, or a razor slash in a nigger crap game. Let something like that happen, and all white town would clamor for Pepe's to close.

Mose went through side streets until he came to the county courthouse, an ugly pile of red sandstone and brick built when Oklahoma was still Indian Territory. It covered most of a square in the oldest part of Columbus. The entrance was flanked on either side by hitching posts cast in iron like black horses' heads. The space once reserved for horses was now marked off by neat white parking lines.

Though it was still early morning, a row of white men lined the concrete wall around the square, talking, whittling, spitting. Mose stayed close to the curb and kept his eyes straight ahead. His shoes touched spots of brown tobacco juice splattered on the sidewalk.

Mose climbed the worn sandstone steps and entered the courthouse. He walked straight ahead through the corridor that led to Sheriff Kelly's office. A dozen white men lounged on benches outside the Sheriff's door. Mose walked straight ahead until he stood in front of a varnished railing, behind which a white man in Stetson hat and cowboy boots shuffled papers on a table.

"What you want?" the man demanded.

"I want to see Mr. Kelly."

"What you want to see him for?"

"It's a private matter."

The men on the benches stopped their joking to listen. The deputy in the Stetson stared at him skeptically and raised his voice. "Might as well tell me. The Sheriff's busy. He don't keep no secrets from me nohow—leastways secrets a nigger's got to tell him."

Mose was firm. He had come to see Sheriff Kelly and did not mean to be put off. "What I've got to say has to be said to Mr. Kelly," he insisted.

"Oh, all right. Hey, Hub," he shouted into the next room, "they's a coon out here wants to talk to you."

"What's he want?"

"He won't say. Says he's got to talk to you. He's that nigger schoolteacher from Happy Hollow."

"Oh, all right. Send him in."

As Mose stepped through a door in the railing, opened for him by the deputy, he heard one of the men on the benches say, "Bet some other nigger's been fooling with his wife."

Mose shut the words out of his mind and went into the Sheriff's office.

Hub Kelly sat behind a pine-plank desk studying the face on a "man wanted" circular—a Negro face made ape-like in profile. Mose looked at the lean fingers holding the magnifying glass, and then at the lean face above them. Kelly put the photograph aside and turned toward Mose.

"Good morning, sir." Mose spoke first.

"Good morning. Have a seat. I'll be through here in a minute."

Mose, surprised at the invitation to sit down during their interview, took a chair near the end of the desk and waited for Kelly to finish making a note on the circular.

"What do you want to talk to me about?" Sheriff Kelly asked at last.

"I want to talk to you about Pepe's Tavern."

"Pepe's Tavern?"

"Yes, sir."

His tone was neither friendly nor unfriendly. It was businesslike, reserved. Mose understood why people had confidence in Sheriff Kelly.

"Last night," he began, "I found out that my son was down there playing the piano—not for money, but just down there to play for anybody that wanted to listen. I went to get him and take him home. What I saw there made me come to you."

"What did you see?"

"Whites, Mexicans, Negroes all mixed together in one room. Like I never saw before in the South. I don't like to see it, sir. It's dangerous in a Jim Crow town."

"What were they doing?"

"Fooling around, drinking beer, talking, dancing indecent dances——"

"Any outright violations of the law?"

"Not that I saw, sir. But I did see women from Mama Jo's hanging around to pick up customers. I saw people drunker 'n they're likely to get on beer. My people tell me Pepe is bootlegging. I saw Mister———"

Mose stopped suddenly, not willing to mention that Alan Carson was at Pepe's, that he believed Alan Carson had been smoking marijuana.

"You got any proof of anything?"

"No, sir, but———"

"I've got to have evidence before I can do anything. I've had complaints about Pepe before, and I've warned him to go easy, but I haven't had enough to warrant closing him up, or make him leave town. He's got good friends over on this side."

Mose, with the door for discussion slightly opened, leaned forward earnestly. "They tell me Columbus is like a powder keg," he said, "waiting for somebody to light the fuse. I'm afraid the fuse is Pepe's Tavern. If I was called on to stomp out trouble, I'd start there. Have you been there yourself?"

"No, I've just seen it from the outside. It's in Blackledge's precinct. I keep asking Blackledge about Pepe. He swears he runs an orderly place."

Mose wanted to tell Sheriff Kelly what all the Negroes knew and felt about Blackledge, but he hesitated. What Sheriff would listen to complaints against his deputy? What chance would a colored man have against a white one?

"What'd you do with your boy?" Sheriff Kelly asked.

"Took him home and told him to stay away from Pepe's. I hope he will, but you can't be sure, the age he is. That's why I came to you. I have three sons. I want them to grow up law-abiding citizens. I don't want to see them hurt because they stepped over the law."

"Well, I cain't do anything for you now, except advise you to keep them at home or working till they get old enough to have some sense." He lowered his voice. "If you do get evidence on Pepe that'll stand up in court, let me know. That's all I can do for you now."

Mose stood up and backed away from the desk.

"One thing before you go," Sheriff Kelly said. He turned to face Mose squarely. "I know what you did when the colored people got stirred up over that killing out at Old Elam. I know if it hadn't been for you, there would have been bad trouble. You quieted them down, so there was nothing left for us to do. Where'd you get the idea of getting everybody to church?"

"I only used what white plantation owners have always used to turn their Negroes' minds from their troubles: Get them together, get them to singing, promise them a better life by and by, and they'll do what you want. It still works." Mose could feel the bitterness creeping into his voice. "In principle," he added, "I despise the method. At that time it seemed necessary."

"Well, it was a good job. Probably saved a lot of black hides."

Hides, Mose thought. What about feelings? Suddenly he was pouring out the whole story of what happened to Thomas that night, of the taunts and Louisiana hot sauce, the burning eyes and seared spirit.

Sheriff Kelly listened with unusual concern. "That's too bad," he said. "Did you make a complaint?"

"No, sir. It would have been no use."

"It might have been—if you had come to me direct. How come he's on the streets at night? Have you told him the danger?"

"Yes, sir. I've tried to get him to stay home, but he doesn't want to—not all the time. I've just got to keep a grip on him till next September. Then I'll send him off to school."

"You'd better keep close watch on him. You know how white folks feel about trouble in Happy Hollow. Your boy'd get it too."

"That's what I fear most."

"Well, we've got to hold things down together," Sheriff Kelly said. "If you get any definite evidence on Pepe, let me know at once."

Outside, on the sidewalk again, with the eyes of the loungers on him, Mose wondered whether he should have told Sheriff Kelly about Alan Carson. He thought of going back, but kept ahead.

Mose walked through side streets to the back door of Carson

Brothers' store. He had to tell John Carson what he had seen at Pepe's Tavern. He would expect John Carson to do as much for him in similar circumstances. He went in the back door, climbed the steps to the balcony office and waited for John Carson to look up.

"Come in, Mose," he invited without laying down his pen. "What can I do for you this morning?"

"Sir," he said as if the words were being wrung from him, "I've come to tell you about Mister Alan."

"Alan? What about him?"

"You know that Mexican beer hall across the tracks."

"Yes."

"You know what kind of place it is?"

"I've heard a lot."

"Last night I had to go there and get Robert. When I got there I saw Mister Alan, sitting at a table by himself, listening to Robert play. He acted at home—like he'd been there a lot of times before. I said to myself, 'I'll bet Mister Carson doesn't know he's here.' I made up my mind last night to come tell you—knowing, sir, it's none of my business."

Mose watched trouble creep into John Carson's face—watched it tighten his mouth, sharpen his eye. "What was going on there, Mose?"

"I didn't see anything wrong. Robert was playing the piano. Mister Alan was sitting listening to him. Some people were drinking beer, some dancing———"

"Any more whites?"

"Not that I saw, sir. Just Mister Alan. Frenchy says white men go there a lot."

"What really goes on there, Mose?"

"I don't know, sir. Folks say it's a bootleg joint. Some say it's a place for tricky women. I saw some girls from Mama Jo's last night."

Shame mingled with trouble in John Carson's face. "Did you see my son with nigger wenches?"

"No, sir. Like I said, he was at a table by himself. Only one I saw him talk to was Robert."

"I know he talks to Robert. That never worries me. I never minded when Robert came to our house to play the piano for him. It does worry me for him to go to nigger town. Anything could happen over there. I don't see what he finds there. He's got every advantage here."

John Carson dropped his pen and stood up. "What can we do?" he asked helplessly.

Mose saw him for the moment, not as John Carson supported by white superiority, but as another father distraught over his son.

"I went to see Sheriff Kelly," Mose said. "I asked him to close Pepe's. He said there had to be proof that it is a public nuisance. I thought maybe you could help."

"I'll do what I can. I'll talk to Hub Kelly and see what he thinks. I'll tell him to make his deputies keep a closer watch."

"The deputy in our precinct is Blackledge."

"I know." He paused long enough to follow a thought to a dead end. "Next time you see Alan over there, will you come tell me at once?"

"Yes, sir." Mose turned to leave.

"Mose," Mr. Carson said, "Miss May was right. You are a good Mississippi nigger. I wish we had more like you in Happy Hollow. We'd have less trouble all around."

Mose accepted the compliment as a white man's compliment and left. With a mingled sense of gain and loss he hurried again toward Happy Hollow. . . .

When Mose arrived at the schoolhouse he found Cenoria Davis standing in a thin strip of shade along the west wall. She had put her hair up severely and was wearing a pale-green chambray dress that heightened the effect of her light skin.

"Good morning, Professor," she said resentfully.

"Good morning, Cenoria. Will you come to my office?"

He opened the door and she stepped quickly past him. Without looking back, she went up the stairs rapidly, the movements of her body free in the flimsy dress. Mose followed her, more conscious than ever that black and white can achieve a dazzling mixture. When he entered his office she was standing at the window looking out over the hot roof tops toward Reservoir Hill.

She turned to him, still sullen and defiant. "Well, Professor," she said, taking the initiative, "say what you got to say and get it over with. I still want to go to Boley."

"Won't you sit down?" he asked, consciously making his voice conciliatory, friendly.

She dusted a chair with her handkerchief and sat on the edge of it.

"Cenoria," he began slowly, "I was surprised to see you at Pepe's Tavern last night—surprised and hurt."

"I've got to go somewhere," she interrupted vehemently. "Somewhere that I can have some fun. Ain't no place in Happy Hollow unless I do go to Pepe's. I go there with Robert—to hear him play the piano. Ain't no harm in that."

"Not if you listen at home, or at school. It's different at Pepe's. That's a bad place. No place for a girl like you."

"Maybe you don't know what it is to be lonely. I do. Teaching kids all day, sitting by myself in my room at the boardinghouse at night, or listening to Lora Dixon talk. I've got to have something different, even if I have to get it at Pepe's. I'm made that way. I taught Robert all the piano he knows. I've got the right to hear him."

"Not at Pepe's. I've forbidden him to go there. I can't forbid you to go, but I can ask the School Board to dismiss you for unbecoming conduct."

"Go ahead! Get me fired. See if I care. I lived before I got this piddling little job, and I can live somewhere else—somehow. Go ahead. Act big. Fire me."

She jerked her head up defiantly and then dropped it to her hands on the desk.

"I'm not going to fire you. Not now anyway. There's too much here for you to do. Too much for both of us. You're a good teacher. You can do a lot for our people teaching. No place needs good teachers more 'n Happy Hollow. I have only one thing to ask you: Keep away from Pepe's. Stick to your own kind and do your work. That's all any of us need to do here."

She raised her face toward his, let a harsh laugh resound through the empty rooms. "Stick to my own kind? Look at me close, Professor. You see what color I am? How can I stick to my own kind?"

"In the South, Cenoria," Mose said, his voice quiet, compassionate, "one drop of Negro blood makes you Negro. You've got more than a drop. You've got plenty to make you Negro—enough to make you want to stick by our people. To be any satisfaction to yourself or anyone else, you've got to stick with our people. No matter where you go, no matter what you do, you're still Negro. How you accept your blood is what counts."

She began to sob—quietly at first and then in quick jerks that tore her slender body. "It's the loneliness," she cried. "Ever since Jackson left me it's been the loneliness. I go to Pepe's to get away from it. I forget for a little while when Robert's playing."

"I know how you feel."

"No you don't. You cain't. You've never been a light girl with black men and white men looking at you like they were taking every stitch off'n you."

Mose stood over her, almost touching her quivering shoulders. He could see flecks of darker pigmentation under her eyes, feel her sway lightly against him.

"I saw Cluris———"

"Cluris!" she shouted angrily. "I ought to kill that black bitch! She took all I ever had."

Mose laid his hand on her shoulder, tried to soothe her. "What about Jackson?" he asked. "Won't he come back?"

"He won't ever come back," she sobbed. "Cluris says he won't ever come back. I went down to Mama Jo's to ask her. She says he's dead."

Mose dropped his arms around her, pulled her against him, trying with soft words and gentle touch to quiet her. Finding her yielding, he pulled her closer, feeling the softness of her skin, the hot rhythm of her pulse. Suddenly all his feelings about her were compounded into a fierce desire to comfort her, to fill the loneliness, to stop her crying. He pulled her to her feet, crushed her against him, felt his own loneliness and longings surge toward her—toward this woman whose pale shoulders became quiet under his stroking hands.

He knew this was what he had wanted since the first time Josie had denied him. He knew she had wanted it to. Her responses, her straining to him—the rhythm of two bodies. His mind was filled with the how, the where.

Suddenly she stiffened and twisted herself free of him. "Professor," she said angrily, "you trying to sweetheart me?"

He dropped his hands to his sides, stunned by what had happened to them.

"I——" he began hesitantly.

"You were," she accused. "You were trying to take advantage of me—like all the other men. You trying to make me like Cluris!"

Her words were like fire splashed over him. She could not mean them, he knew. But they burned nevertheless.

"You don't have anything to say," she said bitterly. "You ain't never going to say things to me again. You ain't never going to fire me. You'd be afraid to."

Mose was suddenly on the defensive. "You won't say——"

"I won't say anything I don't have to. Let's fix it this way. I go with Robert when I want to. You leave me alone. I leave you alone. That way we can both live in Happy Hollow. Any other way, I go straight to Josie."

She smoothed her hair, covered the signs of weeping with rouge and powder. "You had enough of me?"

Mose hesitated.

"Then let me be. I still got time enough to go to Boley for Saturday night."

She ran down the steps, leaving Mose with a heavier burden on his mind, his conscience.

"She tricked me to keep her job," he told himself. But he did not believe what he had said. He knew too much of her loneliness, of her need. He knew also that she had shown greater strength, greater kindness.

"I meant no harm," he said of himself, again without believing.

The feelings rising from his loins measured the depth of his guilt.

For a week Mose kept his sons at home at night. Then, tension lessening, their resentment growing, he let them go to the pool hall and picture show to meet their friends. Thomas was always with Roscoe and Jabbo. As far as Mose could determine, Robert went alone, except for the evenings when he sat at Lora Dixon's talking to Cenoria Davis.

There were nights when Robert did not come home until long after midnight. Mose lay awake those nights worrying about him and often got up to walk to Pepe's Tavern. He stood in the darkness across the street and watched people come and go. He could see that Sheriff Kelly had made no change. He often saw the girls from Mama Jo's waiting for their friends. He sometimes saw Cluris sitting alone at a table, waiting. Once he saw Blackledge go in, speak to Pepe for a few minutes and then come out again.

But he never saw Robert, or Alan Carson, or Cenoria Davis. Their places had been taken by white boys and by Mexican laborers from their boxcar homes on the tracks.

Such nights left Mose with more worry, a stronger feeling that something had to happen. Pepe's could not go on as it was. Something had to burst into the open.

Mornings after such nights Robert would be at home, with a manner of sleepy innocence.

"Where were you?" Mose would demand.

"I played the piano for some friends."

"Where?"

"They said I ain't to say where, and I ain't saying who with."

No matter how often Mose and Josie questioned him, Robert would never say more.

24

ONE day in late August Mose sat in his office listening to the girls' chorus dragging through "Old Folks at Home." Cenoria Davis was preparing a program for the opening day of school and had chosen to present plantation scenes and songs. Every afternoon the girls went through cotton-chopping and picking scenes, trying to re-create a romantic plantation life but using experiences from their own very real life. Their scenes were set to the dreariest of Stephen Foster. Mose could hear Robert impatiently accenting the rhythm to help the children keep up on "All de world am sad and dreary, ebrywhere I roam." He could hear Cenoria Davis counting aloud. They achieved the tempo, but their singing still sounded lifeless. They were no better on "Old Black Joe."

Mose wondered why any Negro in the South would choose to recall plantation life, especially plantation life set to the music of Stephen Foster. He wondered why he had permitted Cenoria Davis to go ahead. He resented the false dialect, the false sentiment. Negroes had too much music of their own, he reasoned, to borrow from the minstrel show. In the future, he resolved, they would use their own.

"Professor."

Mose turned to see Frenchy standing in the door with his cap in his hand and a cigarette between his lips.

"Come in, Frenchy," he said.

Frenchy crushed the cigarette and dropped it out the window. "Guess that ain't allowed here," he apologized.

He dropped into a chair and turned to Mose. "Better close the door," he said solemnly. "What I got to say might burn some ears."

Mose saw that this time Frenchy was neither mocking nor jesting. His face was serious, grave. He picked at his cap nervously.

"What's up, Frenchy?" Mose asked anxiously, his mind already running ahead to Thomas and Robert.

"Trouble's brewing, Professor."

Trouble's brewing. When hadn't trouble been brewing in Happy Hollow? In Little Dixie? Frenchy's voice, manner made this trouble more ominous.

"White-man trouble."

"How do you know?"

"They had me at the courthouse today."

"Who?"

"The Law. Mister Hub Kelly. Blackledge was there too, mad as a hornet."

"How come?"

"Night before last a carload of white boys wus driving through Happy Hollow when somebody put a rock through the windshield."

"Who?"

"I ain't a-knowing. I ain't heard about it till today. Blackledge don't know either. Last night Blackledge was cruising around over here. He said a bunch of nigger boys wus walking along the road looking for trouble. He told them to go home and they sassed him. Then they hid in the dark and he couldn't catch any of them. He's gonna be laying for them."

"Was Thomas with them?"

"I ain't a-knowing. Mister Kelly sent Blackledge out and talked to me. He sho' nuff scared trouble's gonna break out. He wants to know how to head it off."

"What'd you tell him?"

"Nothing a-tall he could use. I ain't knowed nothing to tell him. I usually knows something, but this time I ain't knowed nothing. I told him to wait till I could find out something. I helt off so I could talk to you."

"What can I do?" Mose said.

"Do you know who flang the rock?"

"No."

"Do you know who sassed Blackledge?"

"No."

"If'n you knowed, could you do something?"

"If I only did."

"I ain't saying it was one o' them, but I seen Thomas and Roscoe and Jabbo on the street last night. They been up to something. I could tell by the look."

"I don't know. I'll ask Thomas."

"If'n he says yes, you gonna tell Mister Kelly?"

"I don't know."

"Well, you ain't got to do that. It'd only make more trouble. All you got to do is tell Mister Kelly you'll keep the boys off'n the streets till trouble blows over. Mister Kelly thinks a heap o' you. He say he talked to you once."

"I went to see him the morning after we went to Pepe's Tavern."

"He say you the only man in Happy Hollow that can put down trouble. I say he's right."

"Did you tell him about Thomas? How white boys have deviled the life out of him?"

"I ain't say nothing about him—till I talk to you first. I ain't wanting to make things wuss 'n they is. I told him he could count on you."

"I'll keep on trying. That's all I can do. One thing sure: I'll keep Thomas in. He is going down to Marshall Sunday night. How do things really look to you?"

"I seen 'em wuss, but they bad enough. Something's got to be done. Next thing you know, white boys'll come back to take revenge. If the nigger boys fights back, we got war."

"Have you mentioned this to anyone else?"

"Not yet. I reckon I ought to tell Brother Simpson."

"He ought to know," Mose agreed. "I'll tell him myself if you want me to."

"Might be best."

"We've got to work quietly. Keep your eyes and ears open. Find out everything you can at the courthouse. Listen to folks over here. Give them the names of any of our people causing trouble. We got to get this stopped."

"Yes, sir, Professor. Me, I ain't wanting no white-man trouble. I seen it before. That's how come I left Louisiana."

"Me neither."

"Folks stirs up easy in Little Dixie."

After Frenchy had gone, Mose walked slowly down the stairs. The girls were singing "My Old Kentucky Home." Cenoria Davis had grouped them around what might have represented the front steps of a slave cabin.

Outside, Mose paused as he often paused to admire the red brick and white spire of the Methodist church. Then he went inside, where he found Brother Simpson kneeling at the chancel rail. Mose joined him for a moment and then they sat together in the front pew.

"Brother, I am troubled," Mose said.

He told of Frenchy's visit, of the trouble brewing, of his own fears for his sons.

"Will people never learn?" Brother Simpson asked. "Will they never learn that vengeance is in the hand of the Lord? It ain't that they don't know better. Both sides reads it from the Book."

"I know."

"It's a hard thing to say, but I sometimes believe a lot of our trouble comes from the Book."

"How?"

"White folks read about brotherly love. The Bible don't say anything about the color of a man's skin. White folks mistreat colored folks and get a bad conscience. Then, because their conscience is hurting them, they treat them a little worse to ease the feeling. First thing you know, the Book has split them right down the middle."

"I see, Brother, I see," Mose said.

Mose understood better the white Christian's conscience in a Jim Crow world. That conscience drove some to make gifts to Negro churches, Negro preachers. It drove others to bitterness and bloodshed. There was no comfort for him in the knowledge.

"How we going to stop trouble this time?" Brother Simpson asked.

"Keep our people quiet. Seek peace."

Mose found the old formula disturbing. It had been workable for a long time. But what of the Negro boys growing up? How could they accept it as truth? What would be the outcome if they did not? Mose dared not think.

"Not many to help us in this sort of thing," Brother Simpson said. "Sister Brackett's good. She can tell us what they're saying on the other side. No use in talking to Daddy Splane. He won't be no use to us. You better keep your boys home and tell other folks to do the same."

Mose left Brother Simpson in the church and went home. The house was dim and silent, with the shades drawn.

Mose went straight to the middle room, to the corner where Thomas kept his clothes behind a curtain. He searched a jacket and found a smooth round stone that fitted nicely in his hand. In another pocket he found a hunting knife with blade honed razor-sharp.

Unable to wait until Thomas could come home, Mose went out through Happy Hollow searching for him. He was not at the pool hall or any of the stands. He went to see Roscoe. The boy was not at his home.

"He gone over to Jabbo's," his mother called from behind a half-opened door.

Mose thought of telling her of the trouble, but decided to wait till he had talked to Thomas.

He found Thomas, Roscoe and Jabbo sitting on the front porch making slingshots from leather uppers and cord.

"Come with me, Thomas," he said firmly.

"How come?" Thomas put his slingshot aside and walked beside Mose.

Without speaking, Mose took him to the schoolhouse and to his office. When the door was closed behind them he took out the stone and knife. "Why do you have these?" he asked.

"I like to have them around."

"Tell me the truth. Why do you have them?"

Thomas looked at him and then at the floor. "I'll need them if anybody ever calls me nigger again." His voice shook with anger.

Mose stood up and put his arm around the boy's shoulders. "My son, my son," he said. "I know how it hurts. But you've got to hold in. You've got to stay away from trouble. I know that white boys are looking for trouble. I know Blackledge is making things worse. Did you sass him?"

"I called him the worst thing I could, but that's not as bad as nigger."

"Calling him names won't help. No more than fighting back. Only thing I can see to do now is for you to stay home till your traintime Sunday night. That way, you'll keep away from them."

Mose walked home with Thomas. Then he went to the houses in Happy Hollow where he knew he could get help. It was late at night before he had finished his work of warning parents to keep their children home.

Just before turning into Mulberry Street, he saw a car race along the road from Columbus and then move slowly past him. Blackledge was driving.

"Hell, it's Mose," a voice complained.

25

Mose was up before sunrise the next morning. He went to the hydrant for water. The few people about were quiet. He could see no signs of the tension he had felt the night before. The cars had left the streets; the dust had settled. He drew his pails of water and walked back along the sandy street.

These were days of drought—dog days in a dust-bowl land, a dry year. For days Mose had watched the signs of drought increase: parched grass and leaves, dusty whirlwinds across the prairie, sand hot to the feet at midnight. He had seen how tempers grew short, how people snapped at one another over trifles.

He felt the rising sun hot on his shoulders. Another stifling day, he thought.

Soon after breakfast Zack brought a load of sweet corn from the bottom land. Mose bought the load.

"Got to can it fast," Josie said. "It ain't gonna keep long in this heat."

Mose helped Robert and John shuck and silk the corn. Thomas cut the corn from the cob, slicing off the grains with a sharp knife, scraping the cobs to get all the milk out. Josie boiled the corn in a kettle and ladled it into quart jars.

"Enough to last all winter?" Mose asked.

"It do look like it."

In the middle of the morning Mose went to the hydrant again. As he drew his pails of water, he watched a ball of dust on the road from Columbus.

Brother Simpson came over from the church. "Good morning, Brother," he said to Mose. "Who's that?"

Through the dust Mose could see Sister Brackett's buggy. Sister Brackett was standing at the dashboard, lashing her pony with the reins.

"Must be something bad to make her drive her pony like that," Mose said.

He started toward the road in front of Lora Dixon's house. People ran from porches and yards.

Sister Brackett jerked her pony to a stop, unmindful of the foam that dripped from his mouth and gathered on his flanks. "God have mercy on us," she prayed.

"What is it?"

"White folks is making a mob."

"How do you know?"

"Seen 'em. With my own eyes I seen 'em hanging around the station."

"Many of them?"

"They must a been twenty. I ast Miz Carson. She say some folks is stirred up. They think they got to do something to put niggers in their place. When I seen what I seen, I jest come back fast as I could."

Mose turned to Brother Simpson. He studied the faces around him. He could see anger, resentment.

"What they think we is?" the people asked.

"What can we do?" Brother Simpson asked.

"Don't get excited. I'll go see Doctor Lewis and ask him to help. The others have failed us."

Mose called Frenchy from the pool hall and asked him to go to Columbus.

Sister Brackett climbed down from her buggy and knelt on Lora Dixon's porch. "Oh, Lawd," she prayed, her face turned to the hot sky, "slack not Thy hand from Thy servants. Oh, Lawd, save us po' niggers and help us."

Brother Brackett came and knelt beside her. Louder and louder their voices rose as they begged the mercy of God on the children of Israel. Women sobbed, children wailed. Those who had laughed at holinesses stepped back, no laughter in their eyes now, only grim fear.

As Frenchy turned toward Columbus Mose could hear the people turn to singing:

> "Oh, there's no hiding place down here,
> Oh, there's no hiding place down here
> Oh, I went to the rock to hide my face,
> The rock said, 'This ain't no hiding place,'
> Oh, there's no hiding place down here."

Mose left Frenchy waiting in the taxi and went alone to see Dr. Lewis.

"What's the trouble, Mose?" Dr. Lewis asked.

"White-man trouble."

"I know. I've been hearing about it."

"What can we do? Our people are frightened, stirred up. I'm afraid of an outbreak. You seen the men hanging around the station?"

"Yes, I've seen them. They're the scum of the town mostly. Some are not scum. They're just fools set on keeping niggers in their place. I went down and looked them over. Then I talked to Hub Kelly and some of the other men in the town. They're keeping an eye on them, but they don't expect trouble. There's not a man with nerve in the lot."

"They may egg one another on."

"They could, but Hub Kelly's watching out for that. Black-ledge——"

"I don't trust him."

"I don't either. He's nothing but a sandlapper with a pistol on his hip."

"He's got a mean streak——"

"I know. He's not fit for the job. Hub Kelly's going to get rid of him. Now you go back and tell your people to keep calm and patient. Tell them to stay in their houses. People over here don't want trouble. They wouldn't know how to get along without their help from Happy Hollow. I'll scatter that mob at the station."

Somewhat relieved in mind, Mose went with Frenchy back to Happy Hollow.

"You've got to keep calm," he said to the people at Lora Dixon's. "You've got to keep inside till this blows over. The white people have promised to help us."

The people dispersing, Mose went home to tell his family what had happened and to help them finish canning corn.

That night Mose gathered some men in Lora Dixon's front room. There, with the lights out, they could watch whoever came and went in Happy Hollow.

The only car cruising the streets that night was Blackledge's. Twice an hour the headlights appeared and disappeared on the Columbus road. Blackledge was always driving. Three men were in the car with him. After midnight Blackledge's car came no more.

With a feeling of relief Mose went home. He passed Josie on her pallet, checked to see that Thomas and Robert were in bed and then lay down beside John. For a while he listened to night sounds. Then, hearing nothing else, he fell into uneasy sleep. . . .

Mose was awakened by the sound of a car on the road and doors slamming. He sat up and started pulling on his clothes. It was daylight outside, but the light was dim in the room. He heard voices— voices of white men.

"You sure this is the right house?"

"You goddamned right."

It was Blackledge.

Mose ran to the front room. Josie was standing up in her long white nightgown.

"Who dat?" Josie demanded. "Who dat using cuss words in front o' my house?"

Footsteps on the sand, on the porch, a hand rattling the front door.

"Open up, goddamn it," a voice bellowed. "Open up before I bust the goddamned door in."

Mose looked at Josie helplessly, and then opened the door and stood back. Three men, led by Blackledge, stepped into the dim room. They hesitated a moment, as if waiting for their eyes to adjust to the dimness, or their minds to adjust to what was before them.

"White trash," Josie hissed. She turned her back on them and began rolling up her pallet.

"I told you to keep your boy home," Blackledge said.

"Isn't he in bed?"

Seeing the uncertainty on Blackledge's face, Mose jerked open the door to the middle room. John was asleep on one bed, Robert on the other. Thomas was not in his place.

"I don't know where——"

"He's dead—down by the tracks."

"Dead? Sweet Jesus, no!" Josie's wail filled the room. She dropped on the trunk and covered her face with her hands. Robert and John, wide-eyed with fright, stood in the doorway.

"I had to kill him," Blackledge said as if he were speaking of a strayed animal. "He threatened me. I had to kill him in self-defense. I come to tell you first." He paused.

"Blackledge ain't taking sassing from no nigger," one of the other men said.

"He sassed me and threatened me," Blackledge said. "Him and two other boys."

"Roscoe and Jabbo?" Josie asked.

Blackledge nodded. "They was coming along the road looking mean. I thought they was going over to white town for trouble. When they got to the tracks, I yelled for them to halt. The other two run. Your boy just kept a-walking. When he didn't stop, I shot to kill."

"We're his witnesses," one of the other men said. "He had to shoot. When we searched him, we found a knife on him."

"God a mercy on us!" Josie wept. "My boy's kilt, he's kilt!"

Mose faced them, his eyes on their guns. No way to fight back now. There might never be a way to fight back. "Can we have our boy?" he asked.

"Better let him lay awhile," Blackledge said. "A dead nigger's a mighty good example."

"When can we have him?"

"Oh, middle o' the morning."

Blackledge and his men turned to go. Another car stopped outside and more men got out. Blackledge talked to them a few minutes and then called Mose.

"Mose," he said, "you're the teacher here."

"Yes, sir."

"You ain't never made no trouble yourself."

"No, sir. Now my boy's dead. I don't know what to do. I've got so much trouble——"

"We ain't going to harm you."

"You've done harmed me about as much as a man can stand," he said bitterly.

"We ain't going to harm you no more, if you do what we tell you. If you don't I cain't be responsible for what white men do. You hear me?"

"Yes, sir."

"We had to do what we've done. We had to teach our niggers a lesson. They got too much out of hand. Too uppity. Too sassy. You tell the niggers to hunker down to their jobs and keep their mouths shut."

"Yes, sir." The words came automatically from a numbed mind.

Blackledge took the wheel and the two cars headed back for Columbus.

The cars out of sight, people crept from hiding and came up Mulberry Street. The news spread fast. Some came to add their sympathy, some to curse the white man.

"God pity you, Brother. God pity you, Sister," Brother Simpson said. "May the mercy of God be with you!"

"Amen," the people in the house prayed.

"Murder, by God!" the men in the yard said angrily. "Cold-blooded murder."

Sister Brackett came through the back door. The people made

way for her and she passed among them, praying and blessing as she went. "God a mercy on you, Sister," she said to Josie. "May the victory be yours." To Mose she said, "One to grow."

Then she went to the front porch and raised her arms out over the people. Her veil was thrown back. Her face was calm, majestic in the bright morning light. She sang the depth of her feeling:

> "Nobody knows the trouble I see,
> Nobody knows but Jesus . . . "

A mighty swell of voices took up the song and made it a fervent prayer:

> "Nobody knows the trouble I see,
> Glory hallelujah."

Over and over they sang the words. Mose could hear Josie, high above the others, singing tribble. Unable himself to sing, he ground down his bitterness, saying:

> "We wear the mask that grins and lies,
> It hides our cheeks and shades our eyes . . .
> This debt we pay to human guile;
> With torn and bleeding hearts we smile. . . . "

When those words, too, became comfortless, he bowed his head and wept.

26

AFTER their outburst of grief and wrath, the people settled down to moaning low. While they sang and prayed inside, another group gathered in the street to talk of revenge. Mose and Brother Simpson heard their talk.

"Come on out and join us, Mose," Bo insisted. "Ain't you coming now?"

Mose stood on the porch and judged the time by the sun. "I've got to get my boy now. I can't do anything till I've got my boy."

"We'll wait," Bo said.

Mose went to the middle room, to Josie resting on a bed with Sister Brackett bending over her. "We've got to go," he said simply.

Josie put on a fresh white uniform. She tied a white head rag around her head. She put her arms around Sister Brackett and they wailed together, "Lawd, have mercy on us po' niggers." Then she and Mose stood on the steps together.

"Let me git Frenchy," a man called.

"No," Mose said. "We'll walk."

"We'll go with you."

"No, we've got to walk together—alone. We appreciate your sympathy, but we've got to walk alone."

"We understand, Brother."

"We understand, Sister."

"We understand, Lawd."

"Tell Frenchy to come after us later. We'll need him then."

"We will, Brother."

Lora Dixon stood before them on the ground. "We'll make ready for you."

"Thank you, Sister."

"We got lots to do."

"Amen, Lawd."

Side by side Mose and Josie walked down Mulberry Street. As they went, the crowd separated. A few remained to help Lora Dixon prepare the house. Sister Brackett led her congregation to church. Brother Simpson took the men who would listen to him to his house to talk about the threat of riot among them. Bo led another group to the pool hall to talk of weapons and plans for revenge.

Mose and Josie talked of the hot sun on their shoulders, the hot sand on their feet. They talked of how quiet the road was to Columbus. They heard only the sound of their voices, of their shoes in the gravelly sand. Mose could not bear to talk of Thomas. Once he took Josie's hand and said, "We've got to bear this burden together."

After they had passed Pepe's Tavern, just before they came to the railroad tracks, they came to a line of armed sentries stretched along the dividing line between Happy Hollow and Columbus. Blackledge and two other men sat in his car, listening to the radio.

"White trash," Josie hissed at the sentry in the middle of the road.

He looked to Blackledge.

"Let 'em pass," Blackledge said. He turned his head to avoid their eyes.

A group of white men stood in the shade of a yardhouse at the tracks. When they saw Mose and Josie they drew back and stood silently waiting.

Slowly, reverently, Mose and Josie approached the body of Thomas stretched out in the shade of the warehouse. Someone had folded the hands to honor the Cross and closed the eyes with coins.

"My baby!" Josie wailed. She took his face in her hands and leaned her cheek against it, sobbing.

Mose knelt beside the body and gently stroked the folded hands. The hope of years, begun when he first held this son in his arms, faded away. In its place came the wrath and hatred stored up in a lifetime of trying to do right, of being thwarted by men he had never wronged. Words burned in him until he had to expel the fire.

"God damn white men. God damn white men!"

Alan Carson crossed the sand and stood near Josie. She saw him there, clean, neat, unhealthily pale, and turned her head away.

"Mose," Alan said.

"Good morning, Mister Alan."

"Mose, I'm sorry."

"Thank you, Mister Alan."

"My father said he had gone for his truck and a coffin. He took up a collection. He wanted to do something to help you in—in all this."

"Thank you, Mister Alan."

Mose saw that Alan Carson himself had felt the effect of violence, of fear, that his assurance had been deeply shaken.

Alan stepped back and his place was taken by Sheriff Hub Kelly. "Mose, it's a shame."

"You could have stopped it," Mose said firmly. "If you'd listened to me, you could have stopped it. I tried to tell you about Black-ledge——"

"Blackledge!" Josie sprayed the sand with cottony spit. "How come you got a murderer to do the policing?"

Sheriff Kelly squatted on his heels, facing them. "I want to talk to you—to explain the law. I have tried to find out what happened. I have talked to Blackledge. He seems to have the law on his side. Your boy was close to the tracks. He did have a knife. Blackledge had witnesses that your boy threatened him. That nigh about cinches it for Blackledge. I don't know who to blame. I know things are tough for all of us. I've got to have a man over there I can trust. Folks wanted me to get shet of him." He paused as if to reconsider his own thinking. "He's got the law on his side."

"You won't do anything?" Mose asked.

"All I can. It'll be brought to the attention of the grand jury, but the law's on his side. If you have some new evidence . . . ?"

"No, sir."

"If you get any, will you come to me?"

"Yes, sir."

Hub Kelly stood up. "I'm sorry you lost your boy," he said, and went back to join the group.

A truck stopped by the yardhouse and John Carson got out. It was the delivery truck for the store. A coffin box showed above the sides of the bed.

"Mose," John Carson said, "Mose, I'm awfully sorry for you, and for you, Josie." He took Mose's hand and held it.

"It's a terrible thing that has happened," Mose said.

"Terrible for whites and blacks. It'll take us a long time to get over this."

"I won't ever."

"I know, Mose. I want to help you as much as I can. We got the coffin for you. You don't owe a cent. The driver will take you when you want to go."

Mose helped Josie climb on the truck. She raised the lid of the box and looked at the gray coffin inside. She patted the gray felt tenderly. White men lifted Thomas to the truck and stretched him beside the box.

"Cain't put him in the coffin now," Josie crooned. "He's got to be laid out. I got clean clothes in the trunk. I got a new suit. Wait'll I git them. Here, let me hold him."

She sat on the floor and took his head in her lap. Mose climbed in beside her and the truck ground slowly through the sandy streets of Happy Hollow.

As they went, Mose searched his own conscience. There was a time when he threw the Bible, a time when Cenoria Davis tempted him. Try as he would, he could not blame himself for Thomas. That blame had to be on white men. . . .

Lora Dixon and the women with her had cleaned the house and set up the laying-out boards when they returned. She had sent Robert and John to carry water to fill a washtub for bathing the body. She had sprinkled the front room with camphor and set a bowl of camphor water on the laying-out boards. She had sent men to dig a grave.

"It's nigh a little cedar," she said. "Someday it'll be sheltered from the sun."

When the truck was gone, people came to help, or to mourn. Sister Brackett and Brother Brackett came, bringing a blue glass lamp to set on the grave. Cenoria Davis brought a glass powder jar with a silver lid. "It's one I had in New Orleans," she said.

Josie held it up to catch the light on the cut edges. "It'll look nice at his feet."

The women washed the body and dressed it in fresh clothes. They put on the dark-blue suit bought for the trip to Marshall. Then the men lifted it into the coffin. Women took turns brushing away flies and moistening in camphor water the cloth that covered the face.

To the people coming and going Josie said, "Tell folks we're gonna funeralize him at sundown."

Then she sent Robert and John to catch a pigeon for the grave service. "Git a white one if'n you can," she told them. "It'll look more like a dove."

"You want the dove service?" Sister Brackett asked.

"I sho' does, Sister. I wants to know all I can know. If'n the Lawd wants to tell me my son's going to heaven, I wants to know it now. It'll be balm for my soul."

"What do you think?" Sister Brackett asked Mose.

"I'd rather not have it, but if it will comfort her any, I will not stand in the way. I don't believe that the flight of a pigeon will tell me whether my son is going to heaven or to the other world. I don't believe in it at all—but if his mother can get some comfort from it, I won't object. For her sake, I hope the pigeon flies straight up."

In the heat of the noonday sun a runner came up Mulberry Street. "Mose, Mose," he called. "Bo wants you down at the pool hall."

"What does he want?"

"They want you to help them."

Knowing the help they wanted, drawn by his own loss to aid them, Mose followed the runner down to the pool hall.

The pool hall was full of angry, sweating men. The back door was crowded. More waited in the shade in the back. All morning they had been working themselves up for a rising. Their faces were set toward violence. They fondled their rifles and shotguns and waited for the signal.

Mose paused at the sight. All this was for him. For Thomas. These men were ready to kill and be killed for the death of his son. Pride in his people rose in him. They would not be put on. They would fight back.

Bo took his hand and stood beside him. "You stopped us before," he said, "but you ain't gonna stop us now. It's different when yo' own lies dead."

"That's right, man," the others yelled. "You tell it, man."

"We got it figgered out," Bo continued. "Blackledge is in his car at Pepe's Tavern. I'll drill him between the eyes with my Winchester. Then we'll all rush the sentry line. We can nigh about git shet o' them that's causing trouble."

"Then what?" Mose asked.

"Our minds is made up. If'n they git us, they git us, but we'll take a lot o' the sons o' bitches to hell with us."

He took a rifle from a pool table. "We wants you with us. You need to taste sweet revenge. We got this gun for you."

Mose took the gun and ran his fingers over the polished steel, the varnished wood. He thought of how it would kill the hate growing within him.

"Blackledge is mine," Bo was saying. "I got a long grudge agin him. You git yo' pick after that."

Mose had never anticipated a choice so clearly defined. He had never felt so much power placed in his hand. They could kill, and wipe some of the evil from the face of the earth. The temptation was great. Yet he waited.

Bo let his voice rise again, like a revivalist trying to lead the hesitant to the altar. "Yo' boy is dead—dead and cold in his coffin—and nobody to raise his hand agin his slayer unless'n you do. We've got to go. You got to go with us."

"Give me time——"

"We ain't got no time. Blackledge don't give no time. He didn't give none to Thomas. He won't give none to us."

The others were on their feet chanting. "Le's go. Le's go after 'em."

The sound of a bell rolled across Happy Hollow. The bell was tolling for Thomas. "One... two... three..." Mose was unconsciously counting. But his mind was on the choice before him. On the one hand, bloodshed, death; on the other, more shame and degradation for him and his people for not striking back. He had never before been so surely the leader of his people, he knew.

"Seventeen . . . eighteen."

The tolling ended.

"Le's go!" the men shouted.

They laid hands on Mose and urged him toward the door. Bo walked beside him, clutching a Winchester in his hands. "God give me guidance," Mose prayed. His feet took up the tramping step of the men around him. They tramped on boards and then on sand, gathering momentum as they went.

They circled once past the hydrant and Lora Dixon's. A few more came to join them. They circled again. When they came near the Methodist church Mose could hear Brother Simpson and his followers singing

> "Lay yo' all upon the altar,
> Lay yo' all upon the altar,
> Lay yo' all upon the altar,
> Oh, love, love, love."

Mose broke from the circling group. "I got to go," he cried in anguish. He pushed aside the hands that tried to hold him. With eyes lifted he marched toward the church. He was conscious of the sound of feet in the sand following him.

He marched straight to the altar and leaned his gun against the chancel rail. As he took up the song he knew that his decision had been right. He glanced around the church. Not all the men had followed him, but enough to break up the march on Columbus.

Brother Simpson held them till late afternoon. Then he and Mose went to face Bo and the handful of men who had stayed at the pool hall.

"We cain't fight that way," Brother Simpson told them.

Frenchy came from Columbus. "Blackledge done gone," he told them. "He takened his guard off. Ain't no guns pointing at us now."

His words broke the tension. The men put away their guns.

It was near sunset when Robert and John returned, a white pigeon held tight in their hands. The crowd had waited all afternoon, but Josie would not let the service start without them. The men brought the coffin to the porch. The women pressed closely around it. They had left off moaning and praying for the moment and were singing a happier song, a song that looked beyond death.

> "Oh, wake me early in the morning,
> Before it is too late,
> Just when the day is dawning,
> To swing on the Golden Gates. ... "

Mose pushed aside the memories the song called up. Resolutely he took hold of the coffin. Resolutely he lifted his share of the burden to his shoulder. This last service he must do for Thomas.

Slowly the six men bore the coffin down Mulberry Street and to the graveyard at the foot of Reservoir Hill. Slowly men and women followed, their voices rising in the refrain:

> "Wake me, shake me,
> Don't let me sleep too late;
> Gonna fly away in the morning
> To swing on the Golden Gates."

Sister Brackett, chosen by Josie for the dove service, stood at the head of the coffin. Brother Simpson faced her from the other end. Sister Brackett, with her back to the east, with the glow of the setting sun on her face, raised her hand. The singing and moaning trailed away into a faint murmuring. She pushed her veil back from her face and stretched her hands out over the coffin.

"Peace, Brothers. Peace, Sisters," she said in a voice that echoed from Reservoir Hill. "The peace of God be upon you. Put the strife of the day behind you. Set yo'se'f forward in humility and peace. Kneel down, Brothers. Kneel down, Sisters. Make yo'se'f humble before God in the presence of death." The people wilted to the earth like plants in a hot wind. Some of them groveled in the dust. Seeing them bend to her will, Sister Brackett called, "Now sing, Brothers and Sisters."

Mose could hear Josie taking up the song.

> "Sister Lou, Brother Joe, Aunt Maria
> Done caught that train and gone...."

"That's right, child'en," Sister Brackett shouted above their singing. "They done caught that Gospel Train and gone on to Glory, Glory. They done bought their tickets, got on the train and gone puffing and whistling off to Glory. Now our son Thomas is on that Glory Train. He's paid the heavy price and gone.... Amen, Brothers. Amen, Sisters. Thomas has caught the Gospel Train. Hallelujah!"

"Hallelujah, amen!"

Mose, kneeling near the coffin, trying to pray his own prayer, found his voice stopped with the thought of the awful price Thomas had paid.

"Ain't no time for weeping," Sister Brackett shouted. "Ain't no time for crying. Now's the time for shouting glory hallelujah one more of His precious lambs done gone home. Don't weep for him, Mother. Don't weep for him, Father. Sweet Jesus don't want you to weep."

"Sweet Jesus don't want you to weep," Brother Brackett sang antiphonally.

"If'n you got yo' own ticket for that Gospel Train, don't you weep. Lawd, have mercy on them that ain't bought them tickets...."

Brother Brackett stood near her and held the pigeon up for her to see. He pointed to the sun setting behind Reservoir Hill. The dove service must come when the rim first touched. Sister Brackett stopped her sermon long enough to tell the men to lower the coffin.

"Sing, Brethren. Sing while they lay his precious body in the dust," she said, raising her hands above the grave. "Sing a song of parting." She began the words softly herself.

> "Good-by, I'm sorry to leave you,
> Good-by, I'm sorry to leave you,
> Good-by, I'm sorry to leave you,
> Gonna leave you in His care. . . . "

Mose could not force himself to sing, but he could hear Josie singing tribble in a voice tired from weeping.

"Ashes to ashes," Sister Brackett chanted as the coffin sank to rest. Her voice rose above the song, above the rattle of tools on the coffin box as workers fastened the lid tight. "Ashes to ashes. . . . Dust thou art . . . unto dust shalt thou return. . . . "

When the lid was fastened down, while the people waited in silence, Brother Brackett stepped forward with the pigeon. The frightened bird fluttered in his hands. He stroked it gently, murmuring, "Fly high, sweet spirit, fly high." Slowly he climbed into the grave and stood with his feet on the edge of the coffin box. The people stood up, crowded forward to watch. They leaned forward until those nearest the grave had to scramble to keep their balance. Sister Brackett began moaning low. Josie, standing near her, let her voice take up the haunting melody. Mose stood near Brother Simpson and watched silently, sternly.

Brother Brackett looked at the sun, waited for the rim to touch the trees on Reservoir Hill. He lifted his hand for silence. Then he held the pigeon straight before him. The people watched with indrawn breath.

"Fly, sweet spirit," Brother Brackett said, and tossed the pigeon forward above the coffin.

There was a quick flutter of wings and the pigeon rose in swift flight. It passed just above the heads of the mourners and flew toward Pleasant Valley. People shoved at one another for a clearer view. They wanted to see the pigeon soar. But it did not soar. It skimmed the earth past houses, past trees. Then it dropped to earth where water had dripped a puddle from the hydrant.

There was a moment of awe, of disbelief. Then Josie wailed, "Down in hell—forever tormented in hell!" Women around her broke into wild wailing. They fell to their knees in the dust. Women crowded around Josie where she had fallen and fanned her with leaves and handkerchiefs. Sister Brackett stood above them exhorting them to pray God to have mercy on Thomas' lost soul—to pray for their own deliverance from torment in hell.

Darkness came to still their wailing, to force them back to the safety of their houses. The women took turns carrying Josie.

Mose walked behind them with Robert and John, his mind numbed, his heart full of grief. He could only try to give them comfort he did not feel.

27

Happy Hollow passed a night of shocked quiet. The moving-picture show was dark. The pool hall closed. People stayed in their houses behind closed doors and drawn shades.

"Blackledge may come agin," they said.

Toward midnight, when Robert and John were asleep and Josie's grieving had hushed, Mose walked the roads of Happy Hollow. Often his steps turned toward the graveyard. As often he compelled himself to turn back when the dark acre was just before him, when the few stones shone dimly. The graveyard was of the past. He had to think on the future. His thinking had led him to Happy Hollow. Must it lead him away again?

Where? Of one thing he was sure: he would not return to Penrose Plantation. He could not see Robert and John toiling up and down cotton rows spring, summer, fall to earn a meager living for the winter. To escape the harshness of Oklahoma he could not do that.

Chicago? He remembered pleasant afternoons on the elm-shaded campus. He remembered libraries, books, talks with friends. He forgot the misery he had seen in slums in the Black Belt. He forgot that life there could be insecure, unsafe, at times violent.

As he walked, his mind was made up. He would take his family and go to Chicago at once. They would begin a new life. In new surroundings, new work, they would forget a little the loss they felt.

He passed the school. Monday morning he should be there conducting the opening exercises. He should be listening to Cenoria Davis driving her girls through singing "Old Folks at Home." His mind was made up. He would not be there.

Mose passed the moving-picture show and the pool hall.

"Mose," a voice whispered from the shadows. "Come here."

Mose went to the porch of the pool hall. Frenchy was leaning against a post. His taxi was in the shadow of the building.

"Mister Kelly asked me to keep watch," he said. "He don't want no more trouble."

"Was he over?"

"He come through town once."

"Blackledge?"

"I ain't seen him. I reckon he ain't gonna show up agin for a few days. It's better if he don't."

"Better for us."

Mose looked down Main Street of Happy Hollow to where the lights of Columbus glowed yellow against a prairie horizon. He understood as he had never understood before that it was a one-way road. Down it the white man could strike. The Negro could never strike back. It was better to go. Mose shuffled his feet in the sand.

"Better go home, Mose," Frenchy said. "Better git some rest."

Wearily Mose walked up Mulberry Street and through his kitchen door. At his bed he paused. Robert was in his place, sleeping soundly beside John. Mose forced himself to lie down on the other bed.

Josie called Mose at daybreak. "I'm gonna go decorate the grave," she said.

Mose cooked breakfast for Robert and John and then went to join her.

"I done what I could to make it look nice," she said when he came to her, where she rested in the shade of a cedar.

With her hands she had shaped the red-clay mound and patted it smooth. She had arranged pieces of broken glass and colored beads in patterns of circles and diamonds. At the head was Sister Brackett's lamp; at the foot, Cenoria Davis' powder box. In the middle of the mound she had placed Thomas' flashlight.

"He liked it," she said, "and I wanted him to have it."

"It looks nice," Mose said quietly.

"Next year I'm gonna have yellow roses for his grave. They'll stand the drought. I'm gonna write Miss May and tell her I want some slips from her yellow rosebush for my baby's grave."

As they walked home in the heat of the morning Mose told her of his plans to go to Chicago. "I ain't a-going one step from Happy Hollow," she insisted. "I ain't gonna leave him now. I wanted to go back to Miss May, but you wouldn't. Now I got to mind the grave. The weather's dry and the ground ain't good. I got to stay with him the enduring time."

Once more Mose yielded to her.

On Monday morning Mose presided at the opening exercises of Phillis Wheatley School. He called on Brother Simpson for the invocation. He introduced John Carson and Dr. Lewis, representing the Columbus School Board. He greeted the parents and children. He listened to "Old Folks at Home" and "Old Black Joe." He called on Sister Brackett for the benediction. School was officially opened much as it had been every other year.

Daddy Splane was absent. There would probably be no report of the occasion in *The Neighborhood Eye*. Mose considered that no loss. Dr. Lewis was present. Mose considered that a gain.

The exercises over, Mose went with John Carson and Dr. Lewis on their inspection of the building. They paused briefly at classrooms on the first floor to watch Lora Dixon and then Cenoria Davis at work with the children.

"Good teachers?" Dr. Lewis asked.

"No complaints."

As they started up the stairs they heard giggling that swelled to roaring laughter. The laughter broke. After a pause, a woman's voice climbed the scale in a trilling laugh.

"What's going on?" John Carson demanded.

"That's the Spanish class. I don't know how she's going to make out. They just sent her down from Langston this morning."

The three men stood outside her door.

"We must learn to greet one another in Spanish," she said to the children. *"Buenos días."* She ended again with her trilling laugh.

"*Buenos días.*" The words were lost in a fresh burst of laughter.

Mose, feeling embarrassed, tried to explain. "The School Board said we had to teach Spanish. I tried all summer to get a competent teacher. She's the only one I could find."

"Seems foolish to teach them Spanish," Dr. Lewis said to John Carson.

"It's equal education."

"All right, if we can do some other things as well." He turned to Mose. "Let's not disturb her now. We'll depend on you to make her a good teacher, or get another one. I want to see the outside."

At the back of the building Dr. Lewis paced off a rectangle ten paces by fifteen paces. "I've been talking to the School Board about that addition," he said. "I want space for shops and laboratories. If we can have Spanish, we've got to have chemistry."

"The tax rate will go up," Carson reminded him.

"Let it go up. Educate them better and they'll be better able to pay it."

"You'll have trouble convincing the people of Columbus."

"I know."

Mose walked with them to John Carson's car. Dr. Lewis leaned out a window. "Mose," he said, "we tried to get Blackledge fired, but no luck. Now we're trying to get him moved."

"Thank you, sir."

In the days that followed, their lives took a new pattern. Afternoons Josie went to the graveyard to smooth the grave and weep over the plants that died in the barren clay. Nights she went to Sister Brackett's and sang and danced and prayed till midnight. Sometimes, at Sister Brackett's urging, she went through Happy Hollow seeking new converts for the holinesses. To show that she had accepted the call to evangelism, she wore white robes that trailed in the dust.

Then Sister Brackett asked her to go with her on hominy-selling trips, to help her preach the true Gospel to white ladies. But Josie refused. No sense in her trying to talk religion to white folks. She had enough work to do among her own people—and with her sons.

Sometimes she found Robert playing the piano after school, alone in the house. Then she tried to persuade him to go with her back to Sister Brackett's.

"You ain't happy," she sometimes said. "I see it in your eyes."

"I ain't lost nothing at Sister Brackett's," he would reply, and she could never get more from him.

She rarely talked as pleadingly with John. He seemed to live in another world—a solemn, serious world into which her religion could not reach. Afternoons and Saturdays he worked as janitor at the school. Evenings he sat beside a lamp with a book.

"He do read too much," Josie complained to Mose. "You don't watch out it'll affect his mind. Miss May always say it ain't good to know too much—'specially darkies."

"Leave him alone," Mose said. "He's got work to do."

Frenchy waited for Mose outside the school one afternoon. "Blackledge is gone," he said.

"Gone? Where?"

"Mister Kelly got him a job down at McAlester. He's gonna be a guard at the pen. Folks'll breathe easier here."

"Yes, they'll breathe easier. I'm glad he's gone. With him gone, things might be better."

When Mose drew his next pay check, he found an increase of twenty-five dollars a month. He went from the bank to John Carson's office to thank him.

"We feel you deserve it," Carson told him.

Mose got almost out of the office and then turned back. "Mister Carson," he said, "we've got to feeling at home in our house. We'd like to buy it."

"I hadn't thought of selling."

"I can save a little money now. I'd like to give it to you for a down payment."

With no promise that he would ever sell, John Carson agreed to accept ten dollars a month in a fund from which Mose could draw any time.

28

ONE night in December Sister Daisy came to call Mose out of bed. "The Reverend's mighty sick," she said. "I want you to come set with him a spell. It'd comfort him."

While Mose put on his shoes Sister Daisy stood by the stove and told him what had happened. For several days Brother Simpson had been sniffling with a cold. She had not worried much about it, but in the afternoon he had walked in the rain out to Old Galilee to hold a funeral, and when he came back he had developed sharp shooting pains in his chest.

"I'm scaid of pneumony," she said.

"You called Doctor Lewis?"

"Not yet. I wanted to ask you first."

Mose studied the old woman's face. She was too tired from working and pastoring, he thought. He wondered whether she had eaten a square meal in a month. Now, with Brother Simpson sick in bed, life would be harder for her. With a weary hand she fumbled at the dust cap on her white hair. She pulled a shawl around her head and tied it.

"I'd better start back," she said. "He might be a-wanting me."

Though it was near midnight, Josie had not come home from church. Mose roused John and told him that Brother Simpson was sick. Then he went out into the dark street. He could hear singing at Sister Brackett's; he could hear laughter from behind the new neon sign at the pool hall. The rain had stopped early in the evening, but enough had fallen for mud to ball on his shoes and muffle his steps. A fresh wind blew from the north. Hog-killing weather tomorrow, Mose thought.

Sister Daisy met Mose at the door with a lamp in her hand. She led him to Brother Simpson's bed. He took the old man's hand in his. It was hot from fever. His eyes were glassy, and his breath came in painful gasps.

"It's Mose," Sister Daisy told him.

He roused himself enough to say, "E'ning, Brother. I'm mighty po'ly," and then sank back to sleep.

"I don't want to alarm you," Mose said quietly to Sister Daisy, "but I think we'd better send for Doctor Lewis."

"I'll trust what you say, Mose."

Mose left the house calmly, but he broke into a run as soon as he was hidden by darkness. He would send John and Frenchy for Dr. Lewis.

Back at Brother Simpson's, Mose took up the vigil against death. He brought in wood to keep a fire in the little tin stove. Not finding enough to last till morning, he got out the ax and chopped wood in the stillness of the night, each stroke like a pistol shot on the clear air. He heard the singing at Sister Brackett's stop, heard voices of her people walking in groups through the streets. Chopping warmed his body and tempered the sadness in his thoughts. He forced himself to think of the future. What would the Methodist church do if Brother Simpson died? More important, what would he do? He thought of the many times he had brought his own worries and griefs to the old man. What would he do when that was no longer possible? The North Star hung to the left of him as he chopped. He threw his questions at it and got them back unanswered.

Shortly after midnight Dr. Lewis arrived in Frenchy's taxi, with John on the seat beside him. "You'd think it was a granny case, getting a man out of bed this time of night," he joked.

He laid a hand on Brother Simpson's forehead and then took a thermometer and stethoscope from his saddlebags. He tested the old man's temperature, his heart, his breathing, sharing each step with John, treating John as if he were another doctor called in for consultation.

His examination ended, he beckoned Mose and John outside. "Pneumonia, all right," he said when they were under the stars. "Not much chance for him to pull through."

Mose felt a fullness in his throat, a smarting in his eyes. He had tried to prepare himself for these words. Now that they had come, he knew there could never be a preparation.

"You going to tell Sister Daisy?" Mose asked.

"Somebody's got to. Maybe you should. You've always been pretty close to them."

"Can't you do anything for him?"

"Not much. Important thing's to keep him warm and quiet. I'm going to fix up something that'll ease him tonight—make breathing easier. In the morning I'll send John over with some more medicine. I'll come again myself in the afternoon."

"We'll appreciate what you do, Doctor."

Dr. Lewis turned with his hand on the door. "Mose," he said, "we've seen a lot of things through together in our time."

"That's right, Doctor."

"By a miracle, we might pull him through."

"I hope so."

Mose and John followed Dr. Lewis back to the bedroom. Sister Daisy was sitting by the bed. She kept her face turned from the light, to keep Brother Simpson from seeing her tears. With frightened eyes she watched Dr. Lewis take a hypodermic needle and wash it in alcohol.

"The needle," she whispered, horrified. "Is he that bad off?"

How often in death watches had she seen the doctor use a hypodermic!—to ease the patient off, people said. Mose knew what she was thinking. The needle was the doctor's last skill—or trick. That meant he had given up every other way. That was what people in Happy Hollow believed. When Dr. Lewis used the needle, there was not much hope left.

Mose fought to free his own mind of the belief. "It's all right, Sister Daisy," he whispered. "Doctor Lewis knows what he is doing. We must trust his judgment."

The needle given, the breathing eased, Dr. Lewis packed his saddlebags and left John to watch the patient. When Sister Daisy returned after closing the door behind him, Mose saw in her eyes a new resignation. She had seen the needle's thrust; she knew her husband would die.

Through the night Mose and John sat with Sister Daisy by Brother Simpson's bed. Though it was night and cold, news of his illness, of the needle, spread, and his people began to gather. Mose met them at the door and tried to persuade them to go home. But they would not. They had come to sit with the sick, in country fashion, and no one could send them away. Held by the presence of death, they knelt on the floor and moaned and prayed into muffling hands.

In the afternoon Dr. Lewis came again. He found Brother Simpson resting more easily, in spite of the praying, moaning people gathered to do their duty by the sick.

"Better get them out of here," he told Mose and John. "They'll kill him if you don't."

Mose persuaded Lora Dixon to start a prayer meeting in the front room of her boardinghouse. Weeping and praying, the people filed past the bed and out into the street. There, unrestrained, they let their moaning-low rise in a crescendo.

With John to help him, Dr. Lewis began his examination. He pressed his face, red from cold, to the patient's black chest and listened intently. Then he asked John to listen to see if he could recognize the change.

"The crisis is about past," he told them. "If he can hold out a little longer, we may pull him through."

"Pray God we can, Doctor," Sister Daisy said.

Her voice sounded dull, lacking in fervor. Mose knew that all hope went out of her the night before when Dr. Lewis used the needle.

On the porch, Dr. Lewis gave John and Mose new instructions. Then he went on another call in Happy Hollow.

"He do think a heap of yo' boy," the people said to Mose when he had gone.

Mose, waking from a brief rest, found the house dark, quiet. He pushed the covers back and stood up, fully dressed. He lighted a lamp and went to the kitchen. Josie had left his supper on the table. There were plates for Robert and John, both untouched. John was sitting with Brother Simpson. Robert had gone to Columbus in the afternoon. No telling when he'd come home.

While Mose was still at the table, John came running for him. "Brother Simpson's dying," he said, standing out of breath in the kitchen. "I could hear the death rattle."

Mose grabbed his coat and ran down Mulberry Street. Before he reached the house he could hear Sister Daisy wailing. He knew that the old man was dead. As he ran, his mind worked at the things that had to be done at once: wash the body, get a coffin, ring the bell.

Mose found a crowd of people huddled on the wind-swept porch. He pushed through them to the door and went in. Sister Daisy had fallen forward and buried her face in the blankets. Her wails came like quick, sharp barks. Old women from the church knelt around the bed, moaning.

Mose spoke to them. "Take her to Lora Dixon's."

Without a word they wrapped her in a cloak and carried her out of the house.

Mose went to the bed and looked at the old man. His eyes were half open and his jaw had dropped forward. Mose took a towel and tied it around the head to hold the jaw in place. Tenderly he adjusted the face and lip muscles so they would harden into the face they had known. Then he took two nickels from his pockets. He pulled the eyelids shut and weighted them with the coins. Gently he smoothed marks of the death struggle from cheek and brow. That done, he drew a sheet over the face to wait till they could get a coffin.

From the men who had gathered, Mose chose Joe Johnson and Brother Brackett to go to Columbus for a coffin. They had to depend on what they could buy at a furniture store.

The men gone, the moaning subsiding somewhat, Mose had time to think about the bell. He and Brother Simpson had seen it on the ground in Columbus. Together they had seen it hoisted to the steeple. Mose knew what it had meant to Brother Simpson. Now the time had come for it to toll his death. There was one white man who ought to hear it toll.

Though it was late at night, Mose sent for John. When he came, Robert was with him. Mose stood on the porch and talked to them.

"You know Reverend Martin at the white Methodist church?"

"Yes, sir."

"I want you to go see him. Tell him Brother Simpson's dead. Tell him we're going to lay him out and then ring the bell. Can you tell him that?"

"Yes, sir."

"Go ahead. Don't tarry anywhere. The trouble's gone, but it wouldn't be safe for two colored boys to be caught loitering at night in Columbus. When you get back, we'll ring the bell."

He took the boys by their arms and walked with them past Lora Dixon's where lights glowed dimly in parlor and kitchen. Then he urged them on their way toward Columbus.

Mose went back to Brother Simpson's to prepare the body for the coffin. The house having only two rooms, Mose asked the women to wait in the kitchen. He built a fire in the kitchen stove and put on a tub of water. He sent two men for a long table and set it in the middle of the bedroom. When the water was warm, he and the other men lifted the body from the bed and laid it on the table. Carefully, tenderly, they washed it from head to foot. Mose found Brother Simpson's pulpit clothes and gave them to the women to brush and press.

When they had dressed him in his pulpit clothes they stretched him on the table in an attitude of sleep, his hands folded across his chest and bound with a handkerchief.

"He'll look fine when we git him in his coffin," the men whispered to one another.

The women crept in from the kitchen. "He do look natural," they said.

Suddenly the sound of a church bell came clear and loud on the night air, a sound softened by distance. Mose ran from the house and stood in the street, alone at first and then in the center of huddling bodies. They counted silently at first. Then, as if impelled, they took up the rhythm in subdued voices. When the count reached sixty-seven and they knew that the tolling was over, they fell to their knees on the cold ground, their voices soft in moaning low.

"Now he'll rest in peace," they whispered to one another.

Back in the house they asked Mose how it had happened—why white folks had rung their bell for a colored preacher.

"White folks're like colored folks," he told them. "Some's good, some's bad. A good one rung that bell. . . ."

29

ONE afternoon Lora Dixon came to Mose's office. "Robert sassed me," she said indignantly.

"What about?"

"I ain't a-knowing. He sassed me and went home. I ain't going to stand for no sassing. You want me to straighten him out?"

"No, I'll go get him when I get through hearing my classes."

When Mose came near the house he heard Robert playing the piano. It was not the music he usually played at home. It was blues music, in the rhythm of the "nigger shuffle"—sinful music. Mose stepped inside quietly, waited for a moment for his eyes to adjust from the glare of a warm spring sun. Consciously putting off the time when he must speak to Robert, he crossed the room silently and slipped into a chair. Then he turned his mind to the things he had to say.

His thoughts became a blur of music and musician. Robert bent his tall body low over the piano. With long fingers curved and stiff like pothooks he pounded the keys in a wild, drumlike rhythm. Mose searched through the shower of sounds for the melody, found it, followed it—a wild and wailing melody, from the cotton patch, from the holy-roller meeting. He tapped out the rhythm on the chair arm, found it irregular, syncopated, growing faster and faster, in unnatural swiftness. From the "nigger shuffle" Robert had changed to some incredible primitive dance. His body swayed slightly, his fingers hammered the keys in mad desperation. Mose, sensing that Robert was not at himself, slipped to one side, saw his eyes fixed and glassy. He was in a trance, like a person overcome at a revival meeting. Mose hesitated, reluctant to speak, reluctant to break the spell, though he knew the spell must be broken.

"Robert!"

His voice was a whisper against the crashing noise of the piano. Robert played on, unaware.

"Robert!"

Mose spoke louder, the tenseness of alarm in his voice. The dance was coming to an end in a mighty crescendo. Robert's fingers tore up and down the keyboard in irregular arpeggios and fierce chromatics. His feet, no longer touching the pedals, slapped the floor in the savage dance. It was as if the music was a monster holding him in a mighty grip.

"Robert!"

Mose yelled above the music and shook Robert's shoulder. Robert did not look up, but he let the music break on a seventh. The tones remained hanging, unfinished, in the little room.

Robert suddenly struck Mose's hand from his shoulder and ran out the front door. He turned up Mulberry Street toward Reservoir Hill, running with uneven steps, lurching body. Mose, running after him, repeated to himself, "The weed! The weed! He's been smoking the weed." His fears were realized: Robert had taken to marijuana. The walls of McAlester prison loomed before him.

As if driven by agonizing pain, Robert ran on toward Reservoir Hill, not looking to left or right, not heeding Mose's footfalls close behind him. They passed the last houses and came to where the trail spread wide through blackjack oaks.

"Robert," Mose called. "Wait, son, wait! What's the matter, son?"

Robert did not answer. He left the trail and crashed through underbrush, driven toward the crest of the ridge. Mose ran after him, heedless of thorns that ripped his clothes.

Robert stopped at last in a clump of young elms, his body half hidden in their tender green. "Oh, Lawd," he moaned, "have mercy on me."

He pressed his hands to his eyes. He beat his forehead with the heels of his hands. Then he began tearing at young elm branches. He pulled long slender twigs from the trees and bound them like cords around his head and wrists. He pulled the withes tighter and tighter, till they cut his flesh. He sobbed violently, letting tears flow down his cheeks from eyes pressed shut. His body twisted in a spasm and he fell to the ground. He lay writhing on last year's leaves, his face touching mandrakes just pushing through the earth.

Mose shook off his awe, knelt over his son. "My son, my son," he said softly, but Robert gave no sign of having heard him. He felt the boy's cheeks, breast, wrists. Something had to be done, but what? Robert was too heavy to carry home. If he called for help, chances were against his being heard. If someone came, all Happy Hollow would soon know.

Mose sat on the ground and took Robert's head in his lap. Carefully he loosened the withes from his head and wrists. When Robert started moaning again, he tied a handkerchief around his head and pulled it over his eyes to shut out the light. With shaking hands he chafed the boy's throat and wrists.

As he worked over his son, Mose heard the distant cooing of a dove. He remembered how as a child on Penrose Plantation he would throw himself on the ground and roll over once at the first dove call in the spring. There was luck to be had and a wish to be made. He felt like lifting Robert's head from his lap and rolling over. He needed good luck.

Robert stirred and begged for water. Mose found a trickle among the mandrakes and wet his shirt in it. He wiped Robert's lips and face and wrapped the shirt around his head. He watched the eyes brighten, the lips relax from pain. Darkness was coming on. He would have to get Robert home soon—before Josie could spread an alarm through Happy Hollow.

"Feel better, son?" he asked.

"Yes, sir."

Mose raised him to a sitting position. He rocked back and forth drunkenly but did not fall. Mose squeezed water on his eyelids and lips. He slapped wet palms against the boy's face and throat.

"Want to try to stand?" he urged.

"Yes, sir."

Mose braced himself solidly and pulled Robert to his feet. For a moment the boy leaned helplessly against him. Robert stiffened his body and stepped feebly forward. "Let's go home," he mumbled.

They found the path leading down and took it, with Robert leaning heavily on his father. Behind them was the blackness of Reservoir Hill, before them Pleasant Valley, with its orange squares of lights from cabin windows.

Mose waited until they reached level ground. Then he asked, "What was it, son?"

"Wild grass. I never dragged on it before. I ought to a known better."

"Wild grass? What do you mean?"

"Wild marijuana. It's too strong. Oh, God, my head's splitting! I was feeling down in the dumps. Instead of taking three drags I took the whole stick. I started losing my eyesight and my head was blowing up. Then I got stone deaf. Couldn't hear a damned thing but my veins pounding in my body. I couldn't see a thing in the world but devils, hell, God, hot coals, needles——"

He stopped in the road, his body shaking, his hands grasping at air. Mose put both arms around him to hold him up.

"Oh, God!" Robert prayed. There was a wildness in his voice, a wildness in his eyes.

"Where'd you get it?" Mose demanded angrily.

"From one of them at Pepe's. A railroad spiker. I'm not blaming him. He told me it was wild. I didn't know it was so bad."

Mose thought of all the hours he had spent outside Pepe's looking for Robert. "You still go to Pepe's?" he asked.

"Ain't no other place."

"You don't sit out front with the others?"

"No, sir. Pepe's got a room for us."

"Who?"

"Me. My friends."

"Which friends?"

"Alan Carson. Some other white boys that likes blues. Sometimes some Mexicans to pick the guitar."

"Cenoria Davis?"

"She don't go there no more. She don't go nowhere no more."

"Why do you want to meet the white boys?"

"They're my friends. They understand me better 'n my colored friends do. We play music, listen to records—the kind of music I like."

"Like the music you were playing today?"

"Yes, sir."

"Where do you learn it?"

"You get to feeling right, it comes to you."

"Does marijuana help?"

"Right then it does."

"And afterwards?"

"Headaches—and a good-for-nothing let-down feeling."

"Doesn't hardly pay, does it?" Mose said kindly.

"No, sir."

Side by side they walked down the beginning of Mulberry Street, evening a glow over Reservoir Hill behind them.

"You're not backsliding from the church, are you, son?" Mose asked, his voice grieving, discouraged.

"No, sir. I don't know, sir."

"Stay close to the church, son. It'll always comfort you."

"Yes, sir," Robert replied bitterly. Then, after a few steps, he said, "Alan Carson cain't come to my church. I cain't go to his. Something's wrong somewhere."

"I know, son, but it's too big for us to right it—all at once. You've got to stick to your own color, and let him stick to his. It has to be that way down here."

Not yet ready to face Josie, they walked an extra block, passing cabins alive with humming voices, breathing air heavy with the smell of potatoes and onions frying in cottonseed oil. Mose knew that they had to talk more, that directing their talk lay with him.

"Son," he said thoughtfully, "you've been through a kind of hell tonight—not the hell of fire and brimstone Brother Simpson preached about, but a hell that burns inside you like a fire. It's a fire that never dies. It just burns and burns inside you. You take the weed today to give you ease from pain. Tomorrow you have to take more because the pain is greater. Do you see what I mean?"

"Yes, sir."

"You've got to stop the fire."

Robert's lips struggled with a question, but he remained silent.

"I'm not going to whip you," Mose said. "I'm not going to punish you at all. You're seventeen now—just about grown. You've got to make up your own mind to quit this way of doing."

"Yes, sir."

"Will you promise to stay away from Pepe's?"

"I'll try, sir."

"Will you promise to stay on this side of the tracks—stay away from white folks?"

"Do I have to do that? Cain't I see Alan? He's my best friend—the only one I can talk to."

"It's for the best. In this town, whites are whites and colored folks cheap as dirt. You can't cross the line to where they are. You can't get nothing but harm from trying. You're old enough to know that."

"Yes, sir."

Mose heard defiance in Robert's voice, felt that it was not against him but against Jim Crow.

They came to Mulberry Street again and turned toward home. A lamp was burning in the front room. They could see Josie in her white dress. She had her Bible and was leaning close to the lamp searching for a Scripture.

"I don't want to tell your mother about this," Mose said when they were already in the yard.

"All right, sir."

Mose stopped for a moment and caught Robert by the shoulders. He turned him until the lamp in the window shone on his face. His face was smooth, boyish again; the wild look had gone from his eyes. If they held their tongues, Josie need never suspect what he had been through.

"My son," Mose whispered, "promise me this won't happen again."

"I'll try, sir." With downcast eyes Robert followed Mose into the front room.

Josie turned from the Bible, a thick finger marking the place. "Where you been?"

"We went for a walk up Reservoir Hill," Mose answered.

"How come yo' shirt's in sich a mess?" she demanded.

"I got it wet in the branch," Mose lied uncomfortably.

"Well, it does look to me like you'd know how much washing and ironing I got to do. Don't never git through. And you come in looking like you'd been in with the pigs. Did you see John?"

"No. Where is he?"

"I sent him looking for you—along about dark."

Mose took off his shirt and hung it over a chair to dry. Robert took a chair near the piano, his back to Josie and the light.

"You look a mess," Josie complained. She tied a white head rag around her hair. "I got to go to meeting now. Supper's on the stove. Git whut you want, but don't forgit to cover it up when you all through."

With her Bible held like a lamp, Josie went out into the night. Mose could hear her walking down Mulberry Street singing, "I am a po' pilgrim . . . traveling through this unfriendly world." He sank into a chair and allowed her words to flow through the passages of his mind.

30

THE last song sung, the benediction sounded, Mose stood near the outdoor stage to shake hands with the people who filed by.

"Best exhibition I ever seen in Happy Hollow," they said. "The graduating class sho' done theirselves proud this time. Where's Robert? Ain't he passed?"

"I—I don't know," Mose stammered. "Yes, he passed."

That afternoon there had been a new blue suit on Robert's bed, a freshly signed diploma on Mose's desk. But Robert had skipped. "I ain't seen him a-tall," his classmates told Mose.

Lora Dixon looked at the diploma in Mose's hand. "I know how you feel," she said, "but they ain't no need for you to feel ashamed. You done what you could."

Mose hid his disappointment, his worry as well as he could from the people marching past. When the last had gone, he locked the schoolhouse and went home.

As he walked up Mulberry Street he heard singing at Sister Brackett's. Josie would not be home yet. "She could have gone to his graduation," he said bitterly. Things might be different if she had shown more interest.

He found the house dark, John in bed asleep, Robert and the blue suit gone. Not bothering to light a lamp, he sat down to wait.

Before the singing had ended at Sister Brackett's, Mose heard Robert step lightly on the porch and slip into the house.

"Son," he said, his voice held even.

"Yes, sir."

"You missed graduation."

"Yes, sir."

"Why?"

"I had to play for some friends."

"At Pepe's?"

"Yes, sir."

"You shouldn't have missed the graduation, presentation of diplomas——"

"I cain't see the difference. You can give me the diploma any time. I couldn't play for these friends any time——"

"Son," Mose interrupted, "you still want me to send you to college in September?"

"Yes, sir."

"Well, it does seem——"

Mose interrupted himself. Graduation had passed and Robert had missed it. Nothing he could say would change that. Whatever else he might say could make the gap between them wider.

"You'd better get some sleep," he said instead.

In June, workers began pouring concrete on the new addition to the schoolhouse. Hardly believing what he saw, Mose watched colored laborers, working under white foremen, level the ground, lay out the design, build forms for the concrete. The foremen, working on a rush job, using government money, hired two men for every one needed. Workers swarmed to the job. Idlers swarmed to watch the work go on.

Now they were pouring the great slab that made the first floor.

"They pouring the big slab," people said to one another on the streets. "They gonna finish, if'n it takes all night. Me, I'm gonna watch."

Pouring began at noon, with concrete mixers grinding, with wheelbarrows rattling on board runways. Whites came from Columbus to watch. John Carson came to talk with the foremen.

By nightfall great squares of concrete lay hardening in the hot night air. Still the men worked on, stripped to the waist, their bodies gleaming under hastily hung floodlights, their voices rising above the clatter of machine and gravel.

When Mose returned after supper he had to work his way through a crowd that stretched to the street.

"Let the Professor by," people shouted. "Let him see what a big schoolhouse we gonna have."

Mose tried to count the men with wheelbarrows, lost count, gave up trying to estimate the number of workers smoothing concrete and tending the mixers. You can do a heap with government money, he reminded himself.

The men with wheelbarrows, in the excitement of a big pour, ran back and forth like ants on plank runways. Man and wheelbarrow seemed one inseparable machine. The men sang to their wheelbarrows, talked to them, named them for their women, made love to them to please their women waiting in the crowd.

Mose listened to their words as the men passed by.

"Come on, Deecie, roll yo' wheel."

"Roll, baby, roll, like you rolled befo'."

"Got a jelly roll waiting when I come home."

"Ain't this heaven on earth for a wheelbarrow man."

Waiting on the side line, other men—the new shift coming on, men who had made love to these same wheelbarrows—watched jealously, shouted taunts at the way their wheelbarrows were handled.

"Look out, black boy, how you pushes my Lucy."

"Don't you worry none, Black Gal, papa's coming soon."

"Hey you, Sluefoot, don't you know how to roll a wheelbarrow?"

Raucous, profane, good-natured, the men went on with the pouring, doing their jobs well, pouring a part of themselves into the new schoolhouse addition for Happy Hollow.

Dr. Lewis pushed through the crowd to Mose. "I got another granny case," he said. "Say, this is going to be a good building!"

"It looks like it."

Mose followed Dr. Lewis around the job and back to his car.

Dr. Lewis sat behind the wheel thoughtfully studying the building scene. "We've come a long way," he said.

Mose looked at the lights making the whole prairie glow. "Yes, sir, I have to admit things look better for us—but one Negro's still got a mighty tough row to hoe in Oklahoma."

Dr. Lewis went back to his patient. Mose waited to watch the change of shifts. Then he walked up Mulberry Street alone.

Josie was sitting in the kitchen with a glass of clabber and a chunk of corn bread. He knew that she was waiting up for him, that she had something on her mind. He waited in the doorway for her to speak.

"Mose," she said, "you ack like you outta step with everybody. You not right with any side. You got too much pride. You been trying to put a lot of people straight, but you ain't he'ped yo'se'f— inside. I tell you, it's time you let God grab a-holt of you. He'll make you sing in tune."

She paused, waiting for him to speak, but he remained silent.

"You can go to bed if you want," she said, "but I'm going down on my knees right now and talk to God about you."

From his bed Mose could hear her mumbling, groping prayers. He listened for a time, and then resolutely shut them out.

31

ONE night Mose stopped Josie when she was leaving to go to Sister Brackett's, her robes freshly ironed, her finger at her passage in the Bible.

"Where's Robert?" he asked.

"I ain't a-knowing." Her lips were puffed out, her voice sullen. "He ain't never tell me where he goes."

"When did he go?"

"This e'ening. Right after you went off. Didn't he come to the schoolhouse?"

"I didn't see him. Where does he go all day? What does he do?"

"He ain't said, but he's always on the road to Columbus. He always make out he's got business over there."

"Has Sister Brackett seen him?"

"She has."

"What does she say?"

"She don't say much. She see him sometimes over in Columbus, playing the piano for white folks. He mostly be's at Miz Carson's, she say."

"Has he made any preparations to go down to Marshall?"

"I ain't seen none."

"Well, he's got only two weeks left."

"How come he's got to go to college? He ain't got no interest in it."

"We've been over that before."

"I disremembers most of whut you said."

"Well, he's got to have more than a high-school education if he's going to get ahead in Oklahoma, no matter what he decides to do. He's got to have more schooling than I can give him in Pleasant Valley."

"Hmph! Whut's all that schooling good for? We talked about him being a preacher. I say college ain't gonna make him a mite better preacher. I say he won't be as good. All it'll do is fill his head with big words and Popery. Take Sister Brackett. They ain't no better preacher nowhere 'n Sister Brackett. She ain't *never* been to school. It ain't schooling Robert needs, I'm here to tell you. Whut he needs is the call. He needs a good dost of the Holy Spirit. He needs the Holy Ghost to slap him down good and hard and then raise him up from the miry clay and set him on the solid rock of Christ Jesus. If'n he gits the call—"

"Josie——"

"—whut education he needs he can git on his knees at the moaner's bench. I know whut you want. You want him to follow yo' footsteps in Methodism. Well, I ain't gonna let him—not if I can he'p it. You done caused one of our boys to die. I ain't a-letting——"

"Josie, you can't say——"

"I can say whut I please. You see this Bible Book?" She held her Bible toward him. Its leather binding was worn and broken, its pages ragged from much reading. "This Bible you took in yo' own hand and flang agin the wall. That was blasphemy. Blasphemy's the unpardonable sin. You gotta pay for it, Mose—all the rest of yo' life you gotta pay for it. You lost one son on that debt. Hadn't a been for yo' blasphemy, Thomas'd be alive yet. . . . And God ain't thu with you, Mose. I tell you He ain't. Don't you think for a minute God's thu with you for yo' sin. Unless'n you repent, God's gonna punish you all yo' days—hallelujah, amen. Mose, it's time for you to repent and seek the true religion. It's time for you to cleanse yo'se'f of sin at the moaner's bench and seek the sanctification of the Spirit. It's time, oh, Lawd, it's time. . . . "

Josie lifted her arms above her head and began praying and shouting. Back and forth the length of the room she went. She shook her hands above her head. Her fingers, hanging loose in their joints, flapped limply against the low ceiling. Her feet took up a slow dance rhythm. As the rhythm became faster, the breaks more marked, she jerked her head to accent the syncopation.

"Lawd, have mercy on him," she prayed, her words keeping time with her feet. "Have mercy on him, and save him from the blight of sin. . . . Bring him back, King Jesus—bring him back to the light . . . bring him back to the fold. Forgive him, Precious Lawd, for departing from the path of the righteous. . . . Help him, oh, God, to give up the backsliding ways of Methodists. . . . Lead him, Sweet Saviour, to sanctification in the Holy Spirit. . . . "

Mose looked at Josie resignedly. Once she had started like that, she might go on till midnight, or till she fell in a trance. Unable to face her accusations, her pleas longer, he took his hat and left the house. Her voice followed him the length of Mulberry Street.

He passed the Methodist church, its doors and windows closed and dark, the steeple an indefinite whiteness. He passed Brother Simpson's house. A dim light showed through the kitchen window. Sister Daisy would be sitting alone by the lamp, grieving for her husband. Mose wished for the old man. He needed someone to hear his doubts and fears. He needed help to drive the feeling of guilt from his mind.

In his loneliness Mose took the road to Reservoir Hill. Slowly he climbed to the top of the ridge. From it he looked out over Pleasant Valley. He had sought gain; he had found loss. One son lay in the graveyard at the foot of the hill. Another was, God knew where, among the iniquities of Columbus.

He asked himself the old questions. Was Josie right? Had Thomas been taken to atone for his blasphemy? Was Robert to be wasted because of his weakness? Had he fallen into the error of blaming the whites for everything evil, as a way to escape his own responsibility?

Mose left Reservoir Hill and walked back to the graveyard. In the darkness he found Thomas' grave and stood by it a moment. But he found no answers there.

Pride. Blasphemy. Lust. The accusing finger had pointed to him. He cringed before the finger. Pride? Blasphemy? Lust? The questions whirled in his head and made the pain unbearable.

He left the graveyard and walked back through Happy Hollow. The sound of singing was in his ears—coming from Sister Brackett's church. They were singing "I'm Up on the Mountain and I Cain't Come Down"—singing it happily, confidently, full of peace, blessed assurance.

He crept through the dark streets toward the church. A bright light beamed through the open door, cutting the darkness like a knife. His feet edged forward through the sand, no longer moving at his will.

At last he stood on the doorsill and looked in. The people were singing, dancing, praying—caught together in a moment of spiritual and emotional union, work and worry gone from their faces, in their stead not resignation but happiness.

Josie, in her long white robe, led the singing and dancing. Her face was calm, trance-like, spiritually beautiful. "I'm up on the mountain and I cain't come down," she sang, as if the last leaden burden had been lifted.

Josie saw him and danced toward him, her face and arms lifted in supplication. Feeling his feet take up the rhythm, he stepped away from guilt, doubt, fear. Then they were singing and dancing side by side. "I'm sanctified and holy and I cain't come down," they sang, treading the floor together. Mose gave way first to tears and then to shouts that tore from his throat. As they whirled Josie clapped an off-beat rhythm. "Yes, Lawd, help him, Lawd," she prayed. The shouts changed from pain to exultation.

At last he danced toward the altar, where Sister Brackett, in her black robe, waited to receive him. Facing each other, they danced and clapped till Mose fell at her feet.

Mose came to in broad daylight in his own bed. Dr. Lewis was bending over him with cold packs for his forehead and throat. John was folding towels into packs and wringing them out in ice water. Robert was at the foot of the bed rubbing his feet and ankles.

"Mose?" Dr. Lewis asked. "Mose?"

"Yes, sir."

"You all right, Mose?"

Mose felt as if he had been in a long, deep sleep. He tried to recall what had happened, but areas of his mind seemed to be closed to thought.

"I'm all right."

"You had yourself a good shout."

Dr. Lewis was completely matter-of-fact in his statement, but his words made Mose cringe. His experience of the night before began to be clear in his mind.

"He out'n his trance?" Josie asked.

She came from the kitchen with a square of ice for the basin. She still had on her white robes, and her face was calm with peace and satisfaction.

"Yes. He's all right now. Can you get me a cup of coffee?"

"Yas, suh. Mose drinks his black. How you like it?"

"Black."

Josie put the ice in the basin and went to the kitchen. In a few minutes she returned with two mugs of coffee.

"It's het up," she apologized. "I ain't had no time to make fresh. You want biscuits and butter?"

"No. Just coffee. You go ahead and get your breakfast."

With Josie out of the room, Dr. Lewis drank his coffee and talked. "Mose," he said, "this has made me do some thinking about religion."

"Yes, sir."

"Man is by nature a religious animal. In the South white men have always believed in Christianity. They taught their black slaves Christianity. Because of their need for faith, the slaves accepted Christianity. White Southerners have made a strange thing of Christianity. White preachers repeat 'Suffer little children to come unto me,' meaning little *white* children. They'd be scandalized if a little colored child came. I needn't say this. You know this."

"Yes, sir."

"It's last night I want to talk about. The white conscience is troubled already. When they come to see the absurdity of a Jim Crow heaven, they'll see the absurdity of Jim Crow on earth. That's not the problem you met last night."

"No, sir."

"Christianity is based on a certain amount of emotion. It is natural for people to turn to religion in time of stress—of grief, fear. You went too far last night. You went to the kind of emotionalism that has upset generations of Southern whites and Negroes. It may not be bad in itself, but it leaves out thought. Without thought there can be no progress."

"I know, sir," Mose said humbly.

"I'm not blaming you. You've been through a lot. I'm only telling you. If strong Negroes give way to it, what happens to the others?"

Mose thought of the times he had put forth the same arguments. He saw them now with broader, deeper meaning and with greater sympathy for the Josies, the Sister Bracketts, the countless thousands who held onto emotionalism because they had nothing else.

"I'll try again," Mose said.

Josie came with a pot of coffee, but Dr. Lewis was ready to go.

"Keep him in bed a few days. He'll be all right." Dr. Lewis took his saddlebags and left.

Josie brought Mose his breakfast and made his bed comfortable, humming a spiritual while she worked. Mose could not recall when he'd seen her so happy.

"Sister Brackett's coming over, if you ain't minding."

Mose knew he had to speak at once. "I don't mind if she comes, but I'm still going to the Methodist church."

Josie sighed resignedly. "If you will, you will. I ain't a-stopping you. But I ain't wearied any more. I know you been sanctified, and the world cain't do you no harm."

32

ONE night Robert did not come home at all. It was the night before he was to leave for Marshall, and Mose waited up late for him, packing books, working out a budget. When Robert did not come, Mose went to bed, disappointed, disturbed. Josie came in toward midnight singing under her breath:

> "I been a-listening all the day long,
> Been listening all the night long,
> Been listening all the day long
> To hear some sinner pray...."

She took off her robes in the darkness and was soon sleeping. Mose quieted himself awhile by repeating the words of her spiritual.

> "Some say that John the Baptist
> Was nothing but a Jew,
> But the Holy Bible tells us
> That John was a preacher too...."

The words themselves became disturbing as he repeated them. He began wondering about the unknown singers who had put them together, the questions they had answered for themselves, the faith they had so completely accepted.

> "I know I been converted
> And I ain't gonna raise no alarm;
> My soul is anchored in Jesus,
> And the Devil cain't do me no harm...."

He lay in bed straining his ears for the sound of Robert coming up Mulberry Street. At three in the morning Robert still had not come. Unable to endure his anxiety inactively, Mose got up and dressed. He went over to Josie's bed and shook her.

"Josie," he called.

"Whut you want?" she asked impatiently.

"Robert's not home yet."

"He ain't? Whut time is it?"

"The clock just struck three."

"He sho' ought to a been in before now. Where'd he go?"

"I don't know. To Columbus I reckon. He seems to spend most of his time there lately. Did he say anything to you?"

"Nothing a-tall. He jest snuck off after he got his suitcases packed, without saying word one, like he's been a-doing. I said to myse'f then, 'He's traipsing off after white folks.'" She sat up in bed. "I ain't surprised none, seeing how you set yo'se'f to drive him away from home."

Josie got out of bed and threw a cloak over her nightgown. She sat in a straight chair and rocked back and forth. "You give him his money?" she asked.

"Yes—enough to buy his ticket."

"Uh-oh."

Mose opened the door and peered down Mulberry Street. The street was dark and still. "I'm going to look for him," he said.

"Go ahead—and when you find him, bring him and yo'se'f back to King Jesus. Ain't no other way to make him do right. Him going to college?" she said with scorn. "Him gonna be a great man? Git a lot of schooling——"

Mose took another look at Robert's bed. He looked at John sleeping peacefully in the same room. No need to wake John to ask about Robert. Their paths rarely crossed. They were strangers who slept in the same room, sometimes met at the same table.

Mose closed the door behind him and walked swiftly down Mulberry Street. The sand damp with dew, his shoes made hardly a sound. He passed Lora Dixon's and turned toward Columbus, his eyes drawn by the faint glow of town lights on the horizon. He walked past rows of houses, past junk yards, and came to the railroad tracks. He hesitated a moment, then walked down the tracks till he came to Mama Jo's. The house was dark except for a night light in the bathroom. He walked on past the row of houses where single women lived alone. They were all dark and silent. If Robert was in one of them, Mose had no way of knowing. He ventured as far as the railroad station and then turned back toward Pleasant Valley.

Slowly he retraced his steps in the damp sand, his mind on the two people with whom Robert seemed most involved—Cenoria Davis and Alan Carson. If he could find them, he might get some answer. He made up his mind that as soon as daylight came he would go to Lora Dixon's and talk to Cenoria Davis. Then in the morning he would go to Columbus to see Alan Carson—if Robert had not come home in the meantime.

He stopped at the Methodist church and sat for a few minutes on the steps, but could not rest. Its silence was worse than Josie's complaining. Again he walked the road to Columbus and stood before Mama Jo's, trying to know what lay beyond the dark walls, dark windows. If Robert should be there, bedded down with a tricky woman, who should bear the blame?

Driven, Mose walked toward Pleasant Valley again. Dawn sharpened the outline of Reservoir Hill before him. He went to Lora Dixon's house and tapped lightly.

"Who's that?" she called. "What you want?"

"Mose," he answered. "Mose Ingram. I want to see Cenoria Davis. I want to ask her about Robert. He hasn't come home yet—not all night."

The door opened and Lora Dixon stood behind the screen in her dust cap and wrapper. "I ain't heard Cenoria come home either."

"Where'd she go?"

"I ain't heard her say. She left right after dark. Let's see if she's in her room."

Lora struck a match to a kerosene lamp. It flared dimly in the half-light of the doorway, brighter on the narrow stairs. Mose stood outside the circle of light while Lora knocked. Getting no answer on her second rap, she opened the door. Mose waited for her "Come on in" and then stepped inside. The bed stood smooth, unmussed in a litter of papers and boxes and opened drawers.

Lora drew back a curtain in the corner of the room. "Her clo's is all gone!" she exclaimed.

"Didn't she say anything?" Mose asked, perplexed. "Nothing about leaving—or where she might go?"

"Nothing a-tall. I'd like to know myself where she went, and who went with her."

"Robert, I think," Mose said sadly. "I don't know who else."

"She cain't be gone far. It ain't but a week till school starts. She's got to be back for that."

"If it's what I think, she won't come back for that. I don't believe she'll ever come back here."

They went back to Lora's parlor. Gray light seeped through dust-gray curtains. Lora blew out the lamp and set it on a table. They faced each other helplessly for a moment; then Mose stepped outside and closed the door behind him.

When Mose got back home, Josie had a fire going in the kitchen stove and was beginning to mix biscuits for breakfast. Without holding back anything, Mose told her what he had learned.

"Ain't no more 'n I expected," she said angrily. With quick jerks she stripped biscuit dough from her fingers. With each jerk she heaped more blame on Mose's head.

When Mose went on the street again he saw Sister Brackett on her way to Columbus with a load of hominy. He stopped her and told her about Robert and Cenoria Davis.

"Ain't a-tall surprising," she said. But she did not stop to talk to him, to add her blame. She clucked her pony on toward Columbus.

During the morning Mose searched halfheartedly through Pleasant Valley for some word of Robert or Cenoria Davis, putting off as long as he could the visit to Columbus, when he would have to face John Carson and admit the turn Robert had taken.

Toward noon Mose saw Sister Brackett coming from Columbus at a trot. He had started down Mulberry Street, his mind made up to go to Columbus, but he went back to his front porch to wait. Only big news could bring Sister Brackett home in the morning, before she had made her noon meal in some white kitchen. Josie came out and stood on the steps.

Sister Brackett stopped in the street and climbed out of her buggy. Slowly, majestically, she walked toward the porch. At the steps, she drew herself to full height and boomed in her sermon voice, "He done pitched his tent toward Sodom."

"Who?"

"Robert."

"What's he done?" Josie wailed. "Is he in trouble?"

"He done pitched his tent toward Sodom, like the Good Book say. He done forsook the ways of the righteous and gone in the paths of the godless. He done——"

"Where is he?" Mose demanded, losing patience.

"On the way to Chicago, they say. They say him and Cenoria Davis went together—last night on the North train——"

"How do you know this?"

"Everybody working at the station know it. Some folks in Columbus knows too. Some white folks is asting 'How come?' about Mister Alan Carson. They asting how come he go to Chicago——"

"When did he go?"

"Nearly a month ago. Miz Carson kep' it from me, but today she come right out and said it. Mister Alan's living in Chicago. She pretend not to know everything, but she do. It's breaking her heart—Mister Alan taking up with niggers."

Sister Brackett paced back and forth in the sandy yard, extemporizing a sermon. "Chicago's a awful place. Ain't no town on the face of the earth as much like Sodom and Gomorrah. It's ten times wuss 'n Babylon. It's a place of whores and whoremongers. Yo' son done gone with the wuss slut of them all. Don't you look at me like that, Brother Mose. Cenoria Davis is a slut. They gone off together to meet a white whoremonger. It's awful. In all my pastoring, I ain't heard nothing as bad as this. Brother Mose, Sister Josie, ain't nothing but the hand of God gonna help now. We got to pray that the lamb'll be brought back to the fold—we got to pray now."

She knelt on the steps and let her voice roll through Happy Hollow. Josie knelt with her. Mose left them and went to his room. Thoughtfully he began selecting clothes for a long journey. Sister Brackett finished her praying and drove on home. Josie came to the room and found Mose packing his clothes in a worn suitcase.

"Where you going?" she demanded.

"To find Robert and bring him back."

"To Chicago?"

"To Chicago, if I have to."

"If you go, I'm going with you."

"It's a long hard trip."

"I ain't a-caring about that. It's my boy I'm a-caring about. Every step you go, I'm going with you. And if we find him, it'll be my voice that'll bring him back."

"We don't have enough money for two———"

"I ain't studying the money. When you git enough for two, we'll go."

Tired, despondent, Mose pushed the half-filled suitcase aside and started from the house.

Josie followed him to the porch. "When we going?" she nagged.

"Maybe Wednesday—maybe Thursday. I've got to get money for tickets. I've got to know where to look when we get there. Chicago's a big place. I've got to talk to Mister Carson, if he's not too high and mighty."

33

Having some thinking, some adjusting to do for himself, Mose went to the schoolhouse and sat alone in his new office. From the first floor he could hear the sound of carpenters sawing, hammering, of men clearing away the debris of building. In a few days their work would be finished. In a few days Mose would begin making it a school.

Mose was looking at the drying slopes of Reservoir Hill when John Carson stamped into the office.

"Good e'ening, Mister Carson," Mose said, rising.

"Hello, Mose. I wanted to see how the carpenters 're coming along—if the building'll be ready."

Mose, looking at him, knew that he had been driven to Happy Hollow by something else. At a casual glance, he seemed unchanged. His white hair was as carefully roached, his clothes as carefully kept. But his face looked worried, drawn about the mouth. His eyes darted restlessly, never fixing directly on Mose. Before, when Mose had first come to Columbus, John Carson had been a man with a firm belief in a fixed social order—based on Jim Crow and the Bible. All of a sudden that order had been disturbed, broken.

"Mose," he said when the silence had to be ended, "I've come to see you."

Mose waited. Carson was still unable to say why he had come.

"About Robert?" Mose asked.

"Yes. About Robert . . . and Alan. Mose, my son's gone. He's been gone nearly a month."

"Yes, sir, I heard. My son's gone too. He left last night."

"That's what they say. They say that light-colored schoolteacher went with him."

"That's what they say, sir."

John Carson at last brought himself to look Mose in the face. "My son's in Chicago," he said. "The agent says Robert and the schoolteacher bought tickets to Chicago last night."

"You reckon they'll see each other there?"

"God only knows. Alan's always been taken with your boy's playing. They might see each other sometime. It's the wench I'm worried about."

"The wench?"

"Cenoria Davis. It's her I'm worried about. Mose, you don't know what it's like for a white man to know his son has gone off with a nigger wench."

"I feel mighty bad about Robert, sir."

"I know you do."

"I had great hopes for him, same as you had for Mister Alan. I wanted him to get an education. He turned away from that a long time back, when he got so wound up in music. Now he's run away. I ought to have seen it coming. I ought to have guarded against this."

"Ain't much way of telling about such things ahead of time," John Carson said.

"I reckon not."

For a moment Mose had forgotten the troubled face of the white man. He suddenly felt compelled to apologize for Robert. "I'm sorry, sir, if Robert had anything to do with Mister Alan going off like this."

"I'm not blaming Robert, Mose. I'm mostly blaming myself. I ought to have known Alan was on the wrong track a long time ago, when he first got the jazz fever. I ought to have kept him at home—kept him away from Pepe's Tavern. You warned me, Mose, but I didn't believe anything like this would happen."

"You going to try to bring him back?"

"Not now, Mose. It won't do no good now. I'll wait till he gets short of money. Then maybe he'll talk sense. My God, I hope so!"

Mose waited for Carson to ask his plans. When the waiting turned to dead silence Mose spoke abruptly. "I'm going after Robert."

"You are?" The emphasis in his voice changed to relief, hope. Mose knew what he was thinking. In this case a Negro might accomplish more than a white man. "When?"

"When I get money for tickets."

"Your wife going too?"

"She wants to go so bad I can't leave her behind. She'd never get over it."

"How much you need?"

"A hundred dollars, sir, with what I have saved up. If I could draw that much on the deposit."

John Carson took out his wallet and counted out ten ten-dollar bills. Without looking at Mose, he handed over the money. "No strings attached to this, Mose," he said, his glance out the window, "except don't say anything about where you got it. Not even to Josie. In Oklahoma it's not right for a white man to be beholden to a nigger—and I am, no matter what you do with this money. I don't want folks to know I'm beholden to you."

Mose, sensing how deeply Carson's pride had been hurt, accepted the money without making any restrictions for himself. "Thank you, sir," he said humbly. "I won't tell anybody, and I'll do what I can."

"When do you expect to go?"

"Thursday, on the night train. That'll get me back in time for school to open."

"If you're a day or two late, that'll be all right. I'll see to that. You ought to get back as soon as you can. Folks'll talk, no matter what."

"We can't help that, sir."

With the air of a man who has done all he can for the moment, John Carson turned to go.

"Do you have Mister Alan's address?" Mose asked.

Carson took an envelope from his pocket addressed to Mrs. Carson. From it he copied an address on a scrap of paper.

Mose looked at it and then at John Carson. "That's on the South Side, in the Black Belt," he said.

"I know, Mose," Carson replied shortly.

The workmen had stopped for the day when they went downstairs.

"Mose," Carson said, "I hope you find them. I hope you can persuade them to come home. If your boy'll come, maybe Alan will too. I can't believe he'd stay up there with a nigger wench. I just can't believe it."

"It doesn't seem he would, sir."

At the door Carson stopped. "Mose," he said, as if the words were being dragged from him, "we seem bound up in this life together. It's funny. White man and colored man. It shouldn't be this way, not in Oklahoma, but it is. I've asked you to do me a great favor."

For a moment Mose thought that they would shake hands. But Carson was unsnapping a leather key case.

"I'll do the best I can, sir," Mose promised.

When John Carson stepped outside and walked stiffly toward his car, he was again the white School Board on a regular inspection trip.

34

WHEN Mose arrived at the station he remembered that he had not been on a train since he arrived in Columbus. In fact, he had not been away from Columbus at all. It had been a long time, measured by his experience, but brief indeed in terms of progress. Standing in the colored waiting room, he could see no new benefits at all—only a thicker layer of dirt on floor and benches, a sharper smell from the washrooms. Once he had stood there, the new principal of Phillis Wheatley School. So real it seemed that he could almost hear Frenchy calling, "Taxi? Taxi to Happy Hollow?" But what a distance lay between!

Josie was with him, and their minds were set ahead—to Chicago, to the problem of bringing Robert home. Josie sat on a bench in the waiting room, her flowing white robes carefully drawn around her, making a spectacle of herself, Mose thought. He had tried to persuade her not to wear the robe, but he might as well have saved his breath. Mose looked at the waiting people, saw that they barely noticed her.

Mose knew it would be different on the train, among people unfamiliar with her and Sister Brackett. A trainman checked their tickets at the coach, and then looked Josie up and down before he let them enter. With a suppressed "What a get-up!" he let them pass. Mose, embarrassed at the man's looks, words, hurried Josie to a seat at the front of the Jim Crow car. All along the aisle heads turned, people stared, but no one spoke to them. Josie sat down and wrapped the folds of her robe around her ankles. The train jerked to a start and she had to arrange herself all over again. She tried to look out the window, but it was a dirty black square.

"Sho' hot in here," she complained. "I don't think I can stand it."

Mose opened the window and let the cool night air blow in,

cooler and fresher as the train picked up speed. They both looked out at the lights of Happy Hollow as the train pulled away from town. Josie searched for the lights of their house, where John waited for them. Mose looked into the windows of Mama Jo's and the houses of the tricky women. Then they were on the black prairie, with only a light here and there on farm or ranch. Mose talked to Josie about "the North"—about what they might expect in Chicago, about Robert—anything to pass the time. But she kept her face to the window and remained impassive to all he said.

By the time the conductor called towns in Missouri, the through passengers to St. Louis had settled down in their seats to get what sleep they could.

"You better get some rest," Mose told Josie. "You going to be mighty tired when we get to Chicago."

She turned her face from the window, fixed her eyes on the blank wall before her and remained sitting rigidly upright. Sometimes her mumbled prayers lasted from one station to another. Sometimes she hummed a spiritual under her breath. Toward midnight Mose moved to a vacant seat across the aisle and let the train rock him to sleep.

When he woke, the train was hugging a ridge, over which the sun glowed white and hot. Josie brushed away crumbs dropped from her sandwich and drank a cup of water Mose brought her. She stood up, straightened her robes and spread a white cloth over her head.

"Where's the privy?" she demanded of Mose.

He pointed to the women's washroom at the other end of the coach—pointed over the heads of wide-awake, curious passengers.

Slowly, majestically as she could with the train lurching under her, Josie went down the aisle. Before her were rows of faces, colored faces, men, women, children. It was like church, with many people waiting to hear the Gospel. It was her duty to speak. She stopped and studied the faces near her. Nearest was an old woman in black, with a black bonnet tied tight, half hiding her face. Josie looked into the wrinkled face, the tired eyes.

"Is you a Christian?"

Her words became a chant, low and compelling. "Is you a Christian?"

"Yes, I'm a Christian."

"Praise the Lawd!"

Her song rose to a jump-up shout. Over and over she chanted, "Is you a Christian?" All down the coach people answered, "Yes, I'm a Christian," and together they sang "Praise the Lawd." A few failed to answer her, found themselves overlooked. The spell of a revival meeting was on them. It was broken only when the conductor called "St. Louis next stop" and Mose took Josie by the arm and led her from the coach.

With the help of a redcap they transferred to another train without going into the station. With her lunch box in one hand and her Bible in the other, Josie followed the redcap down a long ramp under the steel-strutted dome. The redcap stopped at their train and Josie went up the steps first, with Mose close behind her. She took a step forward and then turned on Mose.

"Go back," she hissed. "This the white folks' coach."

"Go on in," Mose urged her. "Whites and colored ride together from here on. Ain't no Jim Crow in Illinois."

He took her arm and forced her ahead of him along the aisle. As the passengers caught sight of her white robe, they nudged one another and whispered. Mose wished angrily that he had made her wear a dress, or stay at home. It was like a minstrel show, with him the butt of the joke. But Josie was not concerned with their laughter. She was too angry at being forced to ride with white trash. Mose hurried her, grumbling, to a seat. She straightened her robe and pulled the white cloth around her face like a veil.

"White trash," she whispered in a voice intended for the entire coach. "A carload of po' white trash——"

"They're not trash——"

"Yes, they is. Ain't no decent white folks gonna lower theirselves riding with niggers. Miss May say it, and I know it's the truth."

"Miss May never went up North."

"I ain't caring about that. She know right from wrong, let me tell you that. She know decent white folks ain't going around where niggers is, and decent niggers'll stay away from white folks unless'n they works for them. Miss May banks a heap on right doing."

"If it's double standard."

Mose pointed to the Mississippi River far below the train bridge. He explained that, no matter what existed from Memphis south, there was no Jim Crow across the Mississippi here. He took a timetable and pointed out the boundaries of Jim Crow. He told her that there was a different relationship between whites and colored where there was no Jim Crow. He showed her that her beliefs belonged to slavery times in Mississippi. But she refused to be convinced. Miss May had told her, and Miss May was right. After a while she refused to listen. She turned her face to the flat Illinois prairies and stared at the green-husked corn slipping past.

"Crops is late here," she said, ending all discussion.

It was late afternoon when they at last arrived at an old hotel in what had once been a fashionable part of the South Side. Now it was a rooming house and social club in a colored tenement area. Mose recalled it from his days in Chicago, recalled the taxis and limousines he had seen arriving for the midnight show. He recalled headlines of police raids, of girls arrested.

The doors were closed, the windows shuttered. He took Josie's arm and helped her up the marble steps. A doorman in green suit and cap opened the door to them and, after a hasty glance, ushered them through a dimly lighted lobby.

"What you want?" the man at the desk said without looking up.

"Alan Carson."

"Oh." The man looked up quickly. "Yes, sir. He resides here. You his friends?"

"We know him."

"He's at the club."

He nodded to the doorman, who led them through a back lobby. They passed through a hallway and came to a door, over which a sign glowed red and green: ORIGINAL BLACK AND TAN CLUB.

Another doorman, in white tie and tails, opened the door to them. He saw Josie and drew back. "Good God! What you want? This ain't no store-front church."

"We wants our boy," Josie said.

"He ain't here." He started to close the door, but Mose pushed inside and pulled Josie after him.

"We'll see," Mose said. "We'll ask Alan Carson. The desk man said he was here."

The man stepped aside. "Come on in. Any friend of Mister Carson's is welcome. Your boy play the piano?"

"Yes."

"He's here all right. He's back there."

The man led them past the bar to a back room so dim that at first they could distinguish forms but not faces. Someone was playing blues on the piano. Mose remembered the afternoon he had followed Robert to Reservoir Hill. He remembered the beat of the music, the sight of a face tortured by pain. The tune, the rhythm were the same.

A voice took up the slow beat:

> "Ain't gonna raise no mo' cotton crop,
> Now I'll tell you why I say so——"

"Robert!" Josie yelled above the music.

She ran past dancing couples and threw her arms around him. She bent low over him, almost hiding him in her robes. She pulled his head against her bosom and cried, laughed, crooned baby words. He stopped singing, but his hands kept moving, as if he could not stop the rhythm.

The dancers, trance-like, circled the floor. Mose saw Alan Carson and Cenoria Davis among them, her hand dark against his, her hair falling on his neck and shoulder.

"You!" Robert said to Josie, the word an accent in the rhythm. And to Mose: "You, too." His fingers lingered on a chord. "You were bound to come."

"Yes, we were bound to come."

"I'm not bound to talk to you."

His voice was shrill, his eyes wide, staring. He jerked away from Josie and stood up, leaving the chord unfinished, hanging. The dancers, stopped in awkward poses, stared. He heard a woman laugh. They were making fun of him because of his down-home folks. He started toward a side exit.

"Son!" Mose said angrily, to stop him. He grabbed Robert's arm and jerked him back.

Robert strained toward the door. "Cain't you let me alone?"

Mose released his grip and lowered his voice. "Son, we've got to talk to you."

Robert felt Josie's hand on his shoulder and shrugged it off. "Then talk and get it over with. I'm paid to play."

He looked about the room. Then he walked to a corner table, where Alan Carson and Cenoria Davis waited. The dancers shrank back, but eyed them covertly. Josie gasped and put her hand to her mouth when she saw Alan and Cenoria. "White trash."

Robert paused before them. "My folks've come," he said. "To take me back. I ain't going——"

Mose interrupted. "How're you, Mister Alan? How're you, Miss Cenoria?"

Alan stood up. Cenoria nodded slightly. Alan, flushed, embarrassed, pulled chairs up for Mose and Josie.

"I ain't a-setting down here, Mister Alan," Josie said scornfully. "I ain't never set at table with white folks, and I ain't starting here." She swept three glasses from the table. "Ain't gonna be no boozing while I'm around," she cried.

She watched a mixed group of white and colored, men and women, take a table near them. "Never thought I'd live to see the day," she said, loud enough for them to hear. Then she turned to Robert. "Robert, you been drinking. Yo' breath's strong enough to knock a man down. You all been drinking. God pity you po' sinners. You all on the road to hell fas' as you can go. But you ain't going if'n I can he'p it. I'm here to set you on the straight and narrow before it's too late, hallelujah!"

She stopped and looked around the room. The people stared back self-consciously. "I'm talking to every last one o' you," she shouted.

She shook her fist in their faces and threatened them with hell-fire and brimstone. "What kind o' place you call this?" she demanded.

They shifted silently.

"Ain't make no difference what you calls it, it's black with sin and iniquity." She looked around again. "Sho' dark in here. You folks scaid o' light? It's worse 'n Sodom and Gomorrah—worse 'n Babylon. I ain't never seen a place befo' where niggers and po' white——"

She stopped and looked straight at Alan Carson. He stared back without flinching. She caught her breath. Miss May had not prepared her for this. "I ain't never seen a place where all kinds o' folks sets down together. It's sinful for whites and blacks to mix up together."

"How come?" Cenoria Davis spoke, her voice cold and sharp.

"Miss May say so," Josie snapped. "She say so, and I sho' nuff believe her."

She stopped for breath. Then she turned to Robert, commanding, entreating. "Robert, baby, you coming home with me right now. You hear me?"

"I'm not. I'm never going down home again—long as I live. I'm here and I'm going to stay."

Josie sank to her knees and raised her hands. "Pray to God, son," she implored. "Ast Him to set yo' feet in the right way. You used to be a good boy and go to Sister Brackett's. You give it up. I don't know why, but you give it up. It wus wrong to give it up. God's waiting. Ain't nothing wrong He cain't he'p. He's waiting to take yo' feet out'n the miry clay. . . ."

Her words changed to a prayer, soft and pleading. People who had laughed at her became silent, not knowing what to do. Robert stood unyielding, his eyes hard, feverish.

Mose knew he had to speak now, if ever. Earnestly he began. "Son, do you remember the day I followed you up Reservoir Hill? You told me you'd never touch the weed again. You broke your promise. I know it from the sound of your music, the look in your eyes."

"Why not?" Robert shouted. "I've had promises broken myself. You're goddamned right——"

At the oath Josie got to her feet, crying, her whole body shaking with sobs. Cenoria went to her and tried to support her. "Sister," Cenoria said soothingly.

Josie pushed her away. "Ain't nobody like you gonna 'Sister' me."

With a shrug Cenoria went back to her chair.

Robert looked at Alan and Cenoria, and then at the circle of faces glowing light and dark in the dim lights.

"We have to take it." His voice was calmer, but the hurt, the bitterness made Mose want to take him by the hand like a child and lead him away.

Alan Carson stepped between them. "Mose, you ought to go," he said gently. "This isn't doing anybody any good. Not now."

But Mose was not yet ready to give up. "Robert," he said, "you don't make it any easier running away. Not to this. You ought to go back to Columbus and hold your head high———"

"No!" Robert shouted. "My friends———"

"Yes, where'd I go?" Cenoria interrupted. "There's no place for me down there—not like this." She pointed to the people around them. "Look at them. No two alike. Nobody can look down on anybody else where it's like that."

"You've got a place, back home," Mose said persuadingly. "You've got your job."

"You know what it's like for me down there. I can't trust nobody." Her voice became accusing. "I can't even trust you—no more."

Mose looked at Josie and Robert and knew that they understood what Cenoria meant. But there was nothing he could say. How could they understand that he had paid for his weakness many times over?

"I won't put up with it," Cenoria continued. "My place is here. Our minds run alike. No matter what you say, I won't go back to Oklahoma."

She left them and went over to the piano. Her agitated fingers formed a few broken chords. Mose looked at Robert and knew it was time for him and Josie to go. He took Robert's hand.

"You won't come home?"

"No, sir."

"You could go to school—anywhere——"

"I don't want to. School won't get me over the way I feel. I tried Mama's way, I tried yours. Now I got my own. You've got to leave me to it."

Josie put her arms around him. "Robert——"

The doorman interrupted her. "Let's have some music," he said to Robert. To the bartender he said, "Drinks all round. On the house."

Robert looked at Mose and Josie. "I've got to work," he said.

He went to the piano and took up the same blues tunes. Glass tinkled. Couples moved out on the floor again.

Robert played the melody through once and then began singing

> "Ain't gonna raise no mo' cotton crop,
> Now I'll tell you why I say so,
> Says you work so hard the whole year round
> And cotton prices be so doggoned low...."

Mose, with all the gentleness in him, took Josie by the arm and led her out the side door into the glare of daylight. Alan Carson held the door open for them to pass through. On the sidewalk he took Mose's hand. Suddenly Mose understood how deeply a white man might hate Jim Crow. In the strained face he saw the power of the white man's conscience.

"What do I tell your father?" Mose asked him.

"Whatever you think best." He shrugged and turned away.

Mose hurried Josie down the street to the elevated. Without looking back at the hotel and club, they climbed the stairs and got on a train. They found a seat and squeezed in between colored people who stared at Josie's robe, her grief-washed face. Before they reached the Loop, her grief turned to anger, first at Robert and then at Mose.

"He's lost," she moaned. "Lost to a whore of Babylon. Say whut you will, Cenoria Davis is a whore of Babylon. She taken you in. Now she's taken Robert. I knowed all along you wus having truck with her. I ain't a-minding that now. I ain't a-minding it if'n you git mixed up with a tricky woman yo'se'f. I am a-minding the example you set for our boys. Like I tell you, Robert's lost—bound for *e*ternal tarnation—and nobody to blame but you."

Her voice grew louder, her tone more accusing. People the length of the coach stared at them. A white man left his seat and hung on a strap near them, curious, amused. Mose, knowing well the power of her tongue, tried to stop her, but she would not be stopped.

"Since the day we left Mississippi," she raged, "I been moaning for whut you a-making out'n our children. You say you gonna educate them, and you did. Whut's it got them? Or you? I ask you. I'm telling you whut I told you before: Ain't nothing wuss 'n education for colored folks."

The white man took a pad from his pocket and boldly took notes. Mose stared at him resentfully. Josie kept talking. "You say you gonna make big Methodists out'n them. Hmph! You ain't made Christians out'n them yet. Now look whut you got. Thomas is dead—killed in cold blood by a white man. Robert's gone off and ain't a-coming back. He ain't never gonna be good to himself or nobody else. You still got John. He's nice and study. You better watch yo'se'f or you ain't gonna have him long. Like I said to Sister Brackett, a man ain't got no business fathering children unless'n he's gonna bring them up in the way they ought to go. Trouble with you, Mose, is you got yo'se'f so educated you don't know the right way. You lost yo' own, blaspheming the Book, fuddling with a tricky woman. How can you set yo'se'f up to lead them?"

Mose took up in his own mind the question she had asked him: the question of himself. Her voice ran down to a mumbling, complaining monotone. Mose lost the thread of her talk in his own questionings.

Back at the station, with time to wait for the train, Mose thought of the university, of his pleasant summers there. He thought of Professor Thompson and his encouraging talks. He worked himself into believing that some of his questions could be answered at the university. Hesitatingly he suggested to Josie that they visit where he had gone to school.

"No, you go ahead," she told him. "I ain't a-caring none where you go—jest so's you git back here by traintime. I wants to git on it and go back home. I done had enough enduring this place up here. I wants to go back where I come from. This ain't no place for a nigger like me."

Mose found a seat for her near the women's waiting room. He left her rocking back and forth, singing.

> "I know my robe's going to fit me well,
> I'm going to lay down my heavy load;
> I tried it on at the gates of hell,
> I'm going to lay down my heavy load...."

On the campus, Mose felt strange and self-conscious. The years had made little difference in buildings and grounds, but they had changed him, they had scarred him. Shyly he looked at the faces of students and professors—all strange faces.

He crossed the broad green campus toward the Philosophy Building, standing just as he had remembered it, cold and classical under the great elms. Professor Thompson's office was in a basement corner, shaded by elm trees. Mose saw a light—knew the Professor was there as he had been in the old days, in his hour set aside for callers. Mose saw again clearly the times when he had sat in that office with the Professor, singing spirituals, reading poems, talking of how Negroes should face their problems.

Suddenly Mose knew that Professor Thompson had been wrong —hopelessly, dangerously wrong—not because he was vicious in himself but because he did not understand; he could not get the Negro point of view. All he had said then was made false by the wrong point of view. Whatever he said now would be false, because he did not, could not know what being a Negro meant in Columbus and Happy Hollow.

Without realizing he had turned, Mose found himself across the campus walking toward the elevated station, without having knocked at Professor Thompson's door.

At the station again, Mose sat with Josie, who interrupted her humming to say, "Po' Miz Carson. How's she gonna feel when she know Mister Alan's in the sin line with Cenoria Davis?"

35

TIRED and dirty, heavy-eyed from lack of sleep, Mose and Josie got off the train in Columbus and walked directly through the colored waiting room. On the street they found Sister Brackett waiting for them, holding her pony by the bridle. Mose found her face friendly, comforting.

"Good morning, Brother. Good morning, Sister," she called to them. "I had a mind you all'd come this morning, so I jest waited over here."

People passing by smiled to see the two women, one in white, the other in black, embracing.

"How's John?" Mose asked when their greeting was over.

"He all right. I seen him this morning going over to janitor for Doctor Lewis."

Mose could see curiosity big in Sister Brackett's eyes, could phrase the questions she was eager to ask—about Robert, Cenoria Davis, Alan Carson. They were questions she would ask Josie.

"They's room for you to ride home with me, Sister," she said to Josie.

"Thank you, Sister. I don't mind if I does. My legs sho' ache after that train trip."

She climbed up over the wheel and eased down beside Sister Brackett. Both women tucked their robes around their feet.

"Sister Brackett," Mose asked, "you going to Columbus today?"

"I'm figuring on it. Why?"

"You might say to the white folks that we've come home."

"Is that all?"

"That's all. We've come home."

That was enough, Mose knew, for her to carry the word to John Carson.

Mose watched the buggy cross the tracks toward Happy Hollow. Then he started over the same road on foot, walking slowly, still feeling the burden of questions he could not answer.

He passed in front of the pool hall, where a group of men had gathered on the porch to shelter themselves from the sun. They were laughing when he came near, full, hearty laughter, but they stopped stone-still and waited for him to pass.

"Good morning, Professor," they said to him.

Mose knew the questions that burned them. He knew that they had guessed the truth, or near it, about Robert and Cenoria Davis. But they left their questions unasked.

When Mose had passed he heard a gruff remark, but could not understand the words.

"Hush yo' mouth, boy," he heard a man say. "White folks ain't gonna like no talk like that."

Knowing that his own place in Happy Hollow would be different from now on, Mose walked out of hearing.

Mose waited at the schoolhouse for John Carson to come. He walked through the wide rooms, the locker-lined corridors. The workers had finished; the building was ready for school to open— the best Negro schoolhouse in Oklahoma, Mose felt sure. But everything was strange, unfamiliar.

In the late afternoon John Carson stopped his car in front of the schoolhouse. Mose met him at the door, acknowledged his abrupt greeting. Silently they walked through a long corridor, up polished concrete stairs, to Mose's office. There they turned and faced each other.

"Did you see them?" John Carson asked.

"Yes, sir. In Chicago. At a social club."

"Wouldn't they come back?"

"No, sir."

"What'd they say?"

"Robert said he'd never come back to Oklahoma as long as he lives. He said he couldn't stand it any longer. He said he couldn't stand being down South any longer. I don't think he'll ever come back."

"What'd Alan say?"

"About the same thing. He said he couldn't get any pleasure living in Oklahoma."

"Is that yaller wench with them?"

"Cenoria Davis? Yes, sir, she is."

"Are they living together?"

"Who?"

"Alan and that nigger wench."

"I don't know, sir. They might be. I just can't say. Mister Alan stays at a hotel. They were in a club at the hotel. They all hang out there together."

"Is Alan sleeping with her?"

"I don't know——"

"What do you think?"

"I can't say, sir. Maybe he is, maybe he isn't."

"Goddamn it, you didn't find out much, did you?" Carson's face flushed with rage, with defeat.

"I found out they won't come back. Not any of them. I found out they're drinking a lot, smoking marijuana. That's a lot, sir."

"Yes, that's a hell of a lot. God, what a mess! My son living with niggers. It'll kill his mother."

"We don't feel so good about Robert," Mose reminded him.

"I know, but he's a nigger. Folks don't expect much from a nigger. But my son—Alan Carson. I can't understand what's got into him."

"It's not that whites and colored are living together," Mose said with a mild show of spirit. "It's the kind of life they're living that worries me."

John Carson studied Mose's statement for a moment, then rejected it with an impatient shrug.

"What're you going to do?" Mose asked him.

"What am I going to do? I'm going to get the law on him right now. If I can't keep him away from niggers myself, I'll have the law do it. I'll tell them to bring Robert back too. You want him brought back, don't you?"

"No," Mose said quietly, "not by the law. He'd never do what I want him to if he did come back. There were too many things against me. Now he's chosen his own way, and I don't think any amount of persuasion would change him. I'm afraid it'll be the same with Mister Alan——"

"I'll be goddamned if it will! Not while I'm alive to stop it. Not while there's a string I can pull."

He stamped out of the office and down the stairs. Mose followed him quietly. When Carson got to the front door, he turned, his face blazing with anger. "You keep your goddamned mouth shut about what you've seen," he roared. "I'm not going to have every black son of a bitch in Happy Hollow making jokes about my son. You hear that?"

"Yes, sir."

"If you don't, I'll fire you so fast it'll make your head swim. I'll have you driven out of town with a blacksnake whip."

"Yes, sir."

He went to his car and raced the motor violently. Colored people passing on the streets looked at him briefly and went on, their faces set, emotionless. Mose knew that they were already enjoying laughs at the sorry turn the white man's son had given him.

Carson shut off the motor and came back to the schoolhouse. "Mose," he said, "this thing's getting me. Everything seems turned upside down. I don't know what to make of it. What do you think makes them act like that?"

"I don't know, sir. It may be some folks down here are tired of Jim Crow."

All pride gone from his face, his bearing, John Carson stood in the doorway of the schoolhouse he had built. "Whatever it is, Mose," he said resignedly, "we haven't the power to change it."

In the evening Mose sat alone on his front steps. Josie had gone to Sister Brackett's. John was at school unpacking a shipment of supplies. "It do beat all how that boy wants to study," Josie had said on her way out.

One to grow! Her words had set Mose to thinking of the old saying. It seemed to be turning out as Sister Brackett had prophesied. Mose mused on her prophecy, considering not the faith but the irony.

A car came up Mulberry Street and stopped before his door. It was Dr. Lewis, driving alone in his old car. He got out and walked along the path between Josie's flower beds to where Mose waited.

"Good evening, Mose," he said. He held out his hand and Mose felt hard sinews in his grip.

"E'ening, Doctor. Good of you to come."

"Mind if I sit and talk?"

"Not at all. Not at all. Come on in."

"No, no chair. This is good enough."

Dr. Lewis sat on the edge of the porch and leaned against a post. Mose could barely make out the outlines of his thin face, his ragged hair in the glow of the lights of Happy Hollow. Seeing how at ease the doctor was, Mose felt his own tenseness relaxing.

"John Carson came to my office this afternoon," Dr. Lewis said, getting to the reason for his visit immediately. "He's cut up about this whole business."

"I know, sir. He looked today like it would kill him."

"It won't kill him, Mose. It won't kill you either. It'll hurt you worse than it does him, but it won't kill you. Might help both of you, if you'd let it. That's why I came to talk to you. I'm an outsider, Mose. Maybe I can see this thing clearer than either of you. John Carson was brought up in the belief that God ordained segregation, that through Ham the mark was set on the Negro. He was brought up to believe that any violation of segregation is a sin. In his eyes Alan committed a greater sin breaking the laws of segregation with Cenoria Davis than he did living with her in adultery— if he is living with her. It's a worse blow to his pride. He knows it'll get out. He can't help people knowing his son went off with a high-brown wench. He knows the whisperings and snickering that'll go on behind his back."

He paused a moment as if listening to the sounds that made the pulse of Happy Hollow. "Mose," he began again, "you know a little of what he feels. You were also brought up in the tradition of segregation—on the other side of the line. He can't help looking at the whole thing emotionally. Neither can you. It has been an emotional problem since the day the first slave set foot on American soil. Jim Crow has been kept alive by appeals to the emotions. You know what I mean, Mose?"

"Yes, sir."

"For you, what has happened is not a sin, though the loss is just as great."

"No, sir, it's not a sin. It's a waste of life, talent, hope."

"I know, Mose. It's a terrible price we pay in Oklahoma for the privilege of segregation."

Mose stood up and paced the sandy path. "How long will it last?" he asked. "How long?"

"God only knows. Ten years, twenty, fifty—maybe even a hundred before people understand what it does to them economically, mentally, spiritually. But it has to go. Not all the John Carsons in the world can hold it back."

"He's not the worst."

"No, he's far from the worst."

"I talked with John Carson a long time trying to help him understand. He's still bitter, but he agreed to come to talk to you tomorrow. It'll be a hard thing for him to do, but he said he'd come."

He took Mose's hand and then drove down Mulberry Street.

Mose was alone in his office when John Carson arrived the next morning.

"I had to come back to talk to you, Mose," he began at once. "I have to get things settled in my mind. Last night I was all set to quit the School Board, to let somebody else see what he could make of the situation we've got here. Now I don't know. I used to think I understood colored people. I used to think I knew all about them. I was raised with them. A colored woman nigh about raised me. Now I'm not sure I understand anything at all about them."

He paused uncertainly. His troubled eyes looked past Mose. His sagging, sun-red face seemed weak, old, tired.

"Colored people always have to understand more about whites than whites do about colored," Mose said quietly. "It pays them to. It's like a dog and his master. The dog always knows more about his master than a master knows about his dog. I can show you how it is. When the master comes home at night the dog runs out to meet him. One night he sees a look that makes him jump up on him and paw and lick him. The master says, 'You're a good dog. Here's a bone.' That might happen two or three days in a row. But one night the dog takes a good look. He sees his master is in an ugly mood, so he cringes down on his belly and slinks out of sight. Colored people have to be like that. They have to study the mood of the white man."

"Is that true in Columbus, Mose?"

"It's true in Columbus, sir."

"Then I never understood how things were at all. We always took pride in the things we did for our colored people. We built this school. We helped build your church. Has it all been wrong?"

"No, sir. A lot of it has been right. It's just hard for us to see the right when there's been so much wrong."

"I'm beginning to understand, Mose." John Carson started toward the door and then turned back. "Mose," he said sadly, "I got Alan on the telephone last night. You were right. He's not coming back. He won't ever come back."

"I'm sorry, sir."

"My loss is no greater than yours." He turned again toward the door and Mose walked with him. "All set to start tomorrow?" Carson asked.

"I think so. Not all the teachers have come, but they should be in before morning."

"What time are the opening exercises?"

"Ten o'clock."

"I'll come over. We've got to get the new year started off right."

"Yes, sir."

Mose held the car door open and John Carson climbed in behind the wheel.

"Sir," Mose said, "I wanted to talk to you about the money—the money you let me have to go to Chicago."

"Oh, yes, Mose, I forgot. I had something to say on the matter. Mose, I've made up my mind to let you have the house. I don't want you to pay back the money I let you have then. I'll count that the down payment on the house. You can pay it out by the month. Mister Brown will fix up the notes. You go by the bank and sign them first time you're in town. All right?"

"Yes, sir. Thank you, sir."

"See that you take good care of it."

"I will, sir. My wife'll be thankful to you, sir. She's always wanted her own place."

"That's all right, Mose."

As if afraid of showing too much feeling or of having the moment become embarrassing, John Carson roared his motor and drove down the sandy road toward Columbus.

Mose watched the car through a cloud of dust. "Like Miss May would say, 'He's folks,'" he said softly to himself.

36

Mose lingered late in his office. He looked again at the stack of report cards ready for registration. Today they were blank cards. Tomorrow they would represent boys and girls, names and faces, the countless human problems of a school principal. Today the building was quiet, and a dull brown in color. Tomorrow the quiet would be broken by tramping feet and children's voices; the dull brown would be a background for gingham checks and red hair ribbons and the blue of new denim. Mose found himself looking to the first day of school with quiet pleasure.

He went through all the building for one final look. The old part was much as it had been when he first came to Columbus. He went from it to the new addition. He stopped in the room set aside for homemaking. Fannie Mae Williams now had the best school equipment money could buy. She had stoves and sinks and cabinets. She had sewing machines, sewing tables, dress forms. She had a new assistant, a specialist in training girls to be better homemakers and mothers. They would still teach maiding, but the emphasis would be on the development of women rather than servants. Mose stopped to consider the corner set aside for child care. He tried to estimate the effect ten years of this kind of teaching would have in Happy Hollow.

Next he went to a large room divided by a glass partition. In one side there were twenty typewriters hooded with dust covers. In the other, desks, blackboards, charts. One teacher could set a typing class to work and then teach another class shorthand and general business subjects. There was still not a single job for a

Negro stenographer in Columbus, Mose knew, but things could change.

He came to the general-science laboratory. This was Dr. Lewis' special project. "This is a scientific age," he had argued before the School Board. "We've got to prepare Negroes as well as whites to live in it. You've got labs in the white schools. We'll start with general science this year. Then we can think about adding chemistry and physics."

Mose heard a noise in the storeroom. John was still working, getting supplies ready for the opening of school. Mose looked at the row of desks, each with its Bunsen burner, hot and cold water faucets, electrical connections. Then he went to the storeroom. John was polishing bottles of chemicals and setting them in rows. He had stripped to the waist, and sweat glistened on his dark skin, sharpening the outline of bone and muscle.

"Look nice?" he asked, pointing to the rows of bottles.

"It looks mighty nice. You work it out yourself?"

"Partly. Mostly I followed the chart they sent with the stuff."

He held a chart up for Mose to see. For a moment they stood side by side studying the chart. Mose was aware of how John had grown, almost to his own height. He was aware also of the eagerness in the boy's look, the gentleness in his manner. He put the chart aside and let his hand rest lightly around the boy's hips.

"You're a good boy, son," he said quietly. "I'm mighty proud of you."

John turned to arranging the last of the flasks. "It's going to be a good year," he said.

"Yes, son, in spite of everything, it's going to be a good year."

They walked out of the storeroom and John locked the door. Then they walked together to the corridor that connected the new wing with the old.

"You'd better get along home," Mose said to him, "and help your mammy. I'll be there directly."

As he made a final tour of the building and locked up for the night, Mose reflected on the year before him. He had to make it a good year. He was grateful that John would be with him. For this year they would be together, working together. It was a good prospect.

Mose made his way across Happy Hollow. He paused for a moment at the Methodist church. He passed the picture show and saw by the billboards that a new Western would show on Wednesday. He met people who bowed to him and said, "E'ening, Professor. How you feeling?" He met Sister Brackett on her way home from Columbus. "E'ening, Sister," he said. "E'ening, Brother," she replied, and passed on.

He saw Lora Dixon's boardinghouse and remembered that he had to arrange accommodations for a teacher arriving on the night train. He walked across the road. As he walked he watched a white man in a car on the road from Columbus. He seemed to be asking information of Negroes coming along the road with their totin's under their arms.

Lora Dixon came to the steps and talked to Mose. "Yes, suh, I got a room ready," she said. "Seems like I cain't study nothing but taking care of new teachers."

The white man drove slowly along the street. At last he stopped in front of Lora Dixon's and got out.

"You know where a nigra named Zack lives?" he asked Mose and Lora.

At the word *nigra* Lora gave Mose a quick look and then stared across Happy Hollow. The one word and the tone of his voice had marked his kind.

"You say Zack?" Lora asked.

The man studied a folder of papers in his hand. "That's right. My directions say he lives in the middle of Happy Hollow. He hauls and peddles. I asked a lot of people but nobody seems to know him."

Lora kept her eyes fixed on some spot on Reservoir Hill. Mose waited. The man shuffled nervously through his papers.

"What kind o' business you got with this Zack?" Lora asked.

"I'm an insurance collector. My records show he ain't paid up in eleven weeks. I just been assigned to this area."

Mose and Lora waited till the man returned his papers to the folder.

"No, I ain't know no Zack like that," Lora said in a shrill whine. "You might try some o' the folks back to'ads town."

The man turned his car around in the road and drove back toward Columbus, asking at each house as he went. For a moment Lora looked as if she had brushed away a fly. She and Mose laughed understandingly with each other. Then she asked, "You ready for the opening?"

"Yes. Teachers and children will assemble in their classrooms first. At ten they will march to the auditorium. We've got the School Board coming. Doctor Lewis will give the main talk. After that, teachers will open their classrooms for visitors to pass through and see what's been done."

Mose turned to go.

"I got something to say to you, Mose Ingram," Lora burst out. Mose faced her again, looking up into her eyes. "Mose, you done a good job in Happy Hollow. And you done it without being no handkerchiefhead. I stood up for you in the beginning, and I'm standing up for you now."

Mose took her hand. "Thank you, Lora. You're a great help."

He left her and went up Mulberry Street home. He stepped off the sandy road and onto land he owned. He stepped across the porch and stood under his own rooftree.

Josie was in the middle room getting the beds ready for the night. She was in her white robes. "Make haste, John," she was saying, "and git supper on the table. Prayer meeting'll be starting directly."

Mose crossed the room and stood before her. He put his hands on her arms and they stood breast to breast. "I bought the house," he said quietly.

"You what?"

"I bought the house."

"Well, glory be!" she cried. "I prayed we'd set our feet to rest someday. I prayed to stay right here till the day I die. Now the Lawd's answered my prayers." She held Mose's hands for a moment and then released them while she tramped about the room. She danced back and faced Mose. "How come he sell the house?" she demanded.

"I don't know."

"It ain't got nothing to do with whut we seen in Chicago?"

"I don't know. Maybe."

"Well, it don't matter, long as we got the house."

For the first time since Robert left they sat down to a meal together. Mose asked a blessing. Josie added her amen. They talked of the house and the improvements they would make on it. They talked of the opening of school and of the changes that had been made in Happy Hollow. They did not mention Thomas and Robert. They all seemed to be striving to put the past behind them.

After supper Josie went off to Sister Brackett's. John cleared a space on the table and laid out the new textbooks in general science. Mose took a chair to the front porch and, shirtless and barefoot, sat looking at the lights, hearing the sounds of Happy Hollow. There was laughter at the pool hall and a banjo playing on the porch at Lora Dixon's. Singing started at Sister Brackett's. A woman's voice, high and thin, wailed, "I am a po' pilgrim, traveling through this unfriendly world. . . . "

Mose pondered her words as he pondered the complexities of life in Happy Hollow.

"My people are a happy people, a talented people, a religious people," he said to himself in the darkness. "They have the strength of great faith, the weakness of deep superstition. They have pride, humility, human understanding. They have come a long way since the days of slavery. They have the will to move ahead. God grant me strength to go with them."

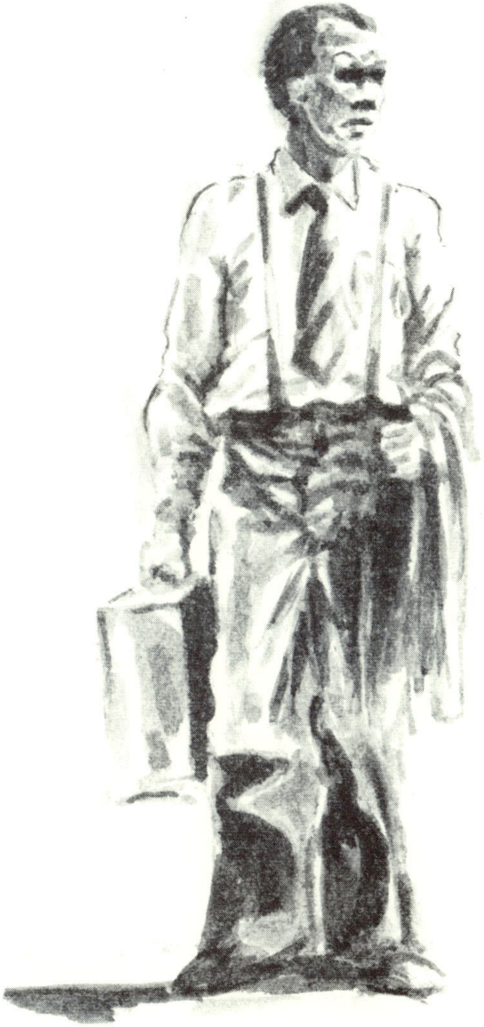

AFTERWORD

Walking on Borrowed Land is William A. Owens's first novel and the first of several books—both novels and non-fiction—that have made him one of the best-known Texas writers. Owens, born in the village of Pin Hook in Northeast Texas, spent the first twenty years of his life escaping from the poverty he was born into in 1905. Owens did farm labor, waited tables, worked in a dime store, filled orders at the big Sears warehouse in Dallas, and worked his way through East Texas State, SMU, and the State University of Iowa before joining the army as a private at the start of World War II. After the war, Owens joined the faculty of Columbia University and began an academic career. His early works were academic in nature and grew out of the folklore research that he began before leaving SMU in the 1930s.

It was his work as a folklorist that led, indirectly, to the writing of *Walking on Borrowed Land*. A member of Army Intelligence early in World War II, Owens was assigned to visit negro churches in the Tulsa, Oklahoma, area to determine whether American blacks were loyal citizens of the Republic. His folklore collecting among the blacks of East Texas during the thirties had made him feel at home in the schools, churches, and homes of the still-segregated negroes of the South.

As Owens tells in the introduction to this volume, it was on his way back to Tulsa after visiting a black congregation that the idea for the novel came to him. However, it was almost a decade and a half before the book which he planned alongside the road in rural Oklahoma was written and published. In the meantime, Owens saw combat in the South Pacific and began his career at Columbia. But his sympathy for the poor blacks of Oklahoma had not diminished at all during the years he spent outside the region. Nor had he forgotten the oppression that scarred East Texas blacks and whites during the years of his boyhood.

Published in 1954, the same year that the Supreme Court (*Brown v. Board of Education of Topeka*) ruled public school segregation unconstitutional, *Walking on Borrowed Land* is a novel that makes an eloquent plea for racial understanding and equality. In order to show segregation at its most oppressive, Owens sets the novel during the middle years of the Great Depression when the blacks constituted a threat to the economic welfare of poor whites and when well-off Southern whites took advantage of the depressed economy to get the full benefit of cheap negro labor. Setting the novel in the thirties also made it possible to show how little progress had been made in the forty or so years since the Supreme Court, in the case of *Plessy v. Ferguson,* had ruled in favor of "separate but equal" education for blacks and whites. The power structure of Columbus, Oklahoma, makes no pretense about the "equal" in separate but equal—and they are certainly deadly serious about the "separate." The town—or rather the town and its "colored quarters"—is operated on the most stringent kind of "apartheid," for the blacks have to cross the tracks and be back in the ironically named "Happy Hollow" before nightfall. It is a classic case of the disgraceful policy many southern towns announced with the signs that said "Nigger, don't let the sun set on you here." Columbus has no signs, but Mose Ingram learns quickly that Oklahoma is not going to be different from his native Mississippi when it comes to separation of the races.

It takes Mose almost no time to see how things are and are likely to remain. When Frenchy the cab driver learns that Mose came to Columbus from college in Chicago, He says "Man, you better go back. You got it easy there. It's rough here—on us folks." But there is no going back for Mose. Bad though Columbus may be, Mose has come to stay. Without making a speech about his duty, Mose knows that he has a mission. He must stay in Happy Hollow and try to teach the children something more than maid work and manual labor, the only subjects that the school board cares about for the city's black citizens.

The evils of segregation are certainly plain to see in Columbus, but the social issue is not the only theme in *Walking on Borrowed Land*. Equally important are the human themes that run through the book. Mose must struggle to overcome more than just the political situation that keeps the blacks of Happy Hollow "in their place." He must find out a way to live with his wife, an uneducated superstitious plantation woman who is easy prey for Sister Brackett of a Holy-Roller church. And he must reconcile himself to what happens to the three sons he is trying to raise to manhood in segregated Oklahoma.

On many levels the novel is about failure. Mose fails to make any headway at all against his wife Josie's ignorance and obduracy. She was trained "right" on Miss May's plantation and was never able to go beyond what she had been taught about her "place." As she tells her sons—contradicting what Mose is trying to teach them—"niggers got to look up to white folks and be humble. Miss May say they ain't nothing worse 'n a uppity nigger." Nor can she be guided away from the superstitions taught in the brand of backwoods religion that helped keep slaves and their descendents from desiring more of the world's rewards than they were given by the Establishment God. She is in complete agreement with Sister Brackett, who says, "I ain't bothering my spirit none about things on this earth. . . . I ain't a-caring if white folks does have everything. . . . I can do without here long as I git to enter the pearly gates, amen." Sister Brackett's speech is an extension of the theme suggested by the title *Walking on Borrowed Land,* which comes from a black spiritual: "I'm walking on borrowed land,/This world ain't none o' my home." Mose also fails to get his three sons to the kind of manhood he envisions for them. The old saying that it takes three seeds to produce one plant proves true in the case of the Ingram offspring. Only John will survive the evils of the segregated world to become the kind of man his father wanted all his sons to be.

But even though there are times when failure seems about to overwhelm Mose Ingram, he never quits struggling. And though it always takes two or three steps backwards to produce one forward,

Mose is so inured to hardship that he never gives up. His efforts to make a better life for his people pass unnoticed most of the time. Only Mose seems to know that he is making a difference in Columbus, and even he has doubts that he is doing much good. It is only at the end of the novel that he gets a commendation for all the good that he has done. Lora, his best teacher and strongest ally in the school, pays him the highest compliment of his life:

> "I got something to say to you, Mose Ingram," Lora burst out. Mose faced her again, looking up into her eyes. "Mose, you done a good job in Happy Hollow. And you done it without being no handkerchiefhead."

Better than an award from the white school board, Lora's words make the struggle worthwhile. And her praise is all Mose is ever likely to get for his efforts. But it is enough. It came from the heart of someone who knew what the effort had been about.

With all the themes that run through the novel, a reader might miss what seems to me to be one of the most important statements the novel has to make: humans are ultimately alone. Mose is. Nobody in Happy Hollow—and certainly no one in Columbus—can make Mose's task easy. What he has to do for his people has to be done in the face of nearly overwhelming odds. Like A. E. Housman's tortured youths, Mose Ingram is "a stranger and afraid in a world he never made." Though Mose is a churchgoer, religion offers him little support. Though he has a wife and sons, the strength to be found in family life is missing for him. Nor can he expect much from government, community, or the members of his race. What Mose realizes is that being a man means taking responsibility for yourself and your actions. Only by deciding what has to be done and doing it himself can Mose stand up to the forces that have been massed against him—ignorance, superstition, prejudice, law, and custom.

Even though the novel is heavily flavored by the dialect that blacks spoke in the South in the 1930s, the reader never has any trouble following the speech. Unlike some novels and stories about black life, *Walking on Borrowed Land* is never so dialect-ridden that a reader has to struggle to get the meaning. Owens manages to do just enough to suggest the speech patterns and the grammar of the poor blacks. He never resorts to the "Yassuh, I'se gwine" kind of dialect representation that some writers think captures the way blacks spoke in the plantation South. The language spoken is unmistakably that of uneducated negroes, but Owens is careful to give the speech a dignity that is missing from the linguistic caricatures of the Stepan Fetchit movies and Uncle Remus tales.

By focusing on Mose's dignity and courage and showing that there is hope for the black race despite all the tribulations, William Owens's novel speaks eloquently for racial justice and understanding. The novel also creates a character who, despite all the forces arrayed against him, is able to keep his dignity intact in a world where the black is expected to be a comic character. Even though Mose Ingram loses more battles than he wins, he finally scores a quiet triumph. And he does it "without being no handkerchief-head."

James Ward Lee
North Texas State University

ABOUT THE AUTHOR

William A. Owens was born in the tiny community of Pin Hook, Texas, in the northeastern section of the state. After a childhood marked by hard work but rich in ballad, song and story, he left the family farm for Dallas. He was educated at Southern Methodist University and received a doctorate from the University of Iowa where his interest was directed toward the study of folklore.

In 1942 Owens entered the armed forces and was assigned to the Counter Intelligence Corps. His duties included reporting on racial friction in several cities, an experience which allowed him to gain further understanding of negroes and their problems. After discharge, Owens enrolled at Columbia University to take writing courses and remained there twenty-eight years as professor of literature and writing. For twelve years, he was dean of the summer sessions.

Known both as a folklorist and a novelist, Owens is one of the literary giants of Texas and one of the few to give voice to the folk culture of East Texas. His books include the autobiographical *This Stubborn Soil* and *A Season of Weathering* and novels *Fever in the Earth* and *Look to the River*. *Walking on Borrowed Land* is his first novel, published in 1954, and reflects his strong feelings about racial achievement and equality, particularly in education.